Discarded

Operation Trumpsformation

ROSS O'CARROLL-KELLY

(as told to Paul Howard)

Illustrated by

ALAN CLARKE

PENGUIN
IRELAND

PENGUIN IRELAND

UK | USA | Canada | Ireland | Australia
India | New Zealand | South Africa

Penguin Ireland is part of the Penguin Random House group of companies
whose addresses can be found at global.penguinrandomhouse.com.

First published 2017

001

Penguin Ireland thanks O'Brien Press for its agreement to Penguin Ireland using the
same design approach and typography, and the same artist, as O'Brien Press
used in the first four Ross O'Carroll-Kelly titles

Set in 12/14.75 pt Dante MT Std
Typeset by Jouve (UK), Milton Keynes
Printed in Great Britain by Clays Ltd, St Ives plc

A CIP catalogue record for this book is available from the British Library

ISBN: 978–0–241–97801–6

www.greenpenguin.co.uk

To Róisín Ingle – for the gift of your friendship

Contents

Prologue

I don't believe it. And I mean that quite literally. The code for the gate has been changed. I put in 2, 0, 0, 9 – the first year that Leinster won the Heineken Cup – but nothing happens. Then I try 2, 0, 1, 1 – the second year that Leinster won the Heineken Cup – except it ends up not being that *either*? So then I try 2, 0, 1, 2 – God, we won a lot of Heineken Cups – and that's when I hear Sorcha's voice coming through the intercom.

She's like, 'What do you want, Ross?' and she sounds more *sad* than angry?

I look up at the security camera and I go, 'Yeah, no, you changed the code.'

She's there, 'I asked you what you wanted, Ross?'

'Er,' I go, 'obviously I want to get in.'

She's like, 'Ross, what part of "Our marriage is over!" do you not understand?'

'I don't accept that it is over. I'm still hoping you can find it in yourself to forgive me for what I did.'

I rode a woman in Dalkey.

She goes, 'We agreed that Saturday was your day to see the children. You can't just turn up randomly like this.'

And I'm there, 'I'm not turning up randomly. I, er, forgot something. When you focked me out.'

'What did you forget?'

'Yeah, no, my Rugby Tactics Book.'

'Your Rugby Tactics Book? Okay, do you actually need it?'

'Is that a serious question?'

'As in, do you need it right now? Could it not wait until the weekend?'

'After my heroics for Seapoint last week, I have to accept that a lot of clubs are going to be sniffing around me now – maybe not as a player, but you'd have to believe there's a coaching role out there for me. That book contains my whole, I don't know, psychology on the game.'

The gate suddenly pops opens, and in I go. I trudge up the gravel driveway towards the gaff. She's standing on the doorstep with her orms folded tightly. I'm a pretty good reader of body language. She definitely still wants me.

I'm there, 'You look well.'

She doesn't. She looks like shit – like she hasn't slept for the past week. I suppose it's possible that she hasn't.

She goes, 'Just take whatever you came for, then go, Ross,' refusing to even look at me.

She turns sideways to let me in. I step past her into the hallway, then up the stairs I go. It's not in its usual spot on the top of my bedside locker. As a matter of fact, I turn the entire bedroom upside-down looking for it, but it's nowhere to be found. Then I just happen to stick my head around Honor's bedroom door, to ask her if she's seen it. And that's when I spot it – on her bed! I'm like, 'Okay, what the fock is it doing in here?' and I stort flicking through it, just to make sure she hasn't written anything rude in it, or drawn dicks all over it, like she's done before.

She hasn't. There's just the stuff I've already Tippexed out. It looks like I got here just in the nick of time. I tip downstairs with the book under my orm. Sorcha is still standing by the front door – again with her orms folded. I'm like, 'So how have you been?'

She goes, 'How the fock do you think I've been, Ross?'

Sorcha *never* swears? Except when she's with her closest female friends and they're all talking dirty, usually about Gordon D'Arcy or one of the Happy Pear goys. Vegward, as I call them.

I'm there, 'I know I'm repeating myself here, but that woman meant nothing. She put it on a plate for me. Made it nearly impossible for me to say no.'

She bursts into tears. She goes, 'You focking ruined everything, you stupid focking . . . focker! And for what, Ross? For what?'

'It doesn't have to be the end, Sorcha.'

'Do you honestly think I can just pretend it never happened?'

'Hey, you've done it before – why not?'

She dries her eyes with the tips of her fingers, then her expression suddenly *hordens*? 'Not this time,' she goes. 'I deserve better.'

I don't think she means that. I notice she's still wearing her wedding and engagement rings. That's hopefully a sign that she might still take me back.

I'm there, 'Can I see the kids?'

She goes, 'You can see them on Saturday – like we agreed.'

'Saturday is days away.'

She lets out a roar at me then. She goes, 'You should have thought of that before you slept with that focking slut!'

I'm there, 'Okay, sorry,' and I'm just about to walk out the door when events suddenly take what might be described as a turn.

I hear a voice – a *dude's* voice? – coming from the kitchen. It's like, 'Are you going to eat your breakfasht, Leo?'

My blood turns cold. Sorcha has another man in the house.

This feeling of total and utter rage suddenly comes over me – it's like the time I said hello to Conor Murray and Simon Zebo in Elverys on Stephen's Green and they pretended not to know me. I'm like, 'Who the fock is that?'

Actually, that's what Simon Zebo said as well.

Sorcha goes, 'It's none of your business who it is, Ross.'

And I'm there, 'None of my business? I've only moved out, what, a week? And already some random dude is giving my children their breakfast?'

'He's not some random dude. His name *happens* to be Magnus.'

'Magnus?'

I don't know if it's the ridiculous name, or the casual way that Sorcha mentions him, or even the memory of Conor Murray laughing at me as I tried on the new Leinster Alternate Test jersey, then discovered, as I tried to pull it down over my belly, that it was actually the fitted women's version. But I head for the kitchen in an absolute rage, with Sorcha following me, going, 'Ross, no! Get out! Get out of this house now!'

I push the kitchen door. Honor is sitting at the table. Brian, Johnny and Leo are in their high chairs. Their faces obviously light up when they see me, but I'm more interested in the total stranger who's trying to get them to eat their unsweetened quinoa porridge with mashed Bortlett pear. What makes it even worse is that the dude – yeah, no, I'm going to admit this – is a seriously good-looking goy. He's, like, blond, square jaw and six-foot-three, possibly six-foot-four in height – which I wouldn't have thought was Sorcha's type. She was always more into backs than forwards.

I somehow resist the temptation to straightaway deck him. Instead, I just go, 'Who the fock are you?'

'Oh my God,' Honor goes, obviously delighted by this development. 'Plot twist!'

'Hey, I'm Magnush,' the dude has the actual balls to go, 'and you musht be Rosh, Shorcha's hushband, yesh?'

I'm picking up an accent – it sounds like Drogheda or somewhere up that way.

'Maybe I should have been more specific,' I go. 'Who the fock are you and what the fock are you doing in my house?'

'Fock you,' Leo shouts, because the triplets are still going through their phase of effing and blinding at every turn and we're still going through our phase of doing fock-all about it in the hope that they'll one day just stop. 'Fock you, you focking cunting fock-fock!'

This Magnus dude goes, 'Well, at thish moment, I am giving the cheeldren their breakfasht. Shorcha, you should eat shome breakfasht, too. I'm shorry to tell you, Rosh, that your wife and I heff been up all night.'

That ends up being the line that snaps my crayons. I literally launch myself across the kitchen at the dude. I don't give a fock how tall he is. I grab him by the front of his shirt and I slam him up against the two-door American fridge-freezer.

Sorcha actually screams. She's like, 'Nooo!!!'

Honor goes, 'Hit him, Dad!' the excitement obvious in her voice. 'Hit him!'

I'm there, 'You've got a neck like Ruby Walsh's understuff, I'll give you that.'

He's tugging at my fingers, trying to loosen the grip I have on him. 'What ish . . . what ish wrong?' he manages to go.

'You and my wife,' I go, 'up all night, were you? And you say it to me in front of my kids?'

Sorcha storts grabbing me, going, 'Ross, it's not what you think!'

But Honor's there, 'It *is* what you think. He said he wants us to think of him as our father. He told me I have to call him Daddy.'

I cock my fist, ready to drive it into the dude's big handsome face, when all of a sudden I feel something crack me across the back of the skull, causing me to release my grip and hit the deck. When my head clears, which takes a good thirty seconds, I notice that it's the Le Creuset cast-iron square Grillit that I bought Sorcha last year. She's certainly getting the use out of it, despite her view at the time that it wasn't a proper Valentine's Day present.

'Get out!' she goes, screaming at me at the top of her voice. 'Get out of this house!'

I'm there, 'Seriously, Sorcha?' climbing to my feet and checking the back of my head for blood. 'I haven't been gone a week and you've already moved on. There's a word for girls like that, Sorcha. I'm not going to say it. But you were the one who mentioned "slut" earlier.'

'Focking slut!' Leo goes.

Sorcha's like, 'I haven't moved on!' still roaring at me, by the way. 'This is Magnus, our new manny!'

Oh, shit.

I'm there, 'Your manny? What the fock is a manny?'

She's like, 'What does it sound like, Ross? He's a male nanny. I said I was going to hire someone to help me with the children while I'm working on the campaign.'

'What campaign?'

'Oh my God, I told you six weeks ago that me and Muirgheal are going to be working for the Yes side in the same-sex marriage referendum.'

Muirgheal is Christian's new squeeze. Her and Sorcha set up the Mount Anville Africa Project, which aims to heighten awareness of how generally shit life is over there by sending more than a hundred transition year students to Botswana every year to see it for themselves.

She's there, 'I told you that once we'd tackled the whole Africa thing, marriage equality was next.'

'Yeah,' I go, 'the whole BGT thing. See, I *was* listening?'

'BGT is *Britain's Got Talent*. The *actual* acronym is LGBT. But then I wouldn't expect you to know that.'

'I thought you were hiring, like, a nanny. I'm not sure I like the idea of another man living under my roof.'

Honor goes, 'I really think you should break his nose, Dad. You would if you were any kind of man.'

Magnus is like, 'Well, you heff nothing to worry about from me on that shcore – right, Shorcha? Becaush I am gay.'

I'm like, 'Gay? Hang on, what did you mean when you said the two of you were up all night?'

'I'm shorry,' he goes, 'shometimes my English ish – how to shay? – not sho good.'

'Where are you even from? I would have put money on Louth. You talk like one of the Kearneys.'

'I'm from Finland.'

'Finland?'

Yeah, no, it's a new one on me as well.

I'm there, 'Random.'

'Not that it's any of your business,' Sorcha goes, 'but he was helping me write a speech. I'm giving a talk this morning to my grandmother's Active Retirement group. We're trying to win over the horts and minds of senior voters who have a more conservative view of marriage.'

Honor goes, 'They're lying, Ross. They've been having an affair. They're laughing at you – like that rugby man when you put on that women's top.'

I'm on the point of nearly apologizing to the dude when I hear a voice in the hall, which I recognize straightaway. It's Sorcha's old man.

'Fock!' Leo shouts, summing up my thoughts exactly. 'Fock this focking focker.'

The door of the kitchen opens and in he walks – the Fresh Prince of Bell-End. Of course, his face drops when he sees his daughter looking all upset and the Rossmeister standing there next to her.

He's like, 'What the *hell* is he doing here?'

I'm there, 'Don't worry, I'm not staying. I just came for my Rugby Tactics Book.'

Sorcha's old dear walks in behind him. *She* decides to have *her* say then? Which is a shame, because I *was* a fan. She goes, 'Sorcha has made it perfectly clear to you that she doesn't want you here anymore.'

Of course, Sorcha decides to give us the full costume drama then – waterworks and everything. Her old dear puts her orm around her and goes, 'Ross, this isn't your home anymore. Please leave.'

I'm there, 'I'm not accepting that it's over. I'm still hoping that we can work it out.'

Sorcha's old man goes, 'Why are we even wasting our breath on him? If you don't leave this house this instant, I shall be forced to phone the Gardaí.'

I'm there, 'Don't worry. I'm going. I'll see you on Saturday, kids.'

'Fock you!' Brian goes. 'You focking wanker!' and out of there I walk, chin up, shoulders back. Of course, Sorcha's old man has to have the last word. A lawyer, bear in mind. He follows me outside.

I go, 'By the way, how are things up in the old Beacon South Quarter?' because I know it's a sore point that he's ended up living there. 'I hear the hospital has taken over one of the vacant aportment blocks for its kidney patients. I'd say it's a cheery focking place to be these days.'

He goes, 'You and my daughter are finished. I don't want you bothering her again.'

I actually laugh. I'm there, 'I think you're terrified that she still might take me back.'

'There isn't a chance in hell.'

'Look, I slept with another woman. It was put in front of me. Gift-horse in the mouth. But Sorcha's still wearing her wedding and engagement rings. What does that tell you?'

'Believe me. All you are to my daughter is a bad memory and some paperwork, which I'm more than happy to do.'

I notice his cor porked in front of the house. A 2007 Hyundai

Santa Fe. A focking tramp wouldn't sleep in it. I look at it and laugh to myself and he pretends that it doesn't piss him off.

'What saddens me,' he goes, 'is that an intelligent girl like Sorcha could have allowed herself to be held back by someone like you for so long.'

I'm like, 'Held back?'

'Sorcha could have done anything with her life. She could have been anyone she wanted to be.'

'Jesus, she did Orts in UCD. Would you wind your focking neck in?'

'Well, luckily, she's still young enough to pick up the pieces and make her mark on the world. Which she will do – you can be sure of that. Once she divests herself of you.'

'*Divests* herself? Is that even a word?'

'Oh, *it's* a word.'

'I'll Google it. We'll see.'

I press the button on my cor key – a brand-new Audi A8 – just to let him know what *I'm* driving these days? He tries to look like it doesn't bother him.

'What you fail to grasp,' he goes, 'is that when it comes to the divorce business, I know every trick in the book. I invented many of them.'

'Divorce hasn't been mentioned yet. All we are is separated.'

'It's over. You're finished here. And by the time I'm done with you, you won't have that fancy car. You won't have a home. You won't have a wife and you won't have your children.'

'Excuse me?'

'I'm going to ruin your life – just like you ruined my daughter's.'

1. Home Sweet Homophobia

The old man is in the jacks. He's standing in front of the mirror, staring at his reflection, going, 'Look at you! You colossus! You winner of hearts! You leader of men!'

I'm just watching him, thinking how much of a knob he's become since he found that wig in Helen's attic and stuck it on his head. He's, like, running his fingers through it, smoothing it across his head and he's going, 'You're a lion! You're strong! You're virile! And this is the moment you were bloody well born for!'

I'm there, 'You know, it's an actual miracle that I turned out to be the genuinely lovely goy that I am.'

He's not even embarrassed to find out that I've been standing there listening to him the entire time. 'Hello there, Kicker!' he goes. 'I'm running through some vocal exercises. *Vox Populi, Vox Dei* and what-not!'

This is in the Morker Hotel, by the way. We're here for the launch of this new political porty of his – New Republic or whatever he's calling it. There must be, like, five hundred people in the main conference room – we're talking reporters from all the papers, radio and TV stations, then a load of just randomers who've turned up to hear Charles O'Carroll-Kelly outline his vision for a new Ireland.

I'm here for the free bor.

He goes, 'I was talking to your mother this morning. She said she hasn't seen you.'

I'm like, 'Er, yeah, that might have something to do with the fact that she's in *prison*?'

'Well, you *could* go and visit her.'

'I've actually got better things to be doing with my time. It might have escaped your attention, but my marriage is in serious trouble.'

'It hasn't escaped my attention, Ross. You're living under my roof. I'm just saying that your mother needs our support at this time.'

He stops smoothing his hair and stares at it for a few seconds. He seems to like whatever way it's sitting because he leaves it then and storts washing his hands. I slip over to the hand-dryer and, when he's not looking, I twist the air nozzle so that it's facing upwards.

'Yeah, no,' I go, 'she should have thought of that before she killed a man.'

He stops what he's doing. He's like, 'Killed a man? You don't seriously think she did it, do you?'

I'm there, 'I wouldn't put it past her. Would you?'

He goes, 'Of course she didn't do it! This is Fionnuala we're talking about! Ari died of a heart attack! She's being fitted up, Ross!'

'Why would they fit her up?'

'Think of the timing! What, I announce that I'm setting up a new political party to challenge the existing order and the following day my ex-wife, who remains a dear, dear friend, is charged with murder? Bit of a coincidence, isn't it?'

'If you say so. Here, don't forget to dry your hands.'

He walks over to the hand-dryer and stands with his hands underneath it. I hit the button and he ends up getting a blast of hot air right in the face. It travels up his forehead and totally messes up his hair, so it looks like he's just walked Dún Laoghaire pier in a hurricane.

'Someone must have turned the nozzle the other way around,' I go. 'Shit one.'

He's like, 'Look at my hair!'

'It's not *actually* hair, can I just remind you?'

He goes back to the mirror and storts trying to smooth it down again, but for some reason it won't go back to the way it was. There's bits of it that insist on standing up, even when he wets his hands and tries to force it down. And he storts getting into a serious flap then, going, 'I can't face the public like this! I look bloody well ridiculous!'

I'm there, 'I'm agreeing with you. It's a bummer.'

He races over to the door, opens it and shouts, 'Hennessy! Crisis!'

and a few seconds later his solicitor comes rushing in, followed by the famous K . . . K . . . Kennet, who's working as his driver these days. It's hilarious – he's got the uniform and everything.

Hennessy's like, 'Jesus, what happened?'

'Never mind the whats and the what-nots,' the old man goes, still going at it but making it actually worse. 'What are we going to do?'

I'm laughing my hole off, by the way.

Hennessy takes out his comb and tries to smooth it down, but it still keeps popping up again in places.

Kennet goes, 'Ine arthur h . . . h . . . h . . . habben an idea, so I am,' and he heads for the door.

'Hurry!' the old man goes. 'I should have been on stage ten minutes ago.'

You can hear the crowd in the function room growing impatient. They're, like, stamping their feet.

Kennet returns with a can of something in his hand. 'It's m . . . m . . . m . . . mousse,' he goes. 'I gorrit offa boord outsoyut.'

The old man goes, 'Well, come on, then, get on with it! I can't leave people waiting all day!'

Kennet sprays a bit into his hand, then – hilarious – storts massaging it into the old man's head while Hennessy goes to work with the comb. They make a complete focking hames of it, though, because the old man ends up with what looks like a really bad comb-over. And the crowd in the conference room is getting seriously pissed off waiting now. They stort a slow-handclap.

'Give me that!' the old man goes, demanding the mousse. He squeezes some of it into his hand and has a crack at trying to fix the damage that the other two have done. He sweeps all of his hair backwards, so now it's suddenly long at the back, like an actual mullet, then he runs his fingers through the sides, slicking the hair back around his ears.

The result is genuinely one of the most ridiculous hairstyles I've ever seen. The old man stares silently at himself for a long time.

'That's it!' he suddenly goes, a smile breaking out across his face. 'That's the look I've been after!'

Hennessy goes, 'It's, er, certainly very different.'

'It's magnificent! Now . . . let's go and share our vision for a new and better Ireland!'

We head for the conference room. I go in first and look for a seat. Helen gives me a wave to tell me there's a free seat next to her. That's what a cool person she is. Way out of my old man's league. I've always said it. The seat is in the middle of a row and the people who are already sitting down do the usual thing of rolling their eyes at the inconvenience of having to let me past, so I do *my* usual thing of accidentally-on-purpose kicking them in the ankles if they don't move their feet out of the way fast enough.

Helen goes, 'Hi, Ross. Is everything okay?' because the crowd are not only slow-clapping now, they're going, 'We want Charles! We want Charles! We want Charles!'

I'm there, 'Yeah, no, he had a bit of a wig malfunction. His head looks a focking state. Wait'll you see it.'

Hilariously, the M.C. for the day ends up being Kennet. M.C. focking Stammer. He steps up to the mic and goes, 'L . . . L . . . L . . . Layuties and gentlemen. Will you p . . . p . . . p . . . pleeyuz p . . . p . . . p . . . put yisser hands togetter for the P . . . P . . . P . . . President of New Republic, Mister Ch . . . Ch . . . Ch . . . Cheerdles O'Cattle-Keddy!'

The audience goes bananas. People love my old man. I've never really understood why. Out he walks, waving to the crowd. And that's when there's suddenly a change in the atmosphere in the room. People are still clapping, but at the same time they're staring open-mouthed at his hair, trying to figure out if it's for real, or if he's ripping the piss.

I turn to Helen and I go, 'It's genuinely funny, isn't it?'

She's like, 'What happened?'

I'm there, 'It was obviously someone's idea of a joke to turn the nozzle on the hand-dryer upside-down. It went all over the place and he ended up putting product in it to try to fix it.'

'He looks like that what's-his-name – in America?'

'Who?'

'He was on the news this morning.'

'I wouldn't make a habit of watching the news, Helen.'

The old man steps up to the mic. Silence falls on the room. His opening line is, 'I love Ireland!'

Which is horseshit, of course. He always says we'd have been better off economically and every other way if we'd stayed port of Britain. He gets a round of applause for it anyway.

'Yes,' he goes, 'I love Ireland! So much so that I stayed here, through years of recessions and economic downturns, even when many of my business friends were saying to me, "Get out, Charlie – the place is bloody well finished!" I never, ever gave up on this country! And today, I'm asking you – the much-put-upon people of this troubled, troubled land – not to give up either!'

There's, like, a giant logo on the wall behind him, which is green, white and orange – a massive N, then underneath it a massive R.

He goes, 'Independence hasn't worked out quite the way we hoped it would! And there's a very good reason for that! We don't choose the best people to lead us! We elect secondary school teachers, barristers who are in love with the sound of their own voices and the intellectually limited sons and daughters of some political dynasty whose name meant something once but doesn't anymore! That's how we've ended up with a Taoiseach with the personality and political gravitas of a County Council Cathaoirleach and a Minister for Finance who should be teaching long division to children in bloody well Dooradoyle!'

There's, like, howls of laughter.

I turn around to Helen. I'm there, 'He has them eating out of the palm of his hand.'

It's very disappointing.

I go, 'By the way, thanks again, Helen – for, like, putting me up?'

She's there, 'It's fine, Ross. Erika's room is empty anyway.'

'Well, it'll only be until Sorcha cops herself on, which will be hopefully soon.'

The old man's still banging on. He's going, 'We have been governed by the same three political parties for the best part of one hundred years and they have done a very bad job of it! Which is why we have to find an alternative to the failed political configurations of the past! We elect Fianna Fáil and they turn out to be crooks, so we give Fine Gael and Labour a shot and they turn out to be useless, so we put Fianna Fáil back in! And on and on and on! We have to break the cycle! That is why I am proud to announce the arrival of an alternative to the parties who have spent the last ten years betraying the Irish people and selling this country out!'

That gets a massive roar of approval.

'These politicians,' he goes, 'who are supposed to be representing *your* interests have instead put you on the hook for billions and billions of euros' worth of debts that have nothing to do with you! Let me repeat that – *nothing* to do with you! And yet you're paying them! Through austerity! Through property tax! Through water rates! Through the Universal Social Charge! Through whatever ruses they can come up with to pick your pockets!'

There's, like, boos from the audience.

He goes, 'Back in 2008, following the inverted commas crash, the Gerhards and the Jean-Claudes called our politicians in and they said, "You're billions and billions of euros in debt! You've got a serious problem here!" That was our time to say, "It sounds to us like *you've* got the serious problem, mein Freund!" But our so-called leaders didn't say that! They were too anxious to be seen as good Europeans, whatever the hell that even means! So they told the suits in Brussels and in Berlin, "Look, we don't know anything! We're just a bunch of simple Irish idiots! Tell us what to do!"

'We surrendered to the IMF, the EU and the EC bloody-well B and their demands that, for the sins of a greedy few, the entire Irish people should be vanquished economically! This idea runs like a red thread through the so-called bailout deal, which seeks, on the one hand, to burden the economy of a great people with an unbearable load and, on the other, to destroy it as much as possible, to cut off all its opportunities, while – with a clever sleight of hand – private debt is turned into public debt!'

There's, like, more boos.

He goes, 'As the leader of New Republic, I am offering you, the people of Ireland, a viable alternative to the failed politics of the past! Which is why the Establishment is already running scared of us! They're terrified of New Republic and what it represents! Some of you may have heard that my wife, Fionnuala, was arrested last week on – I'm going to speak frankly here – trumped-up murder charges in an effort to discredit me, to hurt me, to silence me! Let me say this! They! Will Not! Succeed! I am going to help to prove her innocence – that is a promise!

'I'm also making you, the people of Ireland, a promise! There's going to be a General Election sometime in the next year – and every man and woman in every constituency in this country will have an opportunity to vote for a New Republic candidate!'

Cheers.

'We *can* break the cycle!'

Cheers.

'We *will* break the cycle!'

Cheers.

'Our Programme for Government,' he goes, 'will contain a number of pledges, some of which I can reveal to you today. Once we are elected, we will take immediate steps to abolish water charges . . .'

Roars.

'. . . residential Property Tax . . .'

Roars.

'. . . and the Universal Social Charge!'

Roars.

'We will restore Public Sector Pay!'

Roars.

'We will ensure that our hospitals and our schools are adequately funded!'

Roars.

'We will put Ireland first! And we will make Ireland tremendous again!'

All hell breaks loose. People stort going ballistic. They're on their feet, clapping and cheering. From somewhere near the front, Kennet shouts, 'Ch . . . Ch . . . Ch . . . Cheerles O'Cattle-Keddy for T . . . T . . . T . . . T . . . Taoiseach!'

And, quick as a flash, someone shortens it to, 'CO'CK for Taoiseach!' and within seconds that becomes the chant. Everyone's going, 'CO'CK for Taoiseach! CO'CK for Taoiseach! CO'CK for Taoiseach!'

I turn around to Helen and I notice that she's got, like, tears streaming from her eyes. At first I think it must be, like, *pride*? But when I smile at her and tell her that her husband is full of shit, she points out something that I, for some reason, *missed*?

She goes, 'He called Fionnuala his wife, Ross.'

I'm there, 'Er, I'm pretty sure he said *ex*-wife?'

But she goes, 'He didn't, Ross. He called your mother his wife.'

Little Leo is holding the ball in his two hands. This is in the middle of, like, Herbert Pork.

I go, 'That's it, Leo, get a proper feel for it. Let your, I don't know, subconscience become aware of the weight, the shape and the texture. Now, throw it to me! Come on – throw it back!'

He throws it alright – except not *to* me? He just focks it on the ground in front of him. He goes, 'Focking fockpig!' then he laughs, like a dope.

I look around for the other two. Brian is sitting down on the grass, just shouting, 'Fock you! Fock you! Fock you!' at the top of his voice, while Johnny is walking around in circles singing *Somewhere Only We Know* – the Lily Allen version as well.

I'm not making excuses for myself, but I genuinely don't think I can improve their skills by working with them only one day a week, and I'm pretty sure Joe Schmidt couldn't do it either. If they're going to improve as players, I need access to them three or four days a week. I might need to explain that to Sorcha if this separation continues for much longer.

I'm there, 'Okay, Leo, let's try that again,' scooping the ball up with one hand and giving it back to him. 'But let's see can we do it *right* this time?'

Before I even give him the signal, he just, like, drops it on the ground. I suppose, if you were being charitable, you could say he knocks it on, but the truth is he just drops it out of sheer lack of focking interest. Then he bends down and storts smacking it with his hand. I'm standing there thinking, imagine if Leo Cullen was here right now and saw this kid who I supposedly named after him doing that. The big man wouldn't just be hurt – it'd break his focking hort.

I'm about to give it up for the morning and bring them to Dundrum to fill their bellies with turquoise ice cream, when Honor – sitting on a bench a few feet away – suddenly looks up from her phone and goes, 'Show him – don't tell him.'

Obviously, I'm *thrown* by this? As in, my daughter showing an actual interest in what I'm doing. I'm like, 'What do you mean by that, Honor?'

She stands up and puts her phone away. She picks up the ball, puts it in Leo's hands, then she takes his two shoulders and turns him around, so that he's standing side-on to me. She positions Leo's two hands on the ball. And, by the way, I can't help but notice that she positions them *perfectly*?

'Now, Leo,' she goes, 'you have to spin it as it leaves your hands, okay? Can you do that? Like this,' and she shows him how to perform a pretty good offloading action with his hands. 'On the count of three,' she goes. 'One . . . Two . . . Three!'

And Leo throws the ball. No, he doesn't just throw it. He ends up delivering – honestly? – one of *the* most perfect passes I've ever seen in thirty years of watching and playing the game of rugby. I catch the ball as it hits me hord in the midriff.

Honor goes, 'There!', then she walks back over to her bench, sits down and takes out her phone again.

I'm just, like, staring at her in total wonder. I tip over to where she's sitting, suddenly scrolling down through her Twitter feed. 'Oh my God,' she goes, 'Lena Dunham is *such* a virtue-signalling bitch.'

I'm like, 'Honor, who taught you that?'

She looks at me all defensively. She goes, 'I've been swearing since I was, like, *two*?'

I'm there, 'I don't give a fock about the swearing. I'm talking about the way you just showed Leo how to throw the ball. Oh my God, you were studying my Rugby Tactics Book, weren't you?'

'Yeah. I didn't draw anything on it this time, so don't stort accusing me.'

'I'm not angry with you, Honor. I'm actually impressed.'

'Whatever.'

'I mean it. Here I am, trying to teach the boys the basics, and I might as well be reading rap lyrics to a focking hen. I was on the point of giving up. But you've just helped me believe again in my ability to coach.'

She just shrugs like this means nothing to her one way or the other, then she goes back to her Twitter feed. And that's when it suddenly hits me – the reason for her sudden interest in rugby. I've been so wrapped up in myself that I haven't thought for a minute how this separation might be affecting her. She's trying to make a connection with me – to possibly let me know that she's on *my* side?

I sit down on the bench beside her. It's time for one of our famous father–daughter chats. 'Look,' I go, 'I know the last week or two have probably been difficult for you – especially not having your dad around the house.'

She's there, 'I don't give a shit. I don't like you that much anyway.'

'I know that's not true.'

'It is true. I find you really irritating.'

'I *can* be irritating – I accept that. But there's also a bond between us.'

'I don't think there's a bond.'

'There's a definite bond – even if you don't realize it. Look, I know it can be difficult for children when their parents get separated or divorced.'

That does it. She's suddenly like, 'Are you *getting* divorced?' her face all worried.

I'm there, 'Of course we're not getting divorced! Look, all marriages go through a bad patch. Sometimes it's hord to put your finger on what exactly is wrong.'

'You rode Caleb's mother.'

'Yes, I did ride Caleb's mother. But that's all it was, Honor. Your mother has always found it in herself to forgive me for shit like that. She's always been putty in the hand in terms of my ability to get her to take me back. The difference this time is that her old man is in her ear, poisoning her against me. So it might take me a bit of time to worm my way back in there.'

'When are you coming home then?'

'She just needs time to work shit out. I'd say it'll definitely be within the next two to three weeks, though.'

'Do you promise?'

'Yes, I do. And I'm going to make you another promise as well.'

'Is it money?'

'No, it's not money. My promise is this – until Sorcha decides that I can move home again, I'm going to make sure you get to enjoy the best of both worlds.'

Being a father is something I do well. I don't think anyone's questioning that.

She goes, 'What does that mean?'

I'm there, 'I suppose what it means is that you're going to have me *and* your mother spoiling you. I was thinking we might even hit Dundrum and get you some of that ice cream that looks like Kryptonite.'

'Will you buy me a present for a thousand euros?'

'What is it? Am I allowed to even ask?'

'I don't know yet. I just want you to buy me something for a thousand euros. You and Mom getting separated has left me really, really sad inside. I think I might need counselling.'

'Then a present for a thousand euros is what you shall have. Grab that rugby ball there and let's stick the boys back in the cor.'

She looks a state. But then she always looks a state. The difference this time is that she's finally admitting it.

'Look at my hair!' she goes – this is in the prison visiting room. She grabs a few strands between her thumb and forefinger. 'It's the hard water, Ross! Just look at what it's done to my hair!'

'It's like pubic hair,' I go. 'I'm agreeing with you. You've also put on weight. And I'm only stating that as a fact. A lot of weight.'

'Well, as it happens, I was thinking of going on a hunger strike.'

I crack my hole laughing – no choice in the matter. I'm there, 'It'd be the shortest focking hunger strike in history. All they'd have to do is put a plate of focking pork belly on the landing and you'd eat it through the gap under your door.'

'Ross, must you be so unpleasant?'

'Hey, I came to visit you, didn't I?'

'Yes, you did – and I'm very grateful.'

'Try showing it then. The whole conversation doesn't have to be about you, your hair and the size of your focking orse. I've got shit going on in my own life. The whole world doesn't stop revolving just because you possibly killed a man.'

'I didn't kill anyone, Ross!'

'So you keep saying. Poor Ari. I mean, I thought you were capable of a lot of things, but not actual murder.'

I look around me. There's some rough specimens of humanity in here. The only way to tell the difference between the prisoners and the visitors is the stripy pyjamas. And by that I obviously mean that most of the visitors are wearing pyjamas.

'What the fook are you looking at?' some girl screams at me across the floor after I make the mistake of staring at her for a second or two longer than is polite. 'I'll slash your bleaten throat for you – *and* your fooken ma's.'

It's like being on the last Luas to Fortunestown, I'm guessing.

'That's Pamela,' the old dear goes. 'She's in the bedroom next to mine.'

I'm like, 'Bedroom? Yeah, I'm pretty sure it's called a cell. You're in denial.'

'She's on remand for grievous bodily something or other. Oh, Ross, I can't stand it in here.'

'Well, you better get used to it, because you're looking at twenty years minimum.'

'Twenty years? I can't spend twenty years in this place. I'd be in my sixties when I got out.'

'I'm going to let that go because I know you're having a hord time. The point I'm trying to make is that you're probably never getting out of here.'

'Well, at least your father believes in my innocence. He thinks the entire thing is politically motivated.' She smiles at me. Jesus Christ, she's got a face like a sat-on pomegranate. She goes, 'He's been in to see me every second day, you know?'

I'm there, 'That better not be a dig at me. Like I said, I've got better things to do.'

'Don't be so defensive, Ross. I'm just saying it's nice that he believes I had nothing to do with Ari's death. He looks wonderful these days.'

'It's only a wig.'

'And he's so excited about this new party of his. You know, he reminds me of the old Charles.'

'You say that like it's a good thing.'

'It *is* a good thing. He was the first man I married, remember?'

'Well, unfortunately for you, he's not the one you're going to have to convince that you didn't kill Ari.'

'They're saying I dropped something in Ari's bath to give him that hort attack. A two-bar electric heater, Ross – like poor people use to heat their homes! They're saying that I electrocuted him, then dried him off, dressed him in a tracksuit, dragged him downstairs and left him beside the treadmill. Does that sound like something I would do? Ross, please look at me when I'm talking to you!'

I end up *having* to look at her? It's horrible.

She goes, 'I know that you and I have never been close – and that's mostly my fault. I realize that. But do you honestly think I'd be capable of doing what I've just described?'

I'm there, 'For two billion squids?'

'For any amount of money.'

There's just, like, silence between us then.

'Do you know what I would love?' she goes.

I'm there, 'Don't ask me to smuggle a bottle of gin in here.'

'I would love to see the twins.'

'What twins?'

I genuinely haven't a clue who she's talking about.

She goes, '*Your* twins.'

I'm there, 'They're not twins. They're triplets, you focking drunkard.'

'Triplets! Yes, of course!'

'A handy way for you to remember the number would be to

think to yourself, okay, how many sheets to the wind am I usually by eleven o'clock in the morning? Oh, yeah, it's three.'

'Well, I would love to see them. Do you think you might bring them with you on your next visit?'

'Who said there was going to be a next visit?'

'Ross, please.'

'Twice, so far, I've mentioned that I have shit going on in my life and you haven't even asked what.'

'They're not ill, are they? Those poor little babies!'

'No, it's just that Sorcha has kind of focked me out of the house and I'm now having to live with the old man and Helen.'

'Your father never mentioned that.'

'Doesn't surprise me. He's like you – totally wrapped up in himself.'

'What on Earth has gotten into Sorcha?'

'Hey, I've given up trying to understand the female mind.'

'You poor thing.'

'I rode a woman. With a skinhead. That was a major port of it. So right now I only have access to the kids one day a week.'

'Sorcha is coming to visit me tomorrow. Do you want me to talk to her?'

'It probably wouldn't do any good. Anyway, at the moment we're just separated, although her old man is obviously in her ear. He's using this to convince her to cut me out of her life once and for all.'

'I know exactly how it feels, Ross, to be the victim of an injustice.'

She definitely knows what buttons to press with me.

'Well, my situation is slightly different,' I go, 'in that I did actually ride the woman.'

She puts her hand down on top of mine. She's there, 'So you're saying you do believe me?'

And the truth is, well, I honestly don't know.

Fionn is back from the States.

Yeah, no, he shows up in Kielys while we're having Friday night pints, the usual suspects – we're talking me, we're talking JP, we're

22

talking Oisinn, we're talking Christian. The conversation *had* been about me – and, to a lesser extent, Christian – helping Seapoint avoid relegation to Division 2C of the All Ireland League. Oisinn was actually going, 'You certainly answered your critics with that final kick of the game, Ross – especially the ones who said you were basically a choker who pissed away whatever talent you had.' And that's when Fionn decided to make his entrance – with his glasses and his whole routine.

He walks in and he's all, 'Hey, I thought I might find you in here!' and then suddenly it's hugs all round and the conversation ends up being about his year in New York advising the United Nations on the problem of international piracy and the threat posed by Abu Sayyaf and other Islamic militant groups to merchant ships in the Southern Philippines.

'Yeah, we *were* talking about rugby,' I go, 'and specifically my heroics in the All Ireland League, until you decided to walk in and try to steal the show.'

Even then, he can't acknowledge my achievement in coming back after fifteen years out of the game. He goes, 'Jesus Christ, Ross, I heard about your mother. I'm so sorry. I actually still can't get my head around it.'

'Yeah, no,' I go, 'they're saying she dropped a two-bor electric heater in his bath, the poor focker. Mine's a pint of Heineken, by the way.'

He catches Mary's eye and draws a circle in the air to say same again all round.

He's like, 'This is Fionnuala O'Carroll-Kelly we're talking about. We've known her since we were kids. There's no way she'd be capable of killing someone. I don't think.'

I'm there, 'That's nice to hear. My old man thinks it's an attempt to destroy him politically.'

'Charles is doing a good enough job of that himself,' JP goes. 'He's saying he's going to abolish water chorges, property tax, the USC – and fix the health service. People aren't going to fall for that. No offence, Ross.'

I'm there, 'None taken. I've got enough on my plate anyway

without getting involved in his bullshit. The even bigger news, by the way, is that me and Sorcha have broken up.'

JP goes, 'Shit one,' in fairness to him.

I'm like, 'Yeah, no, me up to my old tricks again. I'll never learn. So we've ended up separated. I'm still hoping I can weasel my way back in there, so don't even think about making a move on her, Fionn.'

Because he would if he thought he had a chance – he'd be on her like a seagull on vomit.

He makes a big point of ignoring this and instead asks Oisinn what he's up to these days. Oisinn tells him he's sort of, like, easing his way back into business – still waiting for the next big thing to come along, whatever that happens to be.

That's when Christian gets a text message. He reads it and goes, 'Hey, Muirgheal's thinking about dropping in – is that cool with everyone?' and he can't keep the smile from his face. We all know that feeling when you first meet a girl and you still haven't found out that she's a focking nightmare like all the rest of them. I end up having to bite my tongue. A boys' night out is a boys' night out. End of discussion.

Fionn goes, 'Muirgheal? Why is that name familiar?'

I'm there, 'Do you remember a bird called Muirgheal Massey? She was in Mount Anville – she went for Head Girl the year Sorcha won it and she was massively pissed off about it. JP rode her on the pitch in Lakelands Pork.'

'It was actually Templeville Road,' JP goes. 'And I didn't ride her – just to say that, Christian. I only kissed her.'

Christian's there, 'Hey, I don't mind. We all have a past!'

I'm like, 'Yeah, no, Lauren's living in France and seeing some cinematographer called Loic, who has zero interest in rugby – isn't that right, Christian? That's the kind of people she's associating with these days. She made her bed. She can focking lie on it now.'

Christian goes, 'So what will I tell Muirgheal? Is everyone cool with her popping in? She's actually outside. She's with Sorcha.'

I'm like, 'Sorcha?' hating myself for sounding so desperate. 'That's very interesting.'

'Yeah, no,' he goes, 'they've been campaigning for marriage equality in Donnybrook all day.'

I'm there, 'Hey, I've no problem with it – marriage equality *or* them swinging in for a drink,' and I'm thinking this might be a great time to persuade Sorcha to give her own marriage another go, especially if I can get her on the Cointreau.

Anyway, they arrive in. And it's not just Sorcha and Muirgheal – they're with the famous Magnus. Oisinn goes, 'Okay, who's that big blond dude with Sorcha?' obviously trying to get a reaction from me. 'The really, really good-looking one?'

I refuse to take the bait. They spot us standing up at the bor and over they trot. Fionn ends up getting all the attention, of course. Sorcha goes, 'Oh my God, you're home!' and it ends up being hugs and UN talk and all the rest of it. She makes a big point of totally blanking *me*, by the way? She's obviously still pissed off with me. She introduces *him*, though – the famous manny. 'Everyone,' she goes, 'this is Magnus.'

And everyone's just like, 'Hey, Magnus!'

He goes, 'Hi, guysh, it'sh gute to meet you.'

The accent is comical. I might sneakily record a few seconds of it and send it to Jerry Flannery. I know he'll get a kick out of it.

Muirgheal goes, 'Oh my God, *what* a day we've had!'

Sorcha turns around to Fionn and goes, 'This is Muirgheal, I don't know if you remember her. We were in Mount Anville together. She was, like, Deputy Head Girl when I was Head Girl?'

No one does passive-aggressive like my wife.

Fionn goes, 'It's really nice to meet you, Muirgheal. And you're campaigning for marriage equality?' showing an actual interest – which is a tactic of his.

Muirgheal's there, 'Yeah, it was actually my idea to torget older voters and try to challenge the traditional view of marriage as being between a man and a woman.'

Sorcha's there, 'In fairness, I think we *both* had the idea? Because I gave a talk to my grandmother's Active Retirement group, remember?'

'I think I did suggest it first, though, even though that's not important. What we're trying to do is get older people to just, like, open their minds and see that love comes in many different forms.'

'And the amazing news is that they're – oh my God – actually listening!' Sorcha goes. 'Do you know what my grandmother said to me after I gave – like I said – the very first talk to the Foxrock and Deansgrange Active Retirement Association? She said that, twenty years ago, the idea of a man marrying a man, or a woman marrying a woman, was as ridiculous to her as the idea of a man marrying his car, or a woman marrying her dog.'

I'm there, 'It does feel a bit random alright – even though I'm obviously one hundred percent cool with it.'

'But then she said, "This isn't for my generation, Sorcha. We've had our time. This is for the next generation. And if this is what they want, then we owe it to them," and my eyes were – oh my God – *literally* welling up with tears?'

'Well,' Muirgheal goes, 'I think I really got through to them at the Donnybrook and District Friends of the Elderly tonight. And tomorrow I'm doing the bowls club in Shankill.'

'Skank Hill,' I go.

Hey, if I don't say it, no one else will.

I'm like, 'Sorcha, do you fancy a Cointreau?'

She's like, 'No, thank you,' without even looking at me. 'Muirgheal, I thought I told you I was going to do the talk at the bowls club?'

'Oh my God, Sorcha, why do you have to turn everything into a competition?'

Oisinn tries to change the subject then. He's like, 'So what's the story with you, Magnus?' and he's got a big, shit-eating grin on his face. 'You're a *friend* of Sorcha's, are you?', implying that there might be something going on between them.

Magnus goes, 'I'm actually working ash a nanny for her. But alsho I am helping with the campaign.'

I'm like, 'Magnus is gay, by the way. He's *a* gay. He's a gay man. Whatever the proper phrase is.'

And suddenly I find everyone staring at me with a mixture of surprise and disgust.

Sorcha goes, 'Okay, *how* is that relevant, Ross?'

I'm there, 'It was just in case they were worried.'

'Worried? Why would Magnus's sexuality worry them?'

'Yeah, no, I only said it just in case they were wondering whether there was anything going on between the two of you. I wanted to put their minds at ease.'

Muirgheal tries to get in on the act then. 'Oh, so you think it's okay,' she goes, 'to define somebody by their sexuality, do you?'

Jesus Christ.

Magnus, by the way, isn't bothered in the slightest. He isn't even following the conversation anymore. He's just, like, staring at the muted TV in the corner of the bor. There's some kind of – I swear to fock – soccer match on the screen. In Kielys, bear in mind! There was a time in this pub when they'd sooner put live animal porn on than soccer. Clearly not anymore.

'Ah,' he goes, 'they are showing the goalsh from Shwanshea againsht Arshenal on Monday night.'

That's what he says. I'm there, 'Whoa, are you saying you're a soccer fan?'

'You mean futebol?'

'No, I mean soccer.'

He's like, 'Of coursh!' and he shrugs his shoulders like it's a ridiculous question to ask anyone. 'I *played* futebol professionally for IFK Göteborg until I wash maybe twenty-shix, twenty-sheven yearsh old.'

'Meaningless.'

'Then, shadly, I wash injured. Alsho, I have five capsh for Finland.'

'And did you mention any of this to my wife? When she interviewed you for the job of minding our children?'

'I didn't conshider that informashion relevant.'

'Yeah, no,' I go, 'I bet you didn't.'

Sorcha goes, 'Ignore him, Magnus.'

I look at the rest of the goys, expecting back-up, but I get none.

JP goes, 'What's wrong with soccer, Ross?' and that's a direct quote.

Er, the ridiculous shape of the ball? The scum of the Earth who play it? Where do you want me to stort?

Then Oisinn, of all people, goes, 'Just because you love rugby, it doesn't mean you have to hate every other sport. We're supposed to be living in an age of tolerance.'

And I'm suddenly made to feel like a bigot for thinking something that it was perfectly okay to think a few years ago, specifically – and I'm just going to come out and say it – I don't want someone who's mixed up in soccer looking after my children. I'm about to say it, but in the end I decide to keep my mouth shut.

As Father Fehily used to say, 'Knowledge is knowing you can push the envelope. Wisdom is knowing it'll still be stationery.'

'Aroyse and f . . . f . . . f . . . foddy Cheerlie, wha?'

Kennet's in cracking form. It's annoying.

'Well, Ine certainly f . . . f . . . f . . . foddying him,' he goes.

I'm there, 'You're paid to follow him – you're his focking dogsbody.'

'Ine saying I'd foddy him to the ends of the Eert. Lot of people will feel the s . . . s . . . sayum way arthur he's speech the utter day. What he said about making Arelunt thremendous again – it's what people want to hee-or, idn't it?'

I've no idea what people want to hear. Especially in this port of the world – namely Finglas. I only drove out here to find out how Ronan was getting on, what with his Leaving Cert being only, like, two weeks away. The answer, by the way, is not great. He's sitting at the kitchen table trying to concentrate on his books, but Rihanna-Brogan is watching an illegal download of *Rio 2 – It's On in the Amazon* on her iPad and she's singing along to the songs, while Shadden is hoovering underneath his feet and Dordeen is sitting at the table, smoking like a crematorium and staring at him like he's a focking dog reading the dishwasher manual.

'How are you fixed?' I go.

Ro's like, 'Not bad, Rosser. Lot of woork to do between now and me foorst exam, but. Ine alreet on Matts, Histody and Biodogy, but I've a feer bit of catching-up to do on the utters – especiady Chemistoddy.'

'Would you not think of maybe going to the library to study, Ro?' just trying to subtly tell Shadden and Rihanna-Brogan to give him some space and Dordeen and Kennet to maybe fock off home to their own gaff. 'It just seems there's a lot going on here.'

Dordeen twists the butt of a cigarette in the ashtray, then takes another one from the packet. She goes, 'I'll teddle you what he'd want to be doing – he'd want to be forgerring all about this stoodying shit. Waste of bleaten toyum. He's gorrra a lubbly geerdle there and a little babby to be looken arthur. Should be out eerding a way-uch, stead of sitting arowunt alt day with he's nose in a buke. It's not natur doddle.'

I'm like, 'What do you mean it's not *natur doddle?*'

'Me and Shadden's fadder, we habn't a single qualification between the boat of us,' and I sit there staring at her for a good ten seconds, waiting to find out what this might be evidence of.

I'm there, 'Is that sentence finished, Dordeen?'

She goes, 'Yeah, it's fidished. What Ine saying is that Shadden shouldn't be expected to spend the next howebber many years of her loyuf waiting arowunt for your son to fidish skewill.'

'It's not *skewill*, it's college.'

Kennet throws his ten cents' worth into the pot then. He's like, 'Alt we're saying is that Ronan would be bethor off putting he's touym and edergy into he's business. There's muddy to be mayud ourrof it.'

Ro set up this, like, *Love/Hate* Tour of Dublin last year. Nudger, Gull and Buckets of Blood are going to run it for him until he finishes college.

'Moy advice to Ronan,' Kennet goes, 'is if you want to go to coddidge, then do – be all mee-uns, gerrit ourrof yisser systoddem – but what you should be concenthraten on is that tewer. It's yisser breath and buthor. It's what puts foowut in that freezer.'

Shadden at least sticks up for him. 'I *wanth* him to go to coddidge,' finally turning off the hoover. 'The *Lub/Hate* thing idn't godda last forebber, especiady when it's been off the teddy a few yeeors. Ronan's got brains to burden. Be a bettor future for us alt if he gets a good educashidden.'

There's no fear of that, I'm tempted to say, trying to concentrate in this focking nuthouse.

'Ro,' I go, 'even if you want to come with me to my old man's for the day. Him and Helen are usually out. You'd have the gaff to yourself. I'd make you tea and blah, blah, blah.'

He's there, 'Nah, I'll be alreet, Rosser. Ine moostard – seerdiously.'

It's at that exact moment that my *phone* ends up ringing? I check the screen and it ends up being – holy shit – Sorcha. My first thought is that she's possibly ringing to apologize for overreacting the night I pointed out that Magnus was – I'm just going to come out and say the word – gay. That's why I end up answering.

I'm like, 'Hey.'

She goes, 'Hi,' even though she still sounds a bit frosty with me. 'I'm looking for a favour.'

Fock. I immediately regret answering.

I'm like, 'A favour?' already trying to come up with an excuse. 'This isn't a great line, by the way. I'm only mentioning it in case I suddenly lose you.'

She goes, 'My grandmother wants to vote today.'

I'm there, 'Vote? Vote for what?'

There's, like, a long silence on the other end.

She goes, 'Today is the day of the marriage *equality* referendum?'

I'm like, 'Oh, yeah, no, I knew that. I definitely knew that.'

'Like I said, I definitely touched a nerve with her and her friends the day I spoke to her Active Retirement group. Do you know what she said to me this morning?'

'Go on. Again, bear in mind –'

'She said, "You've helped me realize something, Sorcha. Marriage is about love. And as a Christian, it's my duty to vote for that over the alternative." Isn't that – oh my God – *such* an amazing thing to say?'

'It doesn't sound like the woman. But yeah, no, I suppose it is.'

She goes, 'I actually tweeted it and it's got, like, thirty Likes already. And six Retweets – one or two of them from people I don't even know!'

'Yeah, no,' I go, 'I'm just wondering – and I'm not being a dick here – but what does any of this have to do with me? There was talk of a favour?'

'Yes, I was going to ask you, would you mind driving her to the polling station?'

'Er, like I said, the line is bad . . . I'm losing you, Sorcha.'

'It's just that I'm going to be tied up all day – mostly monitoring what's happening on social media. There's some amazing, amazing stories out there. And my mum and dad are in Galway – they won't be back until this evening.'

'Hello? Hello?'

'Actually,' she goes, 'don't bother. I can always ask Fionn.'

Don't ever believe, even for a minute, that men are the cleverest of the species. They're not. In fact, if women could open jors, parallel-pork and impregnate themselves, there'd be no need for men at all.

I end up just going, 'Okay, okay, I'll do it.'

Sorcha's granny opens the door and I end up laughing in her face. I know I shouldn't. It's the big, dandelion puffball head on her. I always imagine if you sneezed, her hair would end up flying away.

She goes, '*You're* driving me to the polling centre then, are you?'

I'm there, 'Yeah, no, I'm only doing it as a way of hopefully getting back into Sorcha's good books. Do you want to maybe go to the jacks first?'

The only reason I ask is because she's, like, walking up and down on the spot.

I'm there, 'You seem to be bursting.'

'I don't need the toilet,' she goes. 'It's this thing,' and she pulls up her sleeve to show me her wrist. Again, I laugh, because it turns out she's wearing one of those, like, Fitbits?

I'm there, 'Okay, don't tell me you've fallen for it as well,' because every second focker you meet these days is telling you how many steps he's walked since breakfast and expecting a 'Fair focks!' from you.

She goes, 'The doctor said I needed to get more exercise. He says

I'm too much on that mobility scooter. I have a daily activity goal of one hundred steps per hour. I'm eighty-two, you know!'

I'm there, 'Can you maybe stop doing it for a minute, though? It's actually making *me* want to piss?'

She invites me in, then leads me down to the living room. Her gaff is a typical old person's gaff. It smells of mince and wet wool and you can't turn your head to the side without looking at a picture of Jesus or Mary or one of that crew making you feel guilty about shit you've done or shit you might be thinking of doing.

I'm like, 'So, er, let's get going.'

She's like, 'I'll just get my voting card,' and then she says *the* most unbelievable thing. 'Someone has to put a stop to these gays and their nonsense.'

Now, you can probably imagine my reaction. I'm, like, pretty much lost for words, especially after what she supposedly said to Sorcha about – what was it? – voting for love? I'm like, 'Whoa, whoa, whoa – you're saying you're *against* gay marriage?'

She goes, 'Of course I am. God created Adam and Eve – he didn't create Adam and Panti Bliss.'

'But Sorcha said you were all for it. You told her that it wasn't for your generation, it was for the next generation.'

'I only said that to shut her up. She came to the Active Retirement. I was playing dominos with Mrs Culloty and Mrs Rackard. Oh, she gave us all a big lecture. Said if we were against gay marriage, then we were all homeo phobiacs.'

'I think the phrase might be homophobists?'

'She said if we didn't vote Yes in this referendum, that's what we were. The gall of her to be preaching! I'm eighty-two!'

'You mentioned.'

'Mrs Rackard turned to me and shishee, "Isn't that girl divorced herself?" Says I, "No, she's separated." And shishee, "Who is she to lecture us about marriage so?"'

'That's a very good point. I might end up saying that to her. Store it up in case I ever have to use it.'

'She made a vow. Before God. "Better or worse." I heard her say it. And how many times have you broken up?'

'It's quite a few. I'm not denying that. She gets very jealous.'

Especially when I ride other women.

'And *she's* lecturing *me*,' she goes, 'on what marriage should be.'

I'm there, 'She's got some nerve. I'm tempted to use the word hypocrite.'

'But we didn't want her telling us we were all homeo phobiacs. Oh, you can't say anything these days. Mrs Felton got an earful from her daughter for saying that she'd never tell her Confession to a black priest. So when Sorcha came to the centre, we all said the same thing to her: "Oh, we're with the gays, don't you worry about that! We'll all be voting Yes on the day." '

'But you're actually going to vote No?'

'I'm a Catholic. Gays getting married to other gays is against my faith.'

'Well, maybe *I* could persuade you to vote Yes.'

'You?'

'Yeah, no, the point *I* was going to make is that Sorcha had a lot of gay friends in UCD and every single one of them was sound. And a lot easier to talk to than I expected.'

'You and Sorcha aren't the only ones who know gays. I know gays.'

'What gays do you know?'

'Mrs O'Reilly's grandson is a gay. He does her shopping. He's a radiographer. He gets her bits for her – from SuperValu.'

'See?'

'But he's going to burn in Hell.'

'Jesus.'

'He'll burn in Hell for his carry-on. Unless he repents and stops his nonsense, like the rest of them. Now, wait'll I find my polling card.'

I decide that I can't let her do it. It would literally break Sorcha's hort if she ever found out that her grandmother – who she absolutely *idolizes*, by the way? – voted No.

It'd be ten times worse if she knew that I knew and I let her go ahead and do it.

'Okay,' I go, 'I've got a possible solution.'

She's like, 'A solution? What's this you're saying now?'

'Look, I was planning to vote Yes.'

'That's your business. As long as you know you'll be going to Hell as well.'

'And you're obviously planning to vote No.'

'God created Adam and Eve –'

'Yeah, no, don't say that again. Look, why don't the two of us just not bother our holes voting?'

'What?'

'If you vote No and I vote Yes, we're just going to end up cancelling each other out anyway. So why are we even bothering? Why don't we just stay here and watch . . . is that *Midday* on the TV there?'

'It is. I often put it on. For the company.'

'Well, so do I. I've got a thing for Elaine Crowley. I've told her that to her face.'

'Oh, she's very good.'

'She's better than good. On that subject, we *are* agreed.'

'We could have a glass of Irish Mist, couldn't we?'

Sorcha's granny is murder for the drink – nearly worse than my old dear.

'It *is* after twelve,' I go, then I nod at the bottle on the sideboard. 'You go over and fix us a couple of Irish Mists then. It'll add another few steps onto your total for the day.'

She totters over to the sideboard, then she pours us each a drink while walking up and down on the spot. She has a heavy pouring hand – it's one of the things I've always liked about the woman. She hands me a tall glass filled to the top with whiskey and whatever else is in it, then we both sit down in front of the TV.

'It's nice not having to go out,' she goes.

And I end up having to agree with her. It's actually true what I've heard Sorcha sometimes say – politics definitely is the ort of compromise.

So it's, like, Saturday afternoon and I'm driving the kids home from Dundrum.

'Actually,' Honor goes, staring down at the dozen or so shopping bags at her feet, 'I hope you and Mom never get back together. I'm getting *so* much stuff since you got separated.'

I'm like 'Yes, you are. And there'll be more. This is going to be what it's like every Saturday until your mother hopefully cops onto herself and takes me back.'

We arrive back at Honalee. I pull up on the side of the Vico Road and I press the buzzer. But it's not Sorcha's voice I hear through the intercom speaker. It's actually her old man's. He's forever in the house these days. He answers by going, 'Yes?'

I'm there, 'Yeah, no, it's Ross.'

He goes, 'Who?'

He literally says that.

'You know who it is,' I go. 'Just open the gate, you focking cockwomble.'

Which is what he ends up doing. I hop back into the cor. I turn around to Honor and I go, 'Sorcha's old man is here – again!'

Honor pulls a face. 'I focking hate him,' she goes.

I'm there, 'Well, I just called him a cockwomble.'

She laughs. She's like, 'A cockwomble? That's actually funny!'

I'm there, 'Yeah, no, it just came to me on the spot.'

She goes, 'Good one, Dad!'

I drive through the open gate and up the driveway. 'Oh my God,' Honor goes, 'I totally forgot, *she* asked them to babysit us tonight.'

I'm like, 'Er, *why*? Where's she gone? And where's Magnus? Are – I don't know – Shamrock Rangers playing or something?'

'No, the two of them have gone in to Dublin Castle to hear the referendum result announced – the saps.'

She can be very funny, Honor. As long as you don't get on the wrong side of her.

Brian shouts, 'You focking cockwomble!'

Me and Honor just crack our holes laughing. They really are like sponges at that age. It's lovely.

Anyway, I'm halfway up the driveway when I suddenly see it, porked in front of the gaff – it's, like, a removal lorry? I end up just, like, slamming on the brakes. Because men are lifting shit out of it – we're talking boxes, we're talking a desk, we're talking a sofa – and carrying it all into the house.

I'm like, 'What the fock?' as I climb out of the cor and Honor says something very similar. Sorcha's old man greets us at the door.

I'm like, 'What's all this?'

He goes, 'Oh, just our few, meagre possessions. As you are often wont to remind us, Sorcha's mother and I don't have much in the world. We do have the love of our daughter, however. And, happily, it's not something we have to buy,' and he makes a big point of staring at the ten or fifteen shopping bags swinging from Honor's orms.

I'm there, 'You are not moving into my house.'

'It's not your house anymore,' he goes. 'I told you. You're finished here.'

I whip out my phone and I ring Sorcha.

Honor's there, 'What's happening, Dad?'

And I'm like, 'That's what I'm trying to find out.'

The phone goes straight to her voicemail. I turn on my heel and I head for the cor. Honor's like, 'Dad, where are you going?'

'Fock you,' Brian shouts as I take him and his brothers out of their cor seats. 'You focking cockwomble.'

And I'm there, 'I'm going to Dublin Castle – to find out what's going on.'

'Oh, good,' Sorcha's old man goes, 'because she has a little surprise for you.'

I hear it on the news while I'm in the cor. Ireland has voted to change the Constitution to extend civil marriage rights to same-sex couples and I'm thinking, that's fantastic news – at least I know she'll be in a good mood.

I throw the cor into the Stephen's Green Shopping Centre, then I walk down George's Street and onto Dame Street, where the porty has already kicked off. It's an absolute scorcher of a day and there's, like, a real *carnival* atmosphere on the streets? Men and women are hugging each other. Men and men are hugging each other. Women

36

and women are hugging each other. Everyone seems to be crying – not because they're sad, but because they're happy.

People are driving by and sounding their cor horns as if to say, 'Fair focks and fock the begrudgers who tried to stop this from actually happening.' And I have to say, I feel very proud of what we've just done as a country, even though I didn't bother voting myself.

A massive crowd is gathered outside the gates of Dublin Castle. They're holding up little green signs saying 'Equality' and 'Yes' and '*Tá*' – which is the Irish word for thanks. A bearded man in a dress wraps a rainbow flag around my shoulders and gives me a kiss on the cheek and everyone cheers and I laugh as I push my way through the throng of people to the actual gates. Which end up being locked.

I look through the bors into this, like, courtyord, which again is packed thick with people, waving flags, crying, holding up signs, sitting on each other's shoulders and generally just savouring the moment. In a way, it's, like, *history*?

There's a dude with his back to me who's obviously, I don't know, security of some kind. I'm like, 'Hey – you!' and he turns around. 'Can I get in there, please?'

He's like, 'Do you have a pass?'

There's always one. Give a man a fish and you feed him for a day. Give a man an orange bib, a clipboard and a walkie-talkie and you turn him into an absolute jeb-end.

I pat myself down, going, 'Unfortunately, I think I've lost it. But my wife is inside there – she was involved in the whole, I don't know, *thing*?'

He's there, 'I can't let you in – not without a pass.'

Shit, I'm thinking. I have to get in there to see her. And that's when I hear what could only be described as a loud squeal behind me, followed by, 'Oh my God, Ross!'

I turn around and there's a bird standing in front of me. The face is definitely familiar. I just can't place her. She obviously picks up on my confusion because she puts her hand on her chest and goes, 'Oreanna?'

Oreanna! Now there's a name from the past! I laugh. *She* laughs as well, which comes as a definite relief because during the brief time we dated – we're talking, like, *years* ago? – I accidentally ran over her cat, then accidentally killed her dog.

She's obviously not one to hold a grudge because she gives me a massive hug and goes, 'It's lovely to see you – what a day, huh?'

I'm there, 'Yeah, no, everyone seems to be happy alright.'

Then she turns to the bird standing beside her and goes, 'Eva, this is Ross!'

She's clearly told her one or two stories about the Rossmeister General because Eva's face lights up and she goes, 'Oh my God, *this* is him?', and I can't tell whether she means it in a good way or a bad way.

But Oreanna goes, 'Ross, this is my girlfriend, Eva.'

And I'm like, 'Girlfriend?' because this is obviously new information. 'I didn't think you were –'

She laughs. 'Er, you couldn't tell,' she goes, 'from my general lack of enthusiasm when we slept together?'

I'm like, 'Not really, no.'

I tend not to notice that kind of thing. It might sound sexist, but I'm usually too focused on my own game to care whether the other person is enjoying themselves.

'And you,' she goes. 'I definitely knew *you* were gay,' and she grabs the two corners of the rainbow flag that I'm still wearing around my shoulders and she ties them at the front.

I'm like, 'What?'

She goes, 'Oh, just from the way you went about it. I got a sense that women did very little for you.'

I'm there, 'The thing is, Oreanna, I'm not actually –'

And then I stop, because I notice that she's wearing, like, a laminated badge around her neck and I suddenly see a way of getting through those gates. I'm there, 'So are you, like, *involved* in the whole thing?'

She goes, 'Yeah, I actually work with the Gay and Lesbian Equality Network.'

'Happy focking days. Could you get me in – as in, into the actual courtyord there? It's just that my, er, yeah, no, *boyfriend* is inside?'

'Boyfriend?'

'Boyfriend. Big-time. Bart.'

I don't know why I say Bart. But I do say Bart.

I'm there, 'He's a quantity surveyor.'

Again, I'm just throwing out random shit.

'Oh my God,' Oreanna goes, 'that's so lovely,' and then she turns around to Eva. 'I'll give him a pass,' she goes. 'He did help me realize it was women I liked.'

Jesus, another one. The goys in UCD used to call me Flipper.

Eva just nods. Oreanna reaches into her pocket and pulls out a ticket, which she then just hands to me. I go, 'Thanks so much – you've just made this day even more special for me,' because you've obviously got to make it sound convincing. 'I really want to celebrate this day with, like I said, Bart.'

We say our goodbyes and our good lucks to each other, then ten seconds later I'm through the gates and in the courtyard of Dublin Castle, trying to pick my wife out amid all this happy pandemonium going on around me.

It takes me about twenty minutes to find her. I actually notice this, like, drag queen – who bears an uncanny resemblance to my old dear – turn over on his ankle on the cobbles. It's definitely not the place for heels – in terms of the venue, someone obviously didn't think it through. Anyway, I notice Sorcha and focking Muirgheal lift him back on his feet, then help him fix his skirt.

I'm straight over there and I'm like, 'Okay, Sorcha, what the fock?'

To say she's surprised to see me there, especially wearing a rainbow flag around my shoulders, would be a definite understatement. She's like, 'What are *you* doing here?'

I go, 'Never mind what am I doing here. What are your old pair doing moving their shit into my house?'

'You've got a nerve. You really have.'

'What are you talking about?'

'I'm going to ask you a question, and I want you to tell me the truth.'

'What's the question?'

'Did you bring my grandmother to vote?'

'Yes, I did bring her. Yes, indeed.'

'You didn't, Ross.'

'Excuse me?'

She actually *shouts* it this time? She goes, 'You didn't bring her to vote!'

I once saw Cian Healy emptying loose change from a Jacob's Afternoon Tea biscuit tin into a Coinstar machine in Tesco on the Upper Rathmines Road. The printer must have been out of toner because it spat him out a receipt with no actual writing on it. The look Sorcha gives me is the same look Cian Healy gave that Coinstar machine.

'She didn't move all afternoon,' she goes. 'My mum and dad checked her Fitbit.'

Oh, shit.

I'm there, 'Yeah, no, the thing is . . .' trying to come up with an explanation quickly.

'She only took eight steps,' Sorcha goes, 'between twelve o'clock, which was around the time you arrived, and a quarter to six, when my mum and dad called to her house to find her drunk. Drunk, Ross! In front of *Nuacht*!'

Muirgheal tuts and shakes her head. This has fock-all to do with her – she should stay the fock out of it.

'Okay,' I go, 'if you want the real truth . . . Let me think here . . .'

Sorcha's there, 'You didn't bring her to vote, Ross.'

'That's not true.'

'She told us what happened. She said she was going to vote one way and you were going to vote the other way, so you told her there was no point in bothering.'

'Yeah, no, I'm sorry to have to tell you that that's what actually did happen.'

And that's when I suddenly notice her – the granny – standing a few feet to my left, with Magnus as it happens. The woman is wearing – I shit you not – a t-shirt with the word 'Equality' on it. I'm too in shock to even speak and she takes advantage of my silence to go, 'He said he wouldn't bring me to vote because I told him I was going to vote Yes.'

I'm like, 'What? That's not what . . .'

Magnus shakes his head sort of, like, *disgustedly*?

She goes, 'Live and let live is what I say. Isn't it still love at the end of the day? And who are you to say these gays shouldn't enjoy the same rights as everyone else?'

The sneaky focking cow. I'm there, 'Yeah, no, she's lying, Sorcha.'

Sorcha goes, 'Yeah, I think you've just proven who the real liar here is, Ross. I can't believe you denied her the opportunity to vote in – oh my God – *the* most important referendum in her lifetime.'

'Well, the truth, which you might not want to hear, is that she was actually going to vote No.'

'I don't even want to know your reasons for being against gay marriage, Ross. I had no idea I was married to a bigot.'

By now, of course, there are quite a few people in the courtyord listening in to the conversation? I hope it's not homophobist to say that gay people love a bit of drama.

'She's the one who's the bigot,' I go, feeling like I'm addressing the entire audience in Dublin Castle now. Which, given the level of attention we're drawing, I kind of *am*? 'She only told you she was going to vote Yes because you went to the Active Retirement and bullied her and her mates into it.'

The granny knows what she's doing, though, because she goes, 'I think Sorcha knows which one of us is the liar. You've been doing it your entire marriage.'

Sorcha just shakes her head – like she's more, I don't know, *disappointed* than angry? 'Ross,' she goes, 'this is definitely *the* worst thing you've ever done to me.'

I'm there, 'I hordly think it is, Sorcha. I rode your sister.'

There's a lot of gasps around me. I'm losing this crowd – there's no denying that.

I'm there, 'I'm not saying it in a braggy way. I'm just making the point that we managed to come back from that. Me riding your sister. That's the benchmork.'

And that's when, for some reason, I look down at her hand and I notice that she's not wearing her rings anymore. I actually blurt it out. I'm there, 'You're not wearing your . . .'

She goes, 'Our marriage is finished, Ross. It was from the very minute you drove to Dalkey and had sex with that slut.'

Someone shouts, 'You go, girl!' and there ends up being, like, a round of applause from a hundred or so people.

I'm there, 'Sorcha, please – let's not ruin this day of supposedly celebration by talking about breaking up. Think of all these people.'

It's no good, though. I know what's coming even before she storts fumbling around in her handbag. Then she hands me the envelope. 'That's a letter from my dad,' she goes, 'formalizing our separation and giving you notice that I'm going to be seeking a divorce on the grounds of adultery.'

There's, like, cheers and clapping from the couple of hundred or so people who are tuned in to the conversation. I just look around at all these men and women, here to celebrate. And though I try my best not to be bitter, I end up going, 'Seriously, why would anyone in their right mind want to get married?'

They all stort *booing* me? Which upsets me hugely, because gay people have always, always loved me. As a matter of fact, men who work at skincare counters in deportment stores often look at me when they're answering Sorcha's questions. Sometimes, I can maintain eye contact with them for four or five seconds.

'You know what? I've actually changed my mind,' I go. 'I'm now anti gay marriage.'

I hear people saying to each other, 'He said he's against gay marriage.'

'Why are you even here then?' a man with a pink feather boa shouts. 'Why don't you fock off, you homophobe?'

I'm there, 'I'm saying it for your own good. It's gay marriage today. But you'll be looking for gay divorce next – mork my words. One thing will follow the other.'

'Get out of here,' this big dude with a shaved head goes. 'You're not welcome here.'

And a crowd of maybe two hundred people cheer.

'You must be mad,' I tell them. 'You must all be focking mad.'

2. Eirexit

I'm back in the old man's gaff, sitting at the kitchen table, staring at the letter – and at one word in particular. The D word. I'm there, 'I honestly thought she'd take me back.'

Helen is standing behind me with her hand on my shoulder, being as sympathetic as she possibly can. She goes, 'I expect she feels terribly betrayed, Ross.'

I'm like, 'Yeah, no, keep talking to me like that, Helen. A bit of tough love is probably what I need right now.'

'You cheated on her. You've been cheating on her for years. It shouldn't come as any great surprise that she's finally wised up and decided that she deserves better.'

'Yeah, no, maybe ease off on the tough love, Helen. I might need you to say something positive now to even things up.'

'How many second chances did you think she was going to give you, Ross?'

'Two or three more. I don't know. She carried on wearing her rings until she found out that I didn't bring that stupid cow to vote. There might still be a chance for us if I can persuade her that her granny is a bigot who believes that gay people burn in Hell.'

'I think you need to respect Sorcha's wishes, Ross.'

'She might still change her mind, though. I was thinking about maybe calling over there wearing my *Spicebomb by Viktor & Rolf*, which she can never resist. Another one that definitely gets her juices flowing is *By the Fireplace*, by Replica.'

'Ross, I think you need to accept that your marriage is over.'

'I can't accept it. What am I going to say to Honor? I told her I'd be moving back home within a couple of weeks. I made her that promise.'

'You shouldn't have done that, Ross.'

'Coulda, woulda, shoulda, Helen. The fact is that I did.'

I put down the letter and I end up just shaking my head – I think it's a word – *ruefully*? 'So that's it,' I go. 'It looks like I'm returning to the singles morket.'

Helen rubs the top of my orm in, like, a *soothing* way? She really is great. She's there, 'You don't need to rush out there and find someone else. I don't think it would do you any harm to be by yourself for a while.'

'I know you're trying to help,' I go, 'but you're being ridiculous.'

And that's when the old man suddenly arrives home. Into the kitchen he walks, going, 'Felicitous tidings I bring to thee!' and he slaps the *Sunday Indo* down on the table. 'Feast your eyes on that headline!'

It's like, 'New Republic Ahead of Labour in Poll'.

He goes, 'We're already the fourth largest party in the country behind Fine Gael, Fianna Fáil and Sinn Féin! And that's after one month!'

Helen – in fairness to her – goes, 'Ross is upset, Charlie.'

'Yeah,' I go, 'it doesn't have to always be about you. Sorcha is divorcing me.'

'Divorcing you?' he goes – like the penny has finally dropped. 'Oh, that's rather unfortunate!'

I'm like, 'Is that all you can say?'

And he goes – and I'm quoting him word for word now – 'You know, I heard her on the radio last night talking about marriage rights for the – inverted commas – homosexual community! Came across very well! Even had *me* convinced!'

'Charlie,' Helen goes, 'could you *be* any more insensitive?'

He looks at her and he has literally no idea what she's even talking about. I don't bother my hole explaining it to him, because my phone suddenly rings and I can see from the screen that it's Honor. I stand up from the table and at the same time I answer it. I'm like, 'Hey, you!', trying to put a brave face on shit.

There's no greeting – no nothing. She just goes, 'You lied to me. You *are* getting divorced.'

I laugh out loud. I'm just trying to protect her. I'm there, 'Honor, I swear on my old man's life that me and your mother are not getting divorced.'

I give *him* a long stare, then I step out of the kitchen into the hallway.

Honor goes, 'I heard Mom telling her prick of a dad that she served you with a formal divorce notice in Dublin Castle last night.'

And I'm like, 'Okay, I admit it, we *are* getting divorced. But I'm still hoping to persuade her to give it another go. That's the good news. I know they say don't give your children false hope, but there's a definite chance we'll look back on this one day and laugh.'

There's, like, silence on the other end of the phone. I'm there, 'I hope that's put your mind at ease, Honor.'

She doesn't answer me one way or the other. Instead, she says *the* most unbelievable thing to me. She goes, 'I want to take up rugby.'

I'm there, 'Rugby? The *game* of rugby?'

'Yes,' she goes, 'the *game* of rugby.'

'But you always said rugby was for saps and homosexuals.'

'That was before. Now I've grown to like it.'

'Hey, no offence taken, Honor. Can I just ask you, though, was it my recent heroics for Seapoint that made you want to follow in my footsteps?'

'No.'

'Maybe a little bit? You've heard one or two stories? People are going to talk. I have to accept that.'

'You're such a focking narcissist. I just like the game, that's all.'

I'm suddenly realizing that this all stems from her looking through my Rugby Tactics Book. I've obviously inspired her. I'm there, 'Can I just say, Honor, that I'm absolutely delighted? Because your brothers are turning out to be a massive, massive disappointment to me, certainly in terms of rugby. The next time we're in Herbert Pork, they can stay in their focking stroller and it'll be just me and you throwing the old shaved coconut back and forth.'

She goes, 'I'm not talking about just throwing the ball around in Herbert Pork. I want to play – for, like, a team?'

I'm there, 'An *actual* team?', because there's a bit of me that finds the idea of women playing rugby ridiculous. 'What team are we talking?'

She goes, 'Old Belvedere Minis are having a trial next Saturday. I want you to bring me.'

And I'm like, 'Er, yeah, no, we'll definitely go and check it out.'

When I hang up, the old man is telling Helen that he's asked Hennessy to be his Attorney General if he wins the election and Hennessy has said yes. 'We're going out to celebrate tonight,' he goes, 'with a couple of John Shanahan's finest sides of Certified Irish Angus! And let's see if he doesn't have a bottle of 2004 Échezeaux Grand Cru, Romanée-Conti knocking around!'

Helen totally innocently goes, 'You're not supposed to be eating red meat, Charlie. Or drinking. Remember what the specialist said about your heart?'

'Oh, damn that bloody specialist! Damn his bloody eyes! You can't win an election eating . . . what was that awful thing you made last night?'

'It was brown rice risotto with pumpkin.'

It *was* every bit as disgusting as it sounds, in fairness, and that's not me taking my old man's side.

'Churchill didn't win a war eating brown rice risotto with pumpkin!' he goes. 'It was steak! Every night! Swimming in blood!'

Helen goes, 'Charlie, you've changed since you put that wig on your head.'

But then he suddenly rips into her. He's like, 'Shut up, woman! Just shut the hell up!'

Sorcha opens the door. She looks well. An airtex has always suited her, in terms of showing off her Mister Bigs. She's obviously still pissed off with me because she's got her Out of Office face on.

I go, 'Hey,' playing it über cool.

She's just like, 'The children are ready. They're in the –' and then I watch her little nose twitch. 'Are you wearing *Spicebomb by Viktor & Rolf*?'

I'm there, 'I don't know. To be honest, I just grabbed the nearest bottle to me. Interesting you noticed it was *Spicebomb*, though.'

'Ross, our marriage is finished. You need to come to terms with that fact.'

'Hey, I've every intention of coming to terms with it. You might not want me. I'm sure there's plenty of women out there who wouldn't mind a slice.'

'Let's not do that, Ross. Let's not hurt each other.'

'You were the one who decided to serve me divorce papers in a public place.'

'I was furious with you for stopping my grandmother from voting. I'm still furious. Look, I don't know what you've got against gay people –'

'I love gay people. On the record.'

'It could be a rugby thing. I don't know.'

'I told you, your granny was the one who was going to vote No.'

'But a major port of *being* a liberal – which is something I would definitely, definitely *consider* myself? – is accepting that other people are entitled to their views, however egregious they might be. I was saying that to Fionn last night.'

'Fionn?'

'Yes, we went for dinner. I've wanted to go to Mulberry Gorden for ages.'

'I promised I'd take you.'

'You promised me a lot of things, Ross. The food is – oh my God – every bit as good as they say.'

'So he's back sniffing around you again, is he?'

'Fionn is a friend, Ross. A good friend.'

'Well, he used to be in love with you. I'm just pointing that out so you know what you're doing.'

'Anyway, you can deal with your jealousy on your own time. I don't have to listen to you anymore. I'm just saying I think it's important that you and I don't fall out. For the sake of the children. This divorce is going to be hord enough on them without their parents hating each other.'

'I could never hate you, Sorcha. You look really well, by the way. An airtex has always suited you.'

'We didn't have the perfect marriage, Ross. But who's to say we can't have the perfect divorce? I'm thinking in terms of Chris and Gwyneth and how they handled things.'

'Are these actual people or people on TV?'

'I'm talking about Gwyneth Paltrow and Chris Mortin. I'm talking about the way they consciously uncoupled. I'd love if we could handle things in a similarly civilized way.'

'Consciously uncoupling? Yeah, no, I'd be cool with that.'

'You and I might be finished, but let's not forget that we brought four beautiful children into the world.'

She turns sideways to let me in. The boys already have their coats on. 'Look at this focking prick!' Leo shouts at me from the other end of the hallway. He's putting complete sentences together now. Where do the years go?

Now seems like as good a time as any to say what I have to say. So I go, 'Yeah, no, I was thinking that maybe I'd just take Honor with me this morning.'

Sorcha's there, '*Excuse* me?'

'She wants to take up rugby. I don't know if she mentioned it to you.'

'Rugby? She always said rugby was for –'

'I know what she said, Sorcha. But she's obviously changed her mind. Old Belvedere are having trials this morning for their Minis team and she wants to have a crack at it. Even though I don't fully agree with the idea of women playing the game. My attitude is, what's wrong with hockey?'

Sorcha shakes her head and sort of, like, laughs bitterly. She's like, 'You know why she's doing this, don't you?'

I'm there, 'I'd like to think it stems back to her reading my Rugby Tactics Book.'

'She's doing it to get at me. You know she's barely spoken to me since she found out about the divorce.'

'She's always been a daddy's girl. I'll give her that.'

'Unbelievable! You had sex with that slut – I'm sorry, Ross – and she ends up taking *your* side?'

'That's a lovely thing for me to hear – although I'm still putting it down to the Tactics Book capturing her imagination. There's some pretty amazing ideas in it. I'll tell you one thing, if Matt O'Connor had got his hands on it, he'd probably still be in a job. Anyway, look, whatever her reasons, I promised her I'd take her to this trial this morning. Which is why I was going to ask you if I could leave the boys here?'

'You are *not* leaving them here. Saturday is your access day.'

'I realize that. The point is I'm only going to need access to one of them today. You can hang on to the other three.'

'No way. You are *not* playing favourites with our children.'

'It's not a case of playing favourites, Sorcha. Honor's really keen. I've already seen one or two flashes – she showed Leo how to throw the perfect pass.'

'Fock off!' Brian shouts. 'You focking cockwomble!'

I'm there, 'I've tried playing with the boys. I'm just going to come out and say it, Sorcha – they're shit.'

She's like, 'I beg your pordon?'

'I'm talking about in terms of rugby. Yeah, no, they might get better as they get older, when they learn how to throw and catch a ball properly. But right now, I'm sticking with the word shit. And, to be honest with you, the swearing is becoming a bit of an embarrassment. So what I was going to suggest was that I'd take Honor to rugby training, then maybe come back in the afternoon – no promises – to collect the boys and bring them all to Dundrum. Everyone's a winner.'

'You're taking all four of them, Ross, or none at all.'

'Fine,' I go, 'I'll take the four of them. But I'll probably just leave the boys on the back seat of the cor – obviously with the window open a crack.'

She's like, 'I hope that was a joke.'

'Of course it was a joke!'

It actually *wasn't* a joke? Maybe it's just for *dogs* that it's okay to do that?

Anyway, we don't get the chance to debate the subject any further because that's when my old man all of a sudden shows up. Again, it's totally random, but I see his black Merc crawling up the driveway with the famous K . . . K . . . K . . . Kennet behind the wheel.

I'm like, 'What the fock does this dude want?'

Sorcha looks as confused as I presumably do. She's there, 'I've no idea.'

Kennet pulls up, hops out, then opens the door for the old man, who steps out onto the gravel, combing his hair – even though it isn't *actually* hair? – with his hand. 'Sorcha!' he goes. 'How lovely to see you!'

Sorcha's like, 'Chorles? Oh my God, this is a surprise!' and she keeps looking at me, like she thinks I might know something.

Which I don't.

He doesn't acknowledge me, by the way? It's like I'm not even there. At least Kennet has the social skills to go, 'Howiya, Rosser?'

And I'm like, 'Yeah, whatever – you focking scumbag.'

Instead of his usual driver's hat, I notice, he's wearing a red baseball cap with 'CO'CK for Taoiseach' on the front.

Sorcha goes, 'To what do I owe the –', but she doesn't get time to even finish the question.

'I'm going to cut straight to the proverbial chase!' the old man goes. 'I expect you've heard all about New Republic by now? A sixth force in Irish politics – or seventh if you count Renua, which no one really does.'

'Oh my God, it said in the paper you're already ahead of Labour in the polls.'

'That's only the beginning! Sorcha, we are about to bear witness to a seismic shift in Irish politics! This country has not been at such a critical juncture since the year nineteen hundred and twenty-two! I'm sure Ross here will attest to that – with his keen knowledge of history!'

I got an NG in History. I'm just setting the record straight.

He goes, 'There's a huge groundswell of people out there who've had enough of the old parties who've governed this country since Independence! They're angry! And when people are angry, they're liable to vote for just about anyone! I want New Republic to be that just about anyone!'

'I'd love to say you have my vote, Chorles –'

'I'm not looking for your vote, Sorcha! I'm looking for you to join us!'

'Are you asking me to stand in the next election?'

Where's his focking loyalty? This is the woman who's supposedly divorcing me.

'Why not?' he goes. 'I'm familiar with the work you did on that gay marriage business! I've heard your name mentioned in dispatches as someone who changed the minds of many elderly, conservative voters!'

I say fock-all on the matter. It'd serve no useful purpose.

He's there, 'You convinced hundreds of people – many of them even older than me – to vote for the idea of a man marrying a man!'

'Or a woman marrying a woman,' she goes.

'The very idea of it! We need people of your calibre!'

'I'd love to say yes, Chorles. You know how much I've always loved you – *and* Fionnuala. The problem is that I disagree with your position on water chorges. I'm actually in *favour* of chorging people for water? It's a priceless natural resource, Chorles. And I genuinely believe that if we chorge people for the amount they use, they will learn to treat it more *responsibly*?'

'See? You've just persuaded *me*!'

'Are you saying you've changed your mind?'

'I'm saying you've convinced me that I should give the subject a fuller consideration!'

'Do you have an environmental policy?'

That's hilarious. It's like asking Kennet there if he has a TV licence.

The old man's like, 'A –?'

'An environmental policy,' she goes. 'Because if I do say yes, I'd love to be involved in drawing one up, as well as a White Paper on the future funding of Ireland's domestic water service.'

That'd be typical of Sorcha. She's in the club ten seconds and she's already trying to run things. I'm tempted to say that's Mount Anville for you.

The old man's there, 'How does Sorcha O'Carroll-Kelly – New Republic spokesperson on the Environment – sound to you?'

She goes, 'Could I be Sorcha O'Carroll-Kelly – New Republic spokesperson on the Environment, Community and Sustainability?'

'If that's the price of persuading you to go head to head with Lucinda Creighton, then I'm more than happy to pay it! *Omnia cum pretio!*'

'Lucinda Creighton? Oh my God, she's a role model to me in terms of women's engagement with the political process.'

'Well, that's a pity, because I was rather hoping you would take her seat!'

'You want me to run in Dublin Bay South?'

'Yes. And when I'm Taoiseach, I want you to be my Minister for the Environment!'

'And Community and Sustainability?'

'If you think you can fit those things in as well, by all means! So what do you say?'

'I don't know, Chorles. I'm very busy. I'm a single mother of four children, including three infants.'

'You've got so much talent, Sorcha! So much ability! And loath as I am to make light of your present domestic circumstances, this might be the right time for an – inverted commas – life change?'

What a complete and utter penis.

Sorcha goes, 'I suppose I do have Magnus. And my mom and dad can help out now that they've moved in.'

'You've been talking about going into politics for years, Sorcha! Well, this is your chance! What do you say? Will you help me make Ireland tremendous again?'

She thinks about it for four or five seconds, then goes, 'Okay, Chorles, I'm going to say yes. I would *love* to be the New Republic candidate for Dublin Bay South – as well as the porty's spokesperson on the Environment, Community and Sustainability! And I'm determined to change your mind on water chorges.'

He goes, 'I look forward to many hours of robust debate!'

At that moment, Honor arrives down the stairs with – incredibly – my old Canterbury kitbag slung over her shoulder. 'What's going on?' she goes.

I say fock-all on the matter. But I know that swimming with a shork like my old man is something that Sorcha is going to one day regret. And even though our marriage is over, I possibly owe it to her as a friend to keep a close eye on her.

Honor steps out of the dressing room and walks onto the pitch. She's wearing the little Leinster jersey I bought her for Christmas and I'm suddenly on the point of tears, because I'm remembering her unwrapping it on Christmas morning, then curling her top lip and saying she'd probably end up using it as a focking tanning mitt.

Her exact words.

I'm happy to say that she didn't in the end because it very much suits her.

I'm looking around me. There are plenty of other parents here who are probably every bit as proud as I am. The first thing I notice is that, even though the session is supposedly open, Honor is the only actual *girl* playing?

Leo, Johnny and Brian are sitting in their stroller. Johnny is singing *Everything is Awesome* from the Lego movie, while Leo is shouting, 'They're all focking focks! They're all a pack of focking fockers!'

A few of the other parents seem pretty upset by the language – judging from the way they're staring over and muttering to each other out of the corners of their mouths.

'You pack of pricks!' Brian shouts at them. 'It's all you are – a pack of focking pricks!'

I try to blank it out and just focus on what's happening on the pitch. The dude taking the training session introduces himself as Rob. He picks Honor out of all the other kids and he uses her to demonstrate how to throw a rugby ball. He explains it to her in theory. What he doesn't realize, of course, is that Honor already *knows*? She's grown up steeped in this stuff – plus she's read my playbook from cover to cover. He hands her the ball, takes ten steps backwards and he goes, 'Okay, throw it to me,' which is exactly what Honor ends up doing. It's a perfect pass. As Rob catches it, I can see the look of surprise on his face.

He goes, 'Okay, who taught you to throw like that?'

Honor just shrugs and goes, 'Er, my *dad*?'

And he's like, 'Do you mind me asking, who's your –?' and he follows her line of vision until he sees the Rossmeister General – in other words, me – standing there.

He actually laughs. And I laugh as well. Because I suddenly recognize him just as sure as he suddenly recognizes me. It's Rob Felle. He played inside centre for Belvedere College back in the day and we had some pretty memorable battles, it has to be said. There was one time when I stood on his head in a ruck after he tried to gouge out my eye with his thumb. When we were asked by the IRFU afterwards to make a statement, we both pretended we couldn't remember a thing about the incident.

One word. Rugby.

He goes, 'Ross, how the hell are you? I've been hearing stories about you.'

I'm like, 'Oh, yeah? What have you been hearing? As in, what specifically?'

I'm not fishing for compliments. I just think it might be nice for Honor to hear it in front of the other kids.

'A certain team called Seapoint,' he goes. 'I heard you came out of retirement and saved them from relegation.'

I'm there, 'I didn't do it all on my own,' which would be pretty typical of me, always sharing the credit, even when I deserve all of it. 'Others definitely helped.'

He goes, 'A lot of people who remembered you and wondered whatever happened to you were very, very impressed.'

I'm there, 'I answered the critics. That was my whole reason for coming back in the first place.'

Rob points me out to the sixteen or so kids there and goes, 'See that man over there? He could have been one of the all-time greats.'

I shrug modestly and go, 'Hey, not all heroes wear capes!' and it's a lovely moment for Honor. Beneath the filthy look she's giving me, I'm pretty sure she's bursting with pride.

What happens then is that Rob arranges all the boys and one girl into two teams of eight. They're going to play each other – we're talking ten minutes per half. The idea is to get them used to handling the ball and moving forwards by passing backwards.

The funny thing is that you can see that the boys on Honor's team – the blue team – aren't happy that they're the ones who've ended up with a *girl* on their side? As Rob hands out the bibs, I hear one kid with sticky-out ears and an underbite go, 'It's basically eight against seven – that's, like, *so* not fair!'

I go, 'Don't listen to the critics, Honor! Focus only on what you can affect!' a lesson I learned from my own mentor, the late, great Father Fehily.

Well, the message obviously gets through. The first time Honor gets her hands on the ball, she carries it a good, like, thirty yords. The other team try to tackle her, except she skips away from them with a flick of her hips, or she just ploughs through them – boys who are much bigger than her, bear in mind – and runs on towards the line.

I'm, like, stunned – pleasantly stunned, though. I don't need to tell you who she reminds me of! I'm going, 'Go on, Honor!' literally roaring at her. 'Try in the corner! Try in the corner!'

Unfortunately, she gets dragged into touch five yords from the line.

I'm like, 'Hord luck, Honor!' clapping my two hands together as she climbs to her feet. 'Reset and go again!'

There's a definite change in the atmos around Anglesea Road. Suddenly, no one is complaining about having Honor on their team, since it's straightaway obvious she's in a different league from all the other kids, although I'm not sure that the other parents on the sideline appreciate me pointing out that basic fact.

I'm going, 'She's the best player on display! A focking girl, bear in mind! She's better than all your kids! By a mile!'

Brian goes, 'Yeah, you pack of focking shitheads!' and I don't think the other parents love that either.

The game restorts and it's not long before Honor puts in an unbelievable tackle on this fat kid – she totally knocks the wind out of his lungs – then she picks the ball up and tucks it under her orm. With a sudden acceleration of pace, she burns off two other players and heads for the posts this time. She dummies another tackler with a move I invented – I can actually *see* the page in the book – but as she's heading for the line, this focking ginger kid, who looks like a real dick, puts out his orm and, like, totally clotheslines her.

She goes down.

I'm like, 'Referee!' letting Rob know, in no uncertain terms, that he has a duty – like all referees – to protect the flair players. Rob blows his whistle. He's like, 'That was a bit high, Milseáin.'

He's called Milseáin! I actually laugh out loud. When I was growing up, Milseáin was always a girl's name.

Honor climbs to her feet, rubbing the back of her neck. At the same time, she doesn't make a big issue out of it. You'd have to love her attitude.

'Penalty to the blue team,' Rob goes.

Honor stops rubbing her neck and storts looking around for the ball. But – this is un-focking-believable – the kid on her team with sticky-out ears and an underbite is already in the process of spotting it. I end up suddenly losing it. I push the stroller onto the field, going, 'Whoa, whoa, whoa – what the fock do you think you're doing?'

The kid goes, 'The coach said *I* could take the first penalty?'

'But you didn't win it,' I go. 'Why the fock should you get to take it?'

Rob's like, 'I was thinking maybe they could take it in turns – then they'll all get to have a kick at goal!'

I'm just there, 'Turns?' and I stare him out of it, thinking, yeah, no, that's the give-every-child-a-medal attitude that's destroying modern rugby. That's the you-must-leave-the-field-because-you-got-a-bang-on-the-head-and-your-eyes-are-turned-inwards approach that's turning it into a game for wusses. Rob's old school lost to Cistercian in the Leinster Schools Senior Cup final this year. I'm tempted to mention that to him, but I somehow manage to stop myself.

'Turns my focking hole,' I go. 'My daughter is taking the penalty. No arguments.'

Focking Cistercian. It sounds like a disease that makes cows lame.

I pick up the ball and I toss it to Honor. She's *keen* for it, by the way? She takes it, spots it, then – and this just makes me so proud – she takes four steps backwards and three to the side.

'Okay,' I go, walking back to the sideline with the stroller and having to ignore the seriously filthy looks I'm getting from the other parents, 'make sure there's a forty-five-degree angle between you, the ball and the posts.'

Honor's there, 'Yeah, I know what I'm doing, Dad.'

'Okay, but don't forget to make contact one-third of the way up the ball using your instep.'

'Er, I said I've *got* this?'

And she obviously does, because she looks from the ball to the posts, then back to the ball, then back to the posts again – the exact way I described it on a page headlined 'The Perfect Kick'. There's none of Dan Biggar's horseshit carry-on, even though I have massive, massive respect for him as a number ten. She puts her head down then, takes a run at the ball and sends it up into the air and sailing between the posts.

I'm like, 'Yeeesss!!!'

People often talk about your daughter's wedding day being The Big One in terms of, like, pride. But I doubt if I'll ever feel the same way about Honor as I do at that moment.

All the other parents end up *having* to clap, of course? And I can see all the other kids just staring at Honor – and what I see in their eyes is respect.

I don't know why I didn't see it that day in Herbert Pork, when she showed her brother how to throw the ball. Because now it's so blindingly obvious. My daughter is going to be my rugby player. Not Leo, not Brian, not Johnny. Honor is the true heir to the O'Carroll-Kelly rugby name.

The session eventually ends. Honor goes into the dressing room and I head for the cor. I strap the boys into their baby seats, then I wait for her to finish getting changed. Five minutes later, the front passenger door opens and in she climbs.

'Honor,' I go, 'I am so proud of you.'

She's like, 'Whatever,' full of modesty.

We'll soon knock that out of her.

I'm there, 'You're a natural, Honor,' hoping that it also acts as a subtle motivation to the other three to get their act together. 'Unlike others I could mention.'

I lean forward and I open the glove box. 'I want you to have this,' I go.

I put it in her hands. To say she's surprised would be a definite understatement.

She goes, 'Your Rugby Tactics Book?'

That's what she calls it. Not my Sad Dad's Book or my Loser's Guide to Rugby or my Catalogue of Failure. She calls it my Rugby Tactics Book.

And I go, 'It's not *my* Rugby Tactics Book anymore, Honor. It's yours.'

I ring Ronan – again, this goes back to the whole me being an amazing father thing – to wish him good luck in the Leaving Cert, which storts either tomorrow or it storted yesterday. Or maybe it storted last week.

He's there, 'Alreet, Rosser?'

I go, 'How the hell are you, Ro? How are the exams going – or have they even storted?'

'Steert tomoddow,' he goes. 'English is foorst.'

Ronan has actual potential. His teachers reckon he'll walk into any college he wants.

I'm there, 'English wasn't one of my best. Mind you, who am I kidding – like *I* had a best subject!'

And that's when I notice that he's unusually quiet. I'm there, 'You're not nervous, are you?'

He goes, 'It's not neerbs, Rosser. Ine boddixed, so I am,' and I can suddenly hear that he's on the point of tears.

I'm there, 'Whoa, whoa, whoa – what do mean you're *boddixed*?'

'I should hab listoddened to you when you said to me to foyunt somewhere else to stoody. I caddent concenthrate in that house.'

'Kennet and that focking skank!'

'Him and Dordeen's been cawding arowunt evoddy night, Rosser, wit caddens.'

'Cans? Can they not drink them in their own gaff?'

'Thee said thee wanthed to keep Shadden company while Ine off doing whatebber it is Ine doing – filling me head with shite, Dordeen said.'

'Is that an exact quote?'

'It's what she said.'

'What a focking –'

'So they're thrinking the caddens, then thee put on music – fuddle blast, Rosser.'

'What kind of music are we talking? Not that it's even relevant.'

'Lot of Oasis.'

'I was going to predict Oasis. Jesus, I was going to predict it.'

'Ine habben to listen to, "*Sooo, Saddy can wait . . .*" oaber and oaber and oaber again. And the peerd of them siggin along. And of course then Rihatta-Barrogan wakes up and she's croyun her oyuz out. I habbent slept alt week, Rosser. Beerdly slept. I've English in the morden and I caddent remember a ting. Me moyunt's a blank.'

'Okay, just calm down, Ronan. Do you want me to have a word with them?'

'Doatunt botter your boddicks, Rosser. It's too late now. Ine gonna bleaten fayul.'

I'm sitting in Cinnamon in Ranelagh, which is a bit off the beaten track for me, but I happened to see on Facebook that Sorcha was in the vicinity. It's not stalking, even though it *sounds* like stalking?

Yeah, no, she mentioned that, as the newly announced New Republic candidate for Dublin Bay South, she was going to be spending the morning outside the Luas Station, meeting local people and hearing their concerns – 'We wish we lived in Rathgor!' comes up quite a lot, I'd imagine – and afterwards she was looking forward to having her lunch in this place.

Just after half-twelve, she arrives in. Of course she's pretty taken aback to see me sitting there, drinking a latte and pretending to read a newspaper. The hilarious thing is it's actually upside-down! I'm like, 'Hey, Sorcha! What the hell are you doing here?' making out that it's, like, a massive coincidence.

She goes, 'I was doing a meet-and-greet outside the Luas station . . . The thing is, Ross, I'm actually meeting someone here.'

I'm there, 'It's not Fionn again, is it?' but then, over her shoulder, I suddenly spot who she's talking about. It's Claire from Bray of all places and that long drink of piss she's married to – focking Garret. They must be back for a holiday. Honestly, I've seen more of that pair since they emigrated to Canada than I did when they actually lived here!

Claire's like, 'Oh, em, hi!' with a look of confusion on her face – she's obviously been filled in on our marital situation and she's wondering what the fock I'm doing here.

Sorcha's there, 'I turned up and he was just here,' and it pisses me off that she feels the need to apologize for me.

And Garret's like, 'We could go somewhere else. I'm told Tribeca does a genuinely good pulled-pork sandwich.'

And I'm like, 'Sit the fock down, will you? I'm going to finish my coffee, then I'll be gone.'

So they all sit down at the table with me.

Garret, by the way, has a *Peaky Blinders* haircut and – this is genuinely hilarious – a focking moustache! And I don't mean he has a moustache like my son has a moustache, or even – I'm going to just say it – like my old dear has a moustache. This is one of those ones with the curly ends that hipsters decide to grow when they feel that their passion for independent coffee shops, cross-body bags and bands no one else has ever focking heard of aren't getting them enough attention.

'What the fock is that on your face?' I make a big point of going.

He's like, 'You wouldn't know anything about it – it's called style.'

'Maybe in Toronto it is. In Ranelagh, you look like just another tool who's trying too hord to be noticed.'

He's also wearing shoes with no socks. Jesus Christ, I want to punch him in the face.

Claire goes, 'Okay, you two, don't start! God, I haven't even said hello to Sorcha yet!' but then she does. She stretches across the table and it ends up being air-kisses and all the rest of it.

Sorcha goes, 'How long are you home for?'

And Claire's like, 'Two weeks! Oh my God, it's *so* good to get a holiday! We have been *up* to our eyes with the business!'

She's talking about Wheat Bray Love, the ridiculous organic bakery they opened in Toronto. She takes out her iPad and storts showing Sorcha photographs and Sorcha does her best to sound impressed, while I make a big point of showing no interest whatsoever.

'The big news,' Garret goes, 'is that we've storted opening in the evenings now – doing street food.'

I'm there, 'Street food? Of course, you'd be used to that, Claire, coming from Bray – you were focking reared out of bins.'

'Ignore him,' Sorcha goes. 'Oh my God, I *love* the subway tiles on the wall. And the way you've spelt apple pie on the menu board – with an E, L, and a Y, E!'

Garret goes, 'That's one of the things that Claire and I genuinely love about Canada. Irish people are so literal, aren't they? Whereas over there, you can have fun, experiment, whether that's with how you spell things, what you cook. The street food – Claire will tell you – we're doing root veg curry chips, goat offal patties in steamed brioche buns, then *banh chuoi chien*, which are deep-fried banana cakes. We were the first in Toronto to do those. They're pretty much a delicacy in places like Bangkok. A lot of our menu was inspired by when we did the whole round-the-world thing.'

'It sounds disgusting,' I go. 'The kind of food that would have you shitting Ready Brek.'

He just blanks me, even though it kills him.

'And,' Claire goes, 'we've got this amazing chef, who you're about to meet!'

'Yeah, Broderek just had to find an ATM,' *he* goes.

Then, just as he says it, some dude walks in. It's obviously him because Claire gives him a big wave and over he comes. The best way to describe him is to say that he's a bit Chinesey looking – and I don't mean that in a racist way – except he's not *actually* Chinese because his accent is American slash Canadian. He's like, 'Hiiiiiiii!'

Claire goes, 'Broderek, this is my friend Sorcha, who I've told you – oh my God – *so* much about!'

He's there, 'It's so nice to finally meet you! Finally!'

He's like Gok Wan except with a porkpie hat.

She goes, 'And this is, em, Ross – her ex-husband.'

And I'm there, 'I'm still her focking husband.'

And he's like, 'Oh, er, okay!' and that's when he says *the* weirdest thing. 'So I'm Broderek and I favour they/them pronouns – are you guys cool with that?'

Now, I – honestly? – haven't heard the word pronoun since I sat the Junior Cert. And if I didn't have a clue what it meant then, I'm hordly going to know now.

Sorcha is clearly delighted to hear it, though, whatever the fock it means, because she goes, 'Oh my God, that's amazing! I mean, yes, of course we're cool with it! Good for you, Broderek – I was involved in the recent marriage equality referendum campaign!'

The waitress comes over to take everyone's drink orders. I decide to stick around with the intention of ripping the piss out of Garret and maybe dropping in one or two reminders that I've ridden Claire many, many times over the years. I was the one who stamped her V card, which has always killed him.

I swear to fock, he goes, 'Do you do a turmeric latte?'

The waitress is just like, 'A what?' and she's well within her focking rights.

He's there, 'A turmeric latte. Oh, sorry, I keep forgetting! Ireland!' like even just saying the word is a put-down. 'Okay, I'll just have a Deconstructed Flat White then.'

The poor girl hasn't a clue what he's even talking about. I'm there, 'Why don't you tell her what the fock it is and stop being a dick?'

He goes, 'Can you bring me a beaker of milk, a beaker of boiling water and a beaker with two shots of espresso in it? On a wooden board. With a spoon.'

Claire goes, 'I'll take one of those as well.'

And Sorcha's there, 'I'll try one, too!' because she's easily swayed. 'They sound amazing!'

'By the way,' Garret goes, 'that's another thing we're doing at the moment. Barista classes.'

Jesus, you need to do a focking course now just to make someone a cup of coffee. What's happening to the world?

Broderek's like, 'I'll just have a regular latte.'

And that's the moment when I just happen to go, '*He's* the only normal one out of all of you!'

There's suddenly what would have to be described as a collective intake of breath – you *could* call it a gasp? – around the table.

I'm like, 'What's wrong? I'm saying he's normal because he's having a latte.'

Claire goes, '*They're* having a latte, Ross.'

I'm there, 'What?'

'*They're* having a latte.'

'Who? Broderek's the only one who ordered a latte.'

Sorcha – I swear to fock – *apologizes* for me? She goes, 'I'm *so* embarrassed, Broderek.'

Garret goes, 'See, this is what comes from playing rugby. All those blows to the head he took.'

I'm there, 'Sorry, what's the big deal here? I was just pointing out that he ordered a latte.'

Sorcha goes, 'You were pointing out that *they* ordered a latte.'

'No, I wasn't. I was talking specifically about *him*.'

'About *them*,' Claire goes.

'Sorry, am I having a focking stroke here or something?'

Broderek stands up – in a genuine huff, by the way – and goes, 'Okay, I need to use the restroom,' and off he suddenly focks.

Jesus, the drama.

I'm like, 'What the fock is his problem?'

'*Their* problem,' Claire goes. 'What the fock is *their* problem?'

'Okay, I don't get why everyone's calling him "they". It's like that time Honor had that imaginary friend.'

'When Broderek said they preferred non-binary pronouns,' Garret goes, 'they were asking you to respect their gender identity. And you can't even change your grammatical prejudices to make them feel safe and accepted.'

I'm there, 'I didn't mean any offence to him.'

'You didn't mean any offence to *them*!' Sorcha goes.

'Okay, my head is storting to hurt now.'

Garret's there, 'Well, either way, I think you owe them an apology when they get back from the bathroom.'

They all just shake their heads – like there's something genuinely wrong with *me*? Their deconstructed coffees arrive and our table suddenly looks like a focking laboratory.

There ends up being a bit of chat then.

Claire tells Sorcha it's great that she's finally going into politics because she always thought it was something she'd be totally amazing at. Sorcha says that, at the moment, she's meeting and greeting people in the likes of Ballsbridge, Sandymount, Donnybrook and Rathgor and finding out what they want.

Terenure levelled and Ringsend sacrificed to the sea would be my guess.

Broderek arrives back from the jacks and he still has a face on him.

'Broderek,' Sorcha goes, 'Ross has something he wants to say to you,' putting me on the spot.

I'm like, 'Do I?'

'Yes, Ross, you owe them an apology.'

Jesus Christ.

I end up having to go, 'Look, Dude, I've no idea what the problem is here. I mean, there's stuff that's offensive today that wasn't offensive a year ago, or even a month ago. If you miss the updates, you're suddenly the biggest dick in the world.'

Sorcha goes, 'As a citizen, Ross, it's your responsibility to stay informed. Now, you need to apologize.'

I'm there, 'I'm apologizing to him!'

'You're apologizing to *them*,' Garret goes.

I stand up. I literally can't take any more of this.

'Okay,' I go, 'I'm out of here.'

Sorcha's there, 'Broderek, all I can do is apologize to you on my husband's behalf. Let's just say he has issues when it comes to people with alternate sexual and gender identities.'

I'm like, 'I'm not the one with issues – believe me.'

Then I walk out of there and leave the four of them to it. Or the five of them – if you count Broderek twice.

Ronan is throwing the pints into him – to the point where I'm actually struggling to keep up. We're in The Broken Orms in Finglas, having a few quiet ones to supposedly celebrate him finishing his exams, except he's really going for it. And when I say 'it', I'm talking about oblivion.

'Come on,' I go, 'you don't know that you definitely failed yet.'

He's there, 'Ine arthur fooking it up, Rosser. Enda bleaten stordee.'

'You might end up being surprised.'

'Moost have been mad to think I could go to coddidge. Eer koyunt of people doatunt go to coddidge.'

'Are you talking about people from Finglas?'

'Ine soddy to say that Dordeen was reet. Should be out woorking. Ine no use to Shadden if Ine gonna spend the next howebber many years of me life with me nose stuck in a buke, in addyhow. It was a thream, is alls it was – and the thream is oaber.'

'Well, I don't think it *is* over? Have you thought of possibly repeating in the Institute? I know goys who were thicker than me who got four hundred points in that place.'

'Ine going back woorking on the *Lub/Hate* Tewer of Dublin, Rosser.'

'I don't want you to do that, Ro.'

'Dudn't mattor what you want. I neeyut a weekly wayuch. I've a famidy to feeyut.'

There's, like, silence between us then.

My phone beeps. It ends up being a text message from Sorcha, saying her old man still hasn't had any acknowledgement of his letter, formalizing our separation. I text back, saying I'm still hoping she'll change her mind.

One of the lounge girls tips over. She's a big girl, but at the same time she's quite *pretty*? Around Ronan's age, I'd say. Massive thrups. That's just an observation. She picks up his glass, smiles at him and goes, 'Howiya, Ro?'

He's like, 'Howiya, Jacinta?'

Jacinta. I laugh. I don't know why. It's funny.

She goes, 'Robbie Burden has a free-or on Sahurdee nigh – he's habben a peerty, if you're inthordested.'

He's there, 'I caddent. Ine not free. Soddy, Jacinta.'

She's like, 'It's alreet. I just thought if you were arowunt . . . Anutter thrink?'

She's mad about him. That much is obvious. He goes, 'Yeah, anutter one. Pint of Caddles Birdog.'

And I'm there, 'Yeah, no, Heineken for me.'

She's like, 'We habn't addy Heineken.'

'You do have Heineken. It's just not on *draught*? The manager gets cans in especially for me. They're in the fridge'

She nods, then off she focks to get our drinks. Ronan stares at her humungous yet at the same time not unpleasant orse as she walks away. I possibly have a little look as well.

I'm there, 'Someone's keen. She's obviously gagging for you.'

'Jacinta?' he goes. 'Ah, she's a niece of Buckets of Blood.'

'Niece or not, she wants a piece of you.'

'What?'

'Hey, I'm just putting it out there. Storting a conversation – isn't that the phrase everyone's using these days?'

'I've got a geerdle friend, Rosser. And a thaughter, remember?'

He stares sadly into space. We've all been there. No matter how much you love your kids, there are times when every parent thinks, oh, what I wouldn't do for a focking condom and a time machine.

I'm there, 'I'm just saying it's possible to have a girlfriend and still be doing little bits and pieces on the side.'

He goes, 'And end up like you, wha?'

'Excuse me?'

'Divowerced?'

'We're not divorced yet.'

I check my phone. Sorcha has texted back to say that she's not going to change her mind. It's over between us, and I really need to find a solicitor to handle my side of things.

Ronan goes, 'Toorty-foyuv years of age and back libben in your oul fedda's speer roowum? Oatenly seeing your kids on the week-end? Recommend it, would you, Rosser?'

'Yeah, no, fair enough, Ro. Don't rub it in.'

I watch his attention wander back to Jacinta, who's walking back towards us with drinks, her big bad wolves bouncing up and down underneath her tight black shirt, and there's a look of sad longing in his eyes.

My phone rings. I check the screen and it ends up being Honor. So I answer.

Her opening line is, 'Oh my God! Hill! Air!'

With Honor, of course, that could mean anything. It could be a photo of Katy Perry with sweat patches under her orms or a plane crash in which three hundred people died.

I'm there, 'What's so funny?'

She goes, 'I sent you a link.'

'Yeah, no, I'm having a few pints with Ro.'

'Oh my God, Claire and Garret's friend – that focking sap who looks like Gok Wan . . .'

'Broderek? What about him? Slash them? Slash whatever?'

'He's called you out – on his vlog?'

'Called me out? In what way?'

'Oh my God, Garret just put it on his Facebook page. You've been publicly vlogged! Hill! Air!'

She hangs up. I open Honor's e-mail on my phone, then I click on the link.

Ronan's like, 'What is it, Rosser?' looking over my shoulder.

'Yeah, no,' I go, 'it's this friend of Claire from Bray of all places who I had a run-in with.'

Suddenly, up comes – like Honor said – the famous Broderek, in his glasses and his ridiculous hat, looking seriously focked off.

He goes, 'So . . . I'm in Dublin, Ireland, and I met this person. Okay, I'm going to say he was your typical Ivy League jock type – obviously into sports. So, like, his name was Ross? I won't say his second name. But I met him in this, like, cool café in a really diversity-embracing area called Ranna Lag. And when I was introduced to him, I mentioned that I favoured non-binary pronouns and I said I hoped he was good with that. His wife, Sorcha, who was also there – and who was, can I just say, utterly charming, which is probably why she's in the process of, like, *divorcing* him? – she said that was cool and there was no issue. But this Ross person proceeded to refer to me as "he" and "him", even though I expressly asked him not to and he could see how uncomfortable it was making everyone at the table, but especially me.'

His voice cracks with the emotion of it. Oh, for fock's sake.

Ronan laughs. He goes, 'This is cheerden me up, so it is. You bethor hope it dudn't go voyer dill, Rosser.'

After five or six seconds, Broderek gets it together again. He's like, 'I cannot overstate how triggering and also deeply upsetting I found his attitude towards me as a genderqueer person who made it plain from the outset that I – personally? – find binaries in everyday speech *deeply* offensive. I actually felt, like, *physically* threatened by his refusal to respect my request to use they/them pronouns? But being your typical Biological Essentialist asshole, he let it be known, in no uncertain terms, that he was not going to recalibrate his language to accommodate people who don't identify as one gender or another and to make them feel safe. That is a hate crime. And we have to let homophobic assholes like this Ross person know that hate crimes are not cool. Because if we don't continuously call them out on this kind of thing, then we normalize this behaviour.'

Ronan's just, like, shaking his head, going, 'The bleaten wurdled's gone mad, Rosser.'

Yeah, no, I'm still highly pissed off about it the following day, so I end up driving out to Brayruit with the intention of giving Broderek something to definitely vlog about.

I pull up outside Claire and Garret's gaff in Ordmore Pork. There's a woman – I swear to fock – *sunbathing* on a towel in the front gorden. In a bikini. In the middle of an actual housing estate. I've never said anything about Bray that wasn't one hundred percent warranted.

I ring the doorbell. Once. Twice. Three times. Eventually, *she* comes to the door – as in, Claire?

'Okay,' I go, 'where is he?'

She's like, 'Who?'

'Focking Broderek? I want a word with him.'

'You want a word with *them*.'

'Yeah, I want a word with *them*. Then I want to drag them out onto the road there and break their focking noses.'

'Well, they're not in at the moment.'

'So where is they?'

'They went into town with Garret,' she goes. 'They're checking

70

out a place in Smithfield that's supposed to do a really nice slow-cooked cabrito wrap. It's got amazing reviews.'

And I think, that's it – I know how I'll fix Broderek. I turn to go and that's when I notice that Claire's eyes are red and her mascara is all over the shop. I'm like, 'Have you been crying?'

And that's when the floodgates suddenly open.

'Oh, Ross,' she goes, 'Garret's been sending Facebook messages . . . to this girl . . . he claims she's just a friend . . . but I think . . . I think he has feelings for her . . . I don't know if . . . if I'm imagining it . . .'

'You're probably not imagining it,' I go – any excuse to slag him off. 'It sounds to me like he's cheating on you.'

I notice the woman next-door having a good listen in, her neck extended like a focking periscope. Claire cops it as well, because she goes, 'Come in, Ross. I don't want the whole neighbourhood knowing.'

So in I go.

The house is in bits, by the way. I remember Sorcha mentioned they were renting it out to a bunch of nurses and they made shit of the place.

'I shouldn't have been reading . . . his e-mails,' she goes. 'But this girl . . . her name is Ji Eun . . . she comes into the shop . . . all the time . . . and I know . . . I know she has a thing for him . . .'

Her laptop is open on the kitchen table.

She goes, 'Would you . . . would you mind just reading . . . this message . . . and tell me if there's anything in it . . . or am I being paranoid?'

I sit down at the table. The message is open and I end up just reading it with a sense of already boredom. It's like, 'Hey Ji Eun, it was great to see you the other day! And great to hear all about the trip you're planning to South East Asia!!! I'm SO excited for you, especially having done the trip myself ☺☺☺. You're going to have some amazing experiences and see things that will definitely shape your worldview. What I would say is that Laos, Burma and West Malaysia are ALL worth seeing, as is Brunei and Christmas Island. But what I would also stress is DON'T BE AFRAID TO GO OFF THE BEATEN TRACK!!! Seriously, some of the most rewarding experiences we had were when we threw away the guidebook and just allowed ourselves to 'be' in the moment ☺☺☺.'

I had no idea that Claire was the jealous type. It's actually funny.

'Yeah, no, he's definitely going to ride her,' I go. 'That's if he hasn't ridden her already.'

Claire's like, 'Seriously? Do you think?'

'Take it from someone who prides himself on being a player. All those smiley faces – and what are those things called?'

'Exclamation marks.'

'Exclamation morks. I don't think you're being paranoid at all.'

'There's another message that he sent to her,' Claire goes. 'Tell me what you think of this one.'

Again, there's fock-all in it. It's just like, 'The good news (because I know how much you love your street food ☺☺☺) is that we're planning to add some new dishes to the menu before the end of the summer, including (state secret!!!) rose veal steak burgers, *banh mi* sandwiches and spicy marlin crêpes ☺☺☺. Also (again, PLEASE keep this to yourself!!!) I've entered Broderek's brisket kebab into the Best Snack Food category of the Toronto Street Food Awards. But please don't tell them!!!! ☺☺☺☺☺'

'He's all over her,' I go. 'And he's being totally blatant about it.'

She's there, 'That stuff about the new menu items, Ross – no one was supposed to know that!'

'He's boning her – no question. What a horrible way for you to find out.'

She sits down at the table beside me and the tears come again. She goes, 'This girl –'

I'm like, 'Jai Ho?'

'Ji Eun. She is *such* a bitch, Ross – oh my God, you've no idea. She comes in for her coffee in the morning – double-shot macchiato – and she won't let me serve her. She says she only likes the way Garret makes it.'

'Jesus.'

'And he sometimes gives her an extra chocolate with it.'

'You deserve better, Claire. You definitely deserve better.'

As I'm saying it, I slip my hand onto her knee. I'm thinking, shit, am I going to do this? I think I *am* going to do it! I give it a little squeeze and she looks at me and smiles through her tears.

I'm like, 'Look, I'm biased. I've never liked him. I could never trust someone who doesn't love rugby.'

'Well, he hates you too,' she goes. 'He especially hates that you were my first.'

I'm there, 'Yeah, no, he doesn't love when I bring it up either. I think he's jealous of the connection we have.'

'Connection? What connection?'

'You don't feel a connection?'

'Ross, you throw your eyes up to heaven every time I open my mouth. And the things you say about Bray . . .'

'Maybe that's just me protecting myself.'

'What are you talking about?'

'It drives me mad that you're with him, Claire. Especially when I've got all these feelings for you.'

'Ross, don't.'

'What?'

'The way you're looking at me. The way you've got your hand on my knee. I think you're getting ready to kiss me. And I don't think that would be a good idea.'

'Why not? Your husband seems to be riding all around him.'

'I'm thinking of Sorcha. She's been an amazing, amazing friend to me.'

'Me and Sorcha are finished, Claire. I've accepted that. I'm actually about to get a solicitor on the case.'

'She'd still be hurt if she ever found out.'

'The only two people who'll know are in this kitchen.'

I move in closer and I throw the lips on her. After a few seconds, she responds in kind. She puts her two hands around the back of my neck and storts kissing me greedily – like every mouthful is a little act of payback for Garret. Then, suddenly, we're both on our feet and I'm tearing at her clothes. Off comes her little cardigan, then her blouse, then her bra.

I have a bit of fun with the showgirls and it drives her hog-wild. Then I hitch up her skirt and sit her up on the table. 'No,' she goes, 'not here. Let's go upstairs,' and I don't need an invitation confirmation. I grab her hand and I lead her upstairs to the main bedroom.

And there I'm going to draw a discreet blind on the story to protect both (a) Claire's modesty and (b) my own reputation as someone who doesn't kiss and tell.

All I will say is that we end up going at it like banana time in the monkey house. We do it, then we do it again, then we do it some more. This position. That position. Me on top. Her on top. Our bodies are just a tangle of orms and legs as I bury my head between her big gulps and I sire the girl stupid-faced.

I'd actually forgotten what a cracking little rattle she was and she definitely holds up her end of the deal, pulling off one or two little moves that Sorcha would never even attempt – and, if she did, she wouldn't be able to face me over the brioche the following morning.

One thing I will say about Bray girls is they don't mind being judged.

At a certain stage in the proceedings – and this is all I'm giving away – Claire is sort of, like, sitting astride me and working herself up from a steady canter to a happy gallop when she suddenly stops and goes, 'What did you just say?'

And I'm there, 'I didn't say anything.'

'You said brisket.'

'No, I didn't. Keep going, Claire, in case I go floppy again.'

'Ross, you said brisket.'

'Yeah, no, I sometimes spit out random words when I'm on the job. They never mean anything. Like I said – random.'

She grabs me by the face. 'Ross,' she goes, looking into my eyes, 'I need to know that you're turned on by me and not by the idea of having sex with Garret's wife.'

If women knew half of what goes on in men's heads, they'd be looking for a new planet to live on.

I'm there, 'I'm turned on by *you*, Claire.'

She stares at me for about five seconds, then she obviously sees something in my face that persuades her I'm telling the truth and she goes back to work, until eventually the proceedings come to a sweaty end with her staring slanty-eyed at the ceiling and effing and blinding like Nicki Minaj.

Afterwards, we're enjoying a moment of post-coital getting-our-breath-back before I fock off home. Claire smiles at me and goes, 'What are you thinking about?'

'Just how much I hate your husband,' I go, 'for not properly appreciating you.'

Hennessy greets me like I've arrived to audit him. He goes, 'Jesus Christ!' like even the *sight* of me is a major imposition? 'What the fuck do *you* want?'

His secretary is behind me, going, 'I told him you were busy, but he walked straight past me.'

She's not great, by the way. I'd say most men walk straight past her.

Hennessy tells her it's fine and she focks off. There's, like, a humungous plasma screen on the wall of his office. The lunchtime news is on. He picks up the remote and mutes the sound. I drop the letter from Sorcha's old man on his desk. He gives it the old left to right. Then he laughs – I want to say – *knowingly*?

'What'd I say to you,' he goes, 'before you married that girl?'

I'm there, 'I don't know. I don't remember.'

'I said don't ever piss her off enough that she wants to divorce you – because her old man will fucking crucify you.'

'Yeah, no, he's always hated my guts.'

'And not just in the usual father-in-law, son-in-law, you're-fucking-my-daughter kind of way. *Don't make an enemy of Edmund Lalor*, that's what I said.'

'That ship unfortunately sailed a long, long time ago. He thought she married beneath herself.'

'She did marry beneath herself. Jesus, anyone could see that. She's smart, she's attractive, she's loyal. What have you got?'

'Rugby was a big port of the attraction.'

'You're a sexually incontinent layabout with nothing between your ears and, according to what I hear, even less between your fucking legs.'

75

'Yeah, can I just remind you that you're supposed to be on *my* side?'

Again, he laughs. 'Is that why you're here?' he goes. 'You want *me* to represent you?'

I go, 'Er, yeah – you're the family *solicitor*?'

'I do drink-driving cases. A bit of conveyancing. Edmund Lalor knows family law like I know the gentlemen's cabarets of Pigalle. That's upside-fucking-down and inside-fucking-out. He's the best in the business. And don't forget, this case is especially dear to his heart. So what did you do to bring this on yourself? Or do I even need to ask?'

'We've had problems in our marriage for a while.'

'Well, whoever you screwed, I hope she was the best you ever had. Because you're going to be paying for it for the rest of your life.'

My *phone* all of a sudden rings? I can see from the screen that it's, like, Claire. My first thought is that she's possibly had an attack of the guilts and told Sorcha what happened. In which case, it would be good to know. I go, 'Hennessy, I have to quickly take this.'

He's like, 'Jesus Christ!' obviously considering it rude.

I answer by going, 'Claire, this isn't a great time. What's wrong?'

She's like, 'Nothing, it's just, you know, we're flying back to Canada tonight –'

'I'm aware of that.'

'And, well, me and you haven't actually talked to each other since we –'

'Yeah, no, I've never been one for post-analysis chat, Claire. You of all people should have remembered that.'

'No, it's just that, well, I talked to Garret about Ji Eun, and I think I was probably being paranoid. And now I feel – oh my God – *so* guilty about what we –'

'Do you have any female friends you can discuss this with?'

'What?'

'Look, no offence, but it sounds like the kind of shit you should be discussing with another girl. I'm kind of in the middle of a meeting here.'

'Okay, can I just ask you one last thing?'

76

'Quickly.'

'When you were leaving the other day, you didn't steal my knickers, did you?'

'No,' I go, 'I didn't steal your knickers. Jesus Christ, what kind of a question –?' and then I hang up on her.

Hennessy just, like, glowers at me. He goes, 'You ever take a call when you're in my company again and I will dangle you out the window by your fucking ankles – do you hear me?'

I'm like, 'Er, fair enough,' because he definitely means it. He stares at me for a good ten seconds without saying anything, until I end up having to look away, then he un-mutes the TV again.

'Your father's going to be on,' he goes. 'You should watch this – find out what greatness looks like, since it clearly skipped you.'

Una O'Hagan is reading the news. She goes, 'Charles O'Carroll-Kelly, the leader of New Republic, says his party will fight the next General Election on a promise to take Ireland out of the European Union. In an interview with RTÉ News, Mr O'Carroll-Kelly said that Ireland had been betrayed by Europe and, in particular, the 2008 bailout deal. He said the people were entitled to decide whether they wished to continue paying the price of maintaining what he called the lie of European political union. Paschal Sheehy reports.'

The next thing that pops up on the screen is my old man, chatting to randomers on the main street in Dalkey.

'New Republic are riding high in the opinion polls,' Paschal Sheehy goes, 'on the back of a strong launch last month, at which party leader Charles O'Carroll-Kelly promised to abolish a number of taxes while making improvements to public services. Today, he outlined how that would be achieved if he were to become Taoiseach – by tearing up the 2008 bailout deal and triggering Article 50 of the European Union.'

The next shot is of my old man standing outside The Queens – with his mad hair – going, 'The EU is a failed project! Full point, new par! And it has failed Ireland more than it has failed any other country! The first thing we will do, once we are in Government, is inform the architects of the bailout that they are not getting one cent more from the Irish people! We will then begin negotiations to take the country out of the European Union! This will save us somewhere in the region of €42 billion a year, money which New Republic believes would be better spent funding our hospitals and our schools and making Ireland tremendous again!'

'However,' Paschal Sheehy goes, switching to a shot of Leo Varadkar standing in the RTÉ cor pork, 'the Government was quick to pour scorn on Charles O'Carroll-Kelly's claims that a so-called Eirexit would result in a cash bonanza for Ireland.'

Leo Varadkar goes, 'The figure of €42 billion – he's just plucked that out of the air. Anyone who knows anything about economics would know that we have been net beneficiaries of European membership to the tune of hundreds of billions of euro. Like his promises to scrap water and property tax, this is just more old-fashioned populism. Thankfully, the electorate are smart enough not to take Charles O'Carroll-Kelly either literally or seriously.'

Hennessy laughs. He's there, 'Oh, Leo. You were the brightest and best. Those whom the Gods wish to destroy, they appoint them Minister for Health.'

I go, 'If we pull out of Europe, will we still be in the Six Nations?' but he doesn't bother even answering me.

'Leave it with me,' he goes, putting the letter in his top drawer. 'I'll do what I can to minimize the damage.'

And then I head off. I've a busy afternoon ahead of me on the Internet.

They're standing at the Aer Lingus check-in desk – we're talking Claire, Garret and Broderek. I watch them from a distance, handing over their passports, then lifting their luggage onto the belt. Garret is wearing, I swear to fock, knee-length shorts with red Toms, a white, short-sleeved shirt and – this is the best bit – a focking bow-tie!

Everything about this dude makes me angry.

Broderek is having to take shit out of one of his bags and put it into Garret's case – presumably because he's over the weight limit – and he's obviously pissed off having to do it, because he stares at the bird behind the desk and goes, 'Can I have your name, please?'

The poor girl is about to get the vlog treatment, I suspect.

Once they've checked in, they head for the departures gate with me following at, like, a subtle *distance*? Garret stops so he can take his Beats out of his hand luggage and hang them around his neck – even though he's not actually listening to anything – and that's when I decide to make myself known.

'Thought I'd see you off,' I go. 'Make sure you left the country.'

The three of them turn around. Their faces – yeah, no, definitely – drop when they see *me* standing there? Claire looks the most worried and that's for obvious reasons.

I stare hord at Broderek and I go, 'I saw your vlog. A focking hate crime? You know I could actually sue you for that?'

He goes, 'Syntactic bigotry *is* a hate crime.'

'I just used the wrong word, that's all,' I go.

'Which made me feel threatened.'

'Well, you're about to find out how it feels to be dissed on the Internet. Have you looked at Trip Advisor recently?'

Garret goes, 'What's he talking about?'

I'm like, 'Yeah, no, I'm just commenting – that street food of yours seems to have got a lot of negative reviews lately. Some people have gone on there and absolutely rinsed the place.'

Broderek whips out his phone.

Claire goes, 'Oh my God, Ross, what did you do?'

I'm like, 'Yeah, no, just told one or two home truths of my own.'

Broderek's there, 'Okay, our average rating is down to, like, one star!' and he storts scrolling down through some of the comments I've posted, then reading them out. '*I ordered the aki and saltfish stew, which everyone was banging on about. I ate about five or six mouthfuls before I found out . . . before I found out there was a condom in it.*'

I'm there, 'Everyone's a critic, huh?'

Broderek goes, 'Oh my God, he's written, like, dozens of these things!'

Claire's there, 'Ross, that is our focking *livelihood* you're playing games with?' and she actually roars at me.

'You know,' Garret tries to go, 'we can just report all of those comments as abuse. They'll investigate them and they'll take them down.'

And I'm there, 'By then the damage will have already been done. Word travels fast.'

Claire goes, 'He's right, Garret. People move on. Remember Hasta Siempre that used to do those amazing Cuban sandwiches served in a cigor box? People used to queue outside for hours – now, it's gone! That was, like, one pubic hair!'

I'm like, 'I don't think Broderek is going to be winning any awards for his brisket, by the way. Someone's absolutely gone to town on it.'

Broderek goes, '*I was told the brisket was pretty much good enough to win awards. I ended up getting the squits from it and shitting half a stone of my body weight in about twenty-four hours. Wheat Bray Love? Wheat Spray Love more like! I mentioned this to the chef the next time I was in and HE laughed in my face and then HE told me to fock off. And, oh my God, he's written "he" instead of "they" – and capitalized the H and the E.*'

'Anyway,' I go, 'I don't want to make you late for your flight.'

Garret just shakes his head – like he feels *sorry* for me? He goes, 'You know, Sorcha's had a lucky escape from you,' and he's obviously trying to come up with something to hurt me.

I'm there, 'That's weak.'

'No, I mean it. I hope her old man wipes you out in the divorce.'

'It'll be no skin off my nose. It'll be my own old man who ends up paying.'

'I hope she meets someone else. I genuinely do.'

'What, a single mother with four kids? That's a hord sell – and that's not me being a prick.'

'Maybe someone like Fionn.'

'Fionn? Why are you mentioning Fionn specifically?'

'They seem to be spending a lot of time together these days.'

'They had dinner in that place in Donnybrook where I'd been promising to bring her for years but never bothered. What's your point?'

'We actually met them for a drink last night.'

'Together?'

'Yeah, together. They just seem really comfortable in each other's company.'

'Well, from me to Fionn would be some comedown for the girl – I think even he'd have to admit that.'

'And they've loads in common. Seriously, I'd love if she found happiness with him. Whereas you are going to end up being one sad and lonely old man.'

'Oh, I'll never be lonely, Garret – trust me. Good luck with the street food.'

I turn to leave. But then I suddenly turn back again and I go, 'Hey, I nearly forgot . . .'

And I reach into my pocket and whip out Claire's balled-up knickers.

'I accidentally took these the other day,' I go, 'when I was in your gaff having sex with your wife.'

3. The Bart of the Deal

So I'm officially on Tinder. Big announcement. I've no desire to spend the rest of my life lying in bed jostling the chosen one. So I've downloaded the app and I'm back in the game.

This is how easy it is to hook up these days. I'm flicking through pictures of women – not all of them dogs – until I come to one called Tilly, who I instantly like. She's alright in terms of looks, and girls called Tilly, Milly and Lilly, in my experience, tend to be pretty open-minded, and when I say pretty open-minded, I mean filthy.

So I swipe right. And just as I do, my *phone* all of a sudden rings? No, it's not her. No one's *that* open-minded.

I can see from the screen that it's actually, like, Erika, ringing me from France. I answer by going, *'Buongiorno!'*

She doesn't return the greeting. She just goes, 'I was just talking to Sorcha. She said you're getting divorced,' because the girl likes to keep me grounded – for whatever reason.

I'm like, 'Yeah, no, she's the one who wants it. Although her old man is obviously behind the scenes, pulling the strings.'

'She said you had sex with a woman in Glenageary.'

'It was more the Dalkey end of things, Erika. But the good news is that I'm already back on the dating scene.'

'You're a focking idiot. Anyway, I'm only ringing to tell you that I'm moving back home next week.'

I'm like, 'Whoa!' because it'll be nice having my sister slash half-sister back. She's been studying, I don't know, ort history and appreciation, if you consider that an actual thing. 'Me and you living under the same roof for the first time,' I go. 'I hope it doesn't end up being weird.'

She's there, 'Why would it end up being weird?'

'It shouldn't end up being weird. Forget I said anything.'

'Anyway, I'm ringing to tell you to have your shit cleared out of my room by the time I get back.'

And with that, she hangs up.

A few minutes later, I'm texting this Tilly one to arrange a place to meet when there's suddenly a ring on the door. I decide not to bother my hole answering it on the basis that it's not my focking house. But whoever it is, they seem pretty determined to get an answer because they just keep their finger on the doorbell until I end up having to get out of bed and tip downstairs.

It ends up being Sorcha. I'm like, 'Hey, Sorcha! I was just talking to Erika. You know she's coming home?'

She goes, 'Yeah, she rang me this morning. Is your dad in?'

'He went out about an hour ago. He took his clubs.'

'Okay, that doesn't explain why he hasn't been answering my calls for the past few days.'

'Can I take a message? Can I say what it's in connection with?'

Jesus Christ. Three months ago, we were going at each other like the future of the species depended on it. Now, I'm talking to her like a receptionist. Divorce is focked-up.

'Well,' she goes, 'it's obviously about what he said the other day – about pulling out of Europe? There was no mention of Eirexit – or whatever they're calling it – when I agreed to join New Republic. If we leave the European Union, Ross, Irish students won't be allowed to go away on Erasmus? Can you imagine a world without Erasmus?'

'Not really, no.'

'I genuinely believe that Europe has been an amazing, amazing thing for this country. Do you know if he's read my White Paper, by the way?'

'Your . . . ?'

'White Paper? On the future funding of Ireland's domestic water service? It's just that I gave it to him, like, ten days ago?'

I'm guessing it went straight in the focking bin.

I'm there, 'Yeah, no, he hasn't mentioned it, Sorcha.'

'Because he's still telling people to tear up their water bills,' she goes. 'There was an interview with him in this morning's *Irish Times*. He said the abolition of Irish Water would be, like, a redline issue for the porty in any future discussions to form a coalition Government. This is before we've even discussed the main conclusion of my paper, which is that chorging consumers for water on a metered basis has led to a reduction in wastage in just about every country where it's been tried.'

'I'll definitely mention that to him when he comes home – depending on what state he's in, of course.'

'I'm beginning to think I joined the wrong political porty. Even Fionn thinks I should possibly join the Greens or run as an Independent.'

'Sorcha, I was the one who said it from day one. You're mad having anything to do with him. Even Helen says he's changed since he put that thing on his head.'

'Well, either way, Ross, I can't pretend I'm in favour of pulling out of Europe when I'm actually not . . . Anyway, how are you doing?'

We've always got on unbelievably well. It's a genuine pity that she could never accept the whole me cheating on her thing.

I'm there, 'Yeah, no, I'm good. I miss the kids, though. And I'm not saying that so you'll feel hopefully guilty for only letting me see them one day a week. I'm stating it as a fact.'

'Oh my God, all Honor can *talk* about these days is rugby!'

'She's unbelievable at it, Sorcha. I'm seeing definite flashes of me.'

'And that tactics book you gave her is never out of her hands.'

'You say that like it's a bad thing.'

'It's just not what I had in mind for her, that's all. I thought it was going to be the National Youth Choir and the Mount Anville Junior Runway Fashion Show. I know I'm being silly . . .'

'Let me be the judge of that.'

'. . . but she's stopped taking an interest in her appearance, Ross.'

'Hey, I think we realized a long time ago that Honor wasn't going to be out there winning beauty pageants. She's not great.'

'Yeah, I know she's not pretty in an obvious way. But she's stopped doing her daily skincare regime. And she's storted wearing a beanie – even in the house.'

'A beanie? Jesus.'

'I still think, on some level, she's doing it to punish me.'

'Well, long may it continue, because I think she's going to be a stor, albeit of *women's* rugby? So did, er, Claire from Bray and Garret get off alright?'

'Oh my God!' she goes. 'You haven't heard the goss?'

'What goss are we talking?'

'They've split up!'

'What?'

'The day after they arrived back in Toronto, Garret changed his Facebook status to single, then two days later put up a post saying he was going travelling with some girl called, I don't know, Ji Eun.'

'Random.'

'Random is right. Ross, they seemed – oh my God – *so* loved up when they were here. You saw them.'

'I did. Disgusting.'

'Claire was saying they were talking about storting a family. Although she seemed a little bit off when we met them the night before they went home.'

'We?'

'Me and Fionn.'

'You and Fionn is *we* now, is it?'

'Don't stort, Ross.'

'So any idea what happened? Has Claire said anything or blah, blah, blah?'

'She told me when she was home that there was a girl who was always coming into the shop and flirting with Garret. I'm pretty sure it was this Ji Eun person. He used to give her two chocolates with her coffee.'

'What a scumbag. I can see where *that's* going. So he turned out to be no better than me after all, huh?'

'Claire's obviously devastated because she hasn't replied to any of my messages on Facebook, Twitter, Snapchat or WhatsApp.'

'Scumbag is the only word for him. Here, do you want to come in and wait for my old man? I won't make a move on you. I promise.'

I probably will make a move on her.

'No, I have to get home,' she goes. 'Magnus is going out tonight. I think he has a hot date!'

I'm like, 'With a man?'

'Yes, with a man. He's gay, Ross. It's not something you grow out of.'

'I'm saying fair focks. Who's the dude?'

'That I don't know. But he's been whispering a lot on the phone lately. Then, this morning, he asked me if he could have the evening off! Oh my God, I'd love if he met someone – he is *such* a lovely goy.'

'Very easy to talk to was my analysis. Said it from day one.'

'I know you've a problem with gay people –'

'I've no problem with gay people.'

'Maybe if you weren't so . . .'

'What?'

'Repressed, Ross. Uptight. Do you remember what you said the day I told you that my really, really good friend Jonathan from UCD was gay?'

'No.'

'You said, "Of course he's gay – he went to Gonzaga!" '

'Yeah, that was a joke based on rugby rivalry. I actually love Gonzaga – they're the first school whose results I look out for after obviously Castlerock College.'

'Does it not bother you, Ross, that everything you know about the world you learned in a rugby dressing room?'

'It hasn't done me any horm.'

She's like, 'Hasn't it, Ross?' and then she turns to go. As she's closing the front gate behind her, she looks back at me just to hammer the point home and goes, 'Hasn't it?'

She leaves me with that thought. As she gets into her cor, I get a text message. It's from Tilly. She says half-eight outside Fade Street Social.

Oh, for fock's sake.

Tinder hook-ups should come with a warning. *Women may turn out to be far less foxy than they appear on here.* Tilly is a perfect example of what I'm talking about. Her profile picture was obviously taken in her hotter, but long ago, past. My guess would be that it was on *holidays* somewhere? She has a nice tan, not too much meat on the bones and a smile on her face that suggests she's a good laugh and would pull a few surprises on you once the lights went off.

But the girl who shows up looks fock-all like the girl I arranged to meet.

'You're, er, not blonde,' I go, while we're doing the whole meet-and-greet thing. Of course, what I'm subtly saying is, 'You're not a lot of the things you appeared to be when I swiped right.'

She doesn't pick up on the fact that I'm pissed off at being taken for a mug here. She's pretty happy with me, judging by the delighted look on her face.

All her focking Christmases.

'You're very different from your profile picture yourself,' she has the actual nerve to go to me.

I'm like, 'Pot and kettle. Pot *and* kettle. So what do you want to do?'

She's there, 'Will we get a drink?'

I'm there, 'I don't mind,' which I genuinely don't, even though I'm two or three pints down the road already.

So in we go. I get the first round. It's called being a gentleman. Sancerre for her, Hydrogen for me. And I go, 'So do you go on Tinder a lot?' just to get the old conversational ball rolling.

'No,' she goes, 'I'm actually new to it.'

Yeah, she joined in April 2013, according to her profile. This girl lies like a ten-dollar Rolex.

I'm there, 'Hey, me too. To be honest, I'm sort of, like, easing my way back into the dating game.'

She goes, 'Oh?'

'Yeah, no, I was married there for a while. It's definitely changed, the whole singles scene. It's all apps now, isn't it? I was always a gift of the gab merchant. That's why I've always preferred chatting up women. You have a better idea of what you're getting. And that's not a dig at you.'

It is a dig at her.

I'm there, 'So what about you? Have you ever been married yourself?'

She goes, 'Six years.'

I'm like, 'Any kids?' because I like to know if the water is mined. 'No, no children,' she goes.

I only have her word for that, of course. She could have more kids than Angelina focking Jolie.

We find a table. We have one drink, then another. We chat away. Or rather I let her blab away about various books she's read or intends to read. I think I'm going to do very well back on the dating scene. I'm very good at giving the impression of being interested in what other people are saying.

'I've just finished *Go Set a Watchman*,' she goes. 'It was a lot better than I expected.'

I'm there, 'I wouldn't be much into books myself, even though I'm always saying I should read more. They say the brain is a muscle and it needs exercise – although that's always sounded like horseshit to me.'

Like I said, I've always been a great conversationalist. And it's weird because after about half an hour, Tilly storts to look not quite as bad as I originally *thought*? That could be booze, or it could be the lighting in here. Fade Street Social is like Abercrombie & Fitch. Everything looks different when you get it home. But if I had to describe her, I'd say she's a bit like Cressida Bonas, except chunkier and from Cabinteely.

I do something that's possibly a bit *immature* then? I take a photograph of her when I think she's not looking, the plan being to text it to Oisinn, along with a message saying something along the lines of, 'Onwards and upwards, Oisinn. Look what I'm out with tonight!' and then accidentally on purpose send the message to Sorcha instead.

'Did you just take a photograph of me?' Tilly goes.

I'm there, 'A photograph?', all wounded innocence.

'You're not texting that to one of your friends, are you?'

Jesus, she's hord work.

I'm there, 'If you knew me, Tilly – which you'll hopefully get to – you'd know that wasn't my style.'

'Can we just talk?'

'We've done a lot of talking, Tilly. Well, *you* have.'

'Well, can we talk some more?'

'Hey, whatever flips your pancake. You chat away there.'

Which is what she does. I end up getting her entire life story. She works in, I don't know, some big American firm that does something vital, I'm sure. She says the work is really intense and the management really encourage people to work 'remotely' – which means in the evenings and at weekends for no extra money. They've also installed an area called an Urban Thinkspace, where you can sit on a milking stool, or in a baby's cot, to help you think in original and creative ways. She went off caffeine three and a half months ago and she's honestly never had more energy.

You get the idea. On and on she focking drones – yeah, no, despite the gamey-sounding name, Tilly is about as much fun as a focking mushroom risotto for one.

I decide to try to hurry the conversation along by going, 'So where are we going to take this then?'

And she's there, 'Take it? I don't understand.'

I laugh. I'm there, 'I'm staying with my old man – we're talking Ailesbury Road here,' and I put my hand on her leg.

She picks it off her like it's a wet nappy. 'I'm sorry,' she goes, 'I'm actually a bit of a traditionalist.'

Exact quote.

I'm like, 'A traditionalist? Okay, what do they believe?'

She goes, 'They believe in getting to know someone before progressing to anything else.'

I'm looking at her, just thinking, what the fock are you doing on Tinder then?

I'm there, 'You never mentioned that in your profile. All I'm saying is you're going to get a reputation as a timewaster. I'm making the point.'

Now, in normal circumstances, that would be that. I'd drop her like incriminating evidence. In fact, I'm just about to perform one of my world-famous disappearing acts through the emergency exit when the night takes an unexpected twist.

And not a happy one either.

I'm suddenly aware of someone trying to get my attention across the other side of the bor. It's actually Tilly who first points it out to me. She goes, 'Is that girl waving at you?'

I look over. I don't focking believe it. It ends up being Oreanna. Okay, this town is *too* focking small? I'm there, 'Yeah, no, she seems to be. Actually, would you excuse me just for a minute?'

She goes, 'You're going to leave me on my own while you go and talk to another girl?'

I don't think Tilly's in any position to be playing the wronged woman here.

I'm there, 'Look, she's actually an ex of mine. Oreanna is her name. She, er, still has a thing for me. It might not be safe for you.'

She's like, 'Safe for me?'

'She gets very jealous of other women. She could well glass you.'

'Oh my God!'

'She's a focking nutcase.'

'Okay, well, please don't leave me on my own for long.'

I tell her I'll be two minutes, max. I knock back the rest of my pint, then I tip over to Oreanna, who, it turns out, is here with Eva. They're celebrating their five-year anniversary.

The first line out of her mouth immediately throws me. She's like, 'What about Bart?'

She's a bit pissed. That much is obvious.

I'm there, 'Bart?', and that's when I remember my imaginary boyfriend.

She goes, 'As in, Bart your boyfriend? Who's that girl, Ross?' and she says the word *girl* with total contempt, like she hates even the *idea* of me being straight?

I'm there, 'That girl over there? Yeah, no, she's just a friend.'

'You had your hand on her leg,' she goes.

'Well, she's more of an ex, to be honest. Tilly was the last girl I was ever with before I realized that I was – and it still feels random saying it – *into men*. Into men and in love with Brad. In a big-time way.'

'You mean Bart?'

'I do mean Bart, yeah. In fact, I don't know why I said Brad just there. I still feel sorry for the girl, to be honest. It was a genuine shock to her.'

It's actually Eva who first smells a rat. 'I'm calling bullshit,' she goes. 'You're not even gay. I knew you were totally making it up that day.'

Oreanna's like, 'What?' and she's genuinely furious with me. 'You focking . . . wanker!'

I can see Tilly looking over. She heard her and she's obviously thinking, yeah, no, he wasn't wrong when he said the girl had mental issues.

I end up going, 'I didn't make him up. As a matter of fact, he's around here somewhere,' and I stort looking around me, trying to pick out a boyfriend for myself. Obviously it needs to be someone really good-looking, so as to be believable, but also someone too shit-faced to string a sentence together in the event that Eva and Oreanna want to actually talk to him.

And that's when I spot him. He's standing up at the bor – good-looking, well-built and out of his focking gourd. He's counting out coins on the bor and he's staggering backwards and forwards like a man trying to keep his balance in an airplane toilet in a patch of turbulence. I'm like, 'Ah, there he is! There's my Bart!'

Oreanna looks at him, then back at me and goes, 'You are *so* full of shit!'

I'm there, 'That's him. I swear.'

'Okay,' Eva goes, 'bring him over and introduce us then.'

So I tip over to where the dude is standing. Oreanna and Eva are watching. Tilly is also watching with a look of confusion on her face. I sidle up to him and go, 'Hey.'

'Up Cyahvan!' he goes, trying to focus on me, but his eyes are spinning like I don't know what. 'Up the Lake County! And fuck them Monaghan cunts!'

He's absolutely focking leathered. I'm thinking, this is going to be easier than I thought. I put my orm around his shoulder. He's too horrendufied to even notice. I smile at Oreanna and Eva and their expressions definitely soften, although Eva still looks a *bit* dubious?

'Have you torty cents?' the dude goes. 'I need torty cents for a paint bohull of Bulmers.'

'I'll tell you what,' I go, putting my hand in my pocket, 'why don't I just *buy* you a pint bottle of Bulmers?'

'That'd be fucken migh'hy, so it would. Did you just kiss me on the top of me head?'

'No.'

'Someone kissed me on the top of me head.'

I'm thinking, if only Sorcha could see me – who's repressed now?

He goes, 'I'm thrinking since one o'clock. Up the Lake County and fuck them Monaghan cunts!'

Oreanna and Eva are actually smiling now. Over the other side of the bor, Tilly is definitely *not* smiling. Fock knows what she's thinking. She meets a dude on Tinder, he propositions her, focks off to talk to another woman and now he's standing at the bor with his orm around some drunken bogman, giving him little pecks on the top of the head.

She's not seeing me at my best, I'll give her that.

'Who's them tooy bords looking over hee-or?' the dude goes.

I'm there, 'I actually know them. Do you want me to maybe introduce you?'

'Are they dorty? They look fierce dorty!'

'I don't know about dirty, but the one on the left thinks she possibly knows you.'

The one on the left is Eva.

I'm there, 'She says she was in love with you in college. Is your name Bart?'

'Bayurt? No, tis a cyase of mishtaken idenhihy, so.'

I smile at him – I think it's a word – *speculatively*? 'Hey,' I go, *'she doesn't know that. You could just *say* you're Bart?'

'Mon,' he goes, 'we'll gaw hoaver to them so.'

I'm there, 'Yeah, no, but maybe let me do the talking, will you?'

Over we go. I'm like, 'Girls, this is the famous Bart. And Bart, this is Eva and Oreanna.'

Oreanna hugs him and goes, 'Oh my God, I've been *dying* to meet you? Ross tells me you're a quantity surveyor.'

This obviously means fock-all to him, but he's too pissed to address it directly. At the top of his voice, he goes, 'The Thrumlin Counthy, me fooken hoooooole! Fuck them Monaghan cunts!'

He laughs, puts his orm around Eva's shoulder, then staggers forward, nearly dragging her to the deck in the process. She manages to somehow keep him upright, then she props him up against the bor at an angle where he can't fall flat on his face.

Oreanna is sort of, like, studying him closely, obviously trying to put her finger on what I actually see in him. She can't seem to find it. 'Don't take this the wrong way,' she goes, 'but he's not exactly what I *pictured* for you?'

I'm there, 'What did you picture for me?'

'I don't know. Someone more *like* you. Someone rugby.'

'I never thought a Gaelic football person would do it for me. But I love him.'

And that's when I notice that Tilly is suddenly standing beside me. She goes. 'Okay, what the fock is going on?'

I'm trying to come up with an explanation for her, but Oreanna gets in there first. 'You need to get over Ross,' she goes. 'He has no interest in you.'

And Tilly's there, 'Well, he has no interest in you either! You're the one who can't seem to come to terms with that basic fact.'

Before they get the chance to tease this argument out any further, the dude who's pretending to be Bart suddenly throws the lips on Eva. She reacts by taking a step backwards, then slapping him hord across the face. So *he's* suddenly going, 'Whay did you do that? Are yee Monaghan girls?' and he throws the pint I bought him over Eva. *She* responds by throwing a punch at him – an *actual* punch. Pissed as he is, the dude sees it coming and sort of, like, pirouettes out of the way and Eva ends up punching Oreanna full in the face. Oreanna's nose – seriously? – bursts open like a dropped watermelon. There's, like, blood everywhere.

Tilly, while shocked, goes, 'Well, at least she's saved me the trouble of doing that!' Then Oreanna grabs *her* by the hair and storts swinging her round the bor.

Now, one of the things that made me the rugby player I very nearly could have been was my incredible sense of timing. I'm already moonwalking towards the door as the bouncers arrive and stort trying to pull them aport. I reckon I've got about thirty seconds before they all figure out where they each stand in relation to me.

Oreanna is holding her busted nose with one hand and pointing at Bart with the other. 'You tried to kiss my girlfriend!' she goes.

The dude is like, 'Girlfriend? Is it lesbians yee are?'

And Eva's there, 'Yes – and you're supposed to have a boyfriend!'

He's like, 'A what's that now?'

She goes. 'Er, Ross?'

'Him? I only met that hooer just now when I asked him for torty cents for a paint bohull of Bulmers and he said you wanted the ride!'

Thirty seconds later, I'm in a taxi on the way back to the old man's gaff. I'm telling the driver about my evening and he's laughing so hord at one point, he ends up nearly driving into a lamppost on Lower Leeson Street. I think I'm going to enjoy being back in the singles morket.

As I'm paying the dude, I notice two Gordaí in, like, full uniform standing outside my old man's gaff. There's another dude with them, presumably a *plain*-clothes Gorda? He's the one who actually approaches me.

'Ross O'Carroll-Kelly?' he goes.

I'm like, 'Yeah? What do you want?'

And he's there, 'I'm arresting you on suspicion of being an accessory to murder.'

'Why am I here?' I go – *here* meaning Blackrock Gorda Station. 'I don't have time for this.'

The dude's like, 'Time? Sure you've all the time in the world. I can keep you here for up to forty-eight hours.'

O'Maonaigh is his name.

'Forty-eight hours?' I go. 'That's, like, three days.'

He's there, 'It's two days.'

'*Two* days, then. I'm not staying here for two days.'

'You've been arrested on suspicion of aiding and abetting a murderer and conspiracy to cover up a serious crime.'

'I want a lawyer,' I go, drumming the table with my index finger. 'I want Hennessy Coghlan-O'Hara. You should have his number at the front desk.'

'Oh, we know Hennessy well. And I could interview you in his presence – like I said, over the course of the next forty-eight hours – or you could answer my questions and you'll be out of here within the hour.'

So what choice do I have? I end up going, 'What do you want to ask me?'

'Ari's daughter,' he goes, looking down at his notes, 'Tiffany Blue – she said you told her your mother was capable of anything, including murdering her grandfather for his money.'

'I said that in the course of trying to have sex with the girl. I was chatting her up.'

He looks totally focking baffled – like me having the Nando's ordering policy explained to me for the fiftieth time.

'Then a few weeks later,' he goes, 'the man was found dead in highly suspicious circumstances.'

Okay, I can see the twist he's trying to put on it.

I'm like, 'Dude, I hate my old dear more than anyone. She has a face like a punched doughnut. But despite what I said, I actually *don't* think she'd be capable of killing someone?'

He goes, 'Your mother's account of what happened doesn't add up. Ari takes a bath, then he dries himself off, then he puts on a tracksuit and goes for a run on the treadmill.'

'Your point being?'

'My point being, why would he take a bath *before* he got on the treadmill?'

'Because he wasn't right in the head. The dude was loop the focking loop.'

'Not according to your mother. He was of sound mind – she made a sworn statement to that effect before they got married.'

'She was lying then.'

'She's lying now. Telling all sorts of lies. She's saying now she wasn't home when it happened. She was in Stillorgan Shopping Centre. Then she came home and found him dead.'

'So?'

'But no one saw her when she was out. She has no alibi. She's not even on any security footage from the shopping centre that afternoon.'

'Random.'

'Random – as you say . . . your mother drank half a pint of vodka at lunchtime. Would that be unusual for her?'

I actually laugh. I'm there, 'Lunchtime is pretty late in the day for her to be storting.'

He goes, 'We found the glass in the sink. A tall glass. It had been filled to the top with vodka and her saliva was on it.'

'Yeah, that's called breakfast. The woman is a focking dipso.'

'Do you think she might have needed a bit of Dutch courage if she had something unpleasant to do – like, for instance, drop a two-bar electrical heater into her husband's bath?'

'We've never owned a two-bor electric heater. I've seen them – usually when I've maybe pulled a student and gone back to her bedsit. Or a poor person.'

'So what do *you* think caused the burn mark on Ari's shin?'

'Yeah, no, that actually happened when they were on honeymoon. Supposedly a piece of coal spat out of the borbecue and hit him.'

'Because I've looked through all of their honeymoon photographs. Nearly three hundred of them . . .'

He chuckles to himself.

He goes, 'Some of them are of, shall we say, an intimate nature!'

Jesus Christ, she's a focking disgrace.

I'm there, 'Seriously, don't. I'll get sick all over the floor.'

'There's not one single photograph that suggests the man had a burn on his shin,' he goes.

'So you think it was caused by . . . ?'

'A heater dropped into the bath – yes, I do.'

'Dude, Ari was in his nineties. She didn't need to kill him. He was going to die soon anyway and she'd have inherited everything.'

'He was due to have his mental state assessed two days after he died. And she knew that if he kept that appointment, the marriage would be declared void and she wouldn't get a penny. So she killed him while he lay in the bath, then she dried him off, dressed him in a tracksuit and dragged him downstairs to the basement. She switched on the treadmill, then left him lying beside it.'

'You've no actual proof of that.'

He continues staring at me for a good, like, thirty seconds. Then he goes, 'She's evil, Ross.'

I'm there, 'Hey, I've been saying the same thing for years. You know she has a tail? That's a little-known fact about her. The doctors found it about ten years ago after her gastric band snapped.'

He goes, 'I've met a lot of killers. Most of them never considered themselves capable of killing anyone and regretted it straightaway. I don't see any of that in her. She's cold-blooded. Completely and utterly without human feeling.'

I think back to one of my earliest memories. I was sitting in my high-chair in Sallynoggin slash Glenageary, waiting to be fed, literally screaming with the hunger, while she poured a jor of Dolmio spaghetti sauce and half a bottle of Bombay Sapphire into the blender to fix herself a Bloody Mary first.

I'm there, 'It doesn't mean she'd be capable of, like, murdering someone – does it?'

And that's when the door suddenly flies open and in storms Hennessy with a face like thunder and lightning. He goes, 'What did you tell him?'

And I'm like, 'Nothing – fock-all.'

He points at O'Maonaigh and goes, 'Don't you fucking *ever* interview one of my clients again without me being present!'

O'Maonaigh goes, 'Hello there, Hennessy. Your client is free to go.'

I stand up.

As I'm walking towards the door, O'Maonaigh goes, 'Your mother killed that man in cold blood, Ross. And if I find out you're hiding that two-bar electric heater, I'll make sure you go to prison for a very long time.'

I'm looking at her across the table in the visiting room and I'm thinking about what the dude said – a cold-blooded killer, incapable of human whatever-the-actual-word-was – and this is going around in my head to the point that I haven't even commented on the fact that her hair is purple.

Or maybe that's because, despite everything, I still for some bizarre reason *care* about the woman?

'The focking state of you,' I eventually go. 'You look like a horror clown.'

She's like, 'Yes, it's horrid,' in her usual whiny voice. 'I told you about my troubles with the water in here. Then I heard someone mention this woman – they said she was one of the Scissor Sisters. So I went to see her and I asked her if she had any suggestions for putting some pizazz back into my hair.'

'The Scissor Sisters aren't focking hairdressers.'

'Yes, I realize that now, Ross! Look at me!'

'Hey, watch your focking tone. I was arrested the other day.'

'What?'

'Yeah, no, I was arrested on suspicion of aiding, then another thing called abetting. They think I helped you do it.'

'They're just using you to try to get at me. They think if they keep persecuting the people I love, then I'll make some kind of confession. Your father's right – the entire thing is political. They're terrified that he's going to win the next election and take the country out of Europe. That'll be the end of their plumb jobs.'

'The dude said you drank half a pint of vodka on the morning of the murder,' I go. 'Jesus Christ, I remember you used to at least put tomato juice in it. Of course, that was when you were still *pretending* to be human?'

'Yes, I had a drink, Ross – I had just arrived home to find my husband dead on the floor. I was in shock.'

'You didn't tell me you went out. In fact, you said you were at home when it happened.'

It's obvious that Hennessy's been coaching her.

She goes, 'I was confused. It was only later on I remembered that I went to Stillorgan to see did Donnybrook Fair do those potato latkes that Ari so loved. He was rather homesick, you see – dear, dear Ari.'

'They have CCTV in Donnybrook Fair. Why didn't you show up on that, you focking cyclops?'

'Because when I got out of my car, I realized that I'd left my purse at home, along with my mobile phone and everything. So then I drove back home.'

'And you didn't talk to anyone?'

'Oh, yes, I did. Very briefly. I'd parked in two parking spaces, you see.'

'Why do you always do that?'

'Because I don't want somebody opening their doors and hitting my car. Some awful man told me that I didn't know how to drive. I said something along the lines of, "That's your opinion," and then I drove home. I walked into the house and – yes, that was it – I heard that the treadmill was on. Which I thought rather odd. So I rushed downstairs to find darling, darling Ari . . . oh, I can't even say the word.'

I'm there, 'The word is dead, you focking drama queen.'

'Yes, dead,' she goes. 'And now it's all this. Oh, it's a living nightmare, Ross.'

She storts making the noise of someone crying, although there's no actual water coming out of her eyes. That face has been lifted so many times, her tear glands are halfway down her focking back.

I'm there, 'The dude said he went through your honeymoon photos. They were filthy, he said, some of them. But there wasn't one of Ari with a burn mork on his leg.'

'All of our photographs were from the first two or three days of the honeymoon. Then we stopped taking them. Ari said, "Who the hell are we taking all these photographs for? Why don't we just enjoy our time together while we're both still here?" He meant why don't we just enjoy each other's company and – yes, Ross – each other's bodies –'

'Move on. Quickly.'

'– without having to photograph everything. So I put the camera away and I didn't take it out again.'

All of a sudden, I hear a woman's voice shouting at us across the visiting room. She's like, 'Ah, there thee are – howiya!'

I'd recognize that voice anywhere. It's focking Dordeen.

The old dear screws up her face in disgust, like she swallowed a mouthful of tonic with no actual gin in it. 'Howiya?' she goes. 'Ross, who *is* that awful woman? She seems to think she *knows* us.'

I'm there, 'Yeah, no, that's Shadden's old dear.'

'Who?'

'Shadden? As in, Ronan's girlfriend? As in, the mother of your great-granddaughter?'

She hates being reminded.

'Great-granddaughter,' she goes. 'Oh, don't, Ross – that makes me sound old!'

I'm there, 'You are old. You're older than dirt. And horder to shift.'

Dordeen doesn't like the way we're totally blanking her, because she makes a big point of coming over to our table. She goes, 'Did yiz not heerd me? Ine arthur been shouting at yiz,' and she flicks her head in the direction of the table she's come from. There's a woman sitting at it who I'm guessing weighs about three stone. 'Ine in visitodding a veddy good friend of moyun. Mandy's in for shoplifting – professional, but. Howiya, Fidden Newilla? Hab ya settodled in, hab ya?'

The old dear just stares at her in horror. It reminds me of the time I had a porty in the gaff and one or two Terenure heads crashed it and did a shit in her jewellery box. It's the same look of revulsion on her face.

I go, 'She's asking you if you've settled in,' because I've spent so much time in Finglas over the years that I'm practically fluent.

The old dear still doesn't say shit, so Dordeen changes the subject.

'The utter fedda thinks he fayult he's exaddems,' she goes, sounding delighted about it. 'Probley for the best. Your heer's lubbly, Fidden Newilla. I've been meaden to say to you, if you ebber need athin in hee-or, just gib me a shout, do you wontherstand? If addyone's gibbon you a heerd toyum – athin like that – I've veddy good connect shiddens in hee-or. Do you get me? You oately have to say the woord. We're famidy, arthur awdle . . . Cost you a few bob, but.'

Then off she focks, back to her rake of a mate.

'What a ghastly woman!' the old dear goes. 'PGM, Ross! PGM!' which stands for Poor Genetic Material. I remember the phrase from the time someone on Westminster Road hired a bouncy castle for a children's birthday porty and the old dear took out a High Court injunction to force them to take it down. I laugh. See, she's not all bad – she can be very funny.

I suddenly stand up to go. She's there, 'Is it over already? I didn't hear the bell!'

'Yeah, no,' I go, 'that's because it didn't ring. I'm just bored.'

'Oh, well, you've got a life to lead, I'm sure. Things to do. I'd better get back to my suite.'

'Yeah, it's actually called a cell.'

'Sorcha is coming to visit me on Thursday. Has she seen sense yet?'

'The opposite. She now wants a divorce.'

'A divorce? How awful?'

I'm looking at her closely to see does she actually *mean* it? Does she even *give* a fock, or, like the dude said, does she actually even *have* human feelings? It's impossible to tell. So much of her face is just rubber and polyurethane with a series of levers and pulleys underneath controlling her expressions.

As I go to leave, she reaches for my wrist and squeezes it a little too tightly for my liking. 'I know how it looks,' she goes, 'but I wouldn't have it in me to take someone's life.'

And I have to admit – and this is possibly me being too soft for my own good – but in that moment a big, big doubt definitely enters my mind. She obviously senses it, because she smiles at me. 'I love you,' she goes.

And I'm there, 'I might bring the kids with me next time. You need to do something about your focking hair, by the way. You look like Sharon Osbourne at a hundred.'

Erika looks incredible. And I don't mean that in, like, a *creepy* way? I mean it in the way anyone would pay their sister a compliment. Her legs are brown and well-toned, her honkers look fantastic in that white t-shirt and she's wearing her hair pinned up in a way that always did it for me before we found out that we were technically related.

She's been home five minutes and already the sporks are flying. It's the usual banter between us. She goes, 'Have you been rooting through my underwear drawer?'

I'm there, 'No, I haven't been rooting through your underwear drawer,' and, as I'm saying it, I'm holding little Amelie in my orms. 'Look how big you've grown! Do you remember me? I'm your Uncle Ross, who your mom is presumably always talking about!'

'Ross!' she goes.

I'm like, 'That's right! *Uncle* Ross!'

Erika is unpacking their things. We're in my bedroom – or *her* bedroom, as she's insisting on calling it. She's in terrible form, it has to be said. She goes, 'I can't believe you were rooting through my underwear drawer.'

I'm like, 'Erika, for the last time, I wasn't rooting through your underwear drawer. I might have opened it – yeah, no – just to see what was in there. I see you're still into v-strings, by the way.'

'There's something wrong with you,' she goes. 'There's something seriously, seriously wrong with you. Why haven't you moved all your shit out of my room? I told you I was coming home.'

I'm there, 'Where am I supposed to sleep?'

'There are other bedrooms in this house.'

'Yeah, no, they're all freezing. Why don't we share the room and see how it works out? It might *not* be weird?'

'If your clothes aren't out of this room within the next fifteen minutes, I'm going to throw them out the window, okay?'

Helen and the old man suddenly arrive home. I hear them coming up the stairs, then they're suddenly in the room and it's all hugs and kisses. 'You should have told us what time you were coming in!' the old man goes. 'We would have picked you up at the airport!'

I can see Erika checking out the old man's head. She's like, 'It's the first time I've ever seen you with hair. You look . . . different.'

'And I feel different! Like the old Charles O'Carroll-Kelly! Oh, I've got them all on the back foot! Fianna Fáil and Fine Gael! Sinn Féin and the so-called Labour Party!'

Helen goes, 'Perhaps we shouldn't talk about politics tonight, Charlie!'

I'm getting the impression they've had words.

The old man takes Amelie from me. He's like, 'Will you look at this little one? Oh, she loves her granddad, don't you?'

'Yes!' Amelie goes, clapping her two little hands together.

'Yes, you do! And I don't need a bloody well opinion poll to tell me that much!'

The next thing any of us hears is a voice calling up the stairs, going, 'Hello? I let myself in – I hope that's okay!' and up comes Sorcha.

There's the usual scene out on the landing. Hugs and all the rest of it. Sorcha's there, 'Oh my God, look at you – you're teeny-tiny!'

And Erika goes, 'You haven't changed a bit,' which is a typical Erika line – could be taken either way.

Sorcha's there, 'It's so, so amazing to have my best friend back! And look at Amelie! Oh my God, look at the size of you!' and she takes her out of the old man's orms.

He's obviously still avoiding her because he tries to slip away by going, 'Anyway, I'll leave you all to get reacquainted! I forgot I left poor Kennet outside in the car!'

Sorcha's not so easily fobbed off. 'Chorles,' she goes, 'you haven't been returning my calls.'

He's like, 'The last few days have been horrendously busy, Sorcha, as you can imagine!'

'Did you listen to any of my voice messages?'

I go, 'He didn't need to. I told him you weren't happy about the Europe and the water things, which is why he's been avoiding you ever since.'

She goes, "Chorles, you never said anything about pulling out of the European Union when I agreed to stand for New Republic.'

He's there, 'Europe turned its back on Ireland in its hour of need, Sorcha! They have saddled the people of this country with a debt that little Amelie's grandchildren will be paying!'

Thank fock it's not *us* paying for it – that would pretty much sum up my attitude.

He goes, 'In times of prosperity, friends will be plenty! In times of adversity, not one among twenty! *Amici secundis et plurima* – something, something, something!'

She's like, 'Well, I'm not in favour of Eirexit, or whatever it's called. And I'm saying that as someone who was lucky enough to spend a college term in Annecy. And what about my White Paper?'

'Your what?'

He's already forgotten. I said she'd regret it.

She goes, 'My White Paper on the future funding of Ireland's domestic water service. Chorles, five thousand people die every day for the want of a resource that we take – oh my God – for granted. I genuinely believe that if we knocked on doors and explained to people the environmental benefits that will result from us, as a society, becoming more aware of our water consumption, then nobody would be against paying for water. I think they'd see that they were getting actual value for money.'

'I've given the matter a considerable amount of thought, Sorcha.'

Erika goes, 'Hear her out, Dad.'

He's there, 'I've heard her out,' and he actually shouts it. 'I looked through her – what's this you called it, Sorcha? – your White Paper? And I am still of the view that water charges represent a tax too far! Metering people's water supply runs counter to the New Republic message, which is that ordinary people have been bloody well squeezed enough!'

Sorcha hands Amelie over to Erika.

'In that case,' she goes, 'I have to tell you, Chorles, that I don't think I'm the right person to represent New Republic in Dublin Bay South.'

The old man does the most incredible thing then. He agrees with her. He goes, 'As it happens, Sorcha, you're not alone in that view.'

And suddenly, she's like, '*Excuse* me?'

Helen goes, 'Maybe now isn't the time to have this discussion, Charlie.'

Sorcha's there, 'No, whatever it is, Helen, I want to know.'

'Well,' the old man goes, checking out his reflection in the mirror at the top of the stairs, then fixing his hair with his hand, 'I know you've been out there, pressing the flesh – quote-unquote – on the streets of Ranelagh, Sandymount and so forth!'

'I've been working, like, six or seven hours a day for the porty.'

'We did some private polling, Sorcha! And the feedback we got about you wasn't good!'

Helen goes, 'Erika, are you hungry? We should all go out to dinner tonight.'

But Sorcha's not going to just let it go. She's there, 'What do you mean, the feedback wasn't good?'

'Look,' the old man goes, 'from the soundings we took, we discovered that people in more affluent areas are likely to remain loyal to Lucinda. Which means, to get elected, you would have to win a lot of votes in less affluent areas – your Ringsends and your Harold's Crosses! And unfortunately your approval rating isn't particularly high in those areas! From our research, it's clear that people think you come over a little . . .'

She's like, 'Say it?'

'Pleased with yourself!'

'*Pleased* with myself?'

'Smug is the word that's being used over and over again! Apparently, you keep mentioning that you went to Mount Anville!'

'Only in the context of being Head Girl and how that shows that I have definite *leadership* qualities?'

'The impression people have of you is that you're smug and élitist!'

'There's nothing smug *or* élitist about Mount Anville, Chorles. Oh my God, Mary Robinson went there. Erika, tell him!'

'It all comes down to the impression you create, Sorcha! And you're not creating the right impression! The people of Harold's Cross don't know you like I know you! Bright! Hard-working! Able! Sadly, we live in an age where those things aren't always enough!'

'Well, what do I have to do to win people over?'

The old man is un-focking-believable. She came here to tell him she was leaving the porty and he's somehow managed to turn it around. Because more than anything else, Mounties want to be popular – Sorcha once wrote a four-stor review of a Bodum coffee plunger on Amazon, and she nearly burst with excitement when four people said they found it helpful – and he's totally playing on that.

She goes, 'Okay, Chorles, give me one more chance to try to get my message across to the people.'

He's there, 'How are you going to get your message across to the people if the people can't understand you?'

'Excuse me?'

'You need to work on your accent, Sorcha!'

'Her accent?' Erika goes. 'What's wrong with her accent?'

She's only saying it because she's got the exact same one.

He goes, 'Nothing at all if the fate of Dublin Bay South were to be decided by a vote of female members of tennis clubs in the Sandymount and Clonskeagh areas! Unfortunately, that's not how democracy works! Sorcha, have you ever seen the picture *My Fair Lady*? Starring Audrey Hepburn and the famous Rex Harrison?'

She's like, 'Loads of times. I actually did *Pygmalion* with the Rathmines and Rathgor Musical Society when I was in, like, college.'

'Yes, you probably shouldn't mention that out on the streets either! Well, as you know, *My Fair Lady* is the story of a peasant flower-girl who is taught to speak and act like a member of the upper classes! What I want to do with you is to achieve the exact reverse of that!'

'You're seriously asking me to change the way I speak?'

I'm there, 'Tell him to fock off, Sorcha.'

He goes, 'I'm just asking you to dial the accent up a few post-codes! To beat Lucinda, you are going to have to win a lot of votes in areas like Harold's Cross and Irishtown – to say nothing of Terenure!'

Sorcha and Erika exchange a look.

'Terenure?' Sorcha goes. 'What would I have to say to someone from Terenure? I know nothing of their struggles.'

He's there, 'It matters not what you say, Sorcha – it matters only how you say it! Someone said that once!'

She goes, 'I don't think I could do it, Chorles . . . Erika, I'm trying to think what Miss Barrington, our Speech and Deportment teacher, would think if she even *heard* this conversation?'

Like I said, the old man knows what buttons to press. He goes, 'There have been many brilliant politicians whose careers have foundered because of an inability to relate to ordinary people.'

That seems to do the trick.

'Okay,' she goes, 'I'm prepared to try it. But I want you to know,

Chorles, I haven't given up trying to persuade you that you're wrong about Europe and you're wrong about water chorges.'

Erika's like, 'So who's going to teach her to speak like a skanger? Who's going to be her Henry Higgins?'

And from the bottom of the stairs, we suddenly hear a voice go, 'Are you g . . . g . . . g . . . g . . . godda be long, Cheerdles? Ine d . . . d . . . d . . . d . . . double-peerked down hee-or.'

So I'm back on Tinder. And I arrange to meet – this time? – this bird called Shivail Deasy, who *I* think looks a little bit like Melanie Iglesias, although – again – the thing to remember about profile pics on dating apps is that they're basically a snapshot of the hottest the girl has ever looked or is ever likely to look in her life.

The rule, I've discovered, is that you look at the picture, you try to imagine her twenty to thirty percent less attractive, and you make up your mind on that basis whether you're still interested. In Shivail's case, the answer is yes. She's got what's known in the Paris fashion world as 'big mickey lips', and she lets it be known during an hour of flirty text exchanges that she has a thing for rugby players.

We arrange to meet for a drink in Dakota. And, to cut a long story short, she ends up standing me up, then not answering her phone when I ring her to try to find out why. It might be that she was hoping for a more successful rugby player than one who was last seen plying his trade in Division 2B of the All Ireland League. Or maybe she felt one or two comments I made about her lips crossed a line.

Either way, I end up not giving a fock, because I decide to make a night of it anyway. So I'm walking back up South William Street. It's seven o'clock on a beautiful evening in July and I'm thinking I might hit Bruxelles for one or two and see where the night ends up taking me.

And that's when, all of a sudden, I see something that causes me to lose my train of thought. It's not so much something as someone – or rather *two* someones? – sitting outside, under the awning of Taste! At first, I think, yeah, no, maybe I'm imagining it. But then I realize I'm not. It's Magnus. And he's with Oisinn.

They're looking – I'm going to just come out and say it – weirdly *cosy* together? And I'm suddenly asking myself all sorts of questions, although mainly it's, what the fock? Is this who Magnus has been – oh my God – *seeing*? Hang on, how do they even know each other? I'm thinking, yeah, no, they met that night in Kielys when Magnus arrived in with Sorcha. But Oisinn isn't . . . Or is he? Then I'm thinking, no. Not a chance. Who, Oisinn? He's as straight as I am.

But they're both drinking what look very much to me like fruit smoothies. Not that that's evidence of anything per se. I'm just stating it as a fact. They're both drinking fruit smoothies. On an evening in July. People can make of it what they will.

Just as I'm thinking this, I accidentally catch Oisinn's eye. Oh, shit. Except he's not *embarrassed*? He actually smiles, then Magnus turns and sees me as well. And he smiles, too. Oisinn sort of, like, beckons me over. I mouth the words, 'I've got to go,' but Oisinn pulls a face as if to say, 'Stop being a wuss!' and he beckons me even horder, so I have no choice but to tip over to where they're sitting.

My suspicions are immediately confirmed. It's definitely smoothies they're drinking. I can smell the mango.

I'm there, 'Hey, Oisinn. Hey, Magnus,' for some reason trying to make myself sound more, I don't know, manly. 'How the hell are you goys?'

Oisinn goes, 'What's the story with your voice, Ross?'

I'm like, 'Nothing. What's going on between you two? By that, I just mean what are you up to?'

Magnus smiles at Oisinn and goes, 'Do you want to tell thish guy whatsh going on or will I tell him?'

Oisinn's there, 'I suppose we have to tell him now – we've been busted!'

Magnus laughs. I'm thinking, okay, I'm not ready for this, and that's not me being – what was it Sorcha said? – repressed?

Oisinn goes, 'Ross, you can't tell anyone what we're about to tell you, okay?'

I'm there, 'You don't even have to tell me. Whatever it is. I'm wondering do I actually need to know?'

'Well, you've kind of caught us in the act here,' he goes, 'so we kind of have to tell you. Magnus is my portner now.'

Now, I don't want anyone to think for even ten seconds that I'm not one hundred percent cool with the whole gay thing. It's just that this is coming as a genuine shock to me. At least if Oisinn had texted me the news, I would have had time to process it before facing him – probably with a few funny one-liners to take the sting out of it.

Instead, I'm like a focking gibbering idiot, going, 'Er, yeah, no, em, definitely, yeah, big-time, very good, yeah, definitely, blah, blah, blah.'

Magnus goes, 'Ish everything okay, Rosh? Would you like a shmoothie?'

'No!' I hear myself go. I actually shout it. 'I mean, no thanks. Definitely, yeah, no, big-time, no thanks.'

'Okay,' he goes, 'you jusht look a lidl beet pale, that'sh all.'

'I'm just, I don't know, trying to get my head around it. I'm wondering when did this actually happen? As in, like, you two?'

Oisinn goes, 'Very quickly really. We met that night in Kielys – when was that? Two, three weeks ago? I rang Sorcha and asked her if I could have Magnus's number, then I rang him and said I had a proposition to put to him.'

'Jesus Christ. Keep going. Or don't. I'm equally fine not knowing.'

'So we arranged to meet for a drink. I told him I'd never done anything like this before. I was kind of a virgin in that way. So he'd have to be my guide.'

I'm looking around me, going, 'What did this place used to be before it was Taste! Was it Cook's Café, or was that further down?'

Oisinn goes, 'So we had a few drinks and we talked and we both said, "Okay, let's do it."'

'It might have been Kaffe Moka.'

'Yesh,' Magnus suddenly goes, 'sho now we're in bishinish together.'

Hang on, what did he just say?

I'm like, 'Business?'

Oisinn's there, 'Yeah. I told you we were portners, didn't I?'

I laugh. It's suddenly all clear to me now. I'm there, 'When you said that Magnus was your portner, I thought . . .'

'What?'

'Nothing. It doesn't matter. I thought we were having a totally different conversation. Okay, I get it now.'

Magnus goes, 'Osheen hash the idea to shet up a travel agenshy that will hopefully make Dublin the gay shtag and hen capital of the world!'

I'm there, 'That's an amazing idea,' because it sounds like a licence to print money. 'The whole BLT . . . BFG thing is suddenly massive, isn't it?'

'Alsho,' Magnus goes, 'there ish a lot of good feeling for Ireland ash the firsht country in the world to vote for gay marriage by a referendum.'

'A lot of gays are going to be thinking, fair focks to Ireland – fair, fair, fair, fair focks.'

'Exactly,' Oisinn goes. 'Ireland is now officially *the* most tolerant country in the world. So where better for LGBTQ people to celebrate their last night of freedom? What do you think of the name Gaycation Ireland?'

I laugh.

'Brilliant!' I go. 'Absolutely focking brilliant!'

He goes, 'Thanks, Ross. Anyway, I rang Magnus because, well, he knows the scene. All the best pubs, nightclubs, restaurants – obviously smoothie bors.'

'Osheen hash ashked me to put a broshure together,' Magnus goes. 'Look, I have not yet told Shorcha. Obvioushly, becaush of the bishinish, I will heff to shtop my job of looking after the cheeldren, which of coursh makesh me shad. I would like to tell thish newsh to Shorcha myshelf.'

And I'm there, 'Don't sweat it, Magnus. I won't say a word. I have to say, this is a very different conversation to the one I thought we were about to have.'

I pull up a chair and I sit down. So Sorcha thinks I'm repressed, does she?

'Do you know something?' I go, looking around me for a waiter. 'I might have a smoothie after all?'

Genius. I'm using that word. Honor is touched by genius. She's scored, like, two tries already and she's doing pretty much as she *pleases* out there? The only problem is that, as I remember all too well from my own playing days, there's always someone who wants to clip your wings.

One or two of the parents are moaning, going, 'She's not sharing the ball with her team-mates!', like that's the point of the focking game.

As she's about to go on yet another of her mazy runs, Rob – who's supposedly a qualified *coach*, bear in mind? – goes, 'Offload it, Honor! Offload it!' and this is when there's no one even tackling her.

I go, 'Don't focking listen to him, Honor!', even though I know I'm undermining him here. 'Never offload the ball unless you absolutely, one hundred percent have to!'

But Rob acts like I haven't said a word – someone who's been there and done it and was twice the player that he could ever dream of being. The next time there's a break in play, he turns around to Honor and goes, 'You have to pass the ball, Honor! Some of the other kids haven't even touched it yet!'

I decide that I can't listen to it. I end up having to go, 'Sorry, since when is that the focking object of the game?'

He goes, 'What?'

This is the same bullshit as the last day, when he tried to let some random kid take the penalty that Honor won through sheer talent.

Belvedere College, bear in mind. Belvedere focking College.

I'm there, 'Since when is it important that everyone gets a touch? It's supposed to be a competitive game.'

'You're only a prick!' Brian shouts. 'A focking prick with ears!'

'Ross,' Rob tries to go, 'they're just kids. We're trying to show them that the game can be fun and inclusive.'

I just think, yeah, that's how the Leinster Schools Senior Cup ended up being photographed in a sheep paddock in Roscrea, then splashed all over the Internet.

A couple of the other children's mothers decide to get involved then. 'Sebastian hasn't had the ball once!' one of them goes.

I'm there, 'So focking what? There's players who win Man of the Match awards without ever getting their hands on the ball. What's your point?'

The woman is around my age. She looks a little bit like Val Keil, but she loses points for knowing fock-all about rugby.

'Everyone's supposed to have a turn with the ball,' she goes. 'Your daughter won't give it to anyone else. She seems to want it all the time.'

I'm like, 'Which one is Sebastian?' because I've already got a pretty good idea. 'Is it the kid who looks a bit cross-eyed?'

She's there, 'I beg your pardon?' getting ready to take offence.

I go, 'The kid with the turn in his eye then? I'm sorry to tell you this – because the coach here doesn't seem to want to say it – but your son is no focking good.'

One or two others decide to throw their two yoyos in then.

'Josh hasn't touched the ball either,' this other woman goes – it's mostly *women* complaining, by the way? This one isn't the easiest on the eye either. I'm only mentioning it so you can picture the scene. She looks like Mattress Mick.

'That's because he's shit,' I go, 'and you're having trouble facing up to that basic fact.'

You can see one or two of the fathers – in fairness to them – looking at me and clearly thinking, 'Who is this obvious winner who's not afraid to make the big, big calls?'

Rob goes, 'Ross, none of this is helpful.'

'What does helpful have to do with it? Do you think this is what kids are being taught in New Zealand? That they need to pass the ball in case someone goes home with their feelings hurt? No, they're being taught to be winners from the age of two. Focking killers.'

That's when Honor – with the ball still in her hands – goes, 'It's just because I'm a girl.'

Josh's old dear goes, 'That's ridiculous.'

And I'm there, 'Yeah, shut the fock up, Mattress Mick – you've had your say. Honor, make your point.'

'It's because I'm a girl,' she goes, 'and I'm playing against all *boys*? And because I'm the best player here, I'm expected to apologize for it, or pretend that I'm not as good as I actually am. It's totally sexist.'

God, I love her attitude – she actually *knows* how talented she is?

I'm there, 'It's what they do to great players, Honor – they try to drag you down to their level of ordinariness. I had it for my entire career.'

Mattress Mick goes, 'It's hordly sexism. I'm a woman.'

'Yeah,' I go, 'we only have your focking word for that.'

That ends up being the last straw for Rob. He goes, 'Ross, I can't have you constantly interfering like this. I'm the coach, okay?'

I'm there, 'Coach?' and I laugh. 'You went to a school that lost the Leinster Schools Senior Cup final this year to a school from Tipperary.'

I notice one or two of the dads especially exchange looks of genuine concern.

Rob goes, 'Cistercian Roscrea is technically in Offaly.'

I don't respond to that point because no response is necessary.

I'm there, 'The players took photographs of the cup in a sheep paddock. Look it up. It's all over Google. I drank hundred-year-old Champagne from that cup. Now it's literally in the hands of farm boys with hairy focking gums. It'd be a brave man would ever drink anything from it ever again. And your school let that happen – you who thinks that the most important thing is that everyone gets a touch of the ball.'

'You're only a focking wankbag,' Leo shouts.

Wisely, Rob decides not to get sucked into an argument he can't win. He just goes, 'Okay, can we all just dial it down a notch and remember that this is supposed to be fun!' and he restorts the game.

And being a last-word freak when it comes to rugby, I shout, 'Rugby is like life, Honor. It's shit unless you're winning at it.'

So Magnus has given Sorcha his notice. She looks all sad and goes, 'I can't believe we're losing you! The children are going to be – oh my God – devastated!'

Which is a definite exaggeration. He's only been *on* the scene for, like, a month and I don't think Honor was ever that wild about him.

He's there, 'Like I shaid, the mannying wash alwaysh jusht a shtop gap for me. Thish ish an opportunity to go into bishinish for myshelf.'

She goes, 'I know. I'm being *so* selfish – I haven't even asked you what this business even is yet!'

It's Oisinn who answers. He goes, 'It's kind of a travel agency cum event management company. We're hoping to turn Ireland into a destination spot for gay stag and hen nights.'

'Gaycation Ireland,' Magnus goes.

Sorcha's there, 'Great name! Oh my God!'

We're in Kielys, by the way, and it's all the old crew. We're talking me, Oisinn, Christian, JP and Fionn, then Sorcha, Chloe, Sophie, Amie with an ie, but then also Muirgheal and – like I said – Magnus.

Erika is an hour late. To her own supposed homecoming drinks. We're all standing around waiting for the girl to make her grand entrance. It's just like old times.

Amie with an ie is telling Sophie that her sister is getting married next year and she found this amazing – oh my God – teeny-tiny church in the middle of Wicklow, but they won't let her get married there because of, like, a stupid technicality – the church is, like, Church of Ireland and Amie with an ie's sister and her fiancé are both, like, Catholic. Sophie agrees that it's a disgrace. She goes, 'It's, like, oh my God, Church of Ireland, get over yourselves!'

I hear Muirgheal telling Christian out of the corner of her mouth that Sorcha is a bitch and that she – oh my God – took all the credit for the work they *both* did on the marriage equality referendum and used it to launch her own political career – 'like the sly bitch she was back in school'.

Christian's there, 'Maybe tonight is not the night to bring it up, Muirgheal.'

And Muirgheal goes, 'Oh, don't worry, I'm going to be super-nice to her face!'

Then literally five minutes later, she says to Sorcha that she always knew she'd go into politics one day and that it's a great way for her to refind her pre-marriage identity, now that her marriage has fallen aport. 'And that's not me being a bitch,' she goes. 'I just remember that when Tchaik and I split, I spent the first six months thinking, okay, who was I before?'

I'm tempted to point out that she was the girl who rode JP in either Templeville Road or Lakelands Pork. But I don't out of respect for Christian's feelings. And also because Sorcha is being weirdly frosty to me tonight – as in, she's barely looked at me, for whatever reason.

'I have to admit that politics is – oh my God – so much horder than I *thought* it was going to be?' she goes. 'I'm having to make so many compromises in terms of the way I speak and some of the things I firmly, firmly believe in!'

Muirgheal's like, 'What do you mean by having to compromise the way you speak?'

I'm thinking, don't tell her, Sorcha – she'll only use it against you. But then she *does* tell her? She goes, 'Chorles thinks the reason I'm struggling to get my message across is that a lot of voters can't understand what I'm actually saying. So I'm going to be working on my accent to try to sound a little bit less middle class.'

Muirgheal smiles at her and goes, 'See, that's why *I'm* not cut out for politics? I could never sell out like that – and I'm saying that as a compliment to you.'

Sorcha's like, 'Oh, em . . . thanks.'

Fionn looks at Sorcha – his face all full of concern. 'Don't go compromising too much,' he tries to go. 'Like I said to you before, I'd hate to see you lose sight of the things you're passionate about – the things that made you want to go into politics in the first place.'

He's so trying to get in there, it's embarrassing.

Erika decides to finally make her grand entrance, looking fantastic – let's just get that out of the way. She says her hellos. Sorcha tells her she looks 'Oh my God – amazing!', while the other girls stare at her nervously over the tops of their vodka and cranberry juices.

I'm like, 'Hey, Sis – how the hell are you?' and I give her a big hug.

She goes, 'Yeah, Ross, can you stop pressing your crotch up against my leg?'

Which gives everyone a good old laugh – including Fionn. That's why I decide to put him back in his box. I go, 'Hey,' making sure everyone in the group hears me, 'this must be seriously awks for you, Fionn, is it? First time seeing Erika since she ditched you at the altar. And she's looking well. Very, very well.'

Erika fake-smiles me. Of course, she doesn't know any other way to smile. She goes, 'It's not our first time, Ross. It was Fionn who met me at the airport.'

I'm like, 'What?' because this is news to me.

Fionn's there, 'Yeah, we didn't want things to be awkward when Erika came back. So we talked on the phone and we decided that what happened in the past should be left there and there should be no hard feelings.'

That's annoying news. That's very annoying news. But I try not to let them see how much it pisses me off.

Sorcha introduces Erika to Magnus and says he was – oh my God – *the* best manny in the world, but he's leaving to go into business with Oisinn. Erika says fair play. Oisinn asks her if she has any plans herself. Erika says she's hoping to set up an ort gallery – in fact, she's already seen the perfect unit for it on Duke Street.

The usual ends up happening then. Everyone splits up into, like, little groups. Sorcha, Muirgheal, Christian and Fionn stort talking about – big focking yawn – politics, while JP and Chloe stort bickering with each other out of the corner of their mouths about baby stuff, hoping the rest of us don't notice.

Erika pulls me to one side. She says she wants a word, so we step away from the group, towards the bor.

'Is this about Honor playing rugby? I know she's your goddaughter. You were probably hoping it was going to be showjumping.'

But it ends up not being about Honor at all. She's there, 'What's going on with Dad?'

I'm like, 'What do you mean?'

'What do I mean? He's become so obnoxious.'

'Erika, he was always obnoxious. He's just gone back to being the person he was when he was married to my old dear.'

'My mum is really worried about him. She said he's being really horrible to her.'

'Look, he's just loving being the centre of attention right now. The whole "CO'CK for Taoiseach" thing. I'm sure he'll settle down when everyone goes back to thinking that he's just an annoying penis.'

'I hope you're right. I really do.'

That's when, out of the corner of my eye, I spot something that makes me suddenly lose it. Sorcha throws her orms around Fionn's shoulders and kisses him full on the mouth. I end up reacting – badly.

I race over there, going, 'Whoa, what the fock?'

Fionn goes, 'Calm down, Ross. Sorcha's just asked me to be her campaign manager. Although I have to tell you, Sorcha, I still see you as either a Green or an Independent.'

I'm like, 'Campaign manager? Yeah, that's some slick work, Fionn!'

He's there, 'What are you talking about, Ross?', pretending he doesn't know.

'You're trying to get in there now that you know I'm off the scene. That's why you were totally cool with Erika coming home. You're back in love with my still technically wife.'

That's when Sorcha totally loses it with me – and I end up finding out why she's barely looked at me all night.

'The nerve of you,' she goes, 'to tell me who I can and can't see. I heard what happened, Ross – between you and Claire.'

I'm there, 'Me and Claire? Sorcha, I have literally no idea what you're talking about.'

'You had sex with her. She told me.'

'Oh. That.'

'I can't believe you would do something like that.'

'Sorcha, I know you're not ready to hear this, but it was a spite-ride situation.'

'You're disgusting.'

'Hey, the divorce was your idea. I'm a free agent, Sorcha.'

'And what you did afterwards was just despicable. Going to the airport and putting her knickers into Garret's hand.'

Muirgheal – I swear to fock – decides to stick her hooter in. She goes, 'The thing I don't understand, Sorcha, is how you could have stayed married to someone like him for as long as you did.'

And I'm there, 'Yeah, this coming from the woman who rode JP in either Templeville Road or Lakelands Pork.'

'It was Templeville Road,' JP goes – he's clearly hammered. 'And it wasn't a ride. She just pulled me off.'

Fionn then tries to tell me that *I'm* the one who's out of order. And Christian tells me that I probably should apologize to Muirgheal. So I just go, 'Yeah, whatever! Enjoy your night!' and I end up just walking out of Kielys.

I decide to hit town to grab another drink. There's no cabs around, so I stort walking in the direction of Leeson Street, hoping to possibly flag one down on the *way*? As I'm passing the laneway between Kielys and the Porty Shop, I just happen to glance to my right and I see something that stops me dead in my literally tracks.

Now, I've been around a few corners over the years. I've seen a lot of shit in my life and I thought there was pretty much nothing in the world that could shock me to the point of not being able to even move. But that's what ends up happening. I'm, like, literally rooted to the spot, not wanting to stare, but at the same time, not actually able to turn *away* from what I'm seeing?

Oisinn and Magnus are in the laneway. And they're snogging the face off each other.

4. To the Bleaten Dogs

Erika has kind of hijacked my Saturday afternoon with the kids. Even though I don't mind. It's actually nice, all of us walking around together. We're in Dundrum. Specifically, we're in Office – the shoe place – in Dundrum Town Centre. She offered to buy Honor a present and Honor says she wants this pair of Vans, which look like Kleenex tissue boxes – we're talking big, chunky, slip-on things in black-and-white check, like focking skateboarders wear.

Erika goes, 'Would you not prefer a nice pair of Jimmy Choos?', happy to spend a grand on her.

But Honor's like, 'No, these are the ones I definitely want.'

I'm only half paying attention to what's being said. I'm still thinking about what I witnessed last night. I mean, Oisinn? Gay? I have to admit I'm struggling with it. Not that I have a *problem* with it? I'm just wondering how I didn't notice? How could I not have seen it in, like, twenty-something years of friendship? I always thought he was as straight as me. This is a goy, bear in mind, who rode my mother.

But now I'm suddenly wondering *were* there signs? He was one of the first rugby players in Ireland to bring hair conditioner into the shower. He was never embarrassed about going into clothes shops like normal Irish men. I walked in on him once when he was tweezing his eyebrows. And then, of course, he slept with a hell of a lot of women who looked like men.

I repeat – he rode my mother!

Erika goes, 'Are you still with us, Ross?' and I suddenly snap out of it.

Ronan's like, 'He's in anutter wurdled, so he is.'

I forgot to say that Ronan is with us as well. 'Yeah, no,' I go, 'I was just doing some of my famous deep thinking.'

They all seem to find this for some reason *hilarious*?

Honor goes, 'You said, "He tweezes his eyebrows."'

I'm like, 'Who does?'

'I don't know. You just muttered it to yourself.'

Erika takes Honor up to the counter to pay for the Vans, leaving me with Ronan, little Amelie and the three boys. 'Costa!' Brian shouts. 'Me want focking Costa!'

I'm there, 'We're going to go and grab something to eat now, Brian. Although it'll probably end up having to be Storbucks.'

'Me want Costa!'

'I don't think there's one here, Brian. The nearest one, as far as I know, is Dún Laoghaire.'

Ronan goes, 'Ine gonna head off, Rosser. I've woork this arthurnoon.'

I'm like, 'Work? Jesus.'

No parent wants that for their child – certainly not on this side of the city.

He's there, 'Ine gibbon the tree o'clock tewer. We've got Detective Geerda Ciardon Madden making a guest appearrance on the bus this week. It's prooben veddy populer.'

'It's great watching you make a success of that business. But it breaks my hort watching you having to earn a living at your age.'

'Ine godda have to get used to it.'

'Ro, you haven't got your results yet. You never know.'

'I doatunt need to get them, Rosser. I know I fayult. Enda stordee.'

Erika and Honor arrive back over. Honor has decided to wear her Vans now. She's thrown her Uggs in the bag.

Ronan goes, 'Ine heading off, Edika. It's great habbon you back, so it is.'

She's like, 'You're not coming for lunch with us?', all disappointed. They get on like you wouldn't believe.

He's there, 'No, I was just tedding Rosser there – I've woork this arthurnoon.'

Erika looks genuinely worried about him as he walks off.

Anyway, we end up hitting *Storbucks*? Erika finds a table and sits down with Honor, Amelie and the boys while I go up to the counter to get the drinks. I'm standing in the queue and some random woman turns around to me and goes, 'Is that your family?'

I follow her line of vision over to where they're sitting. I'm like, 'Yeah.'

She's there, 'Your wife is absolutely beautiful.'

And I, for some reason, go, 'Yeah, no, I'm very lucky. She's a ride,' even though it's probably an *odd* thing to say?

I order the drinks and carry them over to the table in two of those little cordboard trays. Honor is asking Erika how many times she's been engaged. The answer, by the way, is six.

'Did you keep all the rings?' Honor wants to know.

Erika just smiles. She's like, 'Yes, I kept all the rings.'

'Which was the most expensive?'

'The one Jeremy bought me was two hundred thousand pounds.'

'Sterling?'

'Yes, sterling.'

'Oh! My God!'

'Me want Sterling!' Leo shouts. 'Me want Sterling, you focking fock!'

Erika sort of, like, smiles to herself. She goes, 'When I told him I didn't want to marry him, he wrote to me every day for a year, begging me to change my mind.'

'Men are *so* lame!' Honor goes.

I end up going into another trance, thinking about Oisinn again. Like, *how* did I not see it? He owned five pairs of shoes – maybe that was a sign. I remember, one time, someone bought him a set of bath bombs for his birthday and he got unnaturally excited about it. Then, another time, when he was in New York, he did the *Sex and the City* tour. I only found out about it because the ticket dropped out of his pocket one night when we were grabbing a kebab from Ismael's on Baggot Street.

Or am I reading too much into shit? Maybe there *were* no signs. It's possible he didn't realize he was gay until the right man came along. Or did he always know? And did I ever crack a gay joke in front of him – which I'm sure I focking did – and was he forced to just, I don't know, laugh along with everyone else just to keep his secret safe?

'I'm sorry,' a voice suddenly goes, 'I'm going to have to ask you to leave.'

I look up. It's some sort of, I don't know, lady manager person. I'm there, 'Excuse me?'

'Your children,' she goes. 'The swearing. We've had complaints.'

'Fock them!' Brian shouts. 'They're only a pack of pricks!'

I'm like, 'Yeah, no, we've decided not to correct them in case it creates taboos around certain words, which then encourages them to use them even more. It's something my wife read in a magazine.'

'Well, I'm sorry,' she goes, 'I have to think of the other customers.'

I notice the woman from the queue earlier looking over with a guilty look on her face. I'm there, 'Was it you who complained?'

She goes, 'I don't want my children exposed to that.'

She's got two with her – a little boy and a little girl.

'Fock you and fock your children!' Brian goes.

'Disgusting language,' the woman goes.

Honor speaks up then – she's very protective of her brothers. She goes, 'You shouldn't be listening in to other people's conversations anyway. The only reason you have to is because your own kids are so focking boring. And, by the way, the 1980s rang – they want their shoulder pads back . . . Mic drop!'

Mic drop?

Like I said, she can be very funny, as long as *you're* not the torget.

Erika stands up and she's like, 'Okay, maybe we'll take these drinks to go.'

The woman from the queue is disgusted. She goes, 'And I was just telling your husband how beautiful I thought your children were!'

Erika goes, 'He's not my husband. He's my brother,' and you can see the look of confusion on the woman's face, given that I described her as a ride.

As I'm strapping the boys into their stroller, Erika's phone rings. 'Oh my God,' she goes, looking at the screen, 'it's Oisinn!'

I suddenly freeze. I don't know why I'm *being* like this? Maybe I just need time to process it?

She answers. She's like, 'Hey, Oisinn – how are you?'

I mouth the words, 'I'm not here!' to her.

She goes, 'A business proposition? That sounds interesting. When?'

Again, I go, 'Not here!' running my finger across my throat.

She's like, 'Okay, I'll see you then. By the way, I'm in Dundrum with Ross, if you want to talk to him.'

She's such a bitch. She'll never change. She looks at me and goes, 'He wants to know why you're not answering your phone. Or why you haven't responded to any of his texts.'

'Because I had to take Honor to rugby,' I go, 'and then we came here.'

Erika's like, 'Did you hear that, Oisinn? Will I put you on to him now?'

And I'm like, 'No!' and I end up actually screaming the word at her. 'Yeah, no, tell him I'll ring him tonight. Or during the week. Or something.'

The lady manager person, who's still standing there, goes, 'I'm sorry, I *am* going to have to ask you to leave.'

And I'm like, 'Yeah, can you not see that we're trying to get our focking shit together here?'

'Costa!' Brian shouts as I wheel the boys out of the shop. 'Me want focking Costa!'

And I think, yeah, no, it'll definitely be *focking* Costa in future.

I swing out to Honalee. Sorcha's old man is not a happy rabbit when I walk into the living room. 'It's not even Saturday,' he goes. 'Why is *he* here?'

Sorcha is still pissed off with me for, well, riding Claire, but she's decent enough not to bring it up. She goes, 'I gave him permission to take Honor and the boys to see their grandmother in prison.'

He sort of, like, harrumphs to himself. 'A fine place to be bringing children,' he goes and he looks at Fionn, her so-called campaign manager. 'A fine place indeed.'

Sorcha's there, 'Whatever problems Ross and I have, Fionnuala is still their grandmother and she's entitled to see them. And can I just remind you that she hasn't been found guilty of anything yet? I know deep down in my hort that she wouldn't be capable of actually killing someone – unless she was really drunk or something.'

Fionn's not happy with me being here either – although he's just worried that I'm here to rip the piss. The famous K . . . K . . . K . . . Kennet and the old man are about to arrive to give Sorcha her first lesson in how to talk like a skanger.

He tries to go, 'You really need to leave, Ross,' in my own house, by the way. 'We're actually working this morning.'

And Sorcha's old man is like, 'Excellent point, Fionn!', suddenly treating him like the son-in-law he never had. 'The only reason he's here is to laugh and jeer.'

Sorcha's old dear steps into the living room then. She's got a face on her as well. She goes, 'I really don't see that this is necessary, Sorcha. There's absolutely nothing wrong with the way you speak.'

'My thoughts precisely,' her old man goes. 'I certainly don't think you need some Henry Higgins character teaching you how to talk like you went to – oh, what's that awful one in Blackrock? – is it called Sion Hill or something?'

'I've explained it to you,' Sorcha goes. 'Chorles says Lucinda Creighton has Dublin 4 pretty much sewn up. He says I need to stort appealing to the voters of Dublin 6W – places like the Kimmage Road.'

'I did not raise a daughter to appeal to people on the Kimmage Road!'

Fionn is such a focking crawler. He goes, 'I agree with your mum and dad, Sorcha. You've already compromised so much – your views on water charges and Europe. Now you're being asked to change your accent.'

'I'm not changing my accent,' she goes. 'I'm just removing some of the polish from it to try to get my message across to a wider audience.'

'I still say you should ask yourself whether New Republic is the right fit for you politically. I think you're good enough to stand on your own two feet.'

Her old man's like, 'That's your campaign manager talking.'

Dick.

There's a ring on the doorbell and Sorcha's old dear goes out to answer it.

Honor goes, 'Can we stay for this? It's going be hill-air!'

I realize that, which is why I'm taking my time putting the coats on the boys.

Five seconds later, in strolls my old man, followed by the famous Kennet, with Sorcha's old dear behind them, still shaking her head like the whole thing is ridiculous.

'Hello there!' the old man goes. 'Well, this is quite the audience, isn't it?'

Sorcha's like, 'Hi, Chorles. Hi, Kennet. Thank you for giving up your time to do this.'

'Norra botter,' Kennet goes. 'It's norra botter arall, Surrogate.'

The old man is full of himself today and we soon find out why. 'Anyone see the poll in this morning's *Irish Times*?' he goes. 'We're up to third – just two points behind Fianna Fáil! And twelve percent of people would like to see Charles O'Carroll-Kelly become the next Taoiseach! It seems most of our politicians have totally under-estimated the depth of the country's disillusionment with Europe!'

'Well,' Sorcha's old man goes, 'I happen to agree with my daughter that EU membership has been good for Ireland. Also, Charles, I'd like to place it on the record that I consider what you're doing here totally unnecessary. Unlearning all that hard work her teachers did to ensure that she speaks the way she does. What was the point of sending her to Mount Anville if she's going to go out into the world talking like – and this is no offence to you, Kennet – the dregs of our society?'

Sorcha *is* up for it, though? She goes, 'I was actually remember-ing, Chorles, when I was in transition year, I played Mary Boyle in *Juno and the Paycock*. I could maybe try to channel some of that.'

God, I remember that production. A lot of parents walked out. They refused to believe that poverty like that ever existed in Dub-lin and, if it did, they didn't see why they should have to pay ten grand a year in school fees to be reminded of it.

'*Juno and the Paycock*,' the old man goes, 'is exactly what we're aiming for!'

Kennet goes, 'Reet, will we gerron wit the j . . . j . . . j . . . j . . . job?' Then he and Sorcha sit down in ormchairs opposite each other.

'So Cheerdles wants me to teach you a few ph . . . ph . . . phray-zuz you moyt neeyut when encountherdin people from airdeyuz

such as – like the man said – Haddled's Cross, Ringsent and Tede-
newer,' he goes. 'N . . . N . . . N . . . Now, the foorst phrayuz is one
you moyt neeyut to use if you're s . . . s . . . s . . . sympatoyzun wit
someone who's goan troo a heert toyum cos of the ecodomy. *The
cunter doddy is arthur goan to the bleaten dogs, so it has.*'

Honor laughs. It is funny, in fairness.

Sorcha's there, 'The country . . .' with a big serious face on her.

'No, no, no,' Kennet goes. '*The cunter doddy . . .*'

'The cunt . . .'

'*The cunter doddy . . .*'

'The cunter doddy . . .'

'That's reet.'

'. . . is author . . .'

'*. . . is arthur . . .*'

'The cunter doddy is arthur . . . goan to the bleeding . . .'

'*. . . to the bleaten . . .*'

'. . . to the bleaten . . . dogs.'

'*. . . so it has . . .*'

'Do I have to say *so it has* at the end? It just feels like the sentence
is already complete.'

'If you want to f . . . f . . . f . . . firrin with the locaddle people,
you'd be bettor off adding it on to the end. So you would. Say it
altogetter now.'

'The cunter doddy is arthur goan to the bleaten dogs, so it has.'

'V . . . V . . . V . . . Veddy good. Now, anutter one. *Things is teddible bad with the austedity and that.*'

She's there, 'Things . . . should it not be things "are" rather than
things "is"?'

'Thrust me, Surrogate. Ine talken this way all me l . . . l . . . l . . .
life, so I am. *Things is . . .*'

'Things *is* . . . teddible bad . . .'

'Keep goan.'

'. . . with the austerity . . .'

'*Austedity.* There's a D in there, Surrogate – d . . . d . . . doatunt be
afraid to use it.'

'Austedity.'

'. . . and that . . .'

'. . . and that.'

'S . . . S . . . S . . . Say it all togetter now.'

'Things is teddible bad with the austedity and that.'

'You're a natur doddle.'

That's when the living-room door suddenly opens and in walks Magnus. Sorcha said he could carry on living here, by the way, until he found himself a new gaff. I haven't set eyes on the dude since I saw him with his head in Oisinn's mouth a week ago. And of course I end up totally overcompensating by going, 'Ah, there's Magnus! How the hell are you, Magnus? Magnus is here, everyone! The famous Magnus!'

He's like, 'Er, hello, Rosh . . . sho, I jusht wanted to give theesh to the boysh. It'sh jusht shome more of thoshe picture cardsh they like.'

He hands a packet of cords each to Leo, Johnny and Brian. Leo opens his, then shouts, 'Lallana!' who I presume is, I don't know, one of the Teletubbies.

Sorcha goes, 'Oh my God, you got your hair cut! Did you go to Brown Sugar like I told you? Magnus has a hot date tonight, everyone!'

I go, 'Date? What date? Is it definitely a date? As such. Blah, blah, blah,' just babbling really.

'Sorry,' Sorcha goes, 'I shouldn't embarrass you, Magnus. I wish you'd tell us who this mystery man of yours is! I'm dying to meet him!'

'Shadly,' he goes, 'it'sh kind of complicated at the moment becaush he hash not told hish family and friendsh that he ish gay. He thinksh hish friendsh especshially might not take it sho good.'

He seems to be staring at me, although I'm possibly *imagining* that? Or has Oisinn told him that I'm the one who'll possibly have a problem with it?

'That's terrible!' Sorcha goes.

I'm there, 'I, er, might head off actually. We don't want to miss visiting time.'

'B . . . b . . . b . . . b . . . back to woork,' Kennet goes. 'Repeat arthur me, Surrogate. *The Gubber Mint? Go on ourra dat – doatunt be thalken to me!*'

★

The old dear has had all of her hair cut off. And I mean that literally –
as in she's, like, totally bald.

'Seriously, what the fock?' I go – because her head looks like a
focking snooker ball.

She's there, 'I decided to shave it all off, Ross. It's impossible to
have good hair in a reformatory like this.'

'Yeah,' I go, 'it's actually a *prison*? You look a bit like –'

'Who?'

'No one. A woman from Dalkey. It doesn't matter. It's too weird.'

She's delighted to see her grandchildren. She's got Brian on her
knee and he's pointing at her going, 'Who's this focker?'

I'm like, 'That's your grandmother.'

She goes, 'Oh, they're absolutely beautiful – a credit to you, Ross.
And do they all have names?'

Jesus Christ. You'd swear they were focking hamsters.

'Of course they all have names,' I go. 'I told you their names.
That's Brian, this is Leo and that's Johnny.'

Honor's looking around the visiting room, going, 'Oh my God,
it's, like, total skanksville in here!'

I'm there, 'Maybe keep your voice down, Honor. Here, tell your
grandmother about your rugby.'

Honor goes, 'Oh my God, I'm playing rugby now – for, like, Old
Belvedere?'

Honor is a big fan of my old dear's. Or as she put it herself during the drive here: 'I find her face really scary but I love that she's
a bitch.'

'Rugby?' the old dear goes. 'Your father played rugby!'

I'm like, 'Understatement of the century, but keep going.'

'He was very good at it.'

'Better critics than you said it. Said more. Anyway, I definitely
think that Honor is going to be the next O'Carroll-Kelly who
everyone talks about in terms of having a big, big future ahead
of her – and that's despite everything I've said in the past about
women's rugby.'

'I'm the only girl on my team,' Honor goes, 'and I'm better than
all the boys.'

I'm like, 'Yeah, no, they're focking terrified of her. Which is nice to see. Honor, tell your grandmother about the match.'

'We're going to be playing a match.'

'An actual sevens match. Against Bective.'

'It's only a friendly.'

'There's no such thing, Honor. In rugby, friendlies are Tests. Just don't go into it with the attitude that it doesn't matter who wins. It always matters. It matters a lot. And don't let Rob Felle try to persuade you that it doesn't.'

The old dear looks suddenly sad. I suppose she's seeing what she's missing out on, being banged up in here. Or it could be alcohol withdrawal. She goes, 'Maybe I'll come and watch you play one day . . . when I get out of –'

Her voice cracks. She puts her hand over her mouth to stop herself from crying.

'Stupid focking bitch!' Leo goes.

I'm there, 'Honor, why don't you take your brothers over to the vending machine and get them some more Skittles?'

'Me want Costa!' Brian goes.

I'm like, 'You won't get a Costa in here, Brian.'

'Me want Kolo Touré!'

'And get them each a Cola-whatever he-said as well, will you?'

I hand her twenty snots, then off they go to the vending machine. I look at the old dear and I go, 'You need to get your shit together.'

She's like, 'I'm sorry. It just struck me that I'm probably going to miss them growing up.'

'I thought you were innocent.'

'I *am* innocent.'

'Then you've got to believe there's a chance that you'll get off.'

'They've set a date. For my trial.'

'And?'

'April of next year!'

'There you are then! If you're not guilty, it'll hopefully come out then.'

'That's what Sorcha keeps saying.'

'She's talking sense.'

'But it's nine months away! I won't survive nine months in here, Ross!'

'Look, you're going through a hord time. Could you maybe get your hands on some of the prison brew? Is it called hooch? It's always called hooch on T V.'

'They won't share it with me, Ross. They hate me in here.'

'Who hates you?'

'The other guests.'

'Yeah, I think you mean *inmates*?'

'They think I'm stuck-up.'

'Well, you *are* stuck-up. It's one of the few things I actually like about you.'

'Snobby bitch. That's what they say about me. I hear them whispering. And when I walk into the dining room –'

'Prison canteen. Continue.'

'– everyone stops talking. I'm so lonely, Ross.'

'Have you tried, I don't know, making friends?'

'These people aren't my friends. My friends are people like Delma.'

'But Delma's not in here.'

'That's what Sorcha said, too.'

'Would you not think of maybe reaching out?'

'To these people? They're skangers, Ross!'

'Skangers or not, they're all you have now.'

Honor arrives back with the boys just as the bell rings. I managed to stay for the entire hour this time. I must be going soft in my old age because I feel suddenly sad to be leaving her here. 'We'll, em, come again,' I go. 'Maybe in a week or two.'

She goes, 'Please do.' We end up hugging each other. It's nice. Move on. 'And how lovely to meet these little boys. I must learn off their names. And goodbye, Honor.'

Honor's like, 'Bye, Fionnuala.'

As she's being led back to her cell, I look back at her – big focking cueball head on her – and I suddenly realize that I'm now fifty-fifty about whether she did it or not. I wouldn't put it past her. But there's suddenly also a port of me that thinks, yeah, no, she possibly *didn't* do it?

★

So I'm in my bedroom – my *new* bedroom, which is freezing, by the way – and I'm fluting around on the laptop, writing, of all things, a fantasy best man speech for Rob Kearney, just in case I'm ever asked to do the honours. There's a knock and the old man goes, 'You home, Kicker?' at the same time sticking his head around the door.

I'm like, 'Yeah,' quickly closing the laptop.

He goes, 'Oh, I hope I didn't, um, disturb anything!'

Jesus, he thinks I was, well, you know what – choking the bald commuter.

'I'm just off to the prison!' he goes. 'To visit your poor mother!'

I'm there, 'Yeah, no, I was in there the other day if that was a hint.'

'It wasn't a hint, Ross! Wasn't a hint at all! Poor Fionnuala, all the same. You see, this is what happens, Kicker, when you challenge certain vested interests.'

'Do you genuinely think that's the only reason she's there?'

'Of course! Not that the media cares! You're not a political prisoner unless you're in a foreign country and your name is Aung San Suu Kyi!'

He's holding a Cohiba the size of a focking rolling pin. I'm there, 'When did you stort smoking?'

He goes, 'I've been smoking cigars since I was little older than Honor!'

'I mean, when did you go back to smoking? What about your hort?'

'I've got the heart of a bloody rhinoceros!'

'You've got the focking neck of one as well. Did you want something, by the way?'

'Oh, yes, quick question for you – what do you know about greyhound racing?'

'Greyhound racing? It's like horse racing, isn't it – except for *poor* people?'

'Yes, that's what I thought!'

'Why are you asking me about greyhound racing?'

'Well, after Sorcha's, shall we say, master class in how to speak like a commoner, I thought it might be a useful exercise to throw her in at the proverbial deep end!'

'Are you saying you're going to bring her to a dog track?'

'There are *two* in the Dublin Bay South constituency, if you can believe that! Talk about hidden poverty! There's Shelbourne Park and Harold's Cross! I think Kennet and I are going to take her to the latter – see how she gets on *in the field*, quote-unquote!'

'Okay, let me know when this is happening. I definitely want to see it.'

'I shall do that! Oh, maybe say nothing to Helen about the, em . . .'

He holds up his cigor. Then off he focks.

I hop out of bed. I grab a quick Jack Bauer, then I head into town to buy Honor a copy of the famous Leinster versus Northampton Saints match on DVD. I never thought I'd be saying that. I even mention it to the dude who ends up serving me in HMV. 'It's actually for my daughter,' I go. 'Can you believe she's never actually seen the famous Miracle Match?'

The dude looks at the cover like it's a new one on him as well. Then he sticks it in the bag while I put my cord in the little machine and key in my pin. It's 2, 0, 1, 1. I'm storting to become a big, big believer in fate.

I'm there, 'I already own it, but I think every child in the country should be given a copy – just so they know what it's possible to achieve if you believe in yourself,' and I suddenly stort to feel a bit emotional. 'Yeah, no, she's playing the game herself these days. She's got a big sevens match coming up. Against Bective. I'd see this as very much port of her preparation.'

He hands me back my cord. 'Yeah,' he goes, 'I've never actually seen it myself. Rugby is a game that's never really done it for me.'

And I'm like, 'Then I pity you,' and I snatch the bag out of his hand. 'And I mean that. I genuinely focking pity you.'

Thirty seconds later, I'm walking up Grafton Street, thinking, how is it even possible that there are people walking around out there who don't know what Johnny Sexton did for us that day? I'm thinking, imagine if Johnny happened to be in HMV and he overheard that? He'd be on the next plane back to Paris, and I wouldn't focking blame him.

Anyway, just as I'm thinking this, I hear a voice go, 'What are you doing in town?'

It ends up being Erika.

I'm like, 'Yeah, no, I was just buying Honor a copy of the Miracle Match.'

She goes, 'The Miracle Match? Is that a movie?'

'Not you as well, Erika. Please, not you as well.'

She changes the subject. She goes, 'Do you want to see my gallery space?'

I'm like, 'Whoa, is it finished?'

She goes, 'Almost. Come on, I'll show you.'

So we wander around to Duke Street. She's looking incredible, by the way. I know I've got to stop thinking about her in that way – or maybe just stop telling her all the time – but it's still a fact. She's definitely doing yoga because I saw her mat when I was having a poke around her room yesterday and you can see that her body looks, I don't know, tighter. Her traffic stoppers have never looked better either, even though she's dropped an actual bra size. I'll leave it at that before I say too much.

She's taken the lease on a unit a few doors down from the Nespresso Boutique. I tell her fair focks because it's the perfect spot for a gallery, although there's no actual pictures in it because they're still fitting the place out. She's got, like, workers in, plastering and painting and sawing and whatever else.

'Come up to the office,' she goes. 'It's a bit tidier up there,' and I follow her up the stairs, staring at her orse in her tight black trousers, like two tunnelling creatures preparing to surface.

I'm like, 'So, what, the whole building is yours?'

And just as we reach the top of the stairs, she goes, 'No, I'm sharing this floor with Oisinn,' and suddenly I'm staring across an open-plan office at my friend who I've been avoiding for the past, I don't know, *however* many weeks?

His opening line is, 'Dude, what the fock?'

And I'm like, 'Oisinn? Er, what do you mean?'

'Have you been avoiding me?'

'Yeah, no, I've been busy.'

'Well, sit down. I want to share something with you.'

'You don't have to, Dude. Keep it to yourself if you want.'

He laughs. He goes, 'I want you to be the first to know. Because I wouldn't have got through the last few years – losing all my money and all the rest of it – without you. So I want to tell you before I tell anyone else –'

'You genuinely don't have to.'

'– that Gaycation Ireland is open for business as and from next week!'

'Oh . . . er, okay . . . fair focks.'

'I'll show you some of the packages we're going to be doing.'

He produces a brochure from his desk drawer. On the cover are three or four dudes with their tops off, wearing Stetsons and drinking shots. It's like, 'Gaycation Ireland – Leading Specialists in LGBTQ Stag and Hen Parties', and then underneath it's like, 'Enjoy One Last Fabulous Weekend of Freedom – in the Most Tolerant Country in the World!'

He storts flicking through the pages – again, full of men in various states of undress – going, 'Look at these packages!'

I'm like, 'Packages?'

I'm a nervous focking wreck.

He goes, 'Travel packages, Ross. These are some of the things we're doing. Look! There's a *Brokeback Mountain*-themed cattle drive from Sneem to Kenmare. An Ugly Dress Competition styled on the Rose of Tralee. That was another one of Magnus's ideas. There's naked skydiving! We're doing that over Roscommon and South Leitrim. Serve the fockers right for voting No in the marriage equality referendum! There's obviously lots of karaoke. Ross, are you okay? Your breathing sounds funny.'

'Yeah, no, it's just very, I don't know, different, isn't it?'

'Different is good, isn't it?'

'Yeah, no, definitely. Definitely, definitely, definitely.'

'Here, I'll give you a laugh. We're also selling all the paraphernalia.'

He stands up and goes to this, like, stationery cupboard in the corner. Suddenly, he storts throwing things at me, going, 'Drama Queen tiaras! Groom-To-Be sashes! NYPD hats in neon pink. Read what it says on the badge, Ross . . .'

It says, 'You Have the Right to Remain Sexy!'

He goes, 'Gay biker moustaches!' and he puts one on. 'And the *pièce de resistance* . . .'

Erika's like, 'Oisinn, don't you dare take that out again!'

But he does anyway. He goes, 'An inflatable hermaphrodite!' and he produces this giant blow-up doll with huge vinyl tits and a big vinyl mickey. He basically attacks me with it, shoving *its* face in *my* face and trying to get me to kiss its puckered mouth.

I stort freaking, going, 'Get away! Get the fock away from me!' and I manage to slip out from underneath it, while Oisinn and Erika both crack their holes laughing.

I'm there, 'That was out of order!' and I end up shouting it. 'We're talking *bang* out of order?'

Erika goes, 'Ross, you're so uptight.'

Oisinn's there, 'I was only breaking your balls, Ross. Anyway, look, we're having a porty to officially launch the business – it's here, a week on Saturday, if you're around.'

'A week on Saturday?' I go. 'Yeah, no, unfortunately, that's my day with the kids. Honor's playing a sevens match against Bective.'

'Come along afterwards. I'd really love you to be there. Magnus would love to see you there as well.'

And all I can go is, 'Er, yeah, no, maybe – we'll see.'

Prison visiting rooms. Greyhound stadiums. I'll tell you something – I've been getting a definite insight lately into how the other half live.

Sorcha looks at me and goes, 'Oh my God, what the fock are you doing here?'

I don't think she's going to forgive me easily for riding Claire and basically breaking up their marriage.

I'm there, 'I'm kind of asking myself the exact same question!', trying to brazen it out. 'I never agree with people who say the dogs is a great night out. I've always looked on it as a kind of holiday in other people's misery.'

Fionn is even *more* annoyed? 'What Sorcha means,' he tries to go, 'is that we're not here to have fun, Ross. We're here to do important constituency work.'

Which is a joke, of course.

I'm there, 'Hey, I'm here to support my – unfortunately for you – still *wife*?'

Sorcha goes, 'I don't focking want you here, Ross.'

But there isn't any more time to debate the matter because my old man suddenly shows up with K . . . K . . . K . . . Kennet in tow. People are literally mesmerized by the sight of him. An actual space opens up around him as he walks towards us. People are shouting, 'CO'CK for Taoiseach!' or they're shouting, 'Make Areluent Thremendous Again!'

Kennet is grinning like a man eating shit at gunpoint. This is very much his kind of crowd, of course. He's like, 'S . . . S . . . S . . . Stordee, Surrogate? Are you m . . . m . . . m . . . mingling or what?'

Sorcha goes, 'I might just need a moment to get my bearings, Kennet,' and she keeps fidgeting with her New Republic rosette. She's clearly kacking it.

I suddenly spot a familiar face coming towards us. I don't actually believe it. It's focking Muirgheal. I'm like, 'Okay, what the fock is *she* doing here?'

Sorcha goes, 'She has more right to be here than you, Ross. She's offered to help me with my campaign.'

I'm there, 'I wouldn't trust her, Sorcha. I genuinely wouldn't trust her.'

'Really, Ross? After what you did with Claire, I'm supposed to take advice from you on who I can and can't trust?'

Fionn says fock-all, although something about his body language tells me that he agrees with my analysis. Sorcha hugs the girl like they haven't seen each other in years. Muirgheal goes, 'I'm *so* excited about watching you in action!'

Then the old man goes, 'Okay, Sorcha, let's meet your people, shall we?' and he collars these three dudes who happen to be walking by – all of them wearing hoodies – and goes, 'Would you chaps like to meet the New Republic candidate for Dublin Bay South? Let me introduce you to Sorcha O'Carroll-Kelly! She's going to tell you what we're planning to do to take Ireland back from the Brussels élite who helped bankrupt this country!'

Sorcha doesn't say shit. She's got obvious stage-fright. She's like – what's that phrase? – a rabbit in the headlice?

One of the dudes looks her up and down and goes, 'She's a lubbly looken boord, idn't she?'

And Fionn pipes up then and goes, 'Never mind what she looks like. Why don't you listen to what she has to say?'

The same dude's like, 'She's not saying veddy mooch.'

Fionn just nods at her and goes, 'Go on, Sorcha!'

And this look of, I don't know, *resolve* suddenly comes over her face? She goes, 'Things is arthur goan down the chewibs, so thee hab. The Gubber Mint doataunt want to know – Enter Keddy and the rest of them habn't boddered their bleaten boddix doing athin abourrit eeben though there's real people is sufferden out theer.'

Jesus Christ, she has the accent to a tee.

Sorcha goes, 'And doatunt talk to me about that shower over in Europe. They're arthur robbing us bloyunt, so thee are – we'd be bethor awp ourrof it altogetter.'

I watch Muirgheal try to keep a smirk from her face.

One of the dudes she's talking to storts actually *clapping?* 'At last,' he goes, 'a poditishidden who wontherstands the concerdens of ordineddy people!'

One of his mates is like, 'I thought you were gonna be one of them stook-up bitches, like what's-her-nayum? You joost *look* it, but!'

And the third dude goes, 'You've moy vote. You're arthur saying there what Ine arthur been saying for yee-ors, except nobody's been listoden to me, so thee habn't.'

They head for the tote to put their bets on for the first race. I hear one of them go, 'I'd royid the bleaten eerse off her as well!'

The old man goes, 'Excellent, Sorcha! Excellent!'

She goes, 'But I didn't actually *say* anything, Chorles.'

'On the contrary,' he goes. 'You sympathized with them in a general way about the state of the country and validated their belief that the political élite, both here and abroad, are doing nothing to serve them, the people!'

'I just feel like I'm pandering to people's ignorance. I still think Europe has been a positive thing for us as a nation. I keep coming back to my point about Erasmus.'

'You've just got yourself three votes there, Sorcha! Mind you, I doubt if they've ever been on the electoral register! Still, it's a very encouraging start!'

A voice comes over through the speaker then. It's like, 'Ladies and gentleman, you're all very welcome to Harold's Cross Greyhound Stadium this evening. The first race is the 6.30, the Vote New Republic Chase.'

I look at the old man. 'You're actually sponsoring it?' I go.

He's there, 'All part of the campaign to win over votes, Kicker! Kennet, I think I'd like a wager on this one! Can you show me how it works? Is it like Leopardstown?'

'V . . . V . . . Veddy simidar,' Kennet goes. ''Mon, I'll show you,' and off they fock to place their bets. Fionn heads off as well for a slash, leaving me with just Sorcha and Muirgheal.

'In Trap One,' the dude goes, 'in red, it's Mannish Jack. In Trap Two, in blue, it's All the Creases . . .'

I lean over the rail – I'm like a focking natural! – while Muirgheal turns around to Sorcha and goes, 'I have to say, I really admire you for what you're doing, Sorcha.'

Sorcha's there, 'What do you mean?'

'Just, you know, setting aside so many of the things you believe in to try to get elected.'

'That doesn't sound like a compliment, Muirgheal.'

I'm there, 'That's because it's not a compliment. She's being a bitch.'

Muirgheal goes, 'I'm not being a bitch. I'm saying it's a very, very brave thing to do.'

Sorcha's like, 'We all have to compromise, Muirgheal.'

'That's the point I'm making. I'm sure even people like Sirikan Charoensiri and Narges Mohammadi have made compromises in their lives that we don't know about. The important thing is to get elected – then you can go back to believing in things like Europe and protecting the environment. If it suits you, of course.'

Sorcha just stares into space. She tries to change the subject by going, 'So how do they make the dogs actually race each other?'

I'm like, 'They don't race each other as such. They chase the hare.'

'Hare? What are you talking about?'

'Yeah, no, I saw it once on *EastEnders*. There's a hare in that box over there. It goes flying around the track and then they all peg it after it. I think it was actually Alfie Moon had a dog in the race.'

'Okay, will you shut the fock up about Alfie Moon? Are you saying the dogs chase an *actual* animal?'

And of course the answer is no. It's, like, an *electric* hare? But I don't get the chance to say that because Muirgheal decides to stick her hooter in and goes, 'Don't make a fuss about it until *after* you're elected, Sorcha! You don't want to go upsetting these people!'

Fionn arrives back from the jacks, while the old man and Kennet arrive back from the tote, just as the first race is about to stort.

'Fionn,' Sorcha goes, on the point of pretty much *tears*? 'They chase a hare!'

And Fionn's there, 'Yeah, but it's not a real –'

But he doesn't get to finish his sentence, because the gun all of a sudden sounds, the traps snap open and suddenly eight snorling dogs are bearing down on the little ball of white fur circling the track on a rail.

'Oh my God, *no!*' Sorcha screams, proving that one or two elocution lessons can't undo three decades of good breeding. 'Don't let them hurt it! Oh my God, don't let them hurt that poor defenceless creature!'

Everyone – and I mean everyone – in the crowd turns around and is suddenly staring at her, their mouths open in literally shock. Then, one by one, they all stort breaking their holes laughing – none more so than Muirgheal. Sorcha bursts into tears.

What can my old man say except, 'She's, um, still a work in progress!'

But Sorcha just shakes her head and goes, 'That's it, Chorles! I quit!'

He goes, 'You can't bloody well quit, Sorcha! Not when we've come this far!'

But she's not going to be talked out of it. She unpins her New Republic rosette and she hands it to him. She goes, 'I've been thinking about it for weeks now, Chorles. Your position on Europe. Your position on water chorges! The stupid voice you're making me do! Bringing me here – Jesus, Chorles – to a dog track?'

He goes, 'You're turning your back on a promising political career, Sorcha!'

She's like, 'I have my beliefs, Chorles. And they mean more to me than getting elected,' and off she walks in a huff.

Under his breath, Fionn goes, 'Good for you, Sorcha!' and he follows her.

The second they've gone, Muirgheal walks up to my old man with her hand out. 'Muirgheal Massey,' she goes. 'I'm a *huge* admirer.'

Ronan isn't returning my calls and I'm pretty sure I *know* why? The Leaving Cert results were out today. And of course I'm now presuming the worst.

I check the time. It's after six o'clock. I try him one last time before I call it a night. Again, it goes to his voicemail.

I go, 'Hey, Ro, it's Ross . . . Rosser . . . I just, em, you know, wanted to let you know that I'm thinking about you. And if you failed, you failed. There's no shame in it. What I'd keep emphasizing, Ro, is that I never passed a single exam in my life and it wasn't the end of the world. Anyway, if you want to talk, my phone will be on all night. Don't worry about the time. I don't care if you wake me. Alright, I'll hopefully talk to you.'

I hang up. My phone instantly rings. It's not Ronan, though. It ends up actually being Honor. Her opening line is, like, properly priceless.

She goes, 'Okay, I need to know, what's a spear tackle?'

I laugh. I'm there, 'A spear tackle? Do you remember a good few years ago – actually, you might not have even been born – Brian O'Driscoll got done by Tana Umaga when he was playing for the Lions and Daddy got very depressed?'

'Was that the time you wet the bed for a month?'

'No, that was when Johnny Sexton moved to Racing Métro. And, in my defence, I was drinking a hell of a lot and I felt it was definitely the wrong move for him in terms of his development as a ten. No, when Drico got done – your old dear will tell you about it – I didn't sleep properly until I knew he'd definitely play again. Anyway, there's a whole section about spear tackles in the Tactics Book.'

'I know,' she goes, 'I'm looking at it here. The Legal Spear Tackle.'

'Yeah, that's a way I came up with to spear tackle someone without getting into shit with the referee. A spear tackle is basically where you pick up another player, turn him upside-down and drop him on his focking head. But the thing is, Honor, you're perfectly entitled to lift an opposing player off his feet – the rule just says it's your responsibility to return him safely to the ground. Well, what I've outlined on that page is a way to make it look like you're returning him to the ground, even though you're technically still smashing him *into* the ground.'

'Oh my God, that is so clever.'

'Hey, thanks, Honor. I know you don't give out compliments for no reason.'

All of a sudden, I hear Sorcha in the background, going, 'Come on, Honor, get off the phone – you've got piano tonight.'

Honor's there, 'I don't want to play the stupid piano. I want to watch Leinster and Northampton again.'

Sorcha goes, 'You're going to your piano lesson, Honor. It's been booked. It's a healthy thing to have a mix of different hobbies and interests.'

I'm in her ear going, 'Don't listen to the woman. She's upset about her political career being over.'

Sorcha's there, 'It can't be just rugby, twenty-four hours a day.'

I'm going, 'It can, Honor. It genuinely can.'

'And change out of those ugly shoes, would you?' Sorcha goes. 'How many pairs of ballet pumps do you own?'

She's there, 'I don't like them. They're too girlie.'

'I thought you *were* girlie. You *used* to be girlie.'

All of a sudden, there's a knock on my bedroom door. Helen sticks her head around it. She mouths the words, 'Ronan's downstairs!' and – I swear to fock – I'm up off that bed like Susan Boyle has just climbed into it beside me. I'm like, 'Honor, I have to go. I'll ring you before you go to bed,' and I hang up on her.

I peg it down the stairs, two at a time. Ronan is standing in the hallway. He looks sad. I'm there, 'Is it bad news?'

He goes, 'Habn't a clue. I habn't opened them, Rosser.'

I'm like, 'What? Why?'

'Ine arthur been walking arowunt alt day, throying to pluck up the cuddidge.'

I notice that he's got the envelope in his hands. I also notice that his hands are shaking.

I'm like, 'Ro, you can do it again. I'll pay for grinds for you. If I have to get a job to pay for them, that's what I'll do. And I'll do it focking gladly.'

He's white in the face.

I'm there, 'Ro, however bad it is, you have to know, okay?'

He just nods, then he offers me the envelope. He goes, 'You open it, Rosser.'

I'm like, 'Me?'

'Please, Rosser.'

So I take the envelope from him and suddenly it's, like, *my* hands that are trembling? I tear it open, then I pull out the A4 piece of paper inside and I unfold it very slowly. Ronan has his eyes closed. I stare at the page for like, twenty seconds, my eyes trying to focus on the letters in front of me.

Shit.

I can suddenly feel tears in my eyes.

'You stupid focker!' I go. 'You really are the stupidest focker I've ever met.'

I fold the page up again. Ronan opens his eyes and he's like, 'I toalt you I fayult, ditn't I?'

'You got seven A's!' I go. 'Ro, you got seven focking A's!'

The old man rings me in practically tears. 'Straight A's!' he goes. 'Across the board! Well, he didn't lick it up off the ground, did he?'

I'm there, 'He must have done because he certainly didn't get it from me.'

'You were intelligent in a different way, Ross! No, you had what's known as a rugby brain!'

'I know that's another way of saying I'm stupid. I don't care, though. My son is a focking genius.'

'What are his plans regarding further education? Has he said yet?'

'He was saying he was thinking of doing possibly Law in UCD!'

'I'll tell you one alumnus who'll be thrilled to hear that news – Mr Hennessy Coghlan-O'Hara!'

'Yeah, no, he hasn't made his mind up yet whether he wants to become a free legal aid lawyer, helping the most vulnerable people in his local community, or a bent solicitor, helping people like the Hutches and the Kinahans evade justice and hang onto the proceeds of their crimes.'

'I'm sure he won't have to decide that until his final year! Anyway, must go! Kennet is about to put young Muirgheal through her paces!'

'Her what?'

'He's giving her elocution lessons!'

I laugh. I'm there, 'What, so Muirgheal is the new Sorcha, is she?'

He goes, 'She's sharp as a tack, Ross! She's going out with young Christian – did you know that?'

''Yeah, I did.'

'Anyway, wish Honor all the best for me, will you?'

I hang up on him just as the kids stort walking out of the dressing room. It's definitely a week for me to feel proud of the job I've done as a father. Honor is the last one out on the pitch – same as me back in the day. There's a whole section in the Tactics Book about the psychological edge you get from making every other focker wait for you.

'Let's kick some orse, Honor!' I go. 'Let's kick some serious orse!'

She just nods at me. She's in the zone in a big-time way.

Brian's like, 'Me want Costa!'

Then Leo joins in. 'Costa mine!' he goes. 'Costa mine!'

I decide to just blank it out. It makes a change from the swearing, I suppose.

The two teams of sevens line up. Old Belvedere on one side of the pitch and Bective on the other. I notice the Bective team is all boys. Honor is actually the only girl out there. She's also the only one who knows how to properly warm up. 'Well done, Honor!' I shout. I know she's only stretching, but again she's learned it straight from me.

That's when Rob Felle tips over to me and tells me he thinks he's possibly tweaked a muscle in his groin. He asks me if I'd be interested in, like, refereeing the match for him. I'm there, 'Yeah, no, I'd love to – if you'll watch the kids for me.'

'No problem,' he goes. 'Obviously, you don't need me to tell you to be even-handed. It's only a bit of fun after all.'

I just hope and pray that's not what his old school is teaching kids. If Cian Healy was here right now, it'd take twenty men to drag him off him.

'Don't worry,' I go. 'I'll try to let the game flow, while obviously making sure the players with genuine skill are protected.'

He's like, 'Er, okay,' and he hands me the whistle. Then he goes over to the stroller.

'Me want Eden Hazard!' I hear Leo shout. 'Me want Eden Hazard!'

I blow the whistle and the match gets underway.

Honor gets the ball in her hands and she storts making some hord yords, except she ends up running straight into this absolute brick wall of a kid, who no more looks nine than I do, by the way. I'm tempted to even say it to him.

Honor hits the deck and the game goes on. I go to help her up except she goes, 'I'm focking capable of standing up by myself, okay?'

She's an unbelievable competitor.

I hear, presumably, this other kid's old man on the sideline going, 'Great tackle, Adam!' and then I decide, fock it, I *will* say it to him? So the next time there's a break in play, I sidle up to the kid – all casual-like – and I go, 'I'm tempted to ask you to go home and get your birth certificate. There's no focking way you're the same age as the rest of these kids.'

He goes, 'I'm nine!'

I'm like, 'A likely focking story. Fortunately for you, I'm going to have to believe it. Bring your birth cert the next day or you don't focking play. Do you understand me?'

He's suddenly shitting himself. He disappears from the game for the next five minutes or so – the little focking fraud – and Honor storts to have things more her own way. As a matter of fact, she manages to score a beautiful try not long afterwards, with Adam missing a vital tackle just before she grounds the ball.

I end up forgetting myself and offering her a high-five as she walks back for the restort. Adam's old man must notice this because he storts getting on his son's case all of a sudden. He goes, 'Don't be afaid to hit her hord just because she's a girl and the referee is her father!'

And that seems to give the kid his confidence back because the next time Honor gets the ball in her hands he absolutely creams her. He sends her flying off the pitch. It's a perfectly legal tackle. But being possibly biased, the next time the ball goes dead, I whisper in the kid's ear, 'I'm watching you. Another tackle like that and you're off. You little focking thug.'

Honor walks up beside me and goes, 'Yeah, I can fight my *own* battles?'

And I'm there, 'I'm just making the point that if Nigel Owens was reffing this match, that kid would be heading for the showers right now with one of Nigel's famous put-downs ringing in his ears.'

She just goes, 'I'll handle it myself, okay?'

Which she does – about a minute before half-time. Adam has the ball in his two hands and he sets off on a run with his eyes fixed on a *try*? Being about two stone heavier and twelve inches taller than everyone else, he's basically ploughing everyone out of the way until finally Honor is the only one standing between him and the line.

I'm not going to lie to you. I'm secretly terrified of my daughter being permanently injured here. But then I notice this look of absolute determination on her face as she puts her head down and readies herself for the impact. Adam is already laughing and he puts his hand out, thinking he's going to just push her over – she's just a girl, bear in mind – but Honor hits him full in the stomach with her shoulder and the wind leaves him like a tyre blowing out. You can hear it.

It's like, 'Wwwooommmppphhh!!!'

Then Honor – this is unbelievable – grabs him around the waist, this fat kid who must weigh, like, ten stone. She loads him onto her shoulder, turns him upside-down, then she slams him into the ground like he's a sledgehammer and she's ringing the bell at the funfair. I'd recognize that move anywhere. The Legal Spear Tackle!

'In your focking face!' I shout, forgetting I'm supposed to be *neutral* here? 'You just got owned!'

'Referee,' Adam's old man shouts, running onto the pitch, 'that was a spear tackle!'

I'm like, 'You don't know what you're talking about!' because it *actually* wasn't? 'She returned him safely to the ground. He moved his head at the last minute. He obviously hasn't been taught how to fall properly.'

Adam's old man clearly knows fock-all about the game. 'My son is hurt!' he goes. 'Stop the match!'

All of the other parents have storted shouting now. I hear the word 'disgrace' mentioned once or twice. Shit, I think. The kid actually *is* hurt? He's clutching his shoulder and howling in agony.

'She's broken his collarbone,' his old man goes after giving him the once-over.

I'm like, 'What are you, a doctor or something?' meaning it sarcastically.

'Yes,' he goes, 'I am. And my son has a broken collarbone.'

He shouts at Rob to phone an ambulance, which is what Rob then does. The game is suddenly forgotten as the sound of a siren fills the air and Adam – who I still think is laying it on a bit thick – is lifted onto a stretcher and put in the back of the ambulance. When it drives off, with Adam and his old man in the back, I turn around to Rob and I go, 'How do I restort the game here?' and he looks at me – I want to use the word – *incredulously*?

'That's one of the most dangerous things I've ever seen on a rugby field,' he goes.

And I'm like, 'If you give me a pen and a piece of paper, I can show you how it's actually technically legal.'

Some of the parents stort calling their children off the pitch then. They're going, 'We don't want our children hurt,' and some of these kids are her actual team-mates.

And that's when Rob turns around to me and goes, 'Get the fock out of here, Ross. And take that daughter of yours with you.'

I'm still furious as I'm strapping the boys into their baby seats. Honor is pretty pissed off too.

'I did it exactly like you said in the book,' she goes – not unreasonably either.

And I'm there, 'Stop blaming yourself, Honor. Blame people who don't understand the basic laws of rugby. And to think, Belvedere used to turn out Tony O'Reillys and Ollie Campbells like there was no tomorrow. Ridiculous.'

I'm just about to stort the cor when my phone all of a sudden rings. It's from, like, a number I don't recognize, but I end up answering it – thinking, like a focking fool, that it's possibly Rob ringing to *apologize* to me?

It ends up being the old dear – obviously ringing from prison. I'm like, 'This is not a good time. Honor's been given a straight red and they've told her to possibly find another club.'

She totally ignores this.

She goes, 'Who was that ghastly woman, Ross? We saw her in the visiting room one of the times you were here.'

I'm there, 'Are you talking about Dordeen?'

'Yes, that's her. I spoke to her, Ross. After what you said about reaching out. She mentioned that she could help me.'

'You don't want her kind of help. She's a focking scumbag.'

'Well, whatever she said or did, everything has suddenly changed! Everybody is all sweetness and light, Ross.'

'What's that going to cost you?'

'Nothing. She said we were family. Is that true, Ross? Are we related to her in some way?'

'I told you, she's Ronan's girlfriend's old dear. Have you been drinking?'

'They gave me a bottle of the prison brew. Oh, it's ghastly.'

'But you drank it anyway.'

'There isn't anything else. Anyway, I've made friends, Ross. Can you believe that? A woman called Something and another woman called Something Else.'

'It sounds like you're bezzies.'

'Like you said, they're nothing like Delma. But it's company, isn't it? Oh, I must go, Ross. I'm about to play table-tennis!'

I laugh, if you can believe that. I actually laugh in spite of everything and I stort to feel a little bit better about shit. I stort to think, yeah, no, this might turn out to be the best thing that could have happened to Honor in terms of her development as a player. Old Belvedere clearly aren't interested in born winners. At least this gives us a chance of finding a different club – a better club – for her. Mary's, for instance, are bound to have a Minis set-up.

I go, 'When you lead Ireland to your first Grand Slam, Honor, I genuinely think we'll look back on this day and laugh. But we're also keeping a list of names.'

She's like, 'Whatever,' still seriously focked off.

From the back of the cor, Brian goes, 'Me want Costa! Me want Costa!'

And I end up suddenly losing it. I'm like, 'Brian, will you shut the fock up about Costa? We're not going to focking Costa!'

And that's when Honor turns around to me and goes, 'He's not talking about Costa the coffee shop. He talking about Diego Costa.'

I'm there, 'What the fock is a Diego Costa?'

And Honor – totally straight-faced – goes, 'He's a soccer player.'

I slam on the brakes. This is just as I'm pulling out onto Ailesbury Road.

I'm like, '*Say* that again?'

'That's what they've been shouting all the time,' she goes. 'Adam Lallana, Kolo Touré – they're all the names of soccer players.'

'How would they know that, though?'

And Honor – as casual as you like – goes, 'Magnus buys them Match Attax cords.'

I immediately get out of the cor and open the back door. Brian is holding – exactly like Honor said – a picture cord with a soccer player on it. A soccer player called Sergio Agüero. I reach into the pocket of his little dungarees and I discover that he's got a whole focking deck of the things. I'm suddenly looking through them. Eden Hazard. Vincent Kompany. Aaron Ramsey. Raheem Sterling.

I've literally never heard of any of them.

I look at Leo, sitting beside him, and he's got a deck as well. I snap them out of his little hand. And so does little Johnny. I do the same. Leo calls me a focking prick-fock. But I can live with that.

I get back into the cor – as angry as I was ten minutes ago, possibly even angrier – and I go, 'Okay, me and that former manny of yours are about to have serious focking words.'

I point the cor in the direction of Killiney, except Honor goes, 'He's not at home. Him and Oisinn are launching their new business today.'

And I remember she's right. It's happening in Erika's new gallery on Duke Street. Sorcha's there as well – the so-called mother of my children who allowed this to happen, who invited a man like that into our home.

I put my foot down and I make it into town in basically record time. I throw the cor onto the taxi rank at Stephen's Green and I'm so pissed off that I end up leaving the kids in it. I end up having to go back for them. I take the stroller out of the boot, take the boys out of their baby chairs, then strap them, one by one, into the stroller. Thirty seconds later, I'm practically running down Dawson Street, then onto Duke Street, pushing the stroller in front of me, forcing people to jump out of the way.

The gallery is absolutely rammers. There's, like, loads of randomers standing around with drinks in their hands and I spot Magnus straightaway. He cops me standing there with the boys and he's suddenly got this big smile on his face. He gives them a little wave.

Brian shouts, 'Me want Romelu Lukaku!' and I end up just glowering at Magnus and going, 'I want a focking word with you!'

There's, like, instant silence in the room, and I'm suddenly aware of the fact that a lot of people are staring at me. I stort to pick out faces I recognize. Sorcha. Erika. Fionn. Christian. JP. Chloe. Sophie. Amie with an ie. Oisinn's old pair.

It's Erika who ends up going, 'Yeah, Ross, Oisinn is in the middle of saying something,' and I realize that I've walked in halfway through his big speech.

'What I was saying,' he goes, 'before I was interrupted, was that up until recently my life has felt incomplete. Things that should have made me happy only made me a little bit happy. Something was missing from my life. And I didn't know what it was until very recently, when I met a man who I fell in love with. Yes, a *man*. Because now I feel like I can finally say it. As a matter of fact, I want to shout it loud enough for everyone in the world to hear. I'm gay. I'm a gay man. I'm in love with Magnus Laakso-Sigurjónsson and I don't care who knows it.'

'Daniel Sturridge!' Leo shouts.

I end up just seeing red. I totally lose it. I'm suddenly pointing at Magnus, going, 'You're focking sick, do you know that?'

Fionn's like, 'Whoa, Ross, you're out of order.'

And I'm there, 'I'm not out of order. I'm far from it. This is something that needs to be said and if no one else is going to say it, then I am. Dude, you're a poisonous influence on people. If that's the kind of warped shit you're into, that's your own business. But when you go corrupting other people – innocent people who aren't wise to the ways of the world – that's when I step in and say no way – not on my watch.'

Sorcha goes, 'Oh my God, Ross, I can't believe you're saying this.'

'And I can't believe you let this man into our home to look after our children. You've always been way too tolerant for your own good.'

It's Oisinn's old dear – at one time, a big, big, big, big fan of mine – who looks at me in shock and goes, 'How can you even think something like that – in this day and age?'

And I'm suddenly thinking, oh shit, because it hits me that they might have thought I was referring to something else.

I'm there, 'Yeah, no, I was actually talking about –'

But Oisinn points at the door and goes, 'Get out of here.'

I'm like, 'Dude –'

But he's just there, 'I said get the fock out of here – right now.'

5. Don't Mention the Wall

I wake up the following day with a feeling of guilt weighing on my head like a bad hangover.

Everyone knows what it's like – that horrible sense that you possibly owe one or two people an apology, but at the same time you wouldn't mind finding out how actually pissed off they are before you go throwing the word 'sorry' around.

I send Oisinn a text and it's just like, 'That all got a bit heated last night! We'll leave it at that! How was the rest of the night?'

Twenty minutes later, there's nothing back from him, but I do notice that I have a text from Sorcha. It's just like, 'Can you come to the house? I have something to give you.'

I stare at it for a good, I don't know, sixty seconds, trying to figure out whether this is likely to be good news or bad. I'm usually a glass-half-full type of goy, but I notice that she hasn't used a single emoji and that is never a good sign with Sorcha.

So I drive out to Killiney to possibly face the music.

The gate is wide open when I get there. I drive through it and up to the house. I ring on the doorbell. It's Sorcha's old dear who ends up answering and it's straightaway obvious from her frosty response that I was right about the absence of emojis. She doesn't say a word to me, just opens the door to let me in.

Upstairs, I can hear one of the boys going, 'Phil Jagielka! Phil Jagielka!' and it breaks my focking hort.

I'm like, 'What's this about, I'm just wondering?'

But she doesn't tell me. She just leads me down to what I used to call the gym but what has now been turned back into a study. 'Edmund wants to talk to you,' she goes. 'I'll go and tell Sorcha you're here.'

I push the door. He's sitting behind his desk and he's on the phone. Big focking serious voice on him. He indicates for me to sit down by just pointing his finger, so I do, while he continues to chat away. It's all talk about, I don't know, clavicles and scapula and other words I don't understand.

I put my feet up on his desk. He eventually hangs up and removes my feet from his desk. Then Sorcha walks in. She sits down on her old man's side of the desk – which is possibly an omen.

'Sorcha,' I go, 'I was actually talking about soccer. I was talking about those cords that Magnus has been buying for the boys.'

She's there, 'We'll talk about that in a minute. That's not why I asked you here.'

And that's when her old man takes sudden chorge of the conversation. He goes, 'Honor broke a young boy's collarbone yesterday.'

Young? Okay, that's debatable.

I'm there, 'She was playing rugby. It's port and porcel.'

He wouldn't know, of course. I remember one time, years ago, he was trying to bullshit me about the game and he storted talking about how well *Roland* O'Gara played against England. I never even bothered my hole correcting him. I thought, let the focker go on saying it. Give him enough rope.

'Part and parcel,' he goes – it's like he thinks we're in court here. 'Deliberately causing a serious injury to another minor. That's allowed under the rules of rugby, is it?'

I'm there, 'Rugby doesn't have rules. It has laws.'

My old man always says the difference between rules and laws is that laws are drawn up by solicitors billing by the hour.

'And trust me,' I go, 'it *was* a legal tackle. I'm not saying it wasn't borderline. She picked him up and she returned him to the ground again. It's just he landed awkwardly.'

He's there, 'As well as a broken collarbone, he has concussion. His father is threatening to sue us for substantial damages.'

'Sorcha,' I go, 'you watched a lot of rugby back in the day. You know that when you get torgeted in a match, you're not supposed to piss and moan about it afterwards. The best players don't, anyway.'

There's no reaching her, though. She just stares straight through me.

He goes, 'What I've since discovered was that this was no accident. This wasn't something that just happened in the heat of the match. This was something premeditated. And it was something that *you* taught her.'

Now, I faced enough citing commissioners back in the day to know how to handle this. I just stick my bottom lip out and shake my head, like I've no idea what he's even talking about. And that's when he produces it. My Rugby Tactics Book. And I can see that it's open on the page headed 'The Legal Spear Tackle'.

I reach across the desk and try to grab it from him, except his hands are too fast, which is something I'm highly embarrassed to admit.

'Oh, no, you don't,' he goes. 'This is evidence.'

I'm like, 'What are you talking about, evidence?'

'I'm going to court to seek a restraining order to keep you away from the children.'

'What? On what basis?'

'On the basis that your influence over them is morally deleterious. Yes, that's also a word, Ross.'

'*Excuse* me?'

'Oh, don't worry, the judge will understand it. He'll understand this, too. The Legal Spear Tackle. There are illustrations and everything. And young Adam's father said he'll provide me with the X-rays of his son's shoulder to put before the court.'

I look at Sorcha and I'm like, 'I thought we said we'd handle this divorce like Gwyneth Paltrow and the dude from Coldplay?'

'I tried, Ross. I genuinely did. It's like I said to Fionn last night after you ruined Oisinn's coming out, I've finally realized that not only do I not love you anymore, I don't even like you. You're not the kind of person I want to be around. And I don't want you damaging the children any further.'

'You never wanted Honor to play rugby. Your nose was out of joint from day one. You'd have preferred if it was, I don't know, *ballet* or something?'

'What you did to Garret and Claire –'

'I've given you my explanation for that and I'm standing by it.'

'Claire has lost her marriage and she's also lost her business. Yes, that's right, Ross. She had to close Wheat Bray Love because of the things you wrote about it on Trip Advisor.'

'Well, the food didn't sound great, in fairness. It actually sounded disgusting.'

'What was disgusting, Ross, was the way you spoke to Magnus last night.'

'I was talking about soccer. I wish everyone would accept that.'

'And, as I said to Fionn, I can't be friends with someone who thinks those things.'

I'm like, 'Oh, yeah, Fionn, I'd say he was fully behind you on that one,' and then I end up giving Sorcha's old man exactly what he wants, in that I suddenly stort *crying*? Hey, it's pretty hord news to take, being told your kids are being taken away from you, especially given the kind of father that I am. I'm like, 'You can't stop me seeing my kids. You can't do it.'

He sits back in his chair and makes a steeple of his fingers. Big smile on his face. He's enjoying watching Sorcha finally turn on me. He's loving every second of it.

Sorcha's there, 'I'm not going to stop you seeing them altogether, Ross.'

Her old man goes, 'My daughter – being far too charitable, in my view – has agreed to allow you to have supervised access.'

'Supervised? What does that mean?'

'It means one hour per week, here in the house, with either Sorcha or her mother or myself present.'

'One hour? What about Honor's rugby?'

'Is that a serious question?'

'Rugby is the one thing I don't joke about. One hour per week? Jesus Christ, that's how often I see my old dear and she's in the focking slammer.'

He goes, 'If I show a judge this book, along with that child's X-ray, believe me, he will grant me a restraining order preventing you from seeing the children at all.'

'Not a judge who understands the laws of rugby.'

'One hour per week. Here in the house. I would strongly recommend that you accept it.'

I have no choice but to go, 'Okay, I'll take it, you total focking knob-end,' and I stand up and I storm out of there. And who do I end up literally bumping into outside in the hall?

Focking Magnus.

I keep forgetting he's still living here. I try to keep the porty polite. I'm like, 'Hey, Dude, I was texting Oisinn earlier – how did the rest of the night go?'

He just, like, glowers at me. He's like, 'Mosht of the time, I do not like to shwear. But thish time, I heff to make an exsheption. You are a fucking ash hole, Rosh. A fucking ash hole. You are very lucky I don't break your noash right now.'

'Dude, when I said you were corrupting innocent people, I was talking about soccer.'

'Get the hell out of my shight.'

The old man is full of it. He's holding up his phone, going, 'You know, Muirgheal has set me up with one of these Twitters!'

All me and Helen can do is look at each other and smile.

'You mean she set you up *on* Twitter,' I go, 'you stupid focking dope.'

He's like, 'Yes, that's the one! You've heard of this thing, have you?'

'Jesus Christ, it's been around for years. Do you not remember that cease and desist letter that Honor got from Caroline Flack?'

'Oh, yes! Didn't Hennessy sort that business out in the end?'

'Yeah, no, he did – but it was *through* Twitter that Honor was trolling slash cyberbullying the woman.'

She had sixty or seventy different accounts at one stage. She was setting them up quicker than poor Caroline could block them. That's the price you have to pay, I suppose, for being in the public eye.

Helen goes, 'Just be careful, Charlie. You hear about people getting into all sorts of trouble on that thing, writing things without thinking them through first.'

She hands me a cup of coffee, then goes back to making my omelette. She really is great – even though the omelette will be barely edible.

'Stuff and nonsense!' the old man goes. 'No, the wonderful thing about Twitters is that I can send my message directly to my supporters without it having to go through the filter of the media – who put a bloody well slant on everything I say! No, as Muirgheal pointed out, this way I'm actually in charge of the message! Oh, she's calling in this morning, by the way.'

Helen's there, 'Calling in? To the house?'

'Yes, I've asked her to replace young Sorcha as the New Republic candidate for Dublin Bay South. Oh, she's very ambitious – and what an operator!'

'Erika doesn't like her. She says she's not a very nice person.'

'Well, thankfully, Erika is only one voter. She's not the entire electorate.'

While this conversation is going on, I'm checking the old man's Twitter feed. It's actually beyond funny. He's posted, like, two messages. The first one, from yesterday morning, is just like, 'Testing testing testing testing,' like he's checking a phone line or a microphone or something.

The second one, from last night, is like, 'Hello, everyone, this is Charles O'Carroll-Kelly speaking!'

The replies are hilarious. It's all shit like, 'Your nothing but a prick!!!!' and 'Scum – well-fed scum!' and 'Why don't you die you waste of fucking skin?'

The usual banter you get on Twitter.

But then – I have to admit – there are other messages as well that are like, 'Water is free, it comes out of the fucking sky, why should we fucking pay for it?' and 'Your the only one speaking the truth, german c**ts telling us what to do, we should say to them you want the money? Then take it out of that you pack of foreign fucks!' and 'Your hair is magnificent, what do you wash it with?'

There's suddenly a knock on the door. He goes, 'Oh, that'll be her – and Hennessy. I asked the famous Kennet to collect them. Ross, answer the door, will you?'

I'm like, 'What's wrong with *your* focking legs?'

Helen's there, 'I'll get it,' but I'm like, 'It's cool, Helen, I'll go,' because she's making me breakfast, in fairness to the woman, and it's hord enough to eat her cooking when it's *not* focking burned.

So out I trot to answer the door. It ends up being – yeah,

no – Hennessy, Muirgheal and K . . . K . . . K . . . Kennet. I let the first two in, then I go to close the door in Kennet's face. He sticks his foot in it. That's the type he is. He goes, 'What are you d . . . d . . . d . . . doing?'

And I'm like, 'You're the help – the help waits *outside*?'

I'm quoting my old dear.

Hennessy goes, 'Charlie needs him this morning. Let him in.'

So I end up *having* to?

I notice straightaway that there's something very different about Muirgheal, although I can't put my finger on what it actually is yet.

'Hennessy,' I go, 'can I talk to you about something?'

And Muirgheal has the actual cheek to go, 'Yeah, we're here to talk about *politics*, Ross?'

Hennessy goes, 'Muirgheal, Kennet, you go talk to Charlie. I'll be two minutes,' and down they go to the kitchen. 'Okay, what do you want?'

'It's Sorcha. Well, it's more her old man. He wants to stop me seeing the kids except for, like, one hour a week *supervised*?'

'I know. I got the letter.'

'Well, presumably we can fight this in the courts?'

'You told your daughter to break another kid's collarbone and almost his neck.'

This is my own solicitor, by the way.

I'm there, 'Surely a judge would understand the difference between a legal spear tackle and an illegal one?'

'I wouldn't be so sure,' he goes. 'A lot of them are hopelessly out of touch with rugby these days. What did you say her old man is offering you?'

'One hour per week – supervised.'

'You're lucky to still have that. Take it.'

Then he follows the others down to the kitchen. And so do I.

Muirgheal has bought the old man a present – oh, she's some operator alright. It's, like, a red tie and it's hilarious because she's actually putting the thing on him when we step into the kitchen. The old man is all embarrassed, the sap. He goes, 'Young Muirgheal's bought me a gift, Hennessy!' his face the same colour as the tie. 'To say thank you for selecting her to run in Dublin Bay South.'

'And by the way,' Muirgheal goes, 'I took the liberty of writing some responses you might consider making to Micheál Martin's comments this morning.'

I notice Helen giving her the evil eye as she puts my omelette down on the table.

The old man goes, 'Michael Martin? What did he say?'

Muirgheal finishes tying the tie, then she looks at it with her head cocked to one side and storts adjusting the knot. 'He called you a dangerous populist,' she goes, 'and he said your views on Europe could set Ireland back one hundred years. There . . . Oh my God, red *so* suits you.'

The old man's like, 'A dangerous populist? The bloody well nerve of the man!'

'Chorles,' she goes, sitting down in *my* seat, 'it's all good. It means he's rattled.'

'Yes, of course! He has to come after me given our position in the polls! Oh, don't worry your head, Muirgheal, I'll deal with our friend in time!'

I can't believe he's *actually* flirting with her. She looks at the omelette, pulls a face and pushes the plate away. It looks focking revolting, in fairness, but actually Helen notices and she gives Muirgheal a long, hord stare.

I end up laughing then because I suddenly realize what's different about Muirgheal. She's blonde.

'Did you *actually* dye your hair,' I go, 'to try to look like Sorcha?'

But she doesn't answer me. She just goes, 'If we're going to work this morning, Charles, can we possibly clear the kitchen?'

The old man – unbelievably – goes, 'Helen, Ross, would you mind –' and he flicks his head to avoid having to say, '– focking off?', which is what he actually means.

Helen is seriously pissed off. She picks up his blue Charvet tie, which she bought him for his birthday and which Muirgheal had dropped on the floor, and goes, 'I happen to think this one suited you better.'

Then she storms out of the room – I swear to fock, in tears. Of course, the old man is totally oblivious to this. He goes, 'Okay, let's start with a basic one, shall we, Kennet?'

And Kennet goes, "Alreet, M . . . M . . . M . . . Muirgheal, repeath arthur me – *the cunter doddy is arthur goan to the bleaten dogs, so it has.*'

I follow Helen out into the hallway, where she just, like, collapses, sobbing, into my orms. I'm there, 'He's a dick, Helen. I was really looking forward to that omelette as well.'

That's easy to say, of course.

'Oh, Ross,' she goes. 'I curse the day he ever found that wig.'

Amelie is thrilled to see me. I'm thinking, at least *someone* is these days? She comes at me with her two orms outstretched, going, 'Uncle Ross!'

It'd nearly give you a big head!

I pick her up and I go, 'At least *someone* is thrilled to see me!'

And Erika, in fairness to her, looks up from her laptop and smiles. 'What do you want, Ross? I'm busy.'

She's busy alright. The place finally looks like an actual gallery. The workmen have gone and the walls are full of pictures slash paintings. I walk around, with Amelie in my orms, checking them out. Most of them, you can tell straightaway what they're supposed to be, which has always been the mork of a good picture slash painting to me.

'You always had a good eye for ort,' I go. 'Here, what are those paintings called in the National Gallery? You're only allowed to look at them in January.'

'Are you talking about the Turner Exhibition?'

'That's them. You only put them out for one month in the year. That's acting the bollocks. I remember I made that point on a school trip once and it wasn't appreciated.'

'It's to protect them from the effects of the sunlight.'

'You say it's that and I say it's acting the bollocks. Of course not everyone in the ort world likes a straight talker – including the staff in that place.'

'Speaking of you being thrown out of galleries, what are you doing here, Ross?'

'Yeah, no, I came to see Oisinn to hopefully apologize properly. Is he upstairs?'

'No, he went out to get a sandwich.'

'I'll, er, stick around if you don't mind.'

'I'm saying I do mind. And I'm not one hundred percent sure he's ready to hear whatever you have to say either.'

'I don't know about that. I can be a bit of a wordsmith when the moment takes me.'

'I know. I heard your little speech during his coming out.'

'When I mentioned Magnus being into warped shit, I was talking about soccer. I wish people would accept that.'

I hand Amelie over to Erika and I change the subject. I'm there, 'By the way, your old dear was in tears earlier?'

She's like, 'Mum? What are you talking about?' and she's furious.

I go, 'Yeah, no, my old man was being a dick to her again. He asked her to leave the room.'

'But it's *her* house.'

'Yeah, it was so Kennet could teach Muirgheal how to talk like a skank. She's replacing Sorcha as his candidate in Dublin Bay South.'

'That girl is a dangerous bitch.'

It takes one to know one – that's what I'm tempted to say. I don't, though. I go, 'Yeah, no, she bought my old man a new tie. Which is the other reason your old dear was upset. He took off the good Charvet one she bought him for his birthday and dropped it on the floor. You should have seen Muirgheal flirting with him.'

She's like, 'Seriously, Ross. She'd cut your throat to get whatever she wants.'

'Who are you telling? Do you remember what a bitch she was when Sorcha won the election for Head Girl in Mount Anville?'

'Well, it sounds like we're about to see a rematch,' she goes.

'What do you mean?'

'Sorcha didn't tell you?'

'Sorcha's not really talking to me. It's because I rode Claire when she was home and I kind of encouraged Honor to break another kid's collarbone.'

'She's planning to run as an Independent candidate.'

I'm like, 'What?' and this sort of, I don't know, dread comes over me. I'm suddenly worried about Sorcha and what Muirgheal might do to her.

But then I don't have time to think about it anymore because Oisinn arrives back and we're suddenly standing face to face. I see the Carluccio's bag in his hand and I go, 'What sandwich did you get?' more to break the ice than anything else. 'I'm a massive, massive fan of the toasted caprese, but then I also like the sausage and ricotta calzone, even though I was dubious about calzones for about ten years after they first came out. I actually refused to recognize them as a thing.'

He just, like, stares me down and goes, 'The only reason I haven't punched you in the face is because there's a child in the room.'

I'm there, 'Dude, I'm trying to say sorry here.'

'I don't want your apology.'

'I was actually talking about soccer when I said that shit to Magnus.'

'At least have the courage to admit what you are.'

'What am I?'

'You're a homophobic bigot.'

'I disagree with that analysis.'

'I mean, your wife even said it. You refused to bring her grandmother to vote.'

'It's her grandmother who hates gay people. She just hides it well.'

'Well, you certainly don't – hide it well, I mean.'

'Dude, Magnus bought the boys these Match Attax cords. I was worried they might be getting drawn down the wrong path. You hate the game as much as I do. Whatever happened to "Tough on soccer, tough on the causes of soccer"? We lived by that rule.'

'You were the one I was most worried about telling.'

'Me? Why?'

'I just knew you'd be the one who'd have a problem with it.'

'I don't have a problem with it. Look, I struggled with it for a few weeks. I'm admitting that.'

'Weeks? What are you talking about?'

'Oisinn, I knew before anyone. I saw you and Magnus in the laneway beside Kielys getting off with each other.'

He laughs, then nods, like this is somehow *evidence* of something? He goes, 'So that's why you were avoiding me for most of the summer.'

I'm there, 'It was a shock, that's all. But now I've actually got my head around it and I'm genuinely thrilled for you.'

He goes, 'Fock you, Ross,' and he walks past me, giving me a serious shoulder nudge on the way. 'You're focking dead to me.'

'Do you know what?' I shout at him as he walks up the stairs. 'Fock *you*, Oisinn! How's about that? Fock *you* instead!'

Erika tries to block Amelie's ears. 'Ross,' she goes, 'I do not want my daughter growing up with the same vocabulary as your children.'

Amelie suddenly bursts into tears.

I'm there, 'No, I'm going to say what I have to say, Erika. Fock you, Oisinn. There's no one outside your family who cares about you more than I do. I was the one who went to Monte Corlo and brought you home, in case you've forgotten, when you did a runner from your debts and you were considering topping yourself. We've been friends since we were, like, thirteen. Jesus, we played rugby together. How could you believe that of me? I have nothing against gay people. Yes, I'm a nervous wreck around them. But one thing I am not is a homophobiac.'

Erika is staring at me with this look of, like, shock on her face. I realize that, just like Amelie, I'm crying too. And I'm also shaking.

'Fock you for believing the worst of me,' I shout up the stairs. 'And fock you even more for taking your focking friendship away.'

Honor can't understand it. She goes, 'It said in your Rugby Tactics Book that even if someone deliberately takes you out, you're not supposed to go pissing and moaning about it afterwards. And this focking wanker sends us an actual *solicitor's* letter?'

I'm there, 'You're preaching to the choir, Honor. When Drico got done on the Lions tour in oh-five, there was a lot of shit he could have said about Tana Umaga and Keven Mealamu – two pricks, by the way. But he didn't. I can quote from his book. He accepted it.'

We're lying on her bed watching *Orange is the New Black* on Netflix. The boys are crawling around on the floor, fighting over their – it kills me to say it – soccer cords. 'My Wayne Rooney. Mine!' Leo goes. 'Mine!'

I genuinely preferred the swearing.

'Who's she?' I go. 'The bird with the glasses?'

Honor's like, 'Oh, that's Alex.'

'She's a bit of a fox. In spite of the glasses.'

'Yeah, she's also a *lesbian*?'

'Cool.'

'So she wouldn't have any interest in the likes of you.'

'One thing doesn't necessarily follow the other, Honor. It's a common mistake to presume that it does.'

'Well, she had a thing with Piper ages before they went to jail. They were, like, *drug* smugglers together? Then Alex basically double-crossed her. But now they're in prison together. And they're sort of getting it on again.'

'Fantastic. I'm delighted for them. See, that's an example of me being totally open-minded about the gay thing. If only that dick-head Oisinn could see this version of me. And Magnus and everyone else who thinks I'm not cool with . . . Jesus, it's very graphic, isn't it?'

'Do you want me to switch it off?'

'No, no, leave it on. I'm actually answering my critics here.'

Sorcha's old man bursts into the room without even knocking. 'Okay,' he goes, looking at his watch, 'your time's up.'

I'm there, 'There's no way that was an hour.'

'It was fifty minutes. You arrived ten minutes late. If you want the full hour, I suggest you arrive at one o'clock as agreed.'

I'm about to call him a dick, but Honor gets there before me. She goes, 'Why don't you go and eat a bowl of Go Fock Yourself?'

I laugh. I'm there, 'Classic, classic Honor!'

He goes, 'If you continue to speak to me in that way, I'll be cutting off your father's access altogether.'

And I'm like, 'Yeah, just give me a few minutes to say goodbye to my kids, will you – you focking dick?'

He goes, 'You have exactly sixty seconds,' and off he goes.

I'm there, 'I better head off, Honor. He's just going to be a prick about things.'

She just nods. I can tell she's hortbroken. So much for the girl who supposedly found me annoying.

I'm there, 'Look, I'll see you next week, okay?'

She looks away, all sad. She goes, 'A week is ages away.'

And I'm there, 'Believe me, Honor, the time goes twice as slowly for me.'

She throws her orms around my waist and holds me like she has no intention of ever letting go. This is, like, *Honor*, bear in mind? I'm there, 'Honor, I really have to go,' and I finally manage to prise myself free.

I go to say goodbye to the boys. Leo holds up a cord and goes, 'Me have John Terry!' and I decide not to even dignify it with a response. In fact, I totally ignore them as I'm leaving. No hugs, no kisses, no goodbyes for them. It's called tough love, and it'll do them no horm in the long run.

I tip down the stairs.

Sorcha's old man already has the front door open for me. As I'm just about to walk out, he goes, 'Oh, by the way, have you seen Sorcha's election posters?'

I should know better than to take the bait. But I end up taking it.

I go, 'What are you shitting on about now?'

He points to five or six lorge packages wrapped in brown paper. One of them is torn open and that's the one he reaches for. He pulls a poster out of it. He's all, 'I think they're rather wonderful,' and he holds it up for me to see it.

The first thing that catches my eye is Sorcha's picture. She's wearing her black Alexander Wang blazer and she has her head tilted slightly to one side and a look on her face that seems to say, 'God, it sounds like things are really shit for you right now!'

Next to her face, it says, 'A Strong, Independent Voice for the people of Dublin Bay South!'

But it's what's across the top of the poster that upsets me the most. It's her name. It doesn't say, 'Sorcha O'Carroll-Kelly'.

It says, 'Sorcha Lalor'.

Sorcha's old man goes, 'Now that's a name you can trust, isn't it?'

I end up totally flipping. And I *mean* totally. I head for the study, where Sorcha and Fionn are having what they called a strategy meeting. I can hear Fionn, through the door, going, 'I think we have to accept that there *is* a conservative element out there that *will* be turned off by the fact that you have a failed marriage behind you. But I think we can turn it to our advantage by playing up the whole single mom, four kids, career woman, environmentalist thing. Let women know that they can have it all. I think it'll play really, really well.'

I don't even bother my hole knocking. I just give the door a shove, the same way her old man does. The two of them are sitting either side of the desk. Fionn, at least, has the decency to not be able to even look me in the eye.

I'm like, 'Your idea, was it? For her to drop my name?'

Sorcha goes, 'You didn't think I was going to go on using your name after we were divorced, did you?'

'We're not divorced yet – that's the point I'm making.'

'Well, we're going to be. I decided to go back to my maiden name to try to put distance between myself and your father, whom I still love, by the way – *despite* our political differences? I just don't want people hearing O'Carroll-Kelly and presuming I believe in any of the things he believes in.'

You never truly know a woman until she's divorcing you.

I say that as well. I'm like, 'You never truly know a woman until she's divorcing you.'

And she looks at Fionn and goes, 'Could you just give us a minute, Fionn? I need to talk to Ross about something.'

He's like, 'Yeah, no problem,' and he stands up and focks off.

Once he has, Sorcha turns around to me and goes, 'Okay, this is awkward – it's about money.'

I'm there, 'Do you need money?' reaching into my pocket for my roll of fifties. 'I keep forgetting that your dad is bankrupt, having focked up badly during the boom.'

'No, I don't need money. It's just there's one or two bills haven't been paid.'

'I usually send everything to the old man.'

'It's just the electricity and the telephone.'

'I'll tell him to stick the funds in my account. I don't know if you heard this, but he's persuaded Muirgheal to run against you – as in Muirgheal Massey?'

'Yes, I heard. I'm following her on Twitter.'

'Yeah, no, she was in the gaff the other day. Kennet was teaching her how to say, "Recover doddy – would ya go wadden ourra tat?" '

Sorcha laughs. She's always found me funny.

'Well,' she goes, 'good luck to her. She always talked about going into politics when we were at school.'

I'm there, 'Hey, I can give you dirt on her if you need it. She wanked JP off in a field. You can have that. Venue to be confirmed.'

'Ross, I have no intention of going negative. Muirgheal and I fought a really clean campaign when we both went for Head Girl in Mount Anville. When I beat her, she could have easily been a bitch about it.'

She was a bitch about it.

'No, no,' Sorcha goes. 'When the time comes, I'll debate her on the actual issues.'

And I'm thinking, yeah, good luck with that.

Ronan's excited. But I'm possibly even *more* so? He's storting in UCD next week.

'I've got something for you,' I go. 'A present.'

We're in my old man's gaff.

He's like, 'What is it, Rosser?'

I open it out for him. It's my old UCD hoodie. He looks at it – he's definitely Scooby Dubious. He's like, 'Eh . . .'

I'm there, 'Try it on – see does it fit!'

It's Erika who tries to burst my bubble. She's like, 'He doesn't want to wear your old clothes, Ross. Look at the state of it.'

'Hey,' I go, 'I got off with you one day while I was wearing it. Obviously before we found out we were related. As a matter of fact, sometimes I think I can still smell you off it.'

I hold it up to my face. 'God,' I go, 'do you remember *ck one*? God, I miss the nineties!'

They're both looking at me like I'm off my head.

Erika goes, 'I have a present for you, too, Ronan.'

Ro's like, 'Ah, Edika, you shouldn't hab!'

'It's outside.'

'Outsoyut?'

'Come on,' she goes, grabbing him by the hand. 'Ross, bring Amelie.'

I pick Amelie up and I follow them out the front door. I'm going, 'Yeah, you better not have upstaged my present.'

But, of course, she *has*?

Ronan's looking around him, going, 'Wheer is it, Edika?'

There's suddenly a beep – from a brand-new, black, Golf GTI porked outside on the road. Ronan's mouth drops open.

I'm there, 'I still think my gift had more, I don't know, *sentimental* value?'

He throws his orms around Erika and goes, 'You're unbeliebable, so you are – you're bleaten unbeliebable!'

My present is definitely more of a slow-burner in terms of being appreciated. Erika goes, 'Well, we can't have you travelling across town on public transport every day, can we?'

She hands him the keys and he gets into it. 'Let's turden her on,' he goes, 'see how she's ticking oaber.'

He doesn't have a licence, of course. Or any experience. Unless you count driving a double-decker tour bus without a Category D permit, and three Juvenile Let-Offs for taking a cor without the owner's consent, as experience.

'I lub it,' he goes, still unable to believe it. 'I lub it, Edika!'

I'm there, 'Hey, you can swing in and collect me on your first day.'

He's like, 'What?'

'Your first day. I'm coming with you. To UCD. Help you get settled in. Show you the famous Orts block and one or two other former haunts of mine.'

'Eh, the thing is, Rosser –'

'As someone who's seen it and done it all before. No arguments, Ro. I'm coming with you.'

Micheál Mortin calls my old man's attitude cavalier and grossly irresponsible. This is while they're debating Ireland's future within the European Union on *Claire Byrne Live*. I'm watching from the wings with Muirgheal and Hennessy. They're here to support him. I'm here because I've got a thing for Claire Byrne.

'All his talk of countries being stronger alone,' Micheál Mortin goes, 'it's like something from the nineteen thirties. Eirexit – as Charles calls it – would leave this country totally isolated on the periphery of the continent.'

'Which is what we are anyway!' the old man goes. 'We have a Vichy Government with a puppet leader! Enda bloody well Kenny! A mere Cabinet Secretary whose sole function is to ensure that Ireland makes its monthly reparation payments to our masters in Europe!'

Claire Byrne gets in there then. She's like, 'Isn't this just populist rhetoric, Charles O'Carroll-Kelly? Ireland can't just walk away from its debt obligations, can it?'

'We can,' he goes, 'and we will!'

'Unfortunately,' Micheál Mortin goes, 'that's not how it works. If we renege on our debts – and the electorate, I think, are smart enough to realize this – it will affect our ability to borrow money, going forward.'

'We won't be borrowing any more money going forward, going backward or going in any other bloody well direction! Under New Republic, we won't need to! Ireland produces enough food each year to feed the population of China. That's a fact. And look at us – we're broke!'

'Even if that's true,' Claire Byrne goes, 'who's going to buy all of this food from us if we leave the European Union?'

She's not taken in by his bullshit.

'We will do our own deals!' the old man goes. 'The rest of the world will be queuing up to trade with us! The point is that we cannot determine our own economic course as long as we are living under the weight of *the* most punitive economic burden placed on any country since the famous Treaty of Versailles!'

Muirgheal goes, 'Oh my God, he talks *such* sense!' and she says it just to suck up to Hennessy. 'He's saying things that other politicians are – oh my God – terrified to even think.'

I'm there, 'Not from where I'm standing. I think he's making a complete tit of himself.'

'And what would you know about politics?' she goes.

I'm there, 'I know enough to see through you. Buying him that tie. Flirting with him. Upsetting Helen, who I happen to have a lot of time for. So what is it you're after – what specifically?'

She looks to make sure that Hennessy isn't listening. Then she turns back to me and goes, 'Deputy Leader.'

I laugh. Straight out. I'm there, 'Seriously?'

'Oh, that's not all,' she goes. 'I want to be the one who actually does it, who goes to Europe and tells them, "Yeah, we don't want to be port of your bullshit anymore," and as I'm doing it I'll be picturing Sorcha sitting at home crying her eyes out.'

Some people just love chaos. I'm there, 'I genuinely don't know what Christian sees in you – aport from obviously looks.'

Then I go back to listening to the interview.

Micheál Mortin's there, 'This kind of rhetoric – all these war references coming from this man – it's dangerous in the extreme. The fact remains that the European Union has helped bring peace, stability and democracy to a continent that, less than eighty years ago – we'd be foolish to lose sight of this – dragged the world into a ruinous war.'

And the old man goes, 'Fortunately, Mister Schoolteacher from Cork, the people of Ireland don't need a history lesson from the likes of you! They're living with the folly of the quote-unquote European project every day! People aren't fooled by all this talk of democracy either! Because they remember that every time they've voted No in a referendum that benefits the larger countries in Europe, they've been told to have another think about it and come back with the right answer in six months!'

'That's not actually what happened. The Treaties you're referring to were substantially –'

'People are tired of having their pockets plundered in the service of a totalitarian European super-state, which despises democracy and from which they feel completely and utterly disenfranchised! But you feel like you must go on defending it because of the role played by Fianna Fáil in agreeing to the Carthaginian peace of the so-called bailout! Because Fianna Fáil agreed to impose austerity on the people of Ireland while we paid out on the losing bets of global bond speculators!'

'We were faced with a set of circumstances in 2008 –'

'Fianna Fáil agreed to impose water charges on the Irish people! Fianna Fáil agreed to impose property tax on the Irish people!'

'We were faced with a set of circumstances – if you'll let me finish – where people would have gone to their ATMs and discovered that they had no money.'

'They have no money now! Because you took it from them! Yes, sir! And you used it to pay private debts that had nothing to do with them! You agreed to a deal that has sucked the life's blood out of our economy and will continue to do so for generations to come! And now you're in opposition, you try to pretend these things had nothing to do with you! You get to criticize the way someone else is cleaning up the mess you created! You are a busted flush, Mister Schoolteacher from Cork! A busted flush!'

Claire Byrne tries to get in, except Micheál Mortin goes, 'Can I just respond to that point? No, you gave Charles plenty of time there to attack me, so I'd like the opportunity to address the issues he's raised. There is something frankly hilarious about this man beside me setting himself up as a sort of champion of the downtrodden masses. Charles O'Carroll-Kelly is a modern-day robber baron, who made tens of millions of euros from – let's be honest about this – corruption. Many of the people he's pitching to are living in communities with problems that he helped to create by subverting proper planning procedures. The hypocrisy of the man is frankly staggering.'

The old man ends up losing the plot. He turns around to Micheál Mortin and he goes, 'You are what I would describe as a typical Cork person!'

Hennessy's jaw just drops. He's suddenly running his finger across his throat and mouthing the words, 'Cut it! Cut it there! Cut it there!'

Micheál Mortin goes, 'Oh, you have a problem with the people of Cork, do you?'

The old's man's like, 'Yes, I do!' as Hennessy puts his head in his hands. 'Coming up here to Dublin and moaning about how we do things! I have a big problem with Cork people! When Cork sends its people, they're not sending their best! They're sending their whingers, their moaners, their complainers! Oh, how I'm sick and tired of that ridiculous, uppy-and-downy accent that makes everything sound like a bloody well gripe! And people are sick to the back teeth listening to it!'

Hennessy turns to Muirgheal and goes, 'That's it – that's the election gone before it's even been called.'

The old man looks directly into the camera. 'I'm making the people of Ireland a promise here tonight!' he goes. 'We're going to build a wall – and nobody builds better walls than Charles O'Carroll-Kelly, believe me! We're going to build a wall around Cork – and we're going to make the people of Cork pay for it!'

I haven't seen my old dear smile in so long, I'd forgotten what her teeth looked like.

Focking horrible, I'm suddenly remembering. The woman could shove an entire pineapple in her mouth, then spit it out chunk by chunk.

I'm there, 'You seem in better form. For some reason.'

She goes, 'You sound annoyed by that.'

'I'm not annoyed. As in, that's not what's wrong with me. I'm actually worried about the old man.'

'Your father? What's happened?'

'You didn't hear? He had a total meltdown on TV last night. He's threatening to build a wall around Cork.'

'About time!'

'Do you think?'

'I'm no fan of rural people in general, Ross. I find them slow-minded and resentful.'

'Yeah, no, so do I.'

'They're different from us. There's no point in pretending otherwise. Yet try telling that to these people are who are trying to force diversity onto us.'

'It's just, I don't know, you can't say shit like that anymore. Everyone's always ready to take offence these days.'

'It's political correctness gone mad. Is he going to put broken glass on the top of this wall?'

'I don't know.'

'He needs to put broken glass on the top of it because otherwise they'll just climb over. People will resort to all sorts of measures in the mistaken belief that they can somehow escape their condition. Speaking of which, I have news – I got a job!'

'A job?'

'Here, in the kitchen!'

'You haven't worked since, like, the seventies.'

'That ghastly woman we met in here –'

'Dordeen?'

'Yes, she had a *word* with someone, as she promised she would. The next thing I knew, I was summoned from my suite –'

'Cell. Continue.'

'– and shown to the kitchen, where the vegetables for the day's dinner were all laid out. And this *wan* – Nathalie, the Head Chef – told me to get peeling. Which I did. Well, I've told you what the food was like in here, Ross. Awful, awful, awful. So while I was peeling the potatoes, I was watching her prepare a beef stew and I simply could not resist making one or two suggestions to her.'

'You were lucky you didn't get stabbed.'

'Oh, she wasn't happy at first. Nathalie has a lot of issues with anger. But I said, "Put the knife down, Nathalie! Just try coating the beef in flour! See what a difference it makes!" So she did put the knife down. Then she did what I said. So then I suggested adding some other ingredients and she ended up following the recipe for my famous artisan workhouse stew to the letter! You remember the one Delma and I cooked for all the street people the year I was looking for one of those Rehab People of the Year statuettes.'

'As if being homeless wasn't hord enough without having to eat your muck.'

She's an incredible cook. I'd never let her know that, though.

She goes, 'Well, everyone ate my workhouse stew. And there wasn't a word of conversation in the dining room.'

'Again, prison canteen.'

'They were all too busy enjoying it. There was one woman who said she imagined this was what it must be like to eat in a restaurant! So at bedtime –'

'Lights out.'

'– one of the assistants who works here –'

'Screws.'

'– came to me and said, "How would you like the job of Head Chef?"'

'How did that go down with – what was she called? – Nathalie?'

'Not well. She's in solitary confinement. Isn't it wonderful, Ross?'

'Shit for her. Great for you.'

'The attitude towards me in here has totally changed. These women smile now when they see me coming. They share their soft toilet paper with me. They pop in to see me and tell me their problems. I've no interest, naturally, but it's nice to feel loved again.'

'You seem happy. I'm accepting that.'

'Most of these women have never tasted good food before. I was telling Sorcha earlier. It's my responsibility to come up with a new menu every day. It's so exciting. These people are a blank canvas for me. Obviously, I'll have to be careful – there are a lot of things that could be too much of a shock to their system. I just feel I have a purpose in here at last. And it's all thanks to you, Ross.'

'Me? I didn't do anything.'

'You did. You told me to reach out.'

'That was only because I was sick listening to you focking moaning. I thought, yeah, no, I'll see can I outsource her misery to someone else.'

'And I just wanted to say thank you, Ross!'

So I'm back home in bed, flicking through the channels, looking for *Home and Away*, when I end up accidentally switching on the RTÉ lunchtime news. And the main headline is about my old man.

It's that dude Aengus Mac Grianna reading it, going, 'New Republic leader Charles O'Carroll-Kelly has reiterated his promise to build a wall around Cork if his party is involved in forming the next Government. Mr O'Carroll-Kelly announced plans for the wall last night in the middle of a heated television debate with Fianna Fáil leader Micheál Martin, who is himself from Cork. Samantha Libreri reports.'

I turn up the volume.

'We're going to build a wall!' Samantha Libreri goes. 'The words of New Republic leader Charles O'Carroll-Kelly during an often bad-tempered debate with Fianna Fáil's Micheál Martin on *Claire Byrne Live* last night. And, having had time to sleep on it, Charles O'Carroll-Kelly wasn't backing down on the threat this morning, despite claims by human rights groups that such a wall would be very expensive. In an interview with *RTÉ News*, Mr O'Carroll-Kelly said that, under a New Republic Government, Cork people wishing to migrate to Dublin and other parts of the country would be subject to extreme vetting procedures.'

Up comes the old man's face on the screen – his hair all over the shop. 'We are not anti Cork,' he goes, 'and I want to make that quite clear! What we *are* against is people from Cork who move to Dublin – and other parts of the country – and refuse to integrate and accept our way of life! We need to be grown-up enough as a society to at least have a conversation about this issue! Young people are leaving Cork for other places, especially Dublin, and they're becoming radicalized! They are conflicted between embracing our ways and their loyalty to their home city, which many of them – let's not dodge this – continue to regard as the true capital of Ireland! We cannot allow the general air of pessimism and disgruntlement that Cork people carry with them as baggage to imperil the happiness of the rest of the country!'

Samantha's there, 'However, his comments have been sharply criticized by several sitting TDs, including Minister for Defence Simon Coveney, a TD for Cork South-Central, who has called on Mr O'Carroll-Kelly to apologize.'

Up comes this Coveney dude, who I myself personally have never heard of. 'I think anyone who was born in Cork, or has Cork ancestry, will find what he said deeply offensive. Cork people don't leave their homes and move to Dublin and other parts of the country out of choice. They do it out of economic necessity. But let me say this, they have contributed in a very substantial and a very positive way to the economic, political, cultural and sporting life of not only Dublin, but of every city where they've been forced, for economic reasons, to make their home. Most Irish people understand this and in all parts of the country, there is – *I* think – a mutual respect for each other's traditions and way of life. This is a cynical attempt by a political party to try to drum up support by sowing discord and creating divisions where they don't exist. I'm happy to say I genuinely believe voters will be clever enough to see straight through it.'

Next, there's all this footage of people milling around what looks very much to me like Liffey Valley Shopping Centre.

'However, among these Dublin shoppers,' Samantha goes, 'there was a broad welcome for the idea of a wall.'

And then you see all these randomers going, 'I don't like Cork people. They don't mix and they've no respect for us or our ways.'

Or it's, 'They want this, they want that – they're never happy. Look at Roy Keane.'

Or it's, 'They bring misery wherever they go. Build the wall. By all means build it. I'd nearly pay for the Jaysusing thing meself.'

Ronan looks at me crooked. 'A pint?' he goes. 'It's not eeben lunch toyum, Rosser.'

Ah, UCD! It's all ahead of him! I'm there, 'You're a third-level student now, Ro – live a little.'

Speaking of which, I'm disappointed to see that the bor is pretty much *empty*?

'When I went here,' I go, sounding like the old fort that I possibly am, 'we were five- and six-deep at the bor trying to get served. That was at, like, one o'clock in the afternoon.'

I think the recession scared a lot of young people straight. There was a year or two there when this campus didn't even *have* a bor? I'd hate to think that the old traditions like being shit-faced in the middle of the day are being lost.

'Here, knock that back,' I go. 'It's not gonna drink itself.'

He isn't wearing his hoodie either, by the way.

He's there, 'The thing is, Rosser, I've a leckchudder at two, so I do.'

I laugh – no choice in the matter. I'm there, 'No one goes to lectures before Christmas. As a matter of fact, I never went to a single focking lecture the entire time I was here.'

He's there, 'You were doing a spowerts schodarship, Rosser.'

'Okay, that was uncalled for. The point I'm trying to make is that you shouldn't set the bor too high for yourself early on – and I mean that in every area of your life – because that's what people will expect of you all the time.'

He turns to the borman and goes, 'Hee-or, can I chayunge this for a Baddygowan?'

I grab the pint before he pushes it across the bor to him. 'Yeah, no, give him a Ballygowan,' I go, 'but leave the pint there. It won't go to waste – I can guarantee that!'

I have an idea then. 'I'll tell you what, Ro, if you're so anti the whole idea of spending your first day in UCD mullered, I could just give you a tour of the campus. Show you where everything is – including the famous Orts block. That's where you'll find most of the pretty girls. God, I went through that place like I don't know what – although the phrase "shit through a goose" comes to mind.'

He goes, 'Look, no offedence, Rosser, but I might go off by meself – do you know what I mee-un? Foyunt me owen way arowunt?'

I'm there, 'Er, yeah, no, fair enough.'

'I've a map I dowunloated off of the intodder net,' he goes, getting up off his stool. 'And like I says to you, Rosser, I've a leckchudder at two. I'll give you a bell later, reet?'

I'm like, 'Yeah, no, whatever,' trying not to sound *too* hurt? 'You do whatever the fock you want, Ro.'

So off he goes, leaving me on my Tobler. I stare at his drink, untouched, then I turn to the borman and I go, 'A Ballygowan, huh? Do they still call it a Bally-go-on, go-on, go-on?'

'I've never heard that before,' he goes.

'When I was in UCD, that was all anyone ever called it. "Can I have a Bally-go-on, go-on, go-on?" they'd say! God, it was funny. I was just trying to explain that to my son. The memories you have while you're here, they stay with you for the rest of your life. He's studying Law, just to mention.'

He goes, 'So, what, you decided to chaperone him on his first day in college, did you?'

I'm there, 'Yeah, no, I thought I'd show him where everything was – although the bor is as far as I ended up getting!'

He just nods. He's all of a sudden got, like, a *serious* expression on his face? I don't like it. He's there, 'I'm just thinking about how I would have felt if my old man had insisted on bringing me to college on my first day.'

I end up losing it with him. I'm there, 'Why don't you mind your own focking beeswax and pour me another pint?'

'You've already got a pint and a half in front of you.'

'Sorry, are we married or something?'

'No.'

'Then you don't get to count my drinks! And give me some change for the focking pool table.'

I slap a Caitlin Jenner down on the bor and he gives it back to me in shrapnel. I grab my – so what? – two and a half drinks and I tip over to the table. I rack up and grab a cue, then I stort potting balls, the old magic coming back to me pretty quickly.

Ronan wasn't embarrassed. I know my son. He was just keen to get to his first lecture, that's all. I'm not going to let that come between us.

I don't even feel the afternoon pass. There ends up being a lot of pool and a lot of pints. Then suddenly, I hear voices. Excited laughter. I look up and I notice that the bor is filling up with young people. It's a genuinely lovely thing to see. Teenagers getting pissed.

And that's when I spot Ronan. He's in the middle of this – *literally?* – gaggle of girls and they're laughing their heads off at something he's saying to them. He's telling them the story of the time when he was six years old and he went into the Bank of Ireland in Finglas and wrote on the back of one of the lodgement slips: 'I have a gun – give me everything in the safe or I'll shoot!' Then he stuck it back in the pile.

That actually happened. Some poor focker walked in to lodge money, filled in his details and passed the slip across the counter. The teller flipped it over and the next thing the dude knew the alorm was going off and he was being tackled to the ground, face-down, by a security gord. It's one of those cutesy kid stories that ends up getting told every time his old dear has a family occasion. Anyway, Ronan's dining out on it now. He's going, 'The poo-er fedda hadn't a bleaten clue what was going on! Thee ended up question idden him for torteen hours!'

And the birds are going, 'Oh! My God! You are *so* funny!'

He's got the definite gift of the gab. It has to be said, it's a lovely thing, as a parent, to see one of the qualities you genuinely love about yourself reflected back at you.

I'm about to tip over to introduce myself to his new friends, and that's the moment when suddenly Ronan cops me. He's obviously surprised to see me still sitting there in the bor. But then I suddenly realize that there's something more than just *surprise* in his face? It's, like, fear. His expression seems to say, 'Please, in the name of fock, don't come over here and ruin this for me!'

And that look, well, it slays me. Because I realize that the borman – even though he was a dick about it – was right. My son is all growed up and I have to accept that. I nod at Ronan and he nods back and this look of, like, understanding passes between us. In some ways, it's, like, goodbye – certainly goodbye to the old Ronan.

He's not a little kid anymore. Not that he ever really was. I knock back a full pint in two mouthfuls, pot the final black ball, then I push the bor of the emergency door and wobble across the campus in search of a taxi.

I pay the driver, then I get out and stagger up the path. Three o'clock in the afternoon and I'm struggling to put one foot in front of the other. I'm feeling incredibly – I want to say – *nostalgish* for my college days? At the same time, I'm remembering what happened to my rugby career.

I manage to get the key in the door at the seventh attempt, then into the gaff I go, already dreaming of a whizz, then bed. And that's when I notice the laundry scattered all over the hallway floor. The old man's suit jacket and trousers and then – Jesus, my stomach's doing somersaults here – his Y-fronts.

I stort kicking all the bits into the corner. There's also a navy skirt, a white blouse and a black bra and – I'm surprised at Helen – a black G-er. But then I also notice, in amongst the spilled laundry, two pairs of shoes, one belonging to a man and one belonging to a woman. And that's when I realize that it isn't laundry at all.

It's *his* voice I hear first? It's coming from the living room. 'That was absolutely first class!' he goes. 'Afternoon deluxe – isn't this what they call it? Inverted commas?'

Jesus Christ. Him and Helen are having sex in the living room in the middle of the focking day. The only thing that stops me from spewing right there on the maplewood floor is the fact that I don't want them to know I'm home. I don't have the skills to handle the conversation that would inevitably follow. So I decide to tiptoe upstairs as quietly as I possibly can.

But suddenly I can't move, as in I'm *literally* unable to put one foot in front of the other – and, for once, it has nothing to do with the amount of Amsterdamage I've put away. It's just that I'm staring at the G-er and it's as thin as the wire they use in Sheridans to cut those big blocks of cheddar and I'm thinking how out of character it seems for Helen to wear something like that.

And that's when I hear a woman's voice go, 'Hey, let's do it again!' and I realize straightaway that it isn't Helen.

The old man's like, 'What a wonderful idea! I shall look at my desk diary and see if I can't find an opening one afternoon next week!'

I wander over to the living-room door and I listen through it.

'I'm not talking about next week,' the woman goes, at the same time laughing. 'I'm talking about right now!'

I don't want to know anything about what's happening beyond the door. But there must be some small port of me that does because I end up grabbing the handle, then bursting into the room. The old man is sitting in his favourite ormchair. And straddling him, storkers like the day she was born, is the New Republic General Election candidate for Dublin Bay South.

They're shocked to see me – well, *he* is. He goes, 'What in the name of Hades –?' and he lifts Muirgheal off him and at the same time he stands up, so that I get a full view of him, we're talking full focking frontal, and he's wearing literally nothing except – in the name of fock! – that red tie that she bought him.

185

I'm there, 'Okay, what *is* this?' not wanting to believe the evidence of my eyes – suddenly knowing what it feels like to be Sorcha.

Muirgheal barely bats an eyelid. She just goes, 'Are you really that slow?'

He at least has the decency to be embarrassed about it? He's there, 'It's not what you think, Ross! What happened was we were, em, discussing my first cabinet as Taoiseach! Yes, that was it! And Muirgheal expressed an interest in the Deputy Leadership! Then it suddenly got very warm in here!'

I'm like, 'Dude, there's no excuse you can come up with that I haven't used a hundred times before.'

In other words, you can't shit a shitter.

He still tries to go, 'It's that bloody thermostat! You've heard me complain about it, haven't you, Ross?'

I'm thinking, I never had my old man down as a philanderer. I genuinely didn't think he had it in him.

I'm there, 'Is there any focking chance you could at least cover yourself up?'

He's like, 'Yes, of course!' and he reaches for a cushion – a focking cushion – which he holds in front of his nether bits, at least sparing me any more of that view.

I look at Muirgheal and I go, '*Let's do it again?* At his age? Yeah, you were focking dreaming if you thought that was going to happen.'

She just smiles at me with literally no shame. She reminds me of my old dear – she just doesn't have that particular gene.

And that's when I hear the front door open. The old man ends up nearly having a prolapse there in the living room. He's like, 'No! She's supposed to be playing bloody well tennis with Erika!'

And then – this is quite funny – he runs and hides behind the long curtains. Again, I've done it a thousand times myself.

Ten seconds later, Helen walks into the living room, going, 'What are all those clothes doing in the –?' And then she suddenly stops. Because she's looking at Muirgheal standing there in her raw with a big fock-you smile on her face.

Erika walks in, holding Amelie, and she's like, 'What the fock –?' and I'm talking about Erika, not Amelie.

Helen looks at me and goes, 'How dare you? This is my home – not some . . . knocking shop!'

Talk about giving a dog a bad name.

I'm there, 'For once, Helen, this isn't down to me.'

She goes, 'What are you talking about?'

And I hate doing it. I really do. But I go, 'Talk to your husband. He's hiding behind the curtains.'

He steps out from behind them, covering himself with the cushion, going, 'Oh, hello there, Helen!' actually trying to brazen it out. 'How's that famous backhand of yours these days?'

He's still wearing the red tie, by the way.

Helen just, like, bursts into tears. She's like, 'Charlie, pack your things.'

Muirgheal's like, 'Okay, I can see you've got things to talk about . . .'

The next thing that happens is that Erika hands Amelie to Helen, then races across the room and grabs Muirgheal by the hair. She drags her – literally screaming and scratching – to the front door and focks her out into the gorden, still totally naked.

Ailesbury Road, bear in mind.

The old man's still trying to talk his way out of it. He goes, 'We were discussing front bench positions and the bloody heat, Helen – well, you've said it yourself, it's like Tahiti at times!'

Helen's like, 'Don't you think you've hurt me enough, Charlie, without compounding it by treating me like a fool?'

He suddenly can't look at her. He's there, 'Helen, I'm sorry!'

She goes, 'I'm sorry, too. Pack your things and go.'

And that's when Erika – who's arrived back in the room – goes, 'You as well, Ross.'

I'm like, 'Me? I didn't do anything wrong. In fact, I'm standing here thinking how great it feels that I'm not the one who's been caught in the act for once.'

Erika goes, 'Ross, this isn't your home. And it's not yours anymore either . . . *Dad*. Get the fock out – both of you.'

6. *Transition Year*

The old gaff smells of something. It could be just damp. It hasn't been lived in for months. But then it's not *just* damp? It also smells of – this could be my mind playing tricks on me – but death. Five and a half months ago, a man died in this house, possibly murdered by my old dear. And now me and the old man are back living here.

I open the fridge. There's, like, meat in there, which smells like a corpse, and vegetables in the crisper that have turned literally black. The old man doesn't seem to care about the state of the place. He's just, like, walking around the living room, looking at old stuff.

'It's kind of missing a woman's touch,' I go. 'And I don't mean that in a sexist way. Even though I probably do. I should ask Sorcha for Brandusa's number. She's an unbelievable cleaner – very thorough – and we found out that she wasn't stealing from us after all.'

He goes, 'God, we had some happy times in this house, didn't we? You, me, and your mother!'

I'm like, 'Speak for yourself. I hated every focking day of it. Would you not just apologize to Helen, then we can all move back to Ailesbury Road?'

'It's too late for that, Ross!'

'She was the best thing about you. What the fock were you thinking?'

'I think it's clear I *wasn't* thinking! I think popularity may have gone to my head somewhat! It was just, well, I commissioned a private poll that showed there was considerable support out there for my wall idea – sixty-two percent of people think it's a good idea, Ross, despite your godfather's fears that Charles O'Carroll-Kelly had finally gone and put his bloody well foot in it! Well, I was a bit giddy with the excitement of it and then young Muirgheal asked if I'd considered appointing a Deputy Leader yet! And, well, one thing sort of led to the other!'

'I'm stunned that anything you just said could have led to "the other". Why can't you just admit it? You haven't had one good day since you put that thing on your focking head. Now you've lost everything – your wife, your daughter, your home.'

'*Vitam regit fortuna, non sapientia*, Kicker!'

My phone rings. I can see from the screen that it's, like, Christian. He's obviously heard. I can't believe that it's me cleaning up the old man's mess for once. I'm like, 'How the fock am I supposed to explain this to her supposed boyfriend?'

I answer.

Christian goes, 'Is it true?'

I'm like, 'Is what true? What have you heard?' because it always pays to find out first. It might not even be what you think.

He goes, 'What Erika just told me – about your old man and Muirgheal?'

I'm like, 'Yeah, no, I walked in on them. Well, we knew she was ambitious.'

'I thought it had to be a mistake. I said to Erika, "There's no way in this world that Charles would ride Muirgheal. It must have been Ross."'

'Yeah, thanks for that, Christian. You're a real mate.'

'She said no, it was him. For fock's sake, Ross, I really liked her.'

I stare my old man out of it. He's fiddling with the clock on the mantelpiece – fixing the time.

I'm there, 'Yeah, Christian, I know you really liked her.'

The old man goes, 'I think it was Isaac Newton who said, *Amicus Plato, Amicus Aristoteles, magis amica veritas!*'

I'm there, 'Did you hear that, Christian?'

He's like, 'Yeah.'

I go, 'Did it come as any consolation to you?'

And he's like, 'No, it didn't. I need to focking talk to her,' and he just hangs up on me.

I can't even bear to be in the same room as the old man. So I step out into the hallway and I head for the kitchen. But then I stop as I'm passing the door that leads down to the basement. I haven't been down there since Ari died.

I stare at the door for a good, like, thirty seconds. Then – I don't *know* why? – I give it a shove with my hand. It opens with a creak. I stand at the top of the stairs, looking down. I've got pretty much goosebumps.

I reach for the switch and I turn on the light. Then I stort walking down the stairs, very, very slowly, seeing the room bit by bit.

Oh, holy shit, there's actual scene of crime tape everywhere – we're talking yellow-and-black tape that's been used to rope off an area in the middle of the room, where the old dear's treadmill used to be but isn't anymore. They must have removed it as evidence.

I think to myself, we're some focking family.

Then I see something that – oh . . . holy . . . shit . . . – chills me to the bone. There's the chalk outline of a body on the floor, which must have been where Ari hit the deck after having his hort attack. Or was it where she dragged him, already dead, then went back upstairs and knocked back a glass of Stoli before phoning for an ambulance?

'He turns on the afterburners!' a voice suddenly goes.

Jesus Christ! I get such a fright that I end up practically levitating.

'He turns on the afterburners!'

It's Ryle Nugent's voice. I forgot I changed my ringtone.

'He turns on the afterburners!'

I answer. Then I end up getting another fright because it ends up being *her* – as in, my old dear?

She goes, 'Ross? Where are you?'

And I'm suddenly shitting myself because I'm thinking, does she actually know? Can she somehow see me? Then I think, yeah, no, that's ridiculous.

She goes, 'Can you hear me?'

I'm like, 'Er, yeah, no, I'm in Foxrock. I'm back in the old gaff.'

'Oh?'

'Helen focked us out. The old man had sex with Christian's girlfriend. She's, like, my age!'

She takes this surprisingly in her stride. 'How terribly unfortunate!' she goes. 'How terribly unfortunate for everyone involved!'

I'll say it again. It's a focking miracle that I'm so normal.

She actually changes the subject then. She goes, 'Well, *I* have some wonderful, wonderful news.'

I'm there, 'You're focking unbelievable. Go on, I'm listening.'

'I'm going to do the Nigella Christmas for the girls in here!'

'Er, it's October.'

'Well, as Nigella says, it's all in the planning.'

'The Nigella Christmas, though? Are you sure they can eat shit like that? Would the rich food not kill them?'

'Spiced and super-juicy roast turkey with allspice gravy, redder than red cranberry sauce and four types of stuffing! Ham glazed with Coca-Cola! Potatoes roasted in goose fat with a dusting of semolina! Maple roast parsnips and Christmas sprouts! To be followed by Nigella's famous Ultimate Christmas Pudding!'

'If you definitely think it's safe.'

Her voice drops in volume. 'But I need you to do something for me,' she goes.

I'm like, 'I don't like the sound of this.'

'There's some ingredients that I can't get in here. Star anise, for instance, for the turkey. They've never heard of it before.'

'Could you not just explain to them what it is? Or could they even just Google it?'

'They're suspicious of everything. If you ask for a new ingredient in the kitchen, they presume you want it for what they call a legal high.'

'You can't get high on star anise, can you?'

'No.'

'If anyone would know that, it's you – you focking addict.'

'They won't let me have cherry brandy either –'

'I wouldn't blame them.'

'– for the cranberry sauce.'

'So what's this favour you want me to do?'

'I want you to smuggle them in for me.'

'Excuse me?'

'Oh, they do it all the time in here, Ross. Drugs. Mobile phones. All sorts. Could you bring me in some star anise, a bottle of cherry brandy and some panettone for the stuffing?'

'And how am I supposed to smuggle that lot in?'

'That son of yours might have one or two ideas.'

'Ronan?'

'Well, he's the type, isn't he?'

'That's pretty insulting actually. But yeah, no, I'll ask him.'

There's, like, ten seconds of silence then. As a matter of fact, I'm actually beginning to wonder has she run out of coins for the phone when all of a sudden, out of the blue, she goes, 'Some relationships are just for a particular time, Ross.'

I'm like, 'What are you talking about?'

'I'm saying your father is changing. He's becoming someone else. He's not the man that Helen loved anymore. It happens to people.'

'That's deep. For you.'

'Your father is a leader, Ross. He's finally doing what he was born to do. Helen would have only held him back . . . Don't spend too long down in that basement, Ross.'

I swear to fock, I end up nearly jumping out of my skin. I'm thinking, holy shit, *can* she see me?

I'm there, 'How did you know I was in the basement?'

She goes, 'The signal keeps going in and out. You shouldn't be down there. You'll only upset yourself.'

'They never cleaned up. The Feds, I mean. They left tape everywhere. And a chalk mork in the shape of –'

'– Ari's body.'

'I wasn't going to say it, but yeah.'

She doesn't really say anything after that except, 'Ableforth's is the best cherry brandy. They'll have it in Mitchell's,' and then the pips go and she gets cut off.

It's, like, Saturday afternoon on Hallowe'en weekend.

Me and Honor are sitting on the end of her bed playing – believe it or not – *Call of Duty: Advanced Warfare* on my old Xbox. She's only recently gotten into it, even though she used to think it was – and I quote – lame.

Again, I think, it's her trying to connect with me.

The boys are doing their usual thing. They're toddling around the floor with their soccer cords spread all around. Johnny's going, 'Me have Azpilicueta! Me have Azpilicueta!'

I'm just totally blanking them, although every so often, when they're not looking, I grab a handful of the cords and stick them in the focking bin.

I'm there, 'I heard the manny moved out?'

I was talking to Christian, the poor focker – between my old man riding his girlfriend and me riding his mother, it's a wonder he hasn't murdered one of us – and he said Magnus and Oisinn had moved in together. An aportment somewhere down around Grand Canal Dock.

She goes, 'Yeah, he moved out, like, two days ago?'

I'm there, 'Do you miss him?'

'Not really. He was all, "Honor, I musht tell you, I don't like very much the way you are shwearing at me."'

'That's a good impression. That's a very good impression. I can't believe Fionn is downstairs again. He practically lives here these days.'

I hate using her for information. It's important that I know everything, though.

Honor goes, 'Yeah, no, *he's* just trying to push the two of them together.'

I'm like, 'Who?'

'Her focking dickhead of a dad. There's a zombie! Kill him! Kill him! Kill him!'

Except I don't kill him. *He* ends up killing *me*? I hand Honor the controls. 'Take it,' I go. 'You're much better at this game than me. When you say he's trying to push them together –'

'He keeps telling her how much she has in common with him,' she goes. 'He's all, "You have the same values. You think the same politically. You have many of the same interests, including advocacy."'

I actually laugh. I'm there, 'Advocacy? Okay, when has that ever done it for a girl? I think deep down the man is still terrified that she's going to slip back into her old bad habits – namely me.'

'I hate him.'

'I hate him, too.'

'The other day, I heard him say that he couldn't help but wonder what her life might have been like if she'd got together with Fionn all those years ago.'

'He actually said that?'

'I was listening at the door.'

'And what did she say back to him?'

'She was like, "But then I wouldn't have had Honor and the boys!" and he was like, "Would that really have been such a bad thing?"'

She's going on a rampage here, killing every single focker in sight.

I'm like, 'What a thing to say!'

She goes, 'I got him back later on. He told me to put my dinner plate in the dishwasher and I said, "Why don't you go sit on your thumb, you fock-knuckle?"'

'Fock-knuckle! Brilliant expression, Honor.'

'Mic drop!'

'Mic drop is right!'

'And now he wants me to change my name.'

'Excuse me?'

'Mom's gone back to using her maiden name.'

'I'm aware of that.'

'And *he* wants *me* to be Honor Lalor. He said it'd be simpler all round if we all had the same.'

'I hope you told him to fock off.'

'I did. I was like, *"I'm* an O'Carroll-Kelly! I'm nothing like your focking family, you focking stain! You focking prick with ears."'

'You were well within your rights, Honor.'

'But then *she* rang Mount Anville and said they had to stort calling me Lalor.'

It kills me. It seriously, seriously kills me.

'Look,' I go, 'you'll always be an O'Carroll-Kelly, Honor, no matter what name they try to put on you.'

She puts her head on my shoulder while at the same time continuing to massacre every focker within shooting range. She goes, 'I *know* I will?'

Sorcha's old man bursts in at exactly two o'clock. 'Time's up!' he goes. Then he looks at Honor and he's like, 'Will you take that ridiculous hat off indoors?'

She's got her beanie on.

She's like, 'Yeah, why don't you go and swivel, you focking piece of shit?'

I laugh. She's not scared of anyone. It's a lovely thing to see in a child.

He focks off and I give Honor a hug to say goodbye. I'm there, 'I meant what I said, Honor. You'll always be an O'Carroll-Kelly – and that's something to be definitely proud of.'

'Me want Harry Kane!' Leo goes.

The boys are definitely Lalors, by the way. That should have been obvious from the moment I watched them try to play rugby.

I tip downstairs. Then I decide, fock it, I'm going to say something to Sorcha about her forcing Honor to drop my name. I wander down to the study and I listen at the door for a minute. She's in there with Fionn and they're discussing – of all things – my old man riding Muirgheal.

'He's just appointed her the Deputy Leader of New Republic,' Fionn goes. 'I suppose having sex with Charles was a price she was prepared to pay. I wish you'd let me put the phrase "the blind leading the blonde" out there in the public domain.'

'I really don't want to go negative,' Sorcha goes. 'Look, all Chorles and Muirgheal have done is connect with people's disillusionment with big bureaucracy and their frustration that the recovery isn't happening quickly enough for them. People love to vent, especially when they're talking to people carrying out opinion polls. But I actually trust them to act responsibly when they walk into the actual polling booth.'

'I think you're right. Charles and Muirgheal, though! I still can't get a visual on it – which is probably not a bad thing. I actually didn't think *he* was the philandering type.'

Sorcha goes, 'Well, as my dad said, like father, like son – as in, maybe that's where Ross gets it from?'

I think about pushing the door and having a go at Sorcha over the whole Honor Lalor thing and then at him for slagging off my old man. But then I think to myself, what would it actually achieve? And instead I fock off home.

So I'm in bed, enjoying a nice lie-in, when I'm suddenly awoken by the sound of my phone ringing. I reach for it. It ends up being Shadden. So I answer.

I'm like, 'Hey, Shadden! It's very early, isn't it?'

She's there, 'It's eleven o'clock in the morden.'

That's what I focking meant. I can hear Rihanna-Brogan crying in the background. It's a bit annoying.

I'm there, 'How the hell are you?' trying to let on that I'm less pissed off than I actually am. I'm such a people pleaser.

She's like, 'Ine grant. C'mere, is Ronan theer wit you?'

I'm like, 'What are you talking about?'

'He sted in yoo-er house last neet, ditn't he – arthur some Haddowe'en peerty?'

'Er, yeah, no, he did. But he, er, went off to college first thing.'

'He idn't ansorden he's pho-un.'

'I think he said he had a lecture. For some reason, I'm thinking of the word Jurisprudence.'

'If you see him, ted him Ine looking fordum, will you?' Then she hangs up.

I hop out of bed, throw on my clothes and I point the cor in the direction of Belfield. Fifteen minutes later, I spot him, walking across the main cor pork – he's actually just about to get into his GTI. I give him a blast of the horn and he turns around and looks at me aggressively, which is Ronan's standard MO until he knows who's actually beeping at him. He sees that it's me and he wanders over to where I'm porked. He goes, 'What the fook are you doing hee-or?'

Yeah, a lovely way to speak to your old man.

I'm there, 'I just wanted to see how college was going? I haven't seen you in weeks.'

I stay sitting in *my* cor, just talking to him through the window.

He goes, 'Could you not have joost reng me, Rosser?'

Seriously, this kid has got more front than Christina Hendricks.

I'm like, 'Yeah, no, I've been trying to phone you all morning, but there was no actual answer. You must have been in a lecture, were you?'

He goes, 'Er, yeah, that's reet, Rosser – I was, er, in a leckchudder, yeah.'

I don't want to frighten him off, so I decide to just keep the conversation casual. 'Here,' I go, 'what's the best way to smuggle stuff illegally into a prison?'

He's like, 'Who's aston?'

'*I'm* asking. It's for my old dear.'

'Gin, is it?'

How well he knows his grandmother!

I'm there, 'No, it's not gin – unbelievably. It's actually a few bits and pieces for a Nigella Christmas dinner.'

He's like, 'Best way is in a nappy, Rosser. Thee doatunt check in nappies. You can smuggle in all sorts that way.'

I'm there, 'Yeah, no, thanks for that information, Ro – it's good for me to have,' and then I very, very casually go, 'So . . . are they the same clothes you were wearing yesterday?'

He goes, 'Soddy?'

He's got a big guilty face on him.

I'm there, 'Yeah, no, I just saw a photograph of you on Instagram – out drinking with your college mates last night. A Hallowe'en porty, wasn't it? I could have sworn you were wearing those same jeans and that same top.'

He's like, 'What are you, a copper now?'

'It was just an observation.'

'It's like *thalken* to a copper. If you moost know, I was in a huddy this morden – rudding late, so I was – so I just grapped the neardest clowiths to me.'

'That would explain it then.'

'Ine tedding you that's what happent.'

'Good. Because I did wonder for a minute whether you might have – oh, I don't know – scored some young one and stayed out all night?'

'Rosser, I hab a geerlfriend and a kid at home.'

'Hey, I had a wife and four kids at home and I still did alright for myself.'

'Well, that's a lesson for you, Rosser – doatunt judge evoddy one by yisser own stanthorts.'

'It was just the fact that, like I said, you're wearing the same threads as you were wearing yesterday. And also the fact that Shadden rang me an hour ago to ask if it was true that you stayed with us last night.'

Ronan's mouth is suddenly flapping around like a focked umbrella in a gale. He's like, 'Wh . . . wh . . . wh . . . what did you say to her, Rosser?' and there's, like, *panic* in his voice?

'Don't worry,' I go, 'I covered for you. I told her you stayed over in Foxrock.'

'Did she belieb you?'

'Of course she believed me. When it comes to lying to women, I'm a professional. Just give me a heads-up the next time. She kind of blindsided me. I hadn't a focking clue what she was talking about at first.'

'There woatunt be a next toyum, Rosser. It was a wood-off.'

Ah, that old lie. What he did is obviously eating him up inside. 'Ro,' I go, 'guilt is like a hangover. It lasts forty-eight hours – absolute max.'

It doesn't seem to cheer him up at all.

He's there, 'I did the doort, Rosser. The foorst time ebber – I did the doort on Shadden.'

'And I know you're not ready to hear it,' I go, 'but I'm saying don't be too hord on yourself. If I have one regret in my life – obviously *non* rugby related? – it's that I should have ridden more women. And I rode loads. So was she nice?'

'Who?'

'This bird you cheated on Shadden with – I'd say she's a total lasher, is she?'

'She was alreet, yeah. Her nayum's Josephine.'

'Josephine? Jesus, she sounds like she might be a –'

'She's from Galtway.'

'Galway? Am I hearing that right?'

'Galtway, yeah.'

'And she's up here studying, what, I'm presuming Agricultural Science?'

'She's doing Eerts, Rosser.'

'Orts? Fair enough. I don't know why I said Agricultural Science. Probably prejudice.'

He storts getting a bit upset then. He's suddenly kicking my tyres, going, 'I caddent belieb what Ine arthur doing, Rosser. Poo-er Shadden.'

In a way, I feel *equally* guilty? Because something is suddenly very clear to me. Ronan didn't inherit my brains – luckily for him. He didn't inherit my looks either – you can't have everything. But the urge to do the dirt might be the only thing I did pass on to him – just as my old man clearly passed it on to me.

'You can't help it,' I go. 'I'm talking about cheating.'

He's like, 'What are you bleaten on about?'

'Sorcha was actually right. Look at you, look at me, look at your grandfather. We're helpless slaves to it, Ro. The temptation to stray is in our genes. It's passed down from one generation to the next. Like rugby.'

'I doatunt belieb that.'

'Trust me,' I go, 'you're just the latest in a long line of Kelly family dirtbags.'

I'm suddenly remembering him that night in The Broken Orms and the way he was staring at Buckets of Blood's niece and her Porky Pigs. But he storts absolutely *ripping* into me then? He's there, 'Mebbe I doatunt *want* to turden out like yous! Mebbe I doatunt want to be a liar and cheat – and end up on me owen like you and me grandda. Hab you fooken thought about that?'

'Hey,' I go, 'you were the one who was up all night riding Peigín Leitir Móir.'

Again, it doesn't come as any consolation to him. He just turns around and walks back to his cor, his two shoulders slumped. He'll hopefully come to accept who he is in time, just like I very quickly did. But I'm worried about him. Guilt – especially if you're not used to it – can make a man do silly things. Like confess. Or buy a ridiculously expensive present that straightaway arouses suspicion.

So when he drives off, I send him a text, just going, 'Keep the head, Ro. Don't do anything stupid.'

*

The last Friday in November is traditionally the night we sit down as a family and write the children's Santa Lists. So Sorcha has given me special permission to be here, even though her old man is insisting that it will have to be *instead* of my hour with the children tomorrow, rather than as *well* as? He really is a focktard of the highest order.

Honor is delighted to see me, though. Throws her orms around me and everything. She's put on weight, by the way. That's not me being a wanker. I'm just calling it as I see it.

Sorcha opens her A4 pad on a clean page, pen at the ready. 'Okay,' she goes, 'boys, do you know what you want from Santa?'

'Footbaw!' Leo goes. 'Footbaw! Footbaw! Footbaw!'

Sorcha's there, 'A football? Is that what you want Santa to bring you?'

I'm like, 'They're not getting a football. End of conversation.'

'If they want a football, Ross, they can have a football.'

'Juan Mata!' Brian goes. 'Juan Mata!'

'Juan Mata? Okay, let's find out what team he plays for?'

She Googles the focker on her phone. 'He plays for Manchester,' she goes. 'Hold on, there's two Manchesters. Okay, why is there a Manchester United *and* a Manchester City?'

I'm there, 'Why is there either? That'd be my question.'

'Okay, Juan Mata plays for Manchester United, it seems. Is that what you want, Brian? Do you want a Manchester United Soccer Club strip?'

'Just don't let him go outside that door wearing it, Sorcha. This is still Killiney. Can we maybe do Honor's list? Just to get off the subject of soccer?'

Honor has a folder in front of her, stuffed with photographs cut from fashion magazines. She's very much on top of things. 'Okay,' she goes, 'I want everything in this photograph. As in, like, the whole look?'

She pushes it across the table at us. It's a picture of Samantha Ronson. Sorcha looks suddenly confused. She actually flips it over, thinking she must be looking at the wrong side. She's wearing, like, a black leather biker jacket over a jumper with black-and-white horizontal stripes, then skinny black jeans, black Hi Top Converse and – to top it all off – a black fedora. Samantha Ronson, not Sorcha.

I'm there, 'Do you want the hat as well, Honor?'

She's like, 'Everything.'

Sorcha pulls a face. She goes, 'Do you not think it's a bit . . .'

'What?' Honor goes.

'I was just going to say that horizontal stripes aren't, like, *super*-flattering?'

Honor just shrugs. She goes, 'I think she looks great.'

'Horizontal stripes aren't slimming is what I mean.'

'I don't care about being slim.'

I mentioned that – she's turning into a bit of a porker.

'But Hi Top Converse,' Sorcha goes, 'are so ugly. Why don't you get the ladies' shoe Converse? I have them in white and I have them in navy and they're – oh my God – *so* pretty.'

'Because I don't want them,' Honor goes. 'I want what's in that focking picture, okay?'

'Okay, okay. Oh my God, Honor!'

I'm there, 'I think that hat is really cool, Honor. I think it's a great look and that's not me sucking up to you.'

It *is* me sucking up to her. I don't want her to turn her anger from Sorcha to me.

She pulls another photograph from her folder. She goes, 'And I want this as well – again, everything.'

It's Leisha Hailey wearing a man's corduroy suit in brown, with a tan-coloured waistcoat underneath, then chunky white basketball runners. Then she whips out another photograph of – okay, I know *way* too many celebrities – Charlene Borja, who's wearing a grey Guns N' Roses t-shirt, with a black leather tie, black skinny jeans and white Vans.

'Not more Vans,' Sorcha goes. 'There are so many prettier shoes out there, Honor. Will we go on Net-a-Porter and see what's on trend at the moment?'

Honor ends up totally flipping. 'Why are you always trying to dress me?' she goes.

Sorcha's there, 'I'm not trying to dress you, Honor. I'm just trying to guide you. I used to be in fashion retail, remember?'

'Well, I'm not a little kid anymore. I want to wear what I want to wear, not what you want me to wear!'

She stands up from the table. She goes, 'This is such a waste of focking time. I'll e-mail you a list of what I want and links to the websites where you can buy them.'

'Yeah,' I go, 'and we'll send those links on to Santa Claus.'

She's like, 'Yeah, whatever!' and out of the kitchen and up the stairs she goes.

'Christian Benteke!' Brian goes and I'm thinking, yeah, shut the fock up.

Sorcha looks sad. She's there, 'I suppose I do have to accept that she has her own sense of style, even if it's not necessarily what I'd choose for her? And, also, I don't think she's making the most of what she has.'

Which isn't very much – that's what she's implying.

'But,' she goes, 'if those are the kind of clothes she wants to wear, then who am I to tell her that she should be looking at the way the likes of Kiernan Shipka dresses. Or even Hailee Steinfeld.'

I stand up from the table. I'm there, 'Maybe I should go and see if she's okay.'

'She'll be fine,' she goes. 'She'll be watching that prison thing she loves.'

I'm like, 'Hey, speaking of which, would you mind – again, I know it's outside of the whole supervised *access* thing? – if I took the kids in to see the old dear next week? Just for Christmas.'

She sighs. She's there, 'I was going to bring them in myself, but I've just been so busy. I'm about to open an actual constituency office in Donnybrook village. Fionn thinks the election is going to be called for the end of February.'

'Is that a yes then?'

'Well, I don't think it'd be fair for Fionnuala not to see her grandchildren at Christmas. Okay, then. I'll talk to my dad.'

As I go to leave the kitchen, Sorcha goes, 'By the way, how's Ronan getting on in college?'

I'm like, 'Yeah, no, he seems to be enjoying it. Especially the social side of things.'

'What do you mean?'

'Shadden rang me the other morning to say he didn't come home the night before. I overheard you and Fionn saying the philandering thing might be genetic. I'm beginning to think you were actually right.'

She goes, 'Don't be ridiculous. Ronan is nothing like you.'

The old dear looks . . . happy.

See, I could have said anything there. I could have said she looks like one of the Famine Memorial statues came to life. Or if Twink had dysentry.

And even though she looks like both of those things, I'm just going to say 'happy' and leave it at that.

She's bouncing Leo up and down on her knee. I think she's trying to see if there's another bottle of cherry brandy in his nappy. The focking lush.

'Careful,' I go, 'you'll give him whiplash.'

She's there, 'Sorry. You just put one bottle in there, did you?'

'One bottle was all you asked for.'

'Yes, of course. One should be sufficient. What's that thing he keeps saying, by the way?'

'I'm pretty sure it's Theo Walcott. Don't ask. Genuinely, don't ask.'

'Well, thank you again for everything.'

She's got the brandy out of Leo's nappy, the star anise out of Brian's and the panettone from Johnny's, although I had to break that up into little pieces and put it into eight ziplock bags.

It actually *looked* like drugs?

'I should have asked you to bring chestnuts,' she goes, 'for the sprouts.'

I'm there, 'I honestly don't know why people bother with sprouts. Or any vegetable that has to be fried in butter with bacon just to take the taste away. Actually, curly kale is another one. Remember we used to have it at Hallowe'en? Any food where you have to stick a cash incentive inside it to get people to eat the focking thing should never have been taken out of the ground in the first place.'

I go to take Leo back from her, except she goes, 'Leave him with me, Ross.'

I'm there, 'I already told you there's not another bottle in there. You don't believe me?'

'I know there's not another bottle in there. I'm just enjoying holding him.'

And she actually *seems* to be? She's stroking his little cheek with her finger. 'I used to do this to you as a baby,' she goes.

I'm like, 'Me? I didn't think we had any moments like that.'

'There were lots of moments, Ross. You just don't remember them. It used to send you off to sleep.'

It's news to me. That's all I'm saying.

Honor comes back from the vending machine with seven or eight bags of Hunky Dorys and puts them down on the table. She goes, 'It's kind of like *Orange is the New Black* in here – except the women are all skanks.'

I'm there, 'That's a good analysis, Honor. Again, maybe keep your voice down, though.'

'Except for you, Fionnuala. You're kind of the Piper Chapman of Mountjoy Women's Jail. She's the only one who *isn't* a knacker?'

'How lovely!' the old dear goes. 'Thank you, Honor!'

'You're more of a bitch, which I love. You're posh like Piper, but a bitch like Alex.'

Then she storts horsing into the Hunky Dorys.

'Well,' the old dear goes, 'I shall take it as a compliment,' and she smiles at me then. She goes, 'How's your father coping?'

I'm there, 'He's pretending it doesn't bother him. Helen was the best thing that ever happened to him. No offence.'

'And what about the girl?'

'Muirgheal?'

'Yes – are they still . . .'

'Yeah, he wishes! She's *my* age. That was a one-off. She gave him a little taste just so he'd make her his Deputy Leader. The one I feel sorry for is Christian. He got royally focked over by her.'

She smiles.

She goes, 'It's lovely to think of you and your father back in the house in Foxrock. I wish I was there with you. It'd be just like old times. When we were all together. When we were all happy.'

I'm watching her still stroking little Leo's cheek. I can see that his little eyes are getting heavy and I suddenly have this flash of memory – it could even be false memory – but it's me sitting on my old dear's lap and her sending me off to sleep in exactly the same way.

'If it's the last thing I do,' I hear myself suddenly go, 'I'm going to prove your innocence.'

She smiles. She has a face like clown sick.

'Are you really?' she goes.

And I'm there, 'Maybe not literally. It was more of an, I don't know, figure of speech.'

So it's, like, three days before Christmas and I'm on my way to Kielys for a few cheeky lunchtime pints with JP. Hook, Lyon and Sinker finished up today and we're both *dying* to go on the serious tear.

I'm passing through Donnybrook in the back of a taxi when I see it. I turn around to the driver and I go, 'Stop the cor, will you?'

I pay him and I get out. I'm suddenly staring across the road at this, like, shop premises – next-door to Hair Club on the actual Donnybrook Road. It's Sorcha's constituency office slash clinic slash whatever you want to call it.

There's a massive photograph of her in the window, looking concerned, which is a good look for her. Then it says, 'Sorcha Lalor!' in humungous letters. 'A Strong, Independent Voice for the people of Dublin Bay South!'

I cross over the road to get a better look at it and that ends up being my big mistake. Because Sorcha is actually in there. I spot her sitting at her desk, tapping away at the keys of her MacBook, while Honor is sitting opposite her, staring at her phone, wearing an expression that I like to call Resting Bitch Face.

Honor looks up in time to see me tipping past the door. Her face lights up. I put my finger to my lips because Sorcha – like most women – never liked the idea of me ever properly relaxing. Whenever she saw me settling down to a few drinks, she'd always try to come up with little jobs for me to do, as if I only drank for the want of something to do rather than the sheer pleasure of being totally wankered drunk.

I've almost cleared the front of the place when she suddenly looks up and sees me. She goes, 'Ross?', her brain already trying to come up with some chore for me to pass the afternoon. I try to ignore her, except she runs to the door and storts shouting up the street after me. 'Ross? Ross? Ross? Ross?' to the point where I can no longer ignore it.

So I end up having to turn around and go back to her. I'm there, 'Hey, Sorcha. I didn't hear you. I'm just on my way to meet –'

'Can you do me a favour?' she goes. 'Can you take Honor to the hairdresser's for her Christmas cut?'

I'm like, 'Er, I'm not supposed to *have* unsupervised access to our children,' and I hate having to make that argument just so I can enjoy a pint in peace. 'Honor nearly broke another kid's neck the last time I was left alone with her. I can't be trusted. I think I've proven that.'

'This is a one-off, Ross. I've been asked to speak at a meeting of the National Association for the Advancement of Lady Theatre People.'

'Who?'

'It's a new advocacy group campaigning for gender equality in the orts and more strong and independent female characters in leading roles, especially in theatre. I wouldn't ask if it wasn't an emergency. I'd ask my mom and dad, but they've taken the boys down to Christmas Island in Rathdrum.'

I'm like, 'The thing is, Sorcha, I've got this important meeting with JP – to discuss, er . . . *Come on, brain –*'

'Ross,' she goes, 'I'm asking you to do this as a favour to me. You said you wanted to prove yourself in terms of deserving increased access going forward.'

'I'm not sure that that's how I *phrased* it?'

'If you did this, it would prove to a lot of people, including my dad, that you *are* capable of behaving like a responsible parent. Please, Ross. This is – Oh! My God! – a really, really important issue for me to be seen to be involved with. I'm going to suggest arranging a morch on the actual Dáil.'

I end up just giving in. Sorcha locks up the constituency office and heads off in her cor, leaving me and Honor standing on the side of the road.

Honor goes, 'Why don't you just go to Kielys?'

I'm there, 'I promised I'd bring you for this famous haircut, which is going to take half the focking day, I'm sure.'

'I *could* just go to the borber's.'

'What? Really?'

'The hairdresser's takes, like, three and a half hours. If you go the borber's, you're in and out in, like, ten minutes.'

'That's what I always think.'

'There's a borber's next-door to Kielys, isn't there?'

'What, Bren's? Too focking right there is. That's where a lot of the Leinster goys go to get their hair cut. It's where Sean O'Brien once gave me a high-five. Unprompted. Didn't say a word either. Didn't need to. He just hung it up there – high-five – then we both went on our way.'

'Why don't you just go to Kielys? I can go and get my hair cut by myself.'

All I can do is smile at her. She is going to make someone an unbelievable wife one day. Although this whole – I think it's a word – *reasonableness* thing will probably be knocked out of her in her teens. But for now she's talking sense. So I do exactly what she suggests.

Kielys is rammers. It looks like it's not only Hook, Lyon and Sinker who finished up for Christmas today. I manage to find JP and his work crowd. He's already a good three pints down the road. He puts his orm around me and goes, 'Here he is! The man! The legend!'

It's all nice stuff for me to hear, even though he's leathered.

I'm there, 'Jesus, you're tanning it, aren't you?'

He goes, 'We've had an unbelievable year, Ross. Un-focking-believable! We're the official agents for Beach Cove in Ballycanew.

Eight years ago, it was a ghost estate. Last week, they were queuing overnight, Ross – *overnight*, do you remember those days? – to put deposits down!'

I'm about to say fair focks when my old man's face suddenly pops up on the TV in the corner. Again, it's the news. I turn around to Mary and I go, 'Here, turn up the volume, will you?' which she does before pulling a pint for me.

The reporter – it's Mortina Fitzgerald this time – goes, 'Gardaí are investigating whether comments by New Republic leader Charles O'Carroll-Kelly about Cork might constitute incitement to hatred. A spokesman confirmed that they had received more than two hundred complaints following a series of interviews in which Mr O'Carroll-Kelly promised to build a wall around the city to regulate the movement of its people to Dublin and other parts of the country. The spokesman said they would be preparing a file for the Director of Public Prosecutions to decide whether or not to initiate criminal proceedings.

'Charles O'Carroll-Kelly was unrepentant today. In one of a series of angry messages posted on the social networking site Twitter, he wrote, "Investigation is a SMOKESCREEN. This is being driven by FIANNA FAILING and its Cork-born leader who are TERRIFIED of our movement!" followed several minutes later by "Open migration between Cork and Dublin has FAILED! We cannot allow our compassion to overrule our common sense on this issue! WE NEED A WALL!" A short time later, he tweeted, "If Cork is as great as Michael Martin and others seem to think, they should have no objection to us walling them in!"

'New Republic Deputy Leader Muirgheal Massey today denied that the party was deliberately drumming up hatred for short-term electoral gain. And she reiterated her party leader's earlier claim that the cost of the wall would be recouped through a series of levies on Cork businesses and homeowners.'

There's suddenly a shot of Muirgheal standing in the middle of Ringsend. And she storts doing the accent, going, 'As poditicians, we have to accept that the open doh-er podicy bethween Cork and Dublin, as well as Cork and utter peerts of the cunter doddy, has fayult. And it's fayult for a number of diffordent reasons, be it Cork people refusing to assimilate, becoming involved in criminality or joost constantly moaning about evoddy thing and lowerding the gener doddle mood of the rest of the cunter doddy. These people are placing a boorden on the local infrastructure in vardious diffordent peerts of the cunter doddy – the helt serbice, housing, soshiddle welfeer – and ordinary, law-abiding people feel they've taken enough. That's why we are determined to build this wall and build it immediately.'

JP's old man sidles over to me. 'Your father's talking a lot of sense,' he goes. 'They've had free and unfettered movement for years – and where's it got us? We've been inundated. And they don't come here to be our friends. They don't want to mix at all. Every Friday, they're on the train back to Kent Station and they bring whatever money they've earned back with them.'

I'm there, 'Well, I personally think the focker has lost it. Helen used to be able to talk to him. Tell him when he was being a knob. Now he doesn't have her anymore.'

'He's only saying what a lot of people secretly think but are too frightened to say. Scared of being called racist.'

I end up having a couple of pints with him and we shoot the shit about old times. After a while, he turns around to me and goes, 'By the way, who's that little boy standing beside you?'

I turn and I look down. It ends up not being a little boy at all. It ends up being Honor. She's had her hair chopped really, really short, then – oh, holy shit – dyed jet black.

I can't keep ignoring Sorcha's phone calls. Or could I? It wouldn't need to be forever. It'd only have to be until Honor's hair grows back – we're talking April, possibly May, next year. But then that would mean not actually seeing my children on Christmas Day. I'm supposed to be calling over in the evening to watch them open their presents. So it's a definite dilemma for me.

But then I think, she's probably just going to keep ringing – they do say that Mounties always get their man – so I decide to just answer the thing, then act as if nothing's wrong. I'm there, 'Hey,

Sorcha. How the hell are you? I can't stay long, by the way. I'm about to go into – believe it or not – church.'

Which is actually true. It's the Castlerock College Old Boys' Thanksgiving Mass – a Christmas Eve tradition.

She goes, 'What kind of a way was that to send your daughter home the other day?'

I'm there, 'Are you talking about the fact that she looks like a boy?'

'I'm talking about the fact that you put her in a taxi.'

'Oh, thank God.'

'What do you mean, thank God? Anything could have happened to her.'

'Look, to be honest with you, I thought you'd have a complete shit-fit when you saw what she'd had done to her hair.'

'Well, yes, as it happens, I can't believe you sat there and watched them do that to her beautiful, blonde curls.'

Honor mustn't have told her about me focking off to Kielys. She's a great kid. There's evil in her definitely. But if she happens to be on your side, you have very little to worry about. Of course, the problem is that you never know when she's going to turn on you.

Sorcha goes, 'Ross, I can't believe you didn't try to talk her out of it. Out of cutting all her hair off.'

I'm there, 'It's impossible to talk Honor out of anything. If you try to stop her, she's just going to hit you with a load of genuinely hurtful comments.'

She just sighs.

I'm there, 'I have to say, you don't sound as pissed off as I expected you to be. I'd have rung you back if I'd known you were going to be this calm about it.'

She goes, 'I cried for five hours straight, Ross.'

'Okay, that's a lot of crying.'

'My mom cried as well. But then, when I thought about it, I just decided, okay, if that's the way Honor wants to wear her hair, then who am I to keep showing her pictures of Sailor Lee Brinckley-Cook? The whole gender fluidity thing is creeping more and more into mainstream fashion. The idea that little girls should dress like little girls is – oh my God – so nineties. Er, hello – Shiloh Jolie-Pitt? And that's not a dig at you, Ross – even though I know you have issues with traditional-gender-non-conformity.'

'Yeah, I don't know what that even means.'

'So I'm just going to have to be the cool parent who accepts that that's just how Honor wants to look. Although I did mention that her new hair possibly de-accentuated her cheekbones and made her face look round. I could have said fat but I said round instead.'

'Yeah, no, let her figure it out for herself. Anyway, like I said, Sorcha, I'm just heading into – literally – Mass here.'

'Okay, I'll see you tomorrow. Come for six o'clock. We'll be finished with our dinner by then.'

I hang up, then into the church I go. It turns out I'm late. It's already half over, in fact. Father Amokachi has just finished reading The Gospel and he's about to give his sermon, which I've always looked on as Mass's version of post-match analysis.

I'm looking around for the goys, then I suddenly spot them, we're talking JP, Fionn, Christian and – fock *him* – Oisinn, all sitting together in a pew towards the back of the church, except there ends up being no room there for me beside them, so I end up having to sit on the other side of the aisle, next to some old dude whose name I don't remember but who captained Castlerock in the 1950s and now smells of parmesan.

'This Christmas,' Father Amokachi goes, 'I'm going to talk to you about history's two most famous refugees.'

Felix Jones and Ian Keatley, I think.

'I'm talking about Joseph and the Virgin Mary,' he goes.

Father Amokachi is from Nigeria, by the way, and I'm not saying that in a racist or any other kind of way. I'm saying it so you can picture him as a black man and maybe do the accent in your own heads.

He's there, 'I want you all to think about the story of the very first Christmas. The long journey that Mary and Joseph made on foot to Bethlehem, where they were refused shelter, refused food and forced to spend the night in a stable, where Mary gave birth to the baby Jesus. And I want us to consider this as a metaphor for our own lives. Are there times when we have behaved as that innkeeper behaved? Have we turned people away who needed us? Have we done it because we lacked basic human compassion? Or because we have a fear of what we might call The Other?'

Holy shit. He's staring directly at someone in the fourth row and I suddenly realize that the someone he's staring at is my old man. It's unbelievable how obvious he's making it. The old man is obviously uncomfortable with the heat he's getting because he keeps turning around in his seat, catching various people's eyes, then shaking his head like the priest is talking out of his hole.

'The Bible is a love story,' Father Amokachi goes. 'It's the greatest love story ever told. Better than *Fifty Shades*.'

Everyone laughs. He's good value, in fairness to him.

'Yes, the greatest love story ever told,' he goes. 'So why do people read it looking for reasons to hate? Paul writes to the Romans and he says you must love The Other. Accept others for the glory of God, he says, especially those who are different than you, because Christ accepted you and all the people for the glory of God. That means accepting and loving The Other, whether they are black, white, gay, lesbian – or even from Cork.'

There's a wave of muttering that makes its way from the front of the church to the back. He's not going to win people over in this port of the world looking for sympathy for people from Cork. His line about gay people, though – that's the one that gets to me. I'm suddenly thinking about Oisinn and the fact that we haven't spoken for, like, months now.

'Ideas are fashions,' Father Amokachi goes, 'just like clothes. They have their time and they are gone. Things that seem absurd yesterday are logical today and things that seemed logical last year are now absurd. Taboos become social norms just as social norms become taboos. One day we love a slogan, and another day it makes us embarrassed, or even ashamed, that we ever thought that way.'

I can see my old man just shaking his head from side to side. He's definitely not buying it. I've got, like, tears in the corners of my eyes, though.

The priest goes, 'We are one of several million species of animal clinging to a rock that is spinning around and around the sun. And the only thing that distinguishes you is how you treat other people in the short time that you are here. That is all that matters to Christ – not how you love, just that you love. And that is my message for Christmas.'

I turn my head and I catch Oisinn's eye and I give him a little – I don't know – nod, just to let him know that I agree with every word he just said, especially the bit about loving as many people as you can get around to in a lifetime. And for a second I think he's about to smile at me, which would be – you know what? – *the* greatest Christmas present I ever got. But in the end he turns to face the front again and storts saying his Apostles' Creed.

The old man has tweeted – I shit you not – seventeen times about Father Amokachi today. Today being *Christmas* Day?

His feed is like, 'Father Amokachi, a highly overrated priest, attacked me at the Castlerock College Old Boys' Christmas Mass last night . . .'

'Father Amokachi is a failing priest and a Michael Martin flunky who is about to lose BIG!'

'More dishonest clergy!'

I'm there, 'I never thought *I'd* be saying this to *you*, but is there any chance you could put your phone away?'

He goes, 'What's that, Kicker?'

'It's Christmas Day and I'm focking storving. Where's my actual dinner?'

'Patience!' he went. 'As I said to the party faithful at our Christmas drinks during the week, good things come to those who wait!'

He promised to do the cooking. That's the only reason I didn't take up Ronan's offer of spending the afternoon with him and Shadden. The old man went, 'It'll be a bachelors' Christmas! You, me and your godfather!'

But now it's, like, three o'clock in the afternoon and all I've eaten is an entire tin of Quality Street, even the shit ones that I actually hate. Now that I think about it, I looked in the fridge earlier and there wasn't even a turkey in there.

The three of us are just sitting around the kitchen, skulling

Courvoisier and watching whatever Christmas movies are on TV. Only Hennessy Coghlan-O'Hara, by the way, could watch *Home Alone* and see Macaulay Culkin as the villain.

'These two guys,' he goes, meaning Joe Pesci and the dude who plays Marv, 'would be fully entitled to sue this little prick's parents for criminal recklessness for any injuries they received during the course of the burglary.'

I'm like, 'Yeah, it's a kids' film, Hennessy,' even though it's also one of my three favourite movies of all time – the others being *Invictus* and *Home Alone 2*.

Marv pulls what he thinks is the cord for the lightbulb and he ends up getting smashed in the face with an iron.

'Two fractured eye sockets,' Hennessy goes, 'broken nose, blurred vision, loss of earnings. I'm going to say a hundred fucking grand.'

The old man goes, 'My comments about Father Amokachi are trending, I'm happy to report!'

Joe Pesci opens the back door, tripping a wire that turns on a blow torch and burns the top of his head.

'First degree burns to the calavarium,' Hennessy goes, helping himself to another brandy, 'requiring months of skin-graft operations and – depending on the degree of necrosis – quite possibly a skull bone transplant. I'm going to say half a million for that one.'

This is basically how Christmas Day passes – me eating my body weight in sweets, my old man constantly refreshing his Twitter feed to see the reaction to him calling out a priest, and Hennessy costing the personal injuries received by two dudes burgling Macaulay Culkin's gaff.

'Okay,' I eventually go, 'I'm going out.'

The old man's like, 'Don't worry, Kicker! I can feel the elbow in my ribs! You're wondering about your dinner, aren't you?'

I'm there, 'I asked you straight out about it twenty minutes ago but you were on focking Twitter. The fridge is empty, by the way. You forgot to buy a turkey, didn't you?'

He goes to the – I shit you not – freezer, then he pulls out three flat boxes, which actually look like *pizza* boxes?

'Who needs to go cooking a turkey,' he goes, 'when you can have one of these?'

I'm like, 'Okay, what the fock?' and I pick up one of the boxes. It says on the front, 'Microwavable Festive Dinner for One!' and – I'm not making this up – it's an actual frozen Christmas dinner, we're talking two slices of turkey, two slices of ham, a tablespoon of stuffing, two little roast potatoes and four sprouts.

I'm there, 'Are you focking shitting me?'

He goes, 'Eight minutes on defrost, then four minutes on full power is all it requires! There's even a little sachet of turkey gravy to pour over the whole thing once it's fully heated!'

It's the saddest thing I've ever seen in my life.

I'm there, 'Is there a piece of paper and little pen in the box to write your focking suicide note afterwards?'

He goes, 'Come on, Ross! Enter into the spirit of the thing!'

This is what a world without women would look like. Within a week, we'll be eating beans straight from the tin and shitting where we sit.

'A full tin of paint,' Hennessy goes, 'has got to weigh ten pounds. That hits you in the face, it's going to break bones, teeth and cause concussion. I'm going to say three hundred grand for that.'

The old man removes the sleeve of a Microwavable Festive Dinner for One. Now, he goes, 'Does anyone know how these bloody well microwave ovens work?'

The old dear rings me just as I'm driving through the gates of Honalee. She rings me from her cell. Yeah, no, to say thank you for cooking them Christmas dinner, the girls – as she's taken to calling them – have given her a present of a mobile phone.

Probably robbed, but it's the thought that counts.

'We're not *supposed* to have them,' she goes, 'but it's lovely to be able to ring you from my suite –'

I'm like, 'Cell.'

'– and wish you a Merry Christmas.'

'How did the Nigella Christmas dinner go down?'

'Absolutely wonderfully. Did you know, Ross, there are women in here who'd never had ham other than that awful sliced one that you see in packets?'

'There's a lot of inequality in the world. Thank God.'

'Anyway, they loved it. They said it was like they'd all died and gone to heaven.'

I laugh. I'm there, 'Sounds like you ate better than we did. I might even join you in there next year.'

'Well,' she goes, 'I'm hoping I won't be here next Christmas. I'm hoping my trial will prove my innocence.'

And I'm just like, 'Yeah, no, I forgot. Anyway, I better go. I've just pulled up outside Honalee. We're about to do the whole opening presents thing.'

'I do hope Sorcha comes to her senses soon.'

'Unfortunately, I'm not sure that she's ever going to. It's like you said when Helen and the old man broke up – some relationships are just for a certain amount of time.'

'Merry Christmas, Ross.'

'Merry Christmas, I suppose, *Mum*?'

It's a word I've hordly ever used. I hang up, then I get out of the cor and I grab the presents from the boot.

He opens the door – as in Sorcha's old man? He's wearing a paper crown and he does this thing where he pretends to be mid-laugh – just to let me know what a great day he's having – then his face goes all serious when he sees *me* standing there. 'One hour,' he goes out of the side of his mouth, 'starting from now.'

Down to the living room I go. Everyone is sitting around – we're talking Sorcha and the kids, we're talking her old pair, and we're talking her sister, who's obviously home for Christmas, even though I still can't remember her name. *She's* actually the most enthusiastic about seeing me, in the sense that she's the only one who gets up out of her seat to say hello. She's like, 'Hi, Ross!' and she gives me a big wet kiss on either cheek, then rubs her hand up and down my stomach.

'Oh my God,' she goes, 'have you been working out?'

I've ridden her four or five times.

'Just the usual thousand sit-ups a day,' I go.

They've obviously been playing board games because I notice the Trivial Pursuit board on the table. On the sideboard, there's a buffet of food laid out. Turkey and ham sandwiches. Pigs in blankets. Mince pies. Christmas cake. I'm instantly salivating.

'So,' I go, 'did everyone have a nice Christmas?'

I'm just making conversation. I don't give a fock one way or the other.

'It was magical,' Sorcha goes. 'Just like the Christmases we had as children.'

Her old man is delighted to hear that – big smug grin on his face. But Honor lets them all down by calling it. 'It was lame,' she goes. 'The entire focking thing.'

Sorcha's old man's there, 'How would you know? You barely left your room all day.'

'That's because you're a pack of focking knobs and I hate being around you.'

I chuckle to myself and I make sure *he* hears it.

The sister – I must check the tags on her presents to see can I find a name – brings me over a plate of food from the sideboard. I'm just about to take it from her when her old man goes, 'Don't you dare give that to him!' and he basically *roars* it at her?

She's like, 'What?'

'He is not here to eat! He is here to watch the children open their presents and then leave after one hour! Food is not part of the deal!'

Sorcha – being essentially a nice person – goes, 'Dad, it's just a few sandwiches.'

Then I go, 'Yeah, which I paid for through my maintenance. You certainly couldn't afford to put on a spread like that, you bankrupt fock.'

Honor laughs.

Sorcha jumps to her feet. 'Okay,' she goes, 'can we all try to get along – just for this one day of the year? Ross, take the food.'

I'm there, 'I don't want the food. I'm not hungry.'

I'm storving.

'Let's just get these presents open,' I go.

I grab the boys and we all gather around the tree, except for Honor. I'm like, 'Honor, are you coming?'

She's there, 'No, I opened all of my presents four days ago.'

Sorcha goes, 'Okay, for the young people, there are Santa presents, there are Mom and Dad presents, there are Nana and Grandad presents, and there are Great-Gran presents.'

Great-Gran! I'm thinking, of course, where the fock is she?

Five seconds later, she walks into the room, going, 'I say the same thing every year: "Don't have Christmas pudding because you know it backs you up!" Was I gone long?'

'About an hour,' Honor goes, without even looking up from her phone. 'And you better not have left a focking smell in there.'

I just glower at the woman. I literally haven't laid eyes on her since that day in Dublin Castle. But she avoids my stare.

'Come on,' Sorcha goes, 'let's do presents! I'm *so* excited about what I got for you, Nana!'

I empty the Mom and Dad presents out of the sack onto the floor. The boys have no interest in them, though. It breaks my hort to say it, but they make a grab for whatever Sorcha's old man bought them – three square boxes. They tear open the paper and I swear to fock it's like he's done it on purpose. He *has* done it on purpose. It's three soccer balls – one for each of them.

Sorcha's old dear takes them out of the boxes and rolls them across the floor to them. Brian squeals with excitement, then he kicks his ball across the living-room floor and scampers off in chase, followed by Leo and Johnny shouting, 'Footbaw! Footbaw! Footbaw!'

It breaks my focking hort.

'That's un-focking-believable,' I go. 'I mean, I've tried giving them rugby balls and they don't know what to even do with them.'

Sorcha's old dear goes, 'I think it's the shape of the rugby ball they don't like. They don't trust the way it moves.'

'Well, they should trust it.'

'What I mean is, I think most children prefer a ball to be round, don't they?'

'And what the fock would you know about sport?'

Sorcha's old man gets involved then. He goes, 'How dare you speak to my wife in that way!'

I'm there, 'She played tennis in Glenageary – badly, as I remember – and now she's an expert on everything?'

But then suddenly everyone is looking at the granny because she's opened her present from Sorcha – and, hilariously, it turns out to be a silk scorf . . . in the gay pride colours.

I laugh. What else am I going to do?

She goes, 'Oh, thank you, Sorcha. That's, em, very, er . . .'

'Wow,' I go, 'look at that! You're going to be the envy of all your friends, aren't you? What with you all being so into the whole gay rights thing.'

I take the scorf from her, then I walk around the back of her chair. I drape it over her shoulders and – I swear to fock – her entire body stiffens, like I've just hung a snake around her neck. 'You can wear it to the Active Retirement, can't you?'

'Oh, yes,' she goes. 'Mrs Hudson has one just like it – except with not as many colours.'

I'm there, 'I have to say, it genuinely suits you, doesn't it?'

Sorcha goes, 'Do you love it, Gran?'

And the granny's like, 'Oh, yes . . . Yes, I do . . . I love all gay things, Sorcha.'

I'm there, 'I must grab a picture of you in it. You can show it to the parish priest.'

She goes, 'No, I'll put it away in the box – just so it's safe!' and she whips it off her before I can get the shot.

Sorcha opens up one of her presents and lets a scream out of her. 'Oh! My! God!' she goes – and at first I think it's *my* gift that she's opened. It's not, though. It ends up being from Fionn. 'It's a first edition of Barack Obama's *The Audacity of Hope*,' she goes. 'And look, it's even signed: "To Sorcha, Yes, you can. Barack Obama." Oh! My God!'

It puts the popcorn-maker I bought her in the focking shade. If I ever needed a sign that he was definitely trying to get in there, I don't anymore. Sorcha's old man goes, 'What a wonderful young man he is. I've been saying it to you, Sorcha, since you were how old?'

She goes, 'Oh! My God! How did he get Obama to sign it?'

'Speaking of coloured people,' I go, trying to subtly change the subject, 'did you see my old man slagging off Father Amokachi on Twitter this morning?'

Sorcha's face just drops. She's like, 'Do you know how – oh my God – *racist* you sounded just there?'

I go, 'Coloured people? I hear you say coloured people all the time.'

'I don't say coloured people. I say people of colour. There's a huge difference, Ross.'

'Is there? Because they kind of sound the same to me.'

'One is a preferred term and the other is one of the worst things you can possibly say about someone who doesn't share your ethnicity. I can't believe that you're actually out there in the world not knowing any of this stuff. You really need to get on the Internet and educate yourself, Ross.'

I don't get the chance to argue my point any further because Sorcha's granny suddenly goes, 'Ross! How could you do something like that?'

Everyone's like, 'What's wrong? What's wrong?' and that's when I get this horrible burning smell in my nostrils.

She goes, 'Ross threw my beautiful gay people headscarf on the fire!'

Now, you can probably imagine my reaction. I'm like, 'What?' obviously more than a bit *confused* by this? 'What the fock are you talking about?'

Then I suddenly notice her rainbow scorf blazing away in the fireplace. I'm there, 'I didn't do that.'

The granny goes, 'Yes, he did, Sorcha. He hates the gays – we knew that about him. He must have thrown it on the fire while you were looking at that book about that person of colour.'

Sorcha goes, 'Oh my God, Ross, why would you –?'

I'm like, 'Sorcha, I swear to God, I didn't do it.'

And that's when her old man sticks his hooter in. 'He did, Sorcha,' he goes. 'As a matter of fact, I watched him do it.'

My jaw goes literally slack. I always knew he hated my basic guts, but I never thought he'd stoop so low as to lie just to fock me over.

The granny goes, 'Oh, he hates the gays does Ross. God didn't create Adam and Panti Bliss. That's what he said.'

And Sorcha's old man is like, 'I know we said he could stay for an hour, but I think it would be best all round if he left now.'

There ends up being the most unbelievable screaming match then. Sorcha, her old pair and her granny are all shouting at me and I'm shouting back at them. I'm going, 'I didn't focking do it! She's the one who hates gay people! I'm all for them!'

Then, all of a sudden, there's a roar and it's louder than any other voice in the room. It just goes, 'I said shut the fock up!'

There's immediately silence.

It's Honor. She's got a face on her that's all business. 'I've got something I want to tell you,' she goes, 'since we're all here together. It's been on my mind for a while now.'

Sorcha's like, 'Honor, what is it?'

And I'm there, 'Yeah, no, is everything okay?' because she looks kind of upset.

She goes, 'I'm a boy.'

Sorcha's there, 'You're a what?'

'I'm a boy. Meaning I identify as male. And I want to change my gender identity.'

You can imagine *my* face. Again, my mouth falls open – as does Sorcha's, by the way, and she's supposedly a lot more open-minded than I am.

The granny goes, 'What's this she's saying?'

Sorcha's there, 'She's saying she was born in the wrong body, Gran.'

'The wrong body?' the granny goes. 'Whose body was she born in?'

'She means that she's not happy with her assigned sex. Is that right, Honor?'

Honor nods.

Sorcha's old man ends up totally flipping. He's obviously dubious. He goes, 'You don't seriously believe her, do you? It's just attention-seeking behaviour. This is more of it now.'

To say I'm confused would be the understatement of the century.

Sorcha's there, 'Dad, Honor is sharing with us the fact that her sense of herself doesn't correspond with the gender attributed to her at the time of her birth. We have to not only respect that but celebrate it.'

'Gender's not something you can pick and choose,' he goes, 'like the colour of your hair or what shoes you wear.'

But Sorcha just blanks him. Pennies are storting to drop for her – all over the place. 'Honor,' she goes, 'how long have you felt this way?'

Honor just shrugs. She's there, 'I don't know. All my life.'

'Oh my God, is that why you've been wearing the beanie all the time? And those awful skateboarding shoes?'

'Er, I *like* my Vans?'

'Oh my God, is it also why you've been so difficult since childhood and why I've never really been able to form the kind of deep friendship with you that I have with my own mom? Was it because you had all of this conflict going on inside you?'

I'm there, 'Do you honestly think that would explain her behaviour?'

'*His* behaviour,' Sorcha goes.

I'm thinking, Jesus Christ, not this again.

Sorcha's there, 'Aren't you listening to what Honor is telling you, Ross?'

I'm like, 'What is she telling me?'

And Honor goes, 'I don't want to be known as Honor anymore. I want you to call me Eddie.'

7. *Dead in the Water*

'Today is the day!' the old man goes. 'I've had it on good authority that our friend Enda – yes, the Permanent Undersecretary of Vichy Ireland! – is going to call the election! On the twenty-sixth day of the second month, in the year two thousand and sixteen, the people will have the opportunity to decide their own destiny! Is there a pot of coffee made?'

That's what he says to me.

'A pot of coffee?' I go. 'Where the fock do you think you are – an episode of *The Gilmore Girls*? If you want coffee, you put a capsule in the Nespresso, put a mug underneath it, then press the focking button – like normal people do.'

There's all of a sudden a ring on the door. 'Ah,' he goes, 'that'll be my driver and my Deputy Leader!'

Focking Muirgheal.

He goes to open the door and I follow him. I'm just curious as to whether there's any sexual tension between them these days. And, just as I expected, there turns out to be zero. She goes, 'That focking bitch's posters are up *everywhere*!' and I'm guessing she's talking about my soon-to-be ex-wife. 'The coast road in Sandymount, the Donnybrook Road, the main street in Ranelagh, all around the RDS. She must have been out all focking night.'

Yeah, no, Muirgheal is clearly all business now that she's got what she wants from the old man. *He's* still a sap for *her*, of course.

'Please don't upset yourself,' he goes, then he calls out to Kennet, who is standing at the front gate, having a smoke. 'Kennet, I want you to drive around this afternoon, all over Dublin Bay South, and wherever you see a Sorcha Lalor poster, I want you to put up two Muirgheal Massey ones – one above and one below.'

Kennet goes, 'I'll d . . . d . . . d . . . d . . . d . . . d . . . d . . . d . . . do that, Cheerdles.'

Muirgheal's like, 'Thank you!' then she storts straightening the knot on the old man's red tie. He sort of, like, blushes and goes, 'That's, um, quite alright, my dear!' and I end up having to laugh.

I'm there, 'She's got you wrapped around her little finger.'

She goes, 'I was also thinking about challenging her to a debate. Like the ones we used to have at school?'

The old man's like, 'You'll have to do the accent, Muirgheal. Everyone's forgetting about Ringsend and Harold's Cross.'

'I doatunt moyunt thalken like this if it meeyuns votes, so I doatunt.'

She laughs. And the old man laughs. Except he's not laughing at what she said. He's staring over her shoulder at something happening out on the road. It ends up being a woman trying to parallel pork.

It *is* funny, in fairness. When is it ever not?

He wanders down to the front gate and watches her attempt the manoeuvre over and over again. 'Turn the wheel the other way!' he shouts through the gate, at the same time laughing. 'She's turning it the same way again, look!'

I turn around to Muirgheal and I go, 'There's a word for women like you.'

She's like, "Women like me?'

'Yeah, who use sex to get what they want. You broke up his marriage. Helen was the one person who brought out the good in him.'

'Oh, please! You know she never blew him in all the years they were together? Neither did your mother, by the way.'

'I don't even want to think about that. You're making me think about things I don't want to think about.'

She goes and joins my old man then. The woman who's trying to parallel pork is obviously becoming more and more flustered now that she has an audience. The old man is going, 'The same thing! Over and over again! Madness!'

And Muirgheal's like, 'Stupid bitch!'

Kennet sidles up to me. He goes, 'Can I hab a quick w . . . w . . . w . . . w . . . woord wit you, Rosser?'

I'm like, 'There's no such thing as a quick w . . . w . . . w . . .

w . . . woord with you. I could go upstairs for a shave, then come back down and you wouldn't have finished what you'd storted saying.'

He goes, 'We're habben a few thrinks in the house n . . . n . . . next week – on account of it being Ronan's d . . . d . . . d . . . d . . . d . . . d . . . d . . . d . . .'

He's trying to say debs. Castlerock College switched theirs to the middle of January two or three years ago. McGahy, the focking dick of a Principal, felt that an extra few months of maturity – and third-level education – might cut down on the number of incidents surrounding it. I'm happy to say that so far it hasn't.

Kennet's still going, 'd . . . d . . . d . . . d . . . d . . . d . . . d . . . d . . .'

'Debs!' I go. 'Jesus Christ, I genuinely thought that one was going to go on forever.'

He's like, 'Yeah, the debs. Shadden's veddy much looken f . . . f . . . f . . . fortwoord to it. Ronan might be enjoying the s . . . s . . . s . . . s . . . s . . . soshiddle life in coddidge. She hasn't been out in m . . . m . . . m . . . munts.'

And that's when we all of a sudden hear the sound of metal grinding on metal and the old man goes, 'What in the name of Hades! She's scraped the side of the Merc, Kennet! And she's bloody well driving away!'

He suddenly doesn't see the *funny* side of it anymore? I tip down to the front gate to check out the damage. She's taken half the side off his cor. It's hilarious.

'Bloody women drivers!' the old man goes.

He's, like, fuming.

Kennet's there, 'D . . . D . . . D . . . Doatunt woody. I know a fedda is a p . . . p . . . p . . . p . . . pattle beathor. Two or three hours and he'll hab her looken like new.'

'Eddie!' Sorcha shouts up the stairs. 'Eddie, your father's here!'

Random doesn't even begin to describe it.

I'm there, 'How has she been? *He* been?'

She goes, 'I know. It's hord, isn't it? I've forgotten once or twice myself.'

'But you're totally cool with it, are you? You seem to be definitely cool with it.'

'How could I not be cool with it, Ross? He's my son.'

'There has to be a word that's *like* random but actually goes even further?'

'Well, maybe this will make you a bit more understanding about the whole LGBTQ thing.'

Then she shouts up the stairs again. She's like, 'Eddie! Eddie, your father's here!'

I'm like, 'So how do I talk to her?'

She goes, '*Him*, Ross'

'*Him*, then. Do I just talk about all blokey stuff?'

'Ross, you talk to him the way you've always talked to him. He's still the same person.'

Fionn suddenly steps out of the study. In one hand, he's holding his phone. In the other, he has my Leinster mug with the words 'Ster Crazy After All These Years' on it.

It pisses me off. Although I'm not so petty that I'd say it to him.

'Sorcha,' he goes, chuckling to himself, 'have you seen what Charles tweeted yesterday?', not even acknowledging me. 'He said if he's elected he's going to force women drivers to sit a competency test every twelve months.'

Sorcha's like, 'Oh! My God! That is *so* offensive to women everywhere!'

'The first official day of campaigning and he's already shot himself in the foot. Listen to this: "New Republic will pass legislation requiring WOMEN to prove ON A YEARLY BASIS that they are sufficiently competent to drive!" and then he says, "WOMEN are causing ACCIDENTS every day! Scraping our cars and driving away! WAKE UP, PEOPLE!" Oh, hi, Ross.'

'That's my focking Leinster mug,' I go. 'You're getting way too comfortable in this house.'

That gets ignored.

Sorcha's there, 'Oh! My God! Whatever about pulling out of the European Union and building a wall around Cork, this is totally different! Women make up, like, fifty percent of the electorate! More!'

'He's finished after this!'

'Isn't there some statistic that women are involved in far fewer crashes than men?'

'Maybe they all just drive away afterwards,' I go.

Again, I'm blanked.

She's there, 'That's an accepted fact, Fionn.'

He's just like, 'Okay, what we need to do now is to pull together all the data that proves that women are far safer on the road than men. That's how we're going to win this election – by exposing, one by one, every single lie that he tells.'

'I could also use it as an opportunity,' Sorcha goes, 'to put Muirgheal under pressure – as in, how does she feel, as a woman, representing a porty that thinks women are inferior at, oh my God, *anything*?'

'We should also stort a thread on Twitter where women can share their stories of how long they've been accident-free. We'll set up a hashtag – #NotAllWomenDrivers or something like that.'

She's like, 'Oh! My God! No one is going to vote for a porty that's, like, openly misogynistic!' then she shouts up the stairs again, 'Eddie! Eddie! Your father's here!' before disappearing back into the study with Fionn.

Honor slash Eddie looks over the top bannister and goes, 'Are you focking deaf? I've shouted "Come up!" about fifty focking times!'

Discovering his true gender identity, I see, hasn't made my son any less of a bitch.

Up the stairs I go.

I'm like a focking jelly, by the way, not knowing how to act around him. I end up sort of, like, rubbing the top of his head and going, 'Hello there, little chap!'

He looks at me like I'm a focking mental patient. He goes, 'What are we, two characters out of *Oliver Twist*?'

I'm there, 'Sorry, Eddie, I just don't know how to greet you these days.'

'Kiss me like you normally do.'

I'm like, 'Okay, Eddie,' and I do – a big one on the cheek. 'There you go, Eddie.'

'You don't have to keep saying my name,' he goes.

'It helps me remember. I'll probably go on saying it, Eddie, if it's all the same to you.'

The boys are kicking one of the footballs Sorcha's old pair bought them around the bedroom. I don't even bother saying hello to them. They'll hopefully learn in time.

Eddie goes, 'Do you want to play *Call of Duty*? We could play Two Player!'

And I'm like, 'Yeah, no, definitely, Eddie. Definitely.'

We sit down on the end of the bed.

Eddie's like, 'Are you shaking?'

I'm there, 'I am a little bit, Eddie, yeah.'

'Why?'

'I'm terrified I'm going to say the wrong thing and you'll flip. Like that focking Broderek.'

'Broderek's not, like, proper trans – he's just an attention-seeker.'

'See, I don't know how any of it works. I'm rugby, Eddie. I've got a rugby brain. It can be a blessing and a curse.'

'Well, why don't you ask me some questions?'

'I wouldn't know where to stort, Eddie.'

He hits the button for Two Players, then off we go on a shooting spree. He goes, 'Well, what do you want to know?'

I'm like, 'I don't know. I suppose, when did you first realize that you were actually a dude?'

'I suppose I've kind of *always* known? I've never been, like, a girly girl. I mean, *she* was always trying to make me look pretty. But I was never pretty.'

'I'm going to disagree with that analysis, Eddie. I just think you're pretty in a way that's not immediately obvious. It takes a bit of effort to see it.'

'You don't have to say that.'

'I'm calling it, Eddie. I'll never stop calling it, Eddie, just because we're now father and son.'

'It's kind of like, when I was born, just because I had a vagina, the doctors presumed that I was a girl.'

'I think it's fair to say we all did.'

'But if I'd been able to talk, I'd have said, "Er, you've made a *mis-take*? I'm actually a *boy*?"'

'Jesus. I'm trying to think what the reaction in Mount Cormel would have been. So are you, like – I'm terrified to even use the word these days – but *gay*?'

'Sexuality and gender are, like, two totally different *things*?'

'Keep going, Eddie.'

'I don't know what sexuality I am yet. I'm only, like, ten years old.'

'Good point.'

'But I think I'm probably going to end up being pansexual.'

'Okay – and what do they believe in?'

'They're attracted to pretty much *everyone* on the gender spectrum?'

'I feel like I need to be writing this shit down. Do you have a pen, Eddie?'

'You don't need to write it down.'

'It'll save me from saying stupid things. I'll write it into my iPhone.'

We're still blasting away here, the two of us.

He goes, 'I don't mind you saying stupid things. This stuff is all new to people of your age. I get that.'

'That's good because I feel like there's about fifteen stupid things in my head that are just waiting for me to say them out loud.'

'Say them out loud. I won't take offence. And ask me any questions you want. *She* hasn't asked me anything, by the way.'

He's obviously talking about Sorcha.

I'm there, 'She's cool with it, though. She had gay friends in college, bear in mind – even though you're saying you're not strictly gay.'

She's like, 'After I told you, on Christmas Day, she spent the whole of the next day on the Internet. Then she came up to my room and she storted, like, dropping words into the conversation that she'd obviously just learned on Google.'

'She's making the effort, Eddie.'

'She's, like, *such* a virtue-signalling bitch. I actually heard her on the phone yesterday, going, "Speaking as the mother of a trans child . . ." She's such a bogus bitch.'

'Well, I'm just glad you said you were born with this thing, Eddie, because ever since Christmas I've been wondering was *I* to somehow blame? As in, was it playing *Call of Duty*, or bringing you into that prison – or even introducing you to rugby?'

'It had nothing to do with any of those things.'

'I was also thinking, if you *are* a boy, will you be allowed to play for Ireland when you grow up – as in *actual* Ireland?'

'You mean the men's team?'

'That's what I said – actual Ireland.'

'I don't know. I'd be surprised if *she* ever lets me play rugby again!'

We both laugh.

I'm there, 'She's definitely anti the idea since you nearly crippled that other kid. Do you know something, Eddie, I don't care if you're a boy, a girl, or whatever else there is on this famous spectrum you mentioned. I just love spending time with you – even if it's just one hour a week.'

He smiles at me. I have to admit, he was never a good-looking girl – he might actually make a better looking boy – but one smile from him could light up the sky at night.

He goes, 'I know I've always been horrible to you – and I'm probably going to do more horrible things in the future – but you're *actually* a really, really cool person?'

And I go, 'I wish everyone thought like you, Eddie. I genuinely do.'

Dordeen hands me a can of something called Hoxha – which is obviously Albanian for 'Not Heineken' – then she tells me that it's all she has in.

'It's alt I hab in,' she goes.

It's like drinking bin juice from the bottom of the Brabantia.

A second or two later, Ronan and Shadden step into the kitchen and it's ooohhhs and aaahhhs from everyone, including all of the neighbours who've stopped in for a nosey.

I can't tell you how proud I am to see him standing there in his tux. He looks the way he's sounded all his life – like a grown man.

'Yiz look lubbly,' all the old dears go. 'Shadden, your thress is oatenly beauriful!'

Shadden's like, 'Tanks veddy mooch!'

Ronan is holding Rihanna-Brogan. They've put her in a dress for the day. She's a gas little one. Her accent is half southside, half northside, on account of her Killiney-then-Finglas upbringing. 'Mom, I want to go the peerteee,' she goes.

Everyone laughs. They laugh at everything she says. She'll grow up with a complex.

Ronan's there, 'You caddent come to the peerty, Ine afrayut. It's for athults oatenly.'

Dordeen goes, 'She's a bleaten cadickter, idn't she?'

They love a character in this port of the world. Ronan's old dear barely smiles, though – Tina is no fan of the Tuites.

'Ah, the debs!' I go. 'God, I could tell you some stories about *my* debs days. Like, for instance, the one where I went to two different debses on the same night. That's a famous one about me.'

Tina's there, 'Thee doatunt waddent to hee-or your stupid stordees.'

But they *do* want to hear them? One of the neighbours goes, 'You took two geerdles to their debses on the same neet?'

'That's right,' I go. 'Picked the first one up from her gaff, where her old pair were having a drinks porty. Took her to Jurys, made some excuse to disappear for an hour, then pegged it out to the other one's gaff. Champagne with the folks – again, gift of the gab and blah, blah, blah. Then I dropped *her* off at the Berkeley Court and laced back to Jurys.'

Dordeen and the neighbours are listening to this with humungous smiles on their faces. Skobie women have always found me for some reason attractive. Let's be honest, if Tina hadn't had a thing for me, there would be no Ronan.

'*You're* veddy fuddy!' one of the *wans* goes.

One of the things I love about myself is that I can fit in absolutely anywhere, even amongst the lowest of the low.

Tina has to try to steal the limelight away from me, of course. She goes, 'Well, at least your son idn't athin like you!'

He can't even look me in the eye when she says that.

I'm thinking, that's what you think, Tina. That's what you think.

Ro tries to change the subject by going, 'Ine godda hab anutter can of Caddles Birdog,' and he goes to the fridge.

I'm there, 'I'm trying to think of some of the other stories of deb-ses I've ruined. Of course, Mount Anville took out an actual High Court injunction banning me from their bash one year.'

Again, Tina tries to take the spotlight off me. She goes, 'Ross, can I hab a woord wit you?'

I'm like, 'Er, yeah?'

'In proyvit?' she goes, pulling me to one side.

I hear one of the neighbours go, 'Probley about her mickey money.'

They're really lovely around here.

'What's goan on wit Ronan?' Tina goes – and she says it in a sort of, like, angry whisper.

I'm there, 'What are you talking about?'

'Ine he's mutter. I know when there's sometin wrong wirrum. He dudn't look well. He's arthur losing weight, so he is.'

'Okay, keep your focking voice down, will you? I'm guessing it's probably just guilt.'

'I said that to me da. He's feeden giddlety that he's in coddidge and Shadden's stuck at howum moynting the babby.'

I'm there, 'Look, I'd love to say, yeah, no, that's it. But the truth is – contrary to what you said a minute ago about him not being like me – he did the dirt on Shadden. Which proves he's very *much* like me?'

She goes, 'He did wha'?'

'With a bird from Galway – who has nothing to do with agricul-ture, before you put your foot in it like I did. Yeah, no, it turns out that the philandering gene is strong in our family.'

'Ine woodied abourrum.'

'Don't be. I had a word with him. He's not used to guilt, you see. It can sometimes make you do stupid things. I think he's going to be okay.'

It's at that exact moment that we hear him go, 'Mon outsoyut for a middute, Shadden. And bring Rhihatta-Barrogan wit you. I want to ast you sometin,' and me and Tina both look at each other with our mouths wide open, thinking, don't do it, Ro. Definitely don't do it.

'What's he bleaten doing?' Dordeen goes.

Everyone is suddenly looking out the window into the back gorden, where Ronan – oh, holy shit – goes down on one knee and Shadden has her two hands over her mouth in shock and little Rihanna-Brogan is handing her a little ring box.

'Will you maddy me?' Ronan goes – I can actually read his lips.

And Shadden's like, 'I'd luven to!'

And all I can think is, what have you just done, Ro? What the fock have you just done?

He's not ready to hear it. But I say it to him anyway when I finally get him on the phone. I'm there, 'You're about to make the exact same mistake I made. Ro, you're not ready.'

I'm driving into town – I'm actually going over Leeson Street Bridge at the time.

He's like, 'Ine ready, Rosser. Ine tedding you Ine ready.'

'I just want to make sure you're not doing it out of guilt.'

'Giddult?'

'Exactly. That girl from Galway – Pegeen Mike or whatever the fock she was called?'

'That was a wood-off, Rosser.'

'Yeah, you're beginning to sound like me. Trust me, Ro, marriage isn't something you enter into lightly.'

'I know that.'

'I always say that marriage is like eating with chopsticks. It's a lot horder than it looks and you're constantly asking yourself, why the fock am I even bothering with this?'

'I know what Ine doing, Rosser.'

I continue on towards town. I'm actually stopped at a red light outside the Shelbourne Hotel when I suddenly see her. I'm talking about Sorcha's granny. She actually crosses the road in front of the cor and all I can suddenly think about is her throwing that gay pride scorf on the fire and blaming me.

I'm like, 'Ro, I'll have to ring you back,' and then I hang up on him.

I reach for the handle of the door, but she just happens to turn her head at exactly the same time and we end up just staring at each other through the windscreen for what seems like sixty seconds but is probably more like *five*?

It's like that scene in *Pulp Fiction*. I'm Bruce Willis and she's Morsellus – except on a mobility scooter.

Suddenly, I hear the angry blast of a cor horn behind me. The traffic light has turned green again. I give the finger to the dude in the blue Nissan Almera behind me and Sorcha's granny takes off like a bat out of hell – if the bat was going at between five and seven miles per hour.

She's already passed Peploe's when I put my foot down and I end up catching up with her at the traffic lights in front of the Stephen's Green Shopping Centre. But just as I'm about to pull over and make a grab for her, she takes a shorp right onto Grafton Street, which is obviously pedestrianized, and I can't just abandon the cor here, which she clearly knows, because as she passes But-ler's Chocolates, she has a look over her shoulder and she actually smirks at me, like a physically incapacitated Bond villain making her escape.

I just think, hey, I've got all day and a full tank of unleaded. It won't be long before her battery-use indicator light is flashing red and that'll be my time to strike. But where's she actually going? That's what I need to find out.

The light turns green and, as I follow the one-way system around the back of the Stephen's Green Shopping Centre onto – eventually – George's Street, I dial Sorcha's number. She answers on the third ring, going, 'Oh my God, I just got a text message from Shadden! Her and Ronan got engaged!'

I'm there, 'Yeah!'

'Is that what you're ringing to tell me? Because I'm kind of *busy* here?'

I can hear all this, like, angry shouting in the background – like a distant avalanche.

'Yeah, no,' I go, 'I just tried your granny's number there, but she's not home.'

She's like, 'Okay – *why* are you ringing my grandmother?'

'I, er, thought I'd maybe apologize for – yeah, no – throwing her gay pride scorf on the fire. Even though I still maintain that I have nothing to apologize for.'

'Oh! My God! That's *so* mature of you, Ross. I'm sure she'll appreciate it. You might also apologize for stopping her from voting in the marriage equality referendum as well.'

'Yeah, no, I'll possibly do that if it comes up. It's just, like I said, there's no actual answer from her phone. I was wondering is she at Mass or has she possibly gone into *town* for some reason?'

'Well, as it happens, I'm going to be seeing her in a few minutes.'

'No! Really? Where are you?'

'We've got this protest today. Do you remember I mentioned the National Association for the Advancement of Lady Theatre People? They're campaigning for more strong and independent female characters in leading roles, especially in theatre?'

I don't.

I'm like, 'Yeah, no, I remember at the time thinking, what an amazing, amazing cause.'

'Well, on this subject,' she goes, 'I'm happy to say that you and my grandmother feel exactly the same way. In fact, she's coming in to join us. She's become quite the activist in her old age!'

I give her a pretend laugh. 'Hilarious,' I go. 'So where actually are you?'

She's there, 'We've just left The Abbey.'

I'm thinking, okay, I'm pretty sure I know where that place is. So I hang up on her, just as I reach the bottom of George's Street. I go through an orange light and make a technically illegal right turn onto Dame Street. As I'm passing the Bank of Ireland on College Green, I spot Sorcha's grandmother up ahead of me but on the path. She's obviously wondering am I still following her, because she keeps looking back, while flooring it, and forcing other path-users to jump out of the way to avoid being mown down.

I'm just about to hit the accelerator when one of Templemore's finest steps out on the road in front of me, waving his orms like he's focking shipwrecked on an island and he's trying to attract the attention of a passing cruise liner. I end up having to slam on the brakes while Sorcha's granny makes her escape up Westmoreland Street.

I wind down the window, going, 'For fock's sake, what?'

'My fill of sorrow,' he goes – obviously from Tipperary, 'you can't take your vehickle this way.'

I'm there, 'You've got to be shitting me. I have to go this way. I'm following a woman on a mobility scooter.'

'Well, you may lose the look of weeping that is on you. You'll not drive up Westmoreland Street this day – for tis closed.'

'Closed my orse. Get out of the focking way.'

'Tis the toe of my boot you'll be getting if you speak to me in that colour again. Tis only a soft shell on you – and you only a gawk of a lad.'

So that's when I decide to go, 'Look, over there – a homeless person pissing against a wall,' and he turns his head, at the same time reaching for his notebook. I use the distraction to slam on the accelerator again and he ends up having to jump out of the way, shouting, 'The seven tasks of the mountain on you!' and other bogger curses that'd be familiar to anyone who's ever played rugby against the likes of Rockwell or St Munchin's, or accidentally sat in Donncha O'Callaghan's pre-booked seat on the Cork to Dublin train.

I floor the accelerator and swing left onto Westmoreland Street. There's literally nothing on the road in front of me. I spot Sorcha's granny. She's crossed over to the other side of the road. She's passing the Westin Hotel – constantly looking over her left shoulder. I'm sure she totally kacks it when she sees me still behind her. I'm about to swing the cor across two lanes to the pavement when I suddenly end up having to slam on the brakes.

In front of me is this, like, posse of women – we're talking three or four hundred of them – and they're quite literally morching towards me on the actual road. I stort beeping my horn and roaring out the window at them. I'm going, 'Get the fock out of the way! You've no right to be on the road! Get the fock –'

And that's when I remember the protest that Sorcha mentioned. Shit, I didn't realize it was an actual morch. The women at the front, I notice, are carrying a banner that says 'More Strong and Independent Female Characters in Leading Roles, Especially in Theatre – Now!'

They all of a sudden stort booing and advancing towards me at a pretty rapid rate. Sorcha's granny, by the way, is well out of sight by now. I decide to turn the cor around, but before I can put it into reverse, the women have suddenly surrounded it and they're screaming abuse at me and banging on the windows, the bonnet and the roof. It's actually terrifying.

But then again it should be – I'm guessing a lot of them are actors.

They stort rocking the cor then – up and down, with me still in it. Someone is slapping the window on the front passenger side with her hand, going, 'This is the backlash we knew to expect, girls! This is the White Male Patriarchy fighting back! This is why we need strong and independent female characters in –'

Then she stops. Because she's suddenly recognized me. Just as I've recognized her.

It's Sorcha.

She takes a step backwards. She's just like, 'Oh! My –' but she's too in shock to even finish her sentence.

So a GIF of the incident ends up trending on Twitter and the whole thing ends up being blown out of all proportion. When I say that, I mean that whoever filmed the incident only put up the bit where I drove towards the lady protestors, braking, then shouting, 'Get the fock out of the way! You've no right to be on the road!', but nothing of what happened either side of the incident – me chasing an elderly woman on a mobility scooter, then me being dragged from my cor while begging for my life.

You can make anything look bad if you edit it the right way.

Lots of people are pointing out that I'm the same Ross O'Carroll-Kelly who performed a homophobic rant at what is now being described as a coming-out porty. One or two have helpfully provided a link to Broderek's vlog about me, and practically every

second person is mentioning that I'm the son of New Republic leader Charles O'Carroll-Kelly, who recently made misogynistic comments about women drivers.

Sorcha retweeted the GIF, I'm sad to see, adding the NotAll-WomenDrivers hashtag, along with a new one: #MenDriversToo.

I'm lying on my bed with the laptop open, reading the comments, which range from 'what a complete tool' to 'what a complete focktard'.

There's isn't one message of support.

Although I do notice that #NotAllWomenDrivers has been pretty much hijacked by men. I'm scrolling down through the feed and it's, like, ninety percent photographs and GIFs of women behaving badly in cors – blocking yellow boxes, pulling out without looking, putting on eyeliner while driving – alongside comments of a usually sexist nature, then the hashtag #NotAllWomenDrivers.

There's some absolute crackers in there as well. I know men are focking idiots behind the wheel – and I'm worse than most – but the things women do tend to be *funnier*?

There's one sixty-second video, obviously taken from a dashcam, of a woman in a red Renault Megane, who keeps changing motorway lanes to block another cor that's attempting to overtake her. I've actually seen Sorcha do that if she thinks the driver behind has been tailgating her.

It's pretty funny. I'm actually watching it for the second time when my phone all of a sudden rings. It ends up being my old dear.

I'm like, 'Hey.'

She goes, 'Ross?'

She's crying – or she's *been* crying?

I'm there, 'What's wrong? Whatever it is, can it wait until my next visit?'

She goes, 'I've lost my job, Ross. In the kitchen.'

'What? I thought they loved your food – even though it's muck.'

It's not. It's incredible.

'Food poisoning,' she goes.

I'm there, 'Food poisoning? I don't know why I sound so surprised. Your Lamb Two Ways should be renamed Lamb Both Ends.

Meaning it's made me vomit and given me the squits at the exact same time.'

Her Lamb Two Ways is one of the nicest things I've ever tasted.

She's there, 'It wasn't anything I cooked, Ross! I was sabotaged!'

I'm like, 'Sabotaged? What are you talking about?', only half listening to her now. I'm back scrolling down through women drivers doing the darnedest things.

'It was Nathalie, Ross. The *wan* I replaced as Head Chef. They let her out of solitary confinement and she told me she'd get her revenge. At the time, I thought she was just going to slash my face in the showers. But she put something in the food, Ross. I know she did! Because seven women were rushed to the Mater with suspected E. coli enteritis. Including Nathalie herself.'

'Okay, why would she poison the food, then eat it herself?'

'Because it's easier to escape from the hospital than from the prison.'

I'm like, 'What? She escaped?'

She goes, 'Six of them escaped. And because it was my food that put them in the hospital, I'm suspected of being involved. So I've been suspended from my kitchen duties indefinitely. Oh, Ross, I don't think I can survive in here without cooking.'

'Shut the fock up.'

'I'm back to square one, Ross, wondering would anyone miss me if I decided to just end it all.'

'I said shut the fock up. I've just spotted something.'

And I *have* spotted something? It's way down the #NotAllWomenDrivers feed. I feel my hort suddenly beating faster and my hands are shaking.

'The day Ari died,' I go, 'you said you were in Stillorgan Shopping Centre.'

She's there, 'I *was* in Stillorgan Shopping Centre.'

'And you said you porked directly in front of Donnybrook Fair. Taking up two porking spaces – like the selfish bitch that you are.'

'I didn't want someone opening their door and damaging my paintwork. That's not selfish, Ross.'

Someone has tweeted a picture of the old dear's Land Rover

porked outside Donnybrook Fair – like she said – right in the middle of two porking spaces. The dude who posted it wrote, 'Watched some milf do this, when i pointed out she was taking up 2 spaces she said go away you focking peasant! #NotAllWomenDrivers.'

The old dear goes, 'What is it, Ross?'

And I'm there, 'Being a self-centred wagon is about to pay off for you. I've just found the evidence that's going to prove your innocence.'

I burst into the old man's study, going, 'She didn't do it! She genuinely didn't do it!'

Him and Hennessy are sitting on either side of the desk, staring at this, like, *map*? The old man suddenly storts rolling it up. He goes, 'Oh, hello, Kicker! What's all this how-do-you-do?'

I'm there, 'The old dear. She was telling the truth when she said she was in Stillorgan Shopping Centre.'

I open the dude's tweet, then I hand my phone to the old man. 'That's her cor,' I go, 'on the afternoon Ari died. The only thing that threw me was his use of the word MILF. But it's definitely hers – look at the reg.'

'Dear, oh, dear!' the old man goes. 'Look at how she's parked it!'

'She can't drive for shit. Never could.'

'You know, I think I'd make Fionnuala sit a Competency to Drive test every month!'

I'm there, 'I DM-ed the dude who posted it. I asked him when the photograph was taken – the day and the exact time. And he checked his phone.'

Hennessy goes, 'And it was the day Ari died?'

I'm there, 'Like I said, he checked, then he double-checked. I told him, whatever you do, do not delete that photograph.'

The old man is delighted. Even Hennessy's face breaks into a smile. It's the first time I've seen him genuinely pleased with me since I set fire to crucial evidence relating to a fraud case he was implicated in while I was doing work experience in his office. I burned it in a barrel five minutes before the Feds kicked down the door.

He's there, 'You did good! You did real good!'

'Real good?' the old man goes. 'Hennessy, this is amazing! Don't you see what this means? It proves her innocence!'

'Not quite. It proves she went out. It doesn't prove that she didn't kill him shortly before she went out or shortly after she came home. It just means the timeframe is shorter. It's a crack in the State's case.'

The old man goes, 'Well done, Kicker! That's the kind of mind you have, you see! Forever questing!'

'I was actually just fluting around on Twitter, looking at women trying to drive. I'll give you this dude's contact details anyway. He said he'd be happy to provide her with an alibi for that afternoon – although he wants to be paid because he said the old dear was a complete bitch to him.'

'Whatever it costs!' the old man goes. 'Whatever it costs!'

I turn to leave, feeling pretty pleased with myself, it has to be said. And that's when I get the feeling that something's not quite right. I remember the old man rolling up the map when I walked in. It was like I caught them in the middle of *doing* something? Like the old man said, I've got a whatever-it-was mind.

I turn back around and I'm like, 'What are you two up to, by the way?'

Hennessy's like, 'Up to? What do you mean?'

I'm there, 'You were looking at a map. The old man rolled it up the second I walked in. The two of you seemed definitely shifty. You still do.'

'It's, em, just an alternative plan we're considering for Cork!' the old man tries to go. 'We're going to move everyone to Limerick, then use it as landfill!'

'Bullshit,' I go. 'What are you two up to?'

I grab the map out of his hand and I open it out. I end up just staring at it. It's all just lines and squiggles and circles and squares to me. The old man sighs and goes, 'You know what we have to do here, Hennessy, don't you?'

I watch Hennessy's eyes drift to the paperweight that he bought the old man for his sixtieth birthday – it's a big glass thing that says 'A good lawyer knows the law. A great lawyer knows the judge,' and I can tell he's thinking about cracking me over the head with it.

'God, not that!' the old man goes. 'No, I was going to suggest telling the chap the truth! Slight case of crossed wires there, old scout!'

I'm just, like, staring at the map, trying to figure it out for myself. Then, all of a sudden, certain words stort leaping off the page at me. We're talking 'prison yord'. We're talking 'borbed wire'. We're talking 'gord tower'.

I'm there, 'Jesus Christ, are you planning to break her out?'

Hennessy goes, 'Yeah, that was it. Now there's no need because you've brought us this evidence.'

Except the old man goes, 'Hennessy, I think we should invite Ross into the circle of trust! It'll be easier that way!'

Hennessy just nods, resigned to it. Then he has another quick look at the paperweight. Then he nods, resigned to it again.

The old man takes a deep breath, then spills everything – except obviously the humungous glass of XO that he pours himself first.

'Hennessy and I are planning to tender for the right to build and operate Ireland's first ever private prison!' he goes. 'It's part of a Government plan – which is to remain secret until after the General Election – to jail people for non-payment of water charges!'

As you can imagine, this means very little to me. I'd be lying if I said I give a shit about anything that goes on in the world.

'Up until now,' he goes, 'the Government has adopted a softly-softly approach on the issue of non-payment – as you know, there's an election in a matter of weeks! But once it's over, well, there's to be a crackdown! Legislation and so forth! Non-payers will be imprisoned in an enormous, purpose-built and privately run Bastille, which your godfather and I are tendering to build on Lambay Island! We're going to call it – wait for it – Aquatraz!'

I actually laugh. 'You two?' I go. 'You're going to run a focking prison? On an island?'

Hennessy's there, 'If our tender is successful, yes.'

'Okay, that's going to be hilarious.'

Then something suddenly occurs to me. 'Hang on,' I go, 'I thought you were telling people *not* to pay their actual water bills?'

'That's our political position!' the old man goes. 'This is business!'

'Okay, I might be as thick as shit, but even I can see how that makes you a total hypocrite.'

'So,' the old man goes, 'you clearly appreciate the sensitivity of what we've just told you! It wouldn't do for the leader of New Republic, a political party that has incited people to resist water charges, to be seen to be profiting from their imprisonment! The optics – as the chap said – would not be good!'

I'm there, 'That's an understatement. So what are you offering me, to buy my silence?'

Hennessy looks at the paperweight again. I'm actually thankful I'm not in this room alone with him. He goes, 'How does joint custody sound to you?'

You can imagine my surprise when he says that. I'm so thrown by it that I forget about the whole Eddie thing. I go, 'Are you talking about joint custody of Honor?'

He's there, 'I'm talking about joint custody of all your children.'

'Oh, the boys as well – yeah, no, I'd definitely want them. And are you saying I might have an actual case?'

'I spoke to an old friend of mine. He's in family law. He says if we can get it in front of a judge who knows his rugby, then Edmund Lalor doesn't have a leg to stand on. And this friend of mine – well, like the paperweight says – he knows the right judge.'

'I see you disgraced yourself again,' Sorcha's old man goes, staring at his watch. 'Publicly.'

He's waiting for the minute hand to move to tell him that it's one o'clock and he can let me into the house to see my kids.

I'm there, 'I wouldn't say I disgraced myself. It was the way it was edited – I think it's a word – *selectively*?'

He goes, 'I said to Sorcha, she should have let those women kill you. It's one o'clock, you may now enter my home. Oh, look at that, my mistake – it's actually five minutes past.'

I refuse to let him provoke me.

'Where's Eddie?' I go. 'Is he upstairs?'

He's like, 'Honor is in the kitchen with her mother and Fionn,' because he obviously still thinks she's doing it for attention. 'The boys are in the garden playing *soccer* with my wife.'

Like I said, I'm not rising to it. He'll get his comeuppance when I drag him in front of a rugby judge and win joint custody of my kids.

I head for the kitchen. Sorcha, Fionn and Eddie are all sitting around the kitchen table. Sorcha and Fionn are doing the whole politics thing. Fionn is on his iPad and Sorcha is on her iPhone. And, madly, Eddie is sitting with them, tapping away on the keys of Sorcha's MacBook. I'm there, 'Hey, Eddie – are we going to play *Call of Duty?*'

He's wearing his Guns N' Roses t-shirt under a leather jacket and a fedora. He doesn't even look at me. He goes, 'Er, I'm *busy* here?'

I'm there, 'Yeah, no, fair enough, I'll wait.'

Sorcha *does* look at me, though. She's obviously still pretty pissed off with me as well, because she goes, 'You've seen it's all over Twitter, have you? You attacking the women's morch in your cor? What is it about strong and independent female characters in leading roles in theatre productions that makes you feel so threatened, Ross?'

I'm like, 'I told you, I was chasing your granny on her mobility scooter to try to get her to admit that she was the one who threw the gay pride scorf on the fire and that she's the one who hates gay people.'

Fionn goes – and I swear to fock, I'm giving it to you word for word – 'Looking back, Sorcha, reverting to your maiden name was one of the best ideas of the campaign.'

And I go, 'Was it, Fionn? Yeah, you're a real focking bro, aren't you?'

'I'm just saying, Ross, the O'Carroll-Kelly name is toxic right now. Did you see what Charles tweeted this morning? He wants to send the Army into all GAA matches to ensure the safety of referees.'

'What's wrong with that? GAA referees are being murdered every day.'

I look out the window. Sorcha's old dear is kicking the ball to the boys and encouraging them to kick it back.

'Footbaw!' Leo is going. 'Footbaw! Footbaw! Footbaw!'

It makes me feel physically ill. I just hope by the time I get joint custody that the damage isn't permanent.

I go, 'Come on, Eddie, are we playing *Call of Duty* or not?'

Eddie's like, 'Dad, I'm trying to write an e-mail here!'

'In the last twenty years,' Fionn goes, looking up from his iPad, 'I can only find two instances in which referees were assaulted at GAA matches. Charles is creating a climate of fear, then attempting to exploit it for electoral gain, and we have to keep pointing that out.'

'Two?' Sorcha goes. 'How many GAA matches have there been in the last twenty years? It must be hundreds.'

'It's hundreds of *thousands*,' Fionn goes. 'You have to keep high-lighting these lies, Sorcha – especially in the debate with Muirgheal.'

I'm like, 'That's actually happening, is it?'

Sorcha goes, 'That's what I'm prepping for here. It's in the RDS next Wednesday.'

I'm there, 'Are you sure that's wise?' because there's a big port of me that obviously still cares for the girl.

She goes, 'Why wouldn't it be wise? It's just two candidates for public office debating local, national and international issues in front of the voters of Dublin Bay South.'

'She can be a real bitch – bear that in mind. I'm thinking about when you beat her for Head Girl in Mount Anville. I'm not sure she ever fully got over that.'

'Well, we've spoken on the phone and we've both agreed not to go negative on the night. Although I *will* be asking her how she can claim to be in favour of pulling out of the European Union when she spent an entire college year in Ferrara and told everyone that she had an amazing, amazing experience?'

'Keep remembering the facts,' Fionn goes. 'Male drivers are twice as likely as female drivers to be involved in a car accident. Cork people are three times as likely as Dublin people to have good personal hygiene. Ireland has benefited from EU membership to the tune of €200 billion. This is how we beat them, Sorcha. We fact-check everything Chorles and Muirgheal say. Every time they tell a lie – like with this GAA referees story – we counteract it with facts. Okay? Facts, facts, facts – that's what people are interested in.'

I *still* believe that GAA referees are being murdered every day.

I'm there, 'Eddie, who the fock are you writing to anyway?' because this is the only time we get to actually spend together and I don't really have the attention span to stand here and talk about shit that doesn't directly affect me.

Eddie goes, 'I'm writing to Mister Wade.'

That's her headmaster. *His* headmaster.

I'm like, 'Er, why?' because it sounds like a waste of perfectly good gaming time.

Sorcha smiles at me – looking more than a bit pleased with herself, it has to be said – and goes, 'It looks like Eddie is following my lead and becoming involved in activism!'

I'm like, 'What are you talking about?'

And Eddie's there, 'There are, like, *no* toilets in my school for people with alternative gender identities.'

'Er . . . okay . . .'

'There's just, like, toilets for the girls. Then there's, like, men's and women's toilets for the teachers.'

'And could you not just use the men's – you know, now that you're a boy?'

Sorcha goes, 'Oh my God, Ross, do you *know* how offensive that is?'

Eddie goes, 'It's fine. It's confusing for some people.'

Sorcha's there, 'Read out what you've written so far, Eddie.'

And Eddie goes, 'Dear Mister Wade. As you will no doubt remember, when I returned to school after the Christmas holidays, I informed you of my new gender identity, which differs from the gender I was assigned at birth. During the course of our conversation, you assured me that my new identity would be respected by the school and that I would receive the full support of the teachers and staff. To this end, I would welcome the opportunity of opening a dialogue with you on the issue of toilets for people of alternative gender identities. Yours sincerely. Eddie Lalor.'

Sorcha goes, 'Oh my God, that is an amazing, amazing letter, Eddie.'

Eddie's there, 'Okay, I'm going to hit Send. Okay, Dad, I'm ready.'

And all I can think, as we head upstairs to play *Call of Duty*, is poor Mister Wade.

Helen smiles and invites me in. She doesn't look great. She goes, 'Thank you for the flowers at Christmas.'

I'm like, 'Hey, it's cool. I just wondered how you were?'

'I'm getting on with things. Will you have some lunch?'

'Yeah, no, definitely. You're an amazing cook.'

You know where I really stand on that.

'It's nothing,' she goes, 'just some chowder from the Butler's Pantry.'

'Oh, thank God,' I go. 'I mean, that'd be lovely. My old man's fine, by the way.'

And she's just there, 'I didn't ask.'

That's the thing about Helen. She's totally sound, but she's also not afraid to let you know when you've crossed the line. She actually reminds me of Gordon D'Arcy, who's an absolute teddy-bear of a goy until you turn up at his Reformer Pilates studio with seven or eight pints on you, intending to rip the piss, and you've suddenly made an enemy you don't need – trust me!

She's there, 'I'm sorry, Ross, I shouldn't take it out on you. I know how Charlie is. I can see him on the news practically every day.'

'He's saying a lot of stupid things,' I go, 'that a lot of people seem to like the sound of.'

'He's talking about Extreme Vetting. You know, my father was from Cork?'

'Jesus. I never would have guessed that. Never in a million years.'

'And the things he's saying about women drivers.'

'I suppose he *is* very old-fashioned in terms of his attutide towards women. You know, he claims he was there the day Ireland got its first ever Lady Bank Teller. It was in the AIB in Deansgrange in 1988. Him and Hennessy went in to watch her count the money and laugh at the very idea of it.'

She laughs as she puts a bowl of chowder down in front of me. She goes, 'He told me that story.'

I'm there, 'Is there any chance for you two, Helen? As in, any way back for him? If it's any consolation, him and Muirgheal was a one-time-only thing. Apparently, she did one or two things for him that, let's just say, *others* weren't prepared to do.'

Helen just shakes her head. 'Muirgheal was just the final straw,' she goes. 'He's not the man I married, Ross. And now I wonder was he ever? Did I make the mistake a lot of people do in relationships of treating him like a canvas that I could project my ideal version of him onto? The version of him I loved all those years ago? I think he tried to be that man, Ross. But you can't hide who you are – not forever.'

I'm there, 'I always said it was an act. I think I might have mentioned it in my best man speech.'

I hear the front door slam, then the sound of high heels on the wooden hallway floor. Erika's home. She puts her head around the door. She's like, 'Hi, Mom,' and then, when she sees me, she goes, 'Euuuggghhh!!!' like she's for some reason disappointed to see me. 'He's not moving back in, is he?'

Helen goes, 'He just called to see how I was doing.'

Erika just nods. I smile at her and I'm there, 'You look great,' which she does. And, again, I don't mean that in a creepy way, although the way Hansel and Gretel are pretty much bursting out of that white shirt would make you nearly forget that you're related.

'Are you talking to me,' she goes, 'or my chest?'

I'm like, 'You . . . both . . . I don't know.'

'I heard Honor's now called Eddie.'

'Yeah, no, since Christmas.'

'It might explain a few things – her confusion over her identity.'

'Everyone's saying that might be why she always was such a focker – *he* was always such a focker.'

'It runs in the family.'

'Are you talking about me or my old man?'

She doesn't answer. Just takes my chowder from me and storts eating it. I love watching her eat from a spoon, even though that might sound strange. I could watch her eat from a spoon all day.

I'm there, 'So how's the gallery?'

She goes, 'It's fine. People are back buying investment pieces.'

'I love to hear that. I love to hear it. And, er, how's Oisinn?'

I surprise myself by asking that question. I'm going to admit it, I miss him. A huge amount. The drafts folder in my phone is full of text messages that I've written to him and then been either too scared or too proud to send.

'You haven't heard?' she goes. 'Him and Magnus are getting married!'

The RDS Main Hall is absolutely rammers and there's a really tense atmosphere in the room. Sorcha Lalor and Muirgheal Massey are about to debate all the important election issues for the voters of Dublin Bay South.

I spot the old man in the front row, with Hennessy on one side of him and K . . . K . . . K . . . K . . . K . . . Kennet on the other. Sorcha's old pair are also up at the front – the proud parents. I'm sitting about ten rows back, the soon-to-be-ex-husband. There's a spare seat next to me, but when I see Fionn walking up the aisle, I lean across it, just in case he has any notions of sitting beside me.

He doesn't, though. He's obviously got his name on one of the reserved seats as well, because he morches to the front, shakes hands with the old man, Hennessy and the other focker, then he sits down beside Sorcha's old pair, after hugs and kisses and all the rest.

Chris Donoghue is going to be putting the questions and making sure the whole thing doesn't turn ugly. I have to say, I've got a hell of a lot of time for Chris Donoghue. Occasionally, if I'm up, and I happen to be in the cor, I'll stick on *Newstalk* while I'm trying to decide what sounds to put on. Sometimes, Chris and Ivan will be talking about, like, world events and I'll pretend to actually understand what's being said, going, 'Oh, good point! Good, good point!' and 'You can't argue with that logic!', especially if I'm pulled up at a red light and a woman is checking me out.

One person who actually loves that story – even though I'm going slightly off the point here – is Jamie Heaslip. I remember a few years back, he'd just been made a brand ambassador for Land Rover and we were taking his new seven-seat Discovery for a spin out to Tayto Pork – 'see what she's made of', in Jamie's words. I happened to be very hungover, so I brought a Domino's pizza with me and Jamie sulked the entire way there, worried about his precious leather seats. During a long lull in the conversation, I told him the story about pretending to know what they were saying on *Newstalk* and he laughed so hord he nearly drove off the road. Ended up being a totally different day.

Suddenly, they're announced onto the stage – first the chair, the famous Chris, then the two candidates – Sorcha and Muirgheal. Sorcha is dressed in a white suit, while Muirgheal is dressed in all black.

The second the clapping stops, I shout, 'I thought they weren't going to go negative!'

It's a cracking line, which just comes to me in that moment. But it doesn't get a laugh. I end up just getting shushed.

Chris Donoghue goes, 'First, I'm going to ask the two candidates to explain what qualities they possess that they believe would make them a good political representative for the constituency of Dublin Bay South. And I'm going to ask Muirgheal Massey to speak first.'

'Thank you for aston me that question,' Muirgheal goes.

I laugh. Can't help it. She's going to do the whole debate in that accent. There are people in this room who are going to need a focking translator.

'Ine arthur doing loads of woork for chaddity and community-based initiatives oabar the yee-ors,' she goes. 'Including the Afferika Paroject, which I founded and which helps bring litter doddy dozens of Transition Year students to Botswana evoddy year to see the mizzer doddy for themselbs foorst hand.'

The accent definitely slips once or twice, but I can see the old man and Kennet nodding at her to encourage her along.

She goes, 'I teach adult litter dossy two nights a week to a class of thorteen, many of them former thrug addicks. I captained the senior hockey tee-um at school, demonsthraten real leadership quadities. I've altso libbed in the airdea me whole life. Which means Ine aweer of the issues more than, say, someone who's libbed all her life on the Vico Roawut in Kill Lioney.'

Sorcha gives her what I call her Hillary Clinton look. The mouth is smiling but the eyes are saying, 'I am going to rip your focking tits off with my teeth!'

And now it's her turn to answer the question.

She goes, 'First, I'd just like to say thank you to Chris Donoghue and the RDS for offering Muirgheal and I the chance to debate the issues in this wonderful, wonderful forum. As to the question – which I'm very grateful to have the opportunity to answer – I would say that my long experience of advocacy and activism, on a local, national and international stage, makes me ideally placed to serve as a TD for the Dublin Bay South constituency.

'As to my specific experience that makes me suitable for the role, I would like to point out that, like Muirgheal, I was involved in the Africa Project. As a matter of fact, I was the only one who actually set it *up*?'

'No, you werdunt,' Muirgheal goes.

Sorcha's like, 'Yes, I did. And I didn't interrupt you, Muirgheal, so I'd thank you to pay *me* the same courtesy?'

This is bringing back definite memories of our school days. I've seen these two be passive-aggressive to each other in English, Irish, German and Italian.

'The reason that *I* decided to set up the Africa Project,' Sorcha goes, 'is because I felt there was a genuine need to raise awareness of the whole Africa situation among young girls in Dublin 4, Dublin 6 and Dublin 6W, who might hopefully be in a position to one day make a difference. And I genuinely hope I've achieved that. It was around the age of ten that I personally storted to become what I would describe as very, very socially aware. I was, for instance, a vegetarian for seven months until I was diagnosed as having a low Bone Mineral Density and I discovered that soy products gave me eczema. I cried the day Mary Robinson was elected President of Ireland and I once got to interview her on Transition Year Radio and she described my questions as 'very to-the-point'. I also cried the day Nelson Mandela was released. At eleven, I was a member of Amnesty International, Greenpeace and the World Wildlife Fund and at fourteen I was involved in picketing a well-known Dublin furrier for two hours every Saturday afternoon for five months.'

There's a fair few mutters among the audience. She's not going

to win friends in this port of the world with that kind of talk –
although the furrier is still there, by the way, and going from
strength to strength.

'But,' she goes, 'it was in my role as Head Girl in Mount Anville
that I really storted to come into my own in terms of showing definite leadership qualities. Muirgheal would have actually seen that
close-up, because she finished second to me in the election and
served as Deputy Head Girl for four weeks until she decided to
resign for whatever reason.'

'Hockey,' Muirgheal tries to go.

'You said hockey at the time and I accepted that as your reason. I
just hope you won't be so quick to walk away from your responsibilities to the people of Dublin Bay South.'

The discussion moves on to the issue of feminism and what goes
wrong in a woman's head when she gets behind the wheel of a car.

Sorcha goes, 'I would like to know how Muirgheal, *as* a woman,
can justify representing a political porty that has policies that are
actually sexist – specifically the pledge to introduce annual driving
test resits for all female drivers?'

'It's veddy simple,' Muirgheal goes, 'I believe in making eer roads
safer. Mebbe you're in favour of mower detts on the roawids, are
you, Sudeka?'

'I don't believe the way to prevent deaths on our roads is to
specifically torget women drivers, who, if I can just quote some
statistics here –'

'If you're about to quote accident statistics, I wootunt bodder.
The definition of a good thriver idn't someone who dudn't have a
crash. There are loawits of ways in which women are bad thrivers
that doatunt involve accidents. Ine guilty of maddy of them meself.
Blocking yeddow boxes, not letting utter keers out at junctions,
texting while thriving, hogging the overtakun layun when you're
nor even overtakun. Addy toyum you ebber see anutter motor-
dist doing addy of those things, ninety-nine percent of cases, it'll be
a woman.'

Jesus, I feel like nearly clapping. At last, a politician who thinks
the same shit as me.

'I don't do any of those things,' Sorcha tries to go.

Sorcha is one of the worst drivers I've ever seen – just to point that out.

Muirgheal goes, 'Well, you doatunt deserb a pat on the back joost cos you doatunt break the law. I joost think, what's the heerm? If it makes women bethor thrivers and at the sayum toyum saves loyuvs, what are you afrayut of?'

Chris Donoghue goes, 'For the sake of time, we might move off this subject for now. Sorcha, on the issue of water charges, you have been unequivocal in your support for water metering.'

Unequivocal. I'd love to know words like that. Chris Donoghue is my idea of a really intelligent person. In fact, if I'd been at school with him, he's the kind of dude I'd have forced to do my homework for me. I can't pay him a higher compliment than that.

'Yes, I have,' Sorcha goes, 'and I very much welcome the opportunity to talk about it here today. I believe that water is a precious, precious natural resource and, as such, should never be *wasted*? I do accept that it's difficult to persuade people who've been affected by the whole economic downturn thing to hand over yet more money, and I'm saying that as someone whose parents lost everything in the crash. But if people understood the environmental benefits that will accrue to us if we, as a society, become more conscious of our water consumption, I genuinely think they would be queuing up to pay their bills.'

My focking hole. That's what everyone's thinking.

She goes, 'Can I quote you a statistic, Chris? Five thousand people die every day for the want of a resource that we take for – oh my God – granted.'

Muirgheal's there, 'There's a mitt going arowunt that what people are looking for is free wathor.'

'A what?' Sorcha goes.

'A mitt.'

'Oh, a *myth*! It's just I'm finding it very difficult to understand you since you storted speaking in that accent about a month ago.'

'There's a mitt that it's free wathor that people is looking for. But people are alretty paying for their wathor in their taxes, which are amongst the highest in Europe. Eer taxes used to cubber serbices like wathor provision, bin collection, all them tings. Suddenly, we're being toalt that thee doatunt cubber them addy mower.'

'That's too simplistic an argument. It's because the supply of water and the disposal of waste have become more complicated in terms of –'

'It's because the Gubberdin Mint gev away eer tax muddy to a bunch of rich men arthur Europe purra gun to theer heads. And the Gubberdin Mint said, "What about seerbices – we've no money left for seerbices?" And Europe said, "Just cheerge people for the wathor coming out their taps and for the houses they're alretty paying through the nowiz to buy."'

'Sorcha,' Chris Donoghue goes, 'Irish Water are refusing to supply exact figures, but we do know that there is a huge rate of non-compliance in relation to these charges. Isn't it true, as New Republic have suggested, that this particular tax is dead in the water?'

She goes, 'I don't see it as a tax, Chris. I see it as a chorge for a vital service. But what I would add is that, as citizens, we are not entitled to just say, "Oh, I consider this tax unfair, or that tax unjust, and I'm not going to pay it." Of all the chorges slash taxes, this is the one we all should be, oh my God, *delighted* to pay?'

At that moment, I just so happen to look at the old man and I see him give Muirgheal a long, deep nod, which seems to be a signal for something. I watch her shuffle her pages, moving one from the bottom of the pile to the top and I suddenly realize that there's some kind of ambush coming. I instantly jump to my feet.

'Okay,' I shout, at the top of my voice, 'let's wrap this up now! I think we've all heard enough!'

Sorcha's like, 'Ross?' because it's news to her that I'm even here.

Her old pair are looking around, going, 'What the hell is he playing at?' and everyone else is thinking pretty much the same thing.

I'm there, 'Thanks for doing a great job, Chris! I think we're all a lot wiser now as to where we stand!'

Chris doesn't take the hint, though. He turns around to me and goes, 'Can you please sit down – whoever you are?'

Whoever you are? Okay, I'm taking back the nice things I said about him. Someone else can do my homework.

Muirgheal fixes Sorcha with a look and she goes, 'Can I ast you a question?'

Sorcha's there, 'As long as it relates to the issues we're debating, yes.'

'Me question is, if you're so in fabour of people paying wathor cheerges, why habn't you paid your owen?'

Sorcha goes, '*Excuse* me?'

'You heert me – you habn't paid addy of your biddles from Irish Wathor.'

There's, like, a low rumble among the crowd.

'That's ridiculous,' Sorcha goes. 'Of course I have.'

Muirgheal's there, 'Ine just goan to read a lethor that was sent to you from Irish Wathor befower Christmas. *Dear Customer, you recently received a biddle from Irish Wathor for wathor serbices. Under the Wathor Serbices (No. 2) Act 2013, you were liable for wathor cheerges. Payment was due within 14 days of the biddle date and eer records show that your account is now overdue.*'

Oh! Holy! Shit!

There's, like, gasps from the audience. People are not happy.

There's, like, five or ten seconds of total silence before Sorcha can even *say* anything? Even then, the best she can come up with is, 'Well, em, the thing is my, er, husband is in chorge of our household bills . . .'

Her old pair turn around and just, like, glower at me. So does Fionn, the cheeky focker. But the look Sorcha gives me is the worst. It's the kind of look Jamie Heaslip gives you when you've spilled melted cheese and pizza sauce all over the seats of his brand-new, seven-seat Land Rover Discovery.

She looks like she wants to kill me.

'Idn't it thrue,' Muirgheal goes, 'that you doatunt pay for athin. That alt your biddles are payut by your fadder-in-law – Chardles O'Caddle-Keddy.'

Again – just gasps.

She's there, 'It's well you can affowurt to be in fabour of wathor cheerges if you nebber hab to put yisser hand in yisser pocket to pay for them yisser self.'

Sorcha tries to go, 'Since my husband and I separated, the paying of our bills has been the responsibility –' but people are suddenly booing her and calling her a hypocrite – a total one – and telling her to get off the focking stage.

Muirgheal's there, 'It's wooden law for you and wooden law for evoddy body else – idn't that right . . . *Sudeka?'*

Sorcha is left standing there with her mouth just open. She knows it and everyone in the RDS knows it – politically, she's dead in the wathor.

I mean water.

8. Wiggyleaks

An opinion poll in this morning's *Irish Times* has put New Republic in second place – ahead of Fianna Fáil and just two points behind Fine Gael – with two weeks to go until the election. That's according to the news on the radio.

He's going to be un-focking-bearable this morning. And so, I suspect, is Sorcha. I haven't actually seen the girl since the night of the debate, but we've been invited slash summoned to Mount Anville to talk to Mister Wade about Eddie's e-mail.

She's waiting for me in the main lobby with a face like thunder. I'm like, 'Hey, Sorcha.'

'Did you know?' she goes.

'Er, I'm not sure I'm following you. You look well, by the way.'

'Did you know that Muirgheal was going to ambush me like that?'

'No, I didn't. I saw my old man sort of, like, signalling to her. That was when I knew something was coming.'

'I was made to look like an – oh my God – hypocrite! That's what people have been calling me on the doorsteps, Ross. Little Miss Do As I Say And Not As I Do. This has cost me the actual election.'

Then I remember Aquatraz. I think about telling her about my old man being a hypocrite as well. Even though it would piss Hennessy off and be the end of the whole joint custody thing. I'm right on the point of telling her. But then she goes, 'My dad is right. I need to ask myself how I ended up married to a man who, at thirty-six years of age, still sends his bills to his father to pay.'

I go, 'They're your bills as well, Sorcha.'

'*Excuse* me?'

'I'm just saying, they're not *my* bills. They're *our* bills? My old man has been paying for our electricity, our phone and our heating since we got married. And you were always pretty happy with that arrangement.'

'Seriously, Ross, this divorce cannot come quick enough for me.'

Eddie comes along then. He's wearing trousers with his uniform these days. 'Yeah,' he goes, 'I could hear you arguing down the focking corridor.'

Sorcha's like, 'Sorry, Eddie. Your father didn't mean to embarrass you. Let's go and see this Principal of yours – find out what his issue is with your simple request.'

Mister Wade is all smiles when we step into his office. He goes, 'Hello, Sorcha! Hello, em . . . Eddie. And hello, Ross – thanks for coming to see me!'

Sorcha isn't a major fan of his – mainly because he didn't include her name on the list of notable alumni on the school website and yet Alison Doody *is* on it?

Sorcha's there, 'Yes,' trying to hurry matters along, 'I'm actually fighting an *election* at the moment? It'd be great if we could find out why you've asked us here today.'

'Of course,' he goes, 'please sit down,' which is what we end up doing. 'I received Honor's e-mail –'

'*Eddie's* e-mail,' Sorcha goes.

She's in foul form.

Mister Wade's there, 'Yes, of course – Eddie's e-mail. I don't know why I keep saying Honor.'

Eddie weighs in then. 'It's because you haven't got your head around the whole gender diversity thing,' he goes.

The man's like, 'I must admit, it is all new to me – as it is to many of us.'

Sorcha's there, 'As an educator, a major port of your job is to stay informed.'

'Yes, well, I've been trying to do that, and that's why I wanted to discuss *Eddie's* e-mail with you today. As a school, let me just say, we fully respect Eddie's new gender identity, which is why we've allowed him to wear a uniform that is consistent with him being a transgender male. We also recognize – again, as a school – that we have a duty to support LB . . . LG –'

'I keep saying BLT,' I go, trying to keep the conversation light. 'Don't I, Sorcha? Or BFG, which is apparently a book. How random is it that I actually know that? Anyway, Dude, don't sweat it – we know what you're trying to say.'

That earns me a serious filthy from Sorcha. And from Eddie.

Poor Mister Wade has to stort referring to his notes then. 'As a school,' he goes, 'we *do* endeavour to foster an understanding of gender identity and create a culture that respects and values all students and prevents transphobic bullying.'

'Bullying isn't going to be a problem,' Eddie goes. It definitely won't. Girl or boy, he rules this school with an iron fist. 'We're here to talk about toilets.'

'And,' Mister Wade goes, still reading from his notes, 'we further acknowledge – again, as a school – that we have a duty to provide students with access to bathroom facilities that correspond *with* their gender identity. The Department of Education has suggested that schools consider perhaps reassigning their Wheelchair toilets as Wheelchair and Gender Neutral toilets.'

'Excuse me?' Sorcha goes.

'This is coming from the Department of Education.'

'You want my son to use the Wheelchair toilets?'

'Well, it wouldn't be a Wheelchair toilet. It would be a Wheelchair and Gender Neutral toilet. It would say that on the door.'

'I haven't got a disability,' Eddie goes.

The poor dude's there, 'I'm aware of that.'

'And I'm not Gender Neutral. I'm Transgender Male. Which means I want access to a Transgender Male toilet.'

'Obviously, I don't want to cause offence, but –'

'It is your responsibility,' Sorcha goes, standing up and roaring at the poor dude, 'to ensure that Eddie feels safe, secure and also valued within his educational environment!'

I'm there, 'I'm going to suggest a compromise here. Eddie, how would you feel about just using the men's toilet? Or maybe switching schools to – much as I hate to say it – Willow Pork?'

Both of these suggestions are shot down. Actually, they end up being totally ignored. Sorcha looks at poor Mister Wade and goes, 'Can I just remind you that Mary Robinson went to Mount Anville?'

'Yes,' the dude goes, 'I'm well aware that Mary Robinson went to Mount Anville.'

'And not *just* Mary Robinson? There have been a lot of other past pupils who've dedicated their lives to social justice and human rights advocacy.'

That Alison Doody thing clearly still stings.

Eddie *also* stands up? He's like, 'Okay, here's what's going to happen. Either you provide me with a Transgender toilet or I'm taking a case against the school for gender discrimination.'

I know I keep saying it but poor Mister Wade. He's just, like, terrified.

'Okay, look,' he goes, 'I'll call the plumber today.'

'Do it now,' Eddie goes.

The dude just nods and picks up the phone.

Outside in the hallway, Sorcha gives Eddie a big hug. 'I'm so proud of you,' she goes. 'The way you stood up for yourself in there. So, so proud, Eddie. I genuinely think activism is going to be your thing as well.'

Eddie's like, 'Hey, I'm just fighting for my rights as a Trans Male,' and then he focks off back to class.

Sorcha turns to me as we walk across the cor pork. 'And you,' she goes, 'were worse than useless – as usual.'

'Hey,' I go, 'I was just trying to keep the conversation easy-breezy.'

'Your father has destroyed me, Ross. And you just stood by while it happened. No one is going to take me seriously now.'

'I know something, Sorcha. Something about my old man. Something he's planning. And if word of this gets out . . .'

A voice goes, 'We have him, Sorcha!'

We both look around. It's focking Fionn. And he's waving a piece of paper.

Sorcha goes, 'Fionn, what are you doing here?'

He's like, 'Your dad told me this is where you were. I've got something here that's going to blow this election wide open.'

'What? What is it?'

Fionn looks at me, like he wants me to fock off first – like I can't be trusted or something.

I'm there, 'Dude, I probably won't even understand what you're talking about.'

Sorcha's like, 'He probably won't, Fionn. Tell me – what have you found?'

'Okay,' he goes, 'let me read this to you. This is what he said at the launch of New Republic: *"This idea runs like a red thread through our so-called bailout deal, which seeks, on the one hand, to burden the economy of a great people with an unbearable load, and on the other, to destroy it as much as possible, to cut off all its opportunities."'*

Sorcha's like, 'Okay, so what?'

'Now,' he goes, 'listen to this. *"A mad theory, but one which runs like a red thread through the whole Versailles Treaty, and which finally leads to the fact that for ten years they have tried, on the one hand, to burden the economy of a great people with an unbearable load, and on the other, to destroy it as much as possible, to cut off all its opportunities."'*

'Oh! My God!'

'Oh my God is right. Charles is channelling Hitler.'

I just shrug. I'm there, 'Our rugby coach at school channelled Hitler. I don't see what the big deal is.'

'When people hear this,' he goes, 'it's going to be the end of Charles O'Carroll-Kelly. And the end of New Republic.'

The function room above The Broken Orms is packed to the gills. There must be, like, two hundred people in the room and the vibe is good. Ronan's criminal friends are all mixing freely with the two or three Community Gordaí who tried to take Ronan under their wings over the years. I even hear the famous Gull turn around to Gorda Ivor and go, 'Ine fuddy behind yous feddas looking for more bread, so I am. Yous hab a veddy heerd job to do.'

There's a bench warrant out for Gull's arrest for assaulting a water-meter installation engineer with his own shovel. Tomorrow, Ivor and his crew will be back kicking down doors looking for him. But tonight, there's a ceasefire. Because Ronan Masters has got himself engaged.

The old man is working the room. K . . . K . . . K . . . Kennet is

leading him around, introducing him to various local heads. Everyone seems to love him.

Buckets of Blood sidles up to me. He goes, 'He thalks a lot of sed-
dents, your oul fedda!'

I'm there, 'I think he's a knob. Always have.'

'The stand he's arthur thaken on the wathor, but.'

'Sorcha says it's easy to take populist positions when you're in
opposition. People aren't stupid enough to fall for it, though.'

'You'd be surproysed. There's no one arowunt hee-or is godda
pay for their wathor. Thee throyed to install the meters and we ren
them.'

'I heard. I can't believe Gull is here. I heard he put a man in
hospital.'

'Sent a messidge. Lowut and clee-or. Wathor's not sometin you
can cheerge people fow-er. It comes from the Jaysusing sky!'

'Again, I'm quoting Sorcha, but she says that metering water is
the only way to persuade people to be responsible about their usage
and to save the North Pole.'

'What use is the Nort Powill to addyone in Finglas?'

'That's a point.'

'And sure habn't we got the Sowt Powill to fall back on? Hee-or,
what you think of Ro getting maddied?'

I'm there, 'Honestly?'

'Hodestly.'

'I think he's making the biggest mistake of his life. He's too
young to decide who he wants to be with for the next, whatever,
sixty years.'

'Won't last foyuv. He's mooben on, Rosser. Going to coddidge
now. Him and Shadden hab nothing in cobbon any mower – except
a kid.'

Buckets is one of my favourite people in the world. He's very like
me, in fact – he can be accidentally *deep* sometimes?

He tells me he's switching to shorts, then he focks off to the bor.

I tip over to Ronan. I'm like, 'Hey, Ro – congratulations again.'

He goes, 'Thanks, Rosser.'

'I'm presuming it's going to be a hopefully long engagement?'

'We're thalken about mebbe doing it in the subber.'

'This summer? Look, I'm not saying I don't think Shadden's great. I'm just making the point that you've only just storted college. And maybe you're doing this because you feel guilty for riding that bird from the country – the one who's *not* doing agricultural science.'

'I ast Shadden to marry me cos I lub her, Rosser.'

'But how do you know she's definitely the one for you?'

He goes, 'When you know, Rosser, you know!' but as he's saying it, I watch his eyes stray to the bor, where Buckets of Blood is ordering a drink from his niece – was it Jacinta? – with the massive Milk Duds.

I'm there, 'Fair focks to you, Ro. As long as you know what you're doing.'

I mingle some more. I'm a genuinely good mingler. I spot Shadden across the room, showing off the ring. A Lizzy Duke special. And I hear Dordeen go, 'You make shurden lerrim know it's not to be a long engayuchment. What use is coddidge to him now?'

I decide to avoid them. But then I end up getting stuck with Tina, who gives me an earful for about an hour. She goes, 'Would you not hab a woord wirrum? You're apposed to be he's fadder!'

I'm there, 'I just had a word with him, Tina. I asked him was he doing it out of guilt but he said no.'

'Shadden's a lubbly geerdle. It's not faird on her to go into a maddidge wit a fedda who's not ready. And I doatunt want to see him stuck in a situation he's norr able to gerrour of.'

'He seems to be saying that the bird he rode in UCD was a one-off. We have to take his word for that.'

The conversation goes back and forth like this for – like I said – an hour. Then I need to piss. Yeah, no, the old back teeth are floating, so I excuse myself and I head for the jacks.

On the way there, I happen to pass this little storeroom, where they keep barrels and shit like that. Through the half-open door, I can hear the familiar sounds of grunting and moaning, compliments uttered and promises made.

And I know it. I know it even before I push the door open an inch

or two more and catch sight of the two of them going at it. Buckets of Blood's niece is sitting on a barrel, her trousers and her knickers in a ball on the ground, and a boy's bony orse is moving backwards and forwards. I know without needing to see any more that the bony orse belongs to my soon-to-be-married son.

'Hitler?' the old man goes. He's on the radio being interviewed by someone or other. This is while I'm in the cor, on my way to visit the old dear. 'I've never heard of anything so absurd in my life!'

Sorcha and Fionn have obviously put the story out there.

The interviewer goes, 'Can you perhaps explain the similarities – which *are* uncanny – between what you said at the launch of your party and what Adolf Hitler said in Berlin in, I believe, 1931?'

It's actually Pat Kenny. He's a man who's not going to just accept my old man's bullshit.

'Mere coincidence!' the old man tries to go.

Pat Kenny's there, 'You spoke of the bailout as a deal which "seeks, on the one hand, to burden the economy of a great people with an unbearable load, and on the other, to destroy it as much as possible, to cut off all its opportunities". Hitler used exactly the same formula of words to describe the Treaty of Versailles.'

'This is common, everyday language, Pat!'

'The Taoiseach, Enda Kenny, has called on you to apologize to the Jewish people. He said he recently met a woman in Dartry –'

'Let me just say, Pat, this is a non-story that's been put out there in an attempt to distract voters from the real issues! We produce enough food every year to feed China, India, Russia and Brazil combined! And look at us! We are broke! We have trillions upon trillions of euros passing through the accounts of Irish registered companies every year that we are not allowed to tax! Meanwhile, we've got Cork people arriving in Dublin by the container-load and GAA referees being murdered at the rate of two per day! And people are being brought before the criminal courts just for driving home from the pub with a few drinks on them!'

'Are you saying you're in favour of decriminalizing drink-driving now?'

'That's exactly what I'm saying!'

'But the drink-driving laws are in place surely to prevent deaths on our roads?'

'Oh, nonsense! Most people who've had a few drinks are perfectly safe to drive – as long as they use the hard shoulder!'

'You're saying you want the hard shoulder to serve as a third lane for drink-drivers?'

'That's *absolutely* what I'm saying!'

'People will say this is a cynical attempt by Charles O'Carroll-Kelly to deflect attention away from the Hitler controversy . . .'

I kill the engine and get out of the cor, then into the prison I walk. I'm about to hand over my phone to one of the screws when it all of a sudden rings. It ends up being Sorcha. I answer it by going, 'Hey, I see you put it out there about my old man quoting Hitler. It's hord to see him coming back from this.'

She goes, 'I'm not going to apologize for it, Ross. A woman walked up to me in the Gourmet Shop in Rathgor yesterday and called me a fraud.'

'Shit one.'

'To my actual face.'

'I'm agreeing with you. I said shit one. Why are you ringing anyway? I'm about to go in to see my old dear.'

'Mister Wade wants to see us.'

'What, again? Jesus Chirst, we only saw him, like, a week ago.'

'He said this time he wants to come to the house – to talk to us alone. I have to say I'm not exactly comfortable with Eddie not being present. I think I'm going to take minutes of the meeting, just to make sure that he's informed of everything that's actually said.'

'What time is he coming?'

'Three o'clock.'

'Okay, I'll be there.'

And I hang up, just thinking, oh, shit, what fresh hell is this?

I'm sitting opposite my old dear and she's telling me how much she'd love to see the children again.

I'm there, 'I'll definitely mention it to Sorcha. As you know, I've only got, like, *supervised* access these days? Although Hennessy has promised to work on that.'

'It would be lovely to see them again. Honor and the *triplets* – you see, I remembered! One, two, three. I think a real bond developed the last day you brought them in.'

'And do you remember their names?'

'One of them is John, I think.'

'Yeah, you're not getting a pat on the back for that. And by the way, Honor's called Eddie now.'

'I *beg* your pardon?'

'Yeah, no, it turns out that Honor is a boy.'

'It turns out? Are you saying they didn't check at the hospital?'

'The way it was explained to me is that you can be born with, you know, the various bits and bobs that make you a girl, but you're actually a boy. And then you can be born with a – I hate saying this word in front of you – penis, but inside you're actually a girl.'

'When did all of this happen? God, I feel like I've been in here for thirty years!'

'I'm telling you. In the future, when someone has a baby, you won't be allowed to ask if it's a boy or girl. The answer will be no one knows for sure. The answer will be they'll decide themselves when they're old enough.'

She looks at me across the table and her face seems suddenly sad. 'I want you to smuggle something in for me,' she goes.

I'm there, 'Is that why you wanted me to bring the kids in again? So I can put shit in their nappies for you?'

'No, I'm really looking forward to seeing . . .'

'I'm not telling you their names again. I thought you lost your job in the kitchen anyway.'

'It's not ingredients I want you to bring to me, Ross. It's sleeping tablets. There's a large bottle of them in my bathroom cabinet.'

'Would they not give you sleeping tablets in here?'

'Not in the quantity I need . . . Ross, I'm going to take my own life.'

'What?'

'Don't try to dissuade me.'

'Don't flatter yourself. I was just making sure I heard you right. You're seriously saying you're going to kill yourself?'

'If the trial doesn't go my way, I have to consider the possibility that a jury might not believe my account. And in that case, I've decided to end it all.'

'Hey, you're going to be found not guilty. What about the evidence I found? That photograph of your cor?'

'I'm very grateful to you for your efforts, Ross. But it doesn't prove my innocence. They've narrowed Ari's death down to a four-hour period that day. I could have had time to go out shopping *and* kill my husband. In theory.'

'But you didn't.'

'We're dealing with what a jury might plausibly believe . . . Hennessy wants me to change my plea.'

I'm in, like, shock. I'm like, 'What? He wants you to say you actually did it?'

'He wants me to accept a charge of manslaughter,' she goes. 'To say I killed Ari during the course of a heated row, or by some accident, and that I tried to make it look like a heart attack and I'm sorry.'

'I thought Hennessy was supposed to be on our side? I mean, *your* side?'

'He is, Ross. But he says we have to be realistic. There is a weight of circumstantial evidence that points to my guilt. I had a clear motive for wanting him dead.'

'Hennessy's supposed to be the old man's best friend.'

'It's Hennessy's job to get me the best result he can, Ross. And the best result he believes is to plead guilty to a charge of manslaughter and serve seven years in prison.'

'Seven years?'

'He says that with remission, I could be out in five. By which time I would be in my mid-fifties.'

'Again, I could call you on that one. I'm not going to. I'm just saying I could.'

'I'd still have a lot of years left when I got out. But I won't do it, Ross. I won't plead guilty to murdering a man I dearly, dearly loved.

So you'll bring me those sleeping pills – and you won't say a word to your father about it.'

'No,' I go, 'I won't. I can't.'

She's like, 'Ross, I'm asking you, as my son, to please, please, please put me out of my misery.'

'There must be more we can do. More evidence we can find.'

'It's done, Ross. The jury aren't going to believe my story. And when the inevitable happens, I want to be ready. To leave this world on my terms.'

The bell suddenly rings and she stands up. She doesn't kiss me or hug me or even say goodbye. She just walks out of the visiting room without even looking back at me, a shadow of the woman who cooked the Nigella Christmas for more than a hundred inmates just six or seven weeks ago.

I walk out of the prison, thinking, there must be more evidence out there? If she definitely didn't do it, there has to be actual proof.

'I don't know if you watch the news,' Sorcha goes, 'but I'm *actually* kind of busy at the moment?'

'I'm sorry,' Mister Wade goes, 'I wouldn't have asked to see you again if I didn't consider it important.'

'And is a home visit *really* necessary?'

'I was just curious as to whether there was anything, well, going on in Eddie's domestic environment that was causing him to – look, it's not the correct phrase – but act out?'

'You're absolutely right, it's not the correct phrase. Ross, are you going to say anything at all here?'

I'm sitting in between the two of them, watching them bat lines back and forth. 'Yeah, no,' I go, 'I saw my role as being more of a *listening* one? And making tea slash coffee if necessary. Do either of you want tea slash coffee?'

'Do you have decaf tea?' Mister Wade goes. 'I try not to take caffeine after lunchtime.'

Sorcha's there, 'Ross, don't you dare touch that kettle. This isn't Storbucks. Mister Wade has just made a very serious allegation.'

'It wasn't an allegation. I'm just concerned that Eddie's recent behaviour may have its roots in perhaps some disturbance in his home life.'

I'm there, 'Well, the one major change in the last year is that me and Sorcha are now separated and getting divorced.'

'Ah!' he goes, at the same time nodding his head. There's also the slightest hint of a smile on his face.

Sorcha totally flips. 'That has nothing to do with it!' she goes. 'How dare you suggest that his – oh my God – courageous, courageous decision to confront his crisis over his gender identity might be a behavioural issue!'

I'm there, 'I actually wondered was it rugby that tipped her over the edge, didn't I, Sorcha? That's when *she* slash *he* storted dressing down – wearing Vans and all the rest of it.'

'We have accepted Eddie's new gender identity,' Mister Wade goes, 'and I'm not suggesting for one minute that he isn't sincere in his claims to be a transgender male. When I mentioned behavioural issues, I'm referring to the demands that he's suddenly making of the school, which we're finding, well, a little on the excessive side.'

I'm there, 'Hang on, I thought you agreed to the new jacks? You were ringing the plumber.'

'Yes,' he goes, 'and he was in the process of partitioning off an area of the existing girls' toilets to create a transgender toilet. That's when Eddie decided there needed to be *two* transgender toilets – Trans Male and Trans Female.'

'FTM and MTF,' Sorcha goes. 'What's your problem with that?'

'Well, in practical terms, we're not sure that two are strictly necessary. The only males we have in the school, apart from obviously Eddie, are teachers and other staff. And none of them are – as you say – transgender MTF.'

'How do you know that? Maybe they are, but they don't feel they can reveal their true gender identity because they're not working in an environment where they feel fully safe and fully supported.'

'That's not true.'

'Maybe they're afraid that they're working with people who aren't interested in the process of social change through transformative education?'

'I can assure you that that is not true.'

'And how do you know you won't employ a teacher in the future who will be transgender MTF?'

'Well, I don't.'

'Well, I think you should be making provision for that. We're living in a different world to the one we lived in when I was in the school.'

'But then it's all these *other* toilets he's demanding as well. I told him I would consider providing a transgender MTF bathroom, then he returned to my office before the end of the day and said what about Agender, Bigender, Gender Questioning and Gender Fluid?'

I'm there, 'Are all of those *actual*? As in, do we know she's definitely not making them up?'

'Yes,' Sorcha goes, 'they are all *actual*, as you put it.'

I'm like, 'It's just one or two of them do sound made up.'

She goes, 'Agender is someone with no gender identity. Bigender is someone with two gender identities. Gender Questioning is someone who is uncertain of their gender identity. Gender Fluid is someone whose gender identity may change from time to time.'

I'm there, 'And do they all need specific rooms to go to the toilet in? Could some of them not double up? The Bigender and the Gender Fluid sound like they could definitely muck in together – no pun intended.'

Sorcha looks mad enough to kill me with her hands.

'Look,' Mister Wade goes, 'I'm just making the point that building six extra toilets would place enormous pressure on our existing space. We need to have a common sense approach to the whole gender bathroom issue.'

'Oh my God,' Sorcha goes, 'you *actually* sounded like a Nazi there!'

'It's a case of us not having enough room.'

'The Nazis said that.'

'I'm trying to come up with a final solution.'

'The Nazis said that as well.'

I can definitely sympathize with the dude. If Eddie keeps this up, there'll be nowhere left to actually teach. It'll just be rooms to piss and shit in.

'You're actually port of what's wrong with our society today,' Sorcha goes. 'Privileged white males like you need to sit down and have a conversation with yourself,' and then she walks to the kitchen door and stands by it – her signal that this meeting is over. 'I can turn this into a national issue if that's what you want? I could arrange a series of day-strikes by students.'

The dude goes, 'Okay, we'll provide the six toilets. We're very keen to accommodate students like Eddie as much as is practicable. But it's just, well, he makes these demands and he refuses to compromise.'

'Good,' Sorcha goes. 'I'm proud of that. Mount Anville used to value people who showed a desire to change the world for the better. These days, you seem to value people who were in, er, *how* many movies? And when was her actual last one? The 1980s?'

So I finally manage to get Ronan on the phone. He's been basically avoiding me since the night of the engagement porty. So when he finally rings me back, I'm in no mood for his bullshit.

I'm there, 'Ro, you're making a terrible mistake – getting married, I mean.'

He goes, 'Why shoultn't I get maddied, Rosser?'

I'm like, 'I saw you, Ro. The night of the engagement porty. You and Buckets of Blood's niece were going at it like the last night in Magaluf.'

'That was a wood-off, Rosser.'

'Another one-off, huh?'

'Ine godda mend me wayuz as soowun as I get maddied, Rosser.'

And before I can tell him that that's exactly the same bullshit promise I made, he ends up hanging up on me.

I tip into the living room. The old man and Hennessy are watching *Telly Bingo*. I can only presume they're waiting for the lunchtime news to stort. I go, 'What's the story, by the way – with the whole custody thing?'

Hennessy goes, 'I got you a date. Middle of March. In front of Jeremy Dawson.'

'Is he a rugby judge?'

'Does he sound like a rugby judge to you?'

He does sound like a rugby judge actually. The old man shushes me then. He goes, 'The news is about to stort, Kicker!'

I end up catching the first few seconds of it. With one week to go until the General Election, Ray Kennedy says, New Republic is leading Fine Gael and Fianna Fáil by one point and five points respectively in the latest opinion poll. He also says that Charles O'Carroll-Kelly has the highest approval rating among all the party leaders, despite claims that he quoted from an Adolf Hitler speech during the launch of his party and is currently the subject of a Garda probe over his controversial views about people from Cork.

My phone rings. It's a number I don't recognize. But I end up answering it anyway. There's, like, five seconds of silence on the other end. Then I hear all this heavy breathing.

At first, I presume it's just Jerry Flannery, ripping the piss out of me as usual.

But then a woman's voice comes on the line. She goes, 'Hello, Ross,' and I recognize her straightaway.

It's Sorcha's granny.

I'm like, 'What the fock do you want?'

She goes, 'I want you to hear what I have to say.'

'Well, I don't want to talk to you. You stitched me up – twice. Three times if you count the day I was nearly lynched by those angry lady theatre people.'

'I talked to the priest this morning,' she goes.

I'm like, 'What?'

'My conscience has been troubling me, you see. I'm a martyr to my conscience. He heard my Confession. And he said I should make restitution with you.'

'Resti– what?'

'He said I needed to apologize to you?'

'Too focking right you do. You also need to tell Sorcha the truth.'

'The priest didn't mention anything about that.'

'Well, I don't want an apology from you unless you're also going to tell Sorcha that you were the one who was planning to vote No and that you were the one who threw that gay pride scorf on the fire.'

'Okay, I admit it, the priest did say that to me too. But the first thing he said I needed to do was to say sorry to you. Will you come to the house? We could have another Irish Mist or two.'

I actually laugh. Despite everything, I can't help but like the woman.

'Okay,' I go. 'I'll see you in a bit.'

I grab a shower, throw on a pair of clean Cantos, then I point the A8 in the direction of Foxrock Grove – or, as my old dear and her mates have always called this side of the dualler, Deansgrange West.

I hop out of the cor and I walk up to the door. I ring the bell – except there ends up being no *answer*? I try it a second, then a third time, then I bang on the door with the heel of my hand. Still nothing. Which is weird because her red Honda Fit is porked in the actual driveway.

I have a look through the living-room window. I can see through the net curtains that she's not in there. Then I remember that she always keeps a spare key in a flowerpot shaped like a big shoe in the back gorden.

So around the house I go. I find the key – it's for, like, the back door – and I let myself into the kitchen. I'm going, 'Hello? Hello?' and I'm actually shouting it, because I don't want to give the woman a fright – just in case she's on the bowl and she can't hear me.

I'm like, 'Hello?'

She's definitely not downstairs because I try every room. So then I tip up the stairs, thinking, why would she tell me to come and then not actually be here?

And then I get my answer. I push the bedroom door open to see her lying in bed with a big stupid grin on her face. And instantly I know that Sorcha's granny is dead.

It's weird because I'm not *freaked* by it? Even though I'm in a small room with an actual dead body, it feels – I don't know – strangely peaceful. I'm looking at that smile and I'm wondering what was going through her head in the final moments of her life that she seemed to find so funny?

I liked Sorcha's granny. I liked her a lot. She always had a lot of time for me, even when Sorcha's old pair openly hated me. She was a big, big Chorlie Haughey fan. 'Oh, he was a rogue!' she'd go, like she genuinely approved – and I think she kind of felt the same way about me.

Poor Sorcha, I think. She's going to be absolutely crushed by this. Her grandmother meant the world to her. And this couldn't have happened at a worse time, what with the election being only a week away.

And it's only then – I swear to God – that I remember her saying that she was going to tell Sorcha the truth about how she was going to vote in the marriage equality referendum and throwing the gay pride scorf on the fire. But now Sorcha's never going to know the actual truth, because the only person who knows it aport from me is dead.

And that's why I do what I end up doing next. You have to understand it in context.

I spot her mobile phone, chorging on her bedside locker. I walk over to it and I pick it up. It's an old Nokia 6210 – doesn't even have the Internet on it. Her attitude towards phones was much the same as her attitude towards homosexuals – she wasn't as much old school as Old Testament.

After thinking about it for ten, maybe twenty seconds, I use it to send Sorcha a text. It's like, 'Hey Sorcha, it's your granny here. There's something that's been bugging me and I need to get it off my chest. Ross was telling the truth about the day of the marriage referendum. He was the one who basically wanted to vote Yes and I was the one who was anti the gays. I was the one who was going to vote No because, as far as I was concerned, God created Adam and Eve, not Adam and Panti Bliss, and all gay people, while some of them are very nice, will burn in Hell. Gran x.'

I hit Send. Then I suddenly feel bad, so I send a second one to her that's just like, 'That was back then. Since then I've had time to think about it and I'm actually cool with the whole gay thing now. I was just scared of people who were different to me. Sure what harm are they doing anyone? I feel bad for the way I blamed Ross for stopping me from voting. He was the one who was basically going to vote Yes. It feels so good to finally tell the truth. Also it was me who threw the scorf on the fire because I didn't want my friends to see me wearing it. Gran x.'

I send that one as well, then I put the phone back down on her locker. I grab her hand and I hold it for a few seconds and I go, 'I know that's what you would have wanted. Goodbye, Sorcha's granny.'

I leave the bedroom, then I tip down the stairs. But halfway down, another thought occurs to me and I end up going back. I pick up the phone again.

'Yeah, no, one other thing,' I write. 'I really think you should give Ross another chance in terms of maybe forgiving him and hopefully giving your marriage another crack. I'm a major, major fan of his and I think he definitely loves you. You won't do any better. Anyway, I'm glad I got that lot off my conscience. I think I'll lie down now because I'm tired. So tired. So, so tired . . .'

Then I hit Send.

There's a rainbow flag draped over her coffin as it's lowered into the ground. A focking ranbow flag! So now I'm obviously wondering did Sorcha even get the texts about her being an actual homophobe? They might have got lost in space. Her granny's phone was a piece of shit and I hope that's not being disrespectful to her memory.

I'm sort of, like, skulking towards the back of the crowd. This is in, like, Deansgrange Cemetery. My old man is to my right, a few feet away, although there's thankfully no sign of Muirgheal. I spot Helen and Erika, then Oisinn and Magnus, then, standing together, JP, Christian, Chloe and – look who's home from France – Lauren. I can't help but notice that Fionn is at the front with Sorcha's family – her old pair and her little ride of a sister. And I spot Eddie, in his skinny black jeans, black Supra Hi Tops, Ramones t-shirt and fedora.

Sorcha's going to say something. I think she originally planned to talk about her in the church, except she ended up being too upset, but now she's steeled herself and she's going to deliver a graveside – okay, I may have totally made this word up – but *eugoly*?

'My grandmother,' she goes, 'was an amazing, amazing woman. She was born in 1934, five years before the world went to war. She saw – oh my God – *so* much change in her life, we're talking social change, we're talking lifestyle change, we're talking technological change. She wasn't afraid of change. She forgot her fear and embraced it. For instance, despite her phobia of developing brain cancer from any piece of technology invented after the gramophone, she started using a mobile phone in her final years.'

It's a pity it was a piece of focking shit, I think.

'She loved that she lived in a world of variety. She was incredibly open-minded. Yes, she was – oh my God – *so*, so religious. She sometimes went to two Masses a day – one after the other. But she was also very spiritual. She didn't believe in – and I don't want to offend the priest – but *dogma*? She didn't need any holy man, any Church, any ancient book, to tell her the correct way to treat people. Just as an example, in the last months of her life, I'm so proud to say that she became an outspoken advocate for gay rights.'

She's looking at Oisinn and Magnus and they're just, like, nodding back at her. If only they knew.

'She believed, most of all, in the right of all people to just be themselves and to love in whatever way they wanted to love. I want to just leave you with a quote. She said many, many memorable things in her life. But this is one I'll – oh my God – never forget. In the final months of her life, she had the opportunity to vote in the marriage equality referendum. As someone who was very, very active in the campaign for a Yes vote, I went to her Active Retirement group and asked her and her friends to maybe consider a different view of marriage from traditional heterosexual marriage, which was all they knew. And my grandmother said, in front of a room full of other strong, strong Catholics: "As a Christian, it's my duty to vote for love ahead of the alternative!" '

That gets a round of applause.

She goes, 'As the mother of a transgender child,' and I watch Eddie roll his eyes, 'I'm grateful to her for the role she played in bequeathing a world of tolerance and love to my children – and to all of our children. Thank you.'

There's a huge round of applause. Massive. Then the priest steps forward and does the necessary. I sidle over to the old man and I go, 'You've got a focking cheek showing your face around here, having stitched her up in a major way.'

'I love Sorcha very dearly, as you know!'

'You've got a funny way of showing it. You destroyed her.'

'That's politics, Ross! A clever man once described it as the art of something something something-else! It may even have been Cicero! Although it doesn't sound like Cicero!'

Then off he goes, back to his cor. Kennet is porked with the engine idling.

I catch Oisinn's eye then and I nod at him, except he just turns his head and blanks me. A few seconds later, Sorcha arrives over to me. She gives me a hug. She already gave me one outside Foxrock Church, but this one is warmer and longer.

She goes, 'We're going back to Fitzpatrick's Castle if you –'

I'm there, 'Thanks, Sorcha. But I'd only ruin the atmos. Your old dear's upset enough about losing her mother without me and your old man kicking off.'

'I really need to talk to you about something.'

'Oh? What is it?'

'Where's your cor?'

'It's porked over there.'

'Okay, let's go for a drive.'

She tells her old pair that she'll see them in the hotel and asks them to take the kids in the funeral cor. Her old man stares hord at me as we get into the A8. Fionn does exactly the same thing. I make sure to give them both a dirty wink, which obviously drives them mad.

I stort the engine and I'm like, 'So where do you want to go?'

She's there, 'Just drive, Ross.'

So I do. I head for Monkstown, where we take the coast road, heading south. She doesn't say shit for a good ten minutes. Then she goes, 'It was all lies, Ross.'

I'm like, 'What was?'

'What I just said about my grandmother. She was a homophobe and she was a liar.'

'Really? Continue on talking.'

'She sent me some texts. It was in the few hours before Mum found her. She must have known she was going to die. She said she wanted to get some things off her chest.'

'What kind of things were *on* her chest?'

'She said you were telling the truth. When you said she was going to vote No. And all that stuff about Panti Bliss – that was her as well.'

'Did she mention the scorf at all? I'm just curious.'

'She said she was the one who put it on the fire.'

'That's interesting because your old man said he witnessed me actually doing it. So she's obviously made a liar out of him.'

'Ross, I feel so bad for the way I treated you.'

We're driving through Dalkey at this point.

'Sorcha,' I go, 'it's fine. I've got big shoulders. I just wish you'd believed me sooner. I'm only allowed to see my kids for one hour a week, bear in mind.'

'That was because you encouraged Eddie to break that child's collarbone. And you had sex with that slut from Dalkey. You're not exactly blameless.'

'Point taken. The thing I can't get over is your old man lying about seeing me burn the scorf. Maybe we should all be focusing on that. What a focking piece of work he's turned out to be.'

'Ross, I can't believe my grandmother was homophobic.'

I feel weirdly guilty. I owe the woman nothing, but I still find myself suddenly defending her. I'm there, 'Maybe she was just scared of, I don't know, people who were different from her. Maybe later on, she did think to herself, hey, what actual horm are they doing?'

'That's exactly what she said, Ross. Those same words.'

'There you are then.'

'I suppose it is some consolation that she changed her mind right at the end. She said something else to me as well.'

'Okay?'

There's, like, silence for a good thirty seconds. For a moment, I think she might have nodded off.

'She said she thought I should give you another chance,' she goes.

I'm like, 'Really? That's a bit random, isn't it?'

'She said I should forgive you and give our marriage another try – even though she really hated you for cheating on me.'

Okay, she's making shit up now. I clearly wrote that she was a major, major fan. I end up nearly saying it to her as well by accident.

I'm there, 'Are you sure she said –? Sorry, keep going.'

'She said you acted like a complete shit, but she said I still should possibly forgive you and take you back. Ross, that was practically the last thought she ever had. You could nearly say it was her dying wish.'

'Random is the only word that seems to do it justice – yet again.'

I'm so, I don't know, tuned in to the conversation that I haven't properly realized that we're suddenly on the Vico Road, a few yords short of Honalee. And that's when Sorcha goes, 'Indicate, Ross.'

I'm like, 'What?'

She goes, 'Indicate,' and at the same time she puts her hand on my leg. I've suddenly got a sink plunger in my chinos.

I go, 'Are you sure?' but that's *after* I've already taken the turn?

'For once in my life,' she goes, 'I'm listening to my hort and not my head.'

I drive through the gates, putting my foot down in a serious way, sending gravel spraying everywhere. Then into the gaff we go.

She's keen. There's no question. She kicks off her shoes, then takes me by the hand and leads me up the stairs.

'Hey,' I go, 'let's do it in your old man's bed!'

She's like, 'Excuse me?'

Yeah, no, I can understand how that might have sounded.

'Doesn't matter,' I go. 'It was just an idea I had for making it a bit more interesting.'

In the end, we make do with *our* old bed?

She pushes me down on it, her hands and her mouth all over me. 'Let's do it like we used to,' she goes. 'Except for longer.'

I'm there, 'Sorcha, I'm not going to make you any promises in terms of duration,' trying to head off her disappointment early on. 'But that's only an indication of how turned on I am right now.'

We knuckle down to business. The equipment is ready and I'm about do the deed when I automatically reach into the drawer of my bedside locker for a nodding sock.

Sorcha's like, 'Why have you stopped?'

'I'm getting a condom,' I go.

'You don't need to use a condom.'

'Seriously? *You've* changed your tune.'

'Ross, you had a vasectomy.'

'Oh . . . er . . . yeah.'

It would be more accurate to say that Sorcha *thinks* I had a vasectomy. Yeah, no, it's a long story. The op was actually booked, but I didn't go ahead with it. The truth is I'm actually still packing live rounds, but I can't help but feel that breaking this news to her might take some of the passion out of the moment.

So I just plough on regordless.

Again, I'm revealing nothing of what actually happens. I'm pleading the fifth. All I will say is that Sorcha ends up finding out what she's been missing these last few months. We bounce each other off every wall and surface in the room and the entire transaction comes to a happy ending with Sorcha lying on her back with her feet around her ears screaming, 'Don't stop! Don't stop! Don't you *dare* stop!' until I eventually do stop, unable to prevent the inevitable any more than Wednesday can prevent Thursday.

She sighs and says that was certainly like the old days. I tell her thanks, then I drift off into a – I'm going to use the word – *blissful* sleep.

I don't know how long I end up being *out* for? But it can't have been that long because Sorcha is awake the entire time. She's stroking my hair and, as I become aware of my surroundings again, I can tell she's wondering what it actually meant? Was it a one-off? Are we back together? Was it a terrible mistake?

'Today is not a day for making big decisions,' she goes. 'I feel very raw right now.'

I'm like, 'Yeah, no, definitely take your time. The second you want me to move my shit back in, though, you just say the word. I'll get on daft.ie and find somewhere for your old pair to live. I'd love to put them in Bray – see how they like them apples.'

'Let's not get ahead of ourselves. Let's move slowly.'

She gets out of the bed. She pulls on her Dan Biggars then covers her num-nums with her hands while searching the floor for her bra.

She goes, 'I better get up to Fitzpatrick's. The funeral porty will be arriving there by now.'

I'm like, 'Jesus, was I that quick?'

She goes, 'It was, em, quite quick, yeah.'

I get out of bed then and stort looking for my own clothes. I'm there, 'Are you doing anything later on?'

'Ross,' she goes, 'I still have an election to fight to –' and then she suddenly stops, sits down on the end of the bed and breaks down in tears. It's an emotional day.

I'm there, 'Hey,' taking her in my orms. 'This isn't the Sorcha I know. The Sorcha I know is strong.'

She goes, 'I'm finished, Ross. People are calling me a cheat and a phoney everywhere I go. And those are just the ones who don't slam the door in my face when they see that it's me standing there.'

'This is just the beginning for you, Sorcha. You're going to go on to do hopefully amazing things. Remember you were talking about becoming a fashion blogger?'

She sort of, like, extracts herself from my embrace. She goes, 'Your dad has to be stopped, Ross. I really love Chorles, but he's a racist and a sexist and a misogynist and a xenophobe. Yet every time he makes one of these, oh my God, *offensive* statements – pulling out of Europe, building a wall around Cork, decriminalizing drink-driving – his popularity actually increases.'

'People have always liked him. I've never understood it.'

I pull on my chinos.

She goes, 'Fionn keeps saying we'll beat him with facts. Just keep emphasizing facts and exposing his lies, he says. He made a speech in Dún Laoghaire last week in which he told four lies.'

I'm like, 'Four? Jesus.'

'I keep telling Fionn, we're running out of time. We have to do something! We need to find something on him!'

And that's when I decide to tell her what I know. I go, 'Sorcha, he's got this thing planned called Aquatraz.'

Her head suddenly spins around like Linda Blair's in *The Exorcist*. She's like, 'Aquatraz? What's Aquatraz?'

I just think, fock the old man and fock Hennessy. It looks like me and Sorcha are almost definitely getting back together, so I'm not going to need to fight for joint custody anymore. 'Yeah, no, apparently,' I go, 'once the election is over, the Government is planning to come down hord on people who haven't paid their water bills.'

She goes, 'So they should.'

'They're talking about jailing all of them in this, like, humungous private prison. Ireland's first, apparently.'

'Well, actually, I've been saying for years that they should consider custodial sentences for people who put ordinary household refuse in the recycling bin.'

I stort buttoning up my shirt. 'Sorcha,' I go, 'the point I'm trying to make here is that the old man and Hennessy are planning to put in a tender to build and then run it.'

She's like, 'Excuse me?'

'I walked in on them a couple of weeks ago. They had the plans out on his desk. Like I said, it's called Aquatraz.'

'But your dad is telling people not to pay their water bills.'

'That's my point.'

'And he stands to benefit financially when they're eventually punished for it?'

'He's a dick, Sorcha. I warned you from day one.'

'Ross, this is explosive!'

'I knew you'd be happy.'

'Where are the plans?'

'I'm presuming they're in his safe.'

I step into my Dubes, ready to go. She goes, 'Do you know the code?'

I'm there, 'Of course I know the code. But I can't let you steal something from my old man's safe, Sorcha.'

And she's like, 'I'm not going to steal anything from his safe. You're going to do it for me.'

I stick on Today FM. Sorcha and the old man are on *The Last Word* with Matt Cooper. It's, like, two days before the election and this is Sorcha's last chance to win over the voters who think she's a hypocrite who's full of shit.

I end up missing the stort of it. By the time I switch it on, the old man is going, 'I didn't say *all* Cork people! You, for instance, Matt, are the kind of Cork person who *is* welcome! You come here to work and you speak in a way that allows you to be easily understood!'

Sorcha – fair focks to her – goes, 'Can I just say, this business of restricting the movement of Cork people to Dublin is typical of how populist politics work. You create an enemy where one doesn't exist and you pander to people's ignorance and fear.'

'Are you denying, Sorcha, that people are coming here from Cork, adopting extreme political and social ideals and aspirations and attempting to undermine the position of Dublin as Ireland's first city?'

Matt doesn't just take his bullshit, though. He goes, 'Let's maybe drop those offensive stereotypes for a moment, Charles, and talk about something that you brought up very late in the campaign, which is this proposal to repeal the ban on drink-driving.'

'It's not a proposal, Matt, it's a promise.'

Sorcha goes, 'Can I just say, Matt, I think this is a cynical attempt by New Republic to win votes in rural areas, where their support is flagging.'

'It's no such thing, Matt!' the old man goes. 'I've been a long-time critic of the way in which people who have no difficulty whatsoever driving while a little tanked up are being unfairly criminalized by our justice system! I want that to stop!'

'Matt, can I just say that today, Muirgheal Massey, New Republic's Deputy Leader, has said she's in favour of decriminalizing other forms of behaviour which pose a huge threat to life on our roads. For instance, she believes that motorists should be permitted to drive in the hord shoulder if they wish to send a text message or apply make-up while driving. This is clearly an effort to win back women voters who have been alienated by the porty's position on annual driving test resits for all women.'

Matt goes, 'We might move onto another issue that I know has figured largely in both your campaigns, and that's the issue of water charges. Sorcha Lalor, can you confirm for our listeners that you have now in fact paid your arrears?'

She goes, 'Yes, I have, Matt, and thank you for offering me the opportunity to clear this matter up once and for all. Given the stresses of preparing for an election, which involves actually inter-facing with the people of Dublin Bay South and listening to their problems and concerns, I was forced to leave a lot of our – let's just say – domestic paperwork to my husband. Unfortunately, in the case of this particular bill, he forgot to pay it. It was simply a bureau-cratic oversight on his port.'

She's made me sound like a fockwit. I don't care, though – she also called me her husband.

I can hear the old man chuckling away in the background.

Matt goes, 'Charles, you seem very amused by this. Your party's position is that Irish Water should be abolished –'

'Will be abolished, Matt! Will be abolished!'

'Well, you've promised to make it a redline issue in any future coalition negotiations. So how does New Republic propose to meet the increasingly expensive cost of providing a twenty-first-century water supply to the country's homes and businesses?'

'By making Ireland the master of its own destiny! It's explained quite clearly in our Programme for Government, Matt! We will rip up the bailout deal and remove the economic millstone that has been placed around the necks of the Irish people! By pulling out of the European Union, we will triple – no, quadruple – the country's export revenue! We will go to those American multinationals who have been using Ireland as a tax haven and we will say, "You owe us! Billions!" We won't need to ask anyone to pay for the water that comes out of their taps!'

I can hear Sorcha clearing her throat. I'm thinking, okay, this is it, and I realize that I'm actually nervous for her. But I don't need to be. She's got this.

'You're telling people to tear up their bills from Irish Water,' she goes. 'I've got something here that I think voters might find interesting!'

The old man goes, 'Okay, what's this?'

I stuck it in a lorge brown envelope for her. My old man is from that generation of men who were once sexually aroused by brown envelopes but now live in fear of them.

She goes, 'This is Chorles O'Carroll-Kelly's tender to build and run Ireland's first private prison, where people will be imprisoned for non-payment of water chorges if the Government is returned to power. Or, presumably, if New Republic gets the overall majority that Chorles considers within his reach.'

The old man goes, 'Those documents are forgeries! I've never seen them before in my life!'

'It's called Aquatraz,' Sorcha goes. 'Chorles, along with Hennessy Coghlan-O'Hara, the man he plans to appoint as his Attorney General, wants to turn Lambay Island into a prison colony for people who don't pay their Irish Water bills. He refers to it in his introduction as: "A Robben Island for the kind of people who don't want to pay for bloody well anything!" It's got machine-gun towers and shorks – actual *shorks*, Matt! – patrolling it.'

'Absolute rubbish!' the old man tries to go. 'We just put those in to give the chaps in the Department of Justice a laugh! The same applies to the quicksand and the crocodile-filled moat!'

Matt Cooper goes, 'So are you saying, Charles O'Carroll-Kelly, that it *is* your plan to build and run this prison, where Irish citizens – a great many of them your supporters – will be jailed for non-payment of water bills, which was something you actively encouraged?'

'What I'm saying, Matt, is that these documents have been obtained by illegal means! It is my intention to go to the High Court – Hennessy, if you're listening, I'll see you in The Chancery Inn in half an hour! – to obtain interlocutory relief to prevent this from becoming a story that detracts from the issues that really matter to voters two days before the most important General Election that this country has ever faced!'

I laugh. I just think, you did it, Sorcha. It's over for him now.

At that exact moment, my phone rings. It ends up being Hennessy. I can hear from his breathing that he's running – presumably in the direction of the Four Courts. He goes, 'You stole those plans . . . you little prick . . . you think I'm going to help you get your kids now?'

I'm like, 'Dude, me and Sorcha are getting back together again. So fock you and fock your joint custody. I don't actually need you anymore.'

He goes, 'You better hope things stay sweet between you and her. Because you and me are fucking finished.'

'Like my old man,' I'm tempted to say.

And then I do say it. I go, 'Like my old man!'

9. Finally Facing My Waterloo (Road)

'This is not the end of Sorcha Lalor.'

That's what she tells Bryan Dobson. But she says it without any real – I don't know – conviction, like one of those boy bands who get voted off *The X Factor* and they go, 'This isn't the end of whatever the fock Simon Cowell decided to call us when it was discovered that our previous band name represented a copyright infringement.'

In other words, she knows she's toast.

Bryan Dobson goes, 'I suppose it's a huge question – and one that's difficult to answer at this early stage – but what happened?'

That's what everyone in the Ballsbridge Count Centre is wondering. And beyond these walls as well, I'm sure. The people weighed up my old man's dodgy business dealings, his hypocrisy on the whole water issue, his attitude towards drink-driving and Gaelic football, his hatred of women drivers and people from Cork, and his threat to pull out of Europe – and they decided that yeah, no, he was the definitely the man for them.

They're still counting in some, I don't know, constituencies, but, according to Bryan Dobson, New Republic has emerged from the election as the biggest porty in the country with a projected fifty-two seats. Muirgheal topped the poll in Dublin Bay South. The old man topped the poll in Dún Laoghaire. Jesus Christ, they even won two seats in Cork, where the locals are now seeing the wall not as a means of keeping them in but as a means of keeping the rest of the country out. That was after the old man offered them a referendum on independence by 2019.

Bryan Dobson's right. You do have to wonder, what the fock?

'I'm still in shock,' Sorcha goes, 'like a lot of other people around the country. Tonight, I'll go home and I'll lick my wounds. And tomorrow, along with my advisors, we'll begin the process of reflecting on why we failed to get our message across to the electorate.'

I notice Sorcha's old man hovering nearby. Then next to him is Fionn, his head hung slightly to the left, a sad smile on his face, like he's sad for her but proud of her at the *same* time? I know I'll have to watch him. Sorcha is going to be very vulnerable now. If anyone's going to take advantage of her, it's going to be me.

I catch his eye and I mouth the words, 'Your focking fault!' and he ends up just giving me a filthy back – as does Sorcha's old man.

Bryan Dobson goes, 'Was it that you failed to get your message across to the electorate or was it simply that the electorate heard your message and didn't think it was any good?'

She got twenty-seven votes, by the way, although it's taken her about four hours to accept that basic fact. She asked for a recount, convinced that someone was going to find a big box of votes that they forgot to count and it'd turn out to contain five thousand votes for her and not just more for Muirgheal.

Sorcha goes, 'Yes, I do have to accept the possibility that people heard what I had to say and rejected it.

'But twenty-seven votes is a very poor showing!' Bryan Dobson goes. He's got the focking courage of CJ Stander.

Sorcha's there, 'Yes, I'm aware of the figures. But I think something far bigger happened today than me losing my deposit. Something dorker. Something more sinister.'

Bryan Dobson's like, 'What do you mean by that?'

I watch her straightening up. Her voice goes up in volume. 'What I mean,' she goes, 'is that populism won. Pandering to the lowest common denominator, playing to people's fears, exploiting people's ignorance – those are the real victors today. We have entered a dangerous phase. I think people will discover very quickly that making the lives of Cork people or women drivers or GAA players more miserable won't make their own lives any happier.'

'And what about the future for Sorcha Lalor? Will you remain in politics?'

'What I'm going to do tonight, Bryan, is go home and love my family a little bit more. And I would urge all of your viewers who are saddened by the hateful direction our country has taken to do the same as me. New Republic might be the biggest political porty in the country but they didn't get the overall majority that they promised they would. Let's not forget that more people voted against them than for them. So let's keep reminding them of that. There are more of us than there are of you! Let's love Cork people a little bit more tonight. Let's love women drivers a little bit more tonight. Let's love people who believe in water conservation a little bit more tonight. Whoever Chorles O'Carroll-Kelly decides is our next common enemy – let's love them a little bit more, too. Let's love each other more and let's love each other horder.'

'Will there be a hashtag?'

'It's too early to say, Bryan.'

She steps away from the camera. She hugs her old man. Then she hugs Fionn, who goes, 'Your interview is already getting a lot of traction on Twitter. Love Horder is an instant hashtag. So is More Of Us Than You. I don't think it'll be long before they're both trending.'

There's no hug for me.

She goes, 'There's no point in winning the election on social media, Fionn. People didn't come out and vote for me.'

I'm there, 'Exactly, Fionn! You've got a lot of questions to answer – election agent, my focking hole!'

My old man arrives over with Muirgheal, Hennessy and Kennet in tow. He's about to go on TV as well. Sorcha shakes his hand and goes, 'Congratulations, Chorles,' and she says the same thing to Muirgheal as well.

Muirgheal just goes, 'Nice speech. Almost as funny as the one you made when you became Head Girl. *I am of Mount Anville – come dance with me!*'

I go, 'Why don't you fock off, Muirgheal, and leave her alone?'

Sorcha goes, 'I'm well capable of fighting my own battles, Ross,' and I'm wondering is she possibly regretting having sex with me the other day?

Some dude runs a microphone lead up the back of the old man's shirt while *he* goes, 'What was it in the end, Sorcha? Twenty votes?'

Oh, he's full of himself.

She's like, 'It was actually twenty-seven.'

'Of course,' he goes, 'I forgot the second recount!' and he sort of, like, chuckles to himself.

Suddenly, the camera is focused on him and he's going, 'Yes, as you say, Bryan, a seismic day! People have rejected the failed political configurations of the past in favour of a new republic! Just a moment ago, I received a phone call of congratulations from An Taoiseach, Enda Kenny, who pointed out to me that, as the leader of the biggest political party in the country, I have been given a mandate to open discussions with interested parties to form a new coalition Government!'

Bryan Dobson goes, 'New Republic was the big winner in this election – that was despite the revelation that you intend to bid for the tender to build a private prison in which water charge non-payers will be jailed.'

'Well, Bryan, I'm just happy to see that the electorate is clever enough to realize that a man's political life and his entrepreneurial life are two entirely separate entities! Now it's time for the entire country to come together and heal the divisions of the past few months!'

Sorcha's there, 'I have to go – where's Fionn?' and I go to follow her.

I'm like, 'I suppose if it's any consolation, you losing means we'll both have a lot more time to give to fix our marriage.'

But she totally ignores me and just walks off. And that's when her old man suddenly steps between us.

He ends up doing the weirdest thing. He pushes something into my hands and it leaves me a little bit speechless, to be honest, because when I look at it, it's, like, a photograph in a frame – a photograph of Sorcha and her grandmother, taken when Sorcha was a child, maybe seven or eight years old. The granny with her big grey Rihanna 'fro and Sorcha sitting on her lap, smiling into the camera.

I'm like, 'Why are you giving me this?'

'I'm not *giving* it to you,' he goes, 'I'm showing it to you. It was supposed to be a gift for Sorcha. For her desk in Leinster House. Turn it over.'

I do. On the back, there's writing. It says, 'Sorcha and Gran' – 6 July, 1988,' and then, underneath that, it's like, 'As a Christian, it's my duty to vote for love over the alternative.'

I actually laugh. I probably shouldn't, but I still *do*? I'm there, 'That quote is total bullshit. You know that. She pretty much acknowledged that before she died.'

I hand it back to him.

'Sorcha's grandmother didn't write those texts,' he suddenly goes.

I freeze. I'm thinking, oh, shit.

I'm like, 'What?' hoping against hope that my face isn't giving me away.

'Those texts,' he goes, 'that came from her grandmother's phone on the day she died. I told Sorcha – her grandmother didn't write them.'

I'm there, 'I genuinely don't know what you're shitting on about. Don't care either. I'm out of here.'

He blocks my way. He's like, 'That wasn't the way she spoke. *I'm actually cool with the whole gay thing* and *He was the one who basically wanted to vote Yes.* There's only one person I know who talks like that, and that person is you.'

I'm there, 'You'd want to get out more. Get on the Luas and open your focking ears.'

'What was the other one? Oh, yes! *I'm a major, major fan of his.* You're not exactly a master forger, are you?'

'You're only bulling because you know she's going to take me back. You know I was with her on the day of the funeral – as in *with* with?'

'You sent her text messages purporting to be from her grandmother, then you took advantage of her grief to get what you wanted.'

'Is that why she's suddenly blanking me? Because you're filling her head with your bullshit?'

'Do you know why I'm laughing? Because you've done it this time. This is the worst thing you've ever done to her.'

'I've done worse. I'm not going to go into specifics because I don't think it'll help the situation. But I've done worse. Way worse.'

'And when she finds out for sure, that'll be the end of it. You won't see her or your children ever again.'

He's so full of shit.

I'm there, 'You've no actual evidence of anything.'

'Oh, I'll get the evidence,' he goes. 'You see, this is what I do, Ross. And you're about to find out just how good I am at it.'

The old man's phone rings. I'm just, like, listening at the study door.

'It's Michael Martin,' Hennessy goes – this is without even answering it. 'Will I tell him to fuck off?'

The old man laughs. He's there, 'No, just let it ring out, Old Bean! Phone his people in a moment and tell them I'm meeting Enda Kenny! Then phone Enda Kenny's people and tell them I'm with Michael Martin! Let's keep them all guessing!'

'On it,' Hennessy goes.

'Let them bloody well stew!' the old man goes. 'Enda's saying he's going to make it a precondition of talks that I offer the people a referendum on Ireland's EU membership! A precondition indeed! Mister Twenty-Nine Seats!'

Hennessy laughs. He's there, 'Michael Martin said this morning that Fianna Fáil won't go into Government with you unless you guarantee that the wall around Cork will be a soft border.'

'What are we going to make it from? Polystyrene?'

They both crack their holes laughing. I suppose they can *afford* to?

I tip back upstairs and my phone rings. It ends up being Sorcha. I'm like, 'Hey, how the hell are you? I see *Love Horder* has become, like, an actual thing – if elections were decided by Likes and Retweets, you'd have topped the poll.'

She asks me the question straight out. She goes, 'Did you write those text messages using my grandmother's phone?'

I'm there, 'No.'

'Because my dad thinks you did.'

'Your old man is just terrified that we're going to possibly get back together again. And I've made it easy for you – I'm admitting that – to always believe the worst of me.'

'I shouldn't have slept with you. It was a mistake.'

'It didn't sound like a mistake at the time. Jesus, the screams out of you.'

'I mean it was an emotional day. And I wasn't in the right frame of mind to make good choices. I'm still not. I've lost my grand-mother and I've just lost an election.'

'Then don't decide anything for now. Give yourself a few weeks. See how you feel then.'

There's, like, silence between us then.

She goes, 'An invitation arrived today from the school. They're having a ceremony to celebrate the opening of the new gender non-binary toilets. Eddie wants you to be there.'

I'm like, 'Yeah, no, I wouldn't miss it for the world.'

She hangs up. So now she's confused. That's still good news. Two weeks ago, she hated my basic guts. Now – having had sex with me – she doesn't know whether she's coming or going. That's progress – although a psychotherapist would probably argue it was the opposite.

About half an hour later, I'm back in bed watching *Shortland Street* when I suddenly hear voices downstairs in the hall. It's all, like, chummy laughter – big hellos and meaty handshakes and all the rest of it. And I could be wrong, but I'm pretty sure I hear a voice I recognize. I step out onto the landing and I have a listen. And I end up in just, like, shock.

It's Fionn.

I'm thinking, what the fock is *he* doing here? Then I hear the old man go, 'Have you played Portmarnock before?'

And Fionn's there, 'Er, no, never.'

'Well, it's a lovely course! Just keep an eye on Hennessy here! Turn your back on him for a moment and he'll put a bloody well kink in your driver!'

'That was an accident,' Hennessy goes. 'I've explained that many times.'

There's more chummy laughter. Then out the front door they go.

I tip down the stairs and watch them through the living-room window. Kennet is loading three sets of clubs into the boot of the Merc. I'm thinking, what the fock is Fionn playing at?

He was always a sneaky focker. I remember when we were in Castlerock, there was a tradition, every January, that if you were named in the Leinster Schools Senior Cup squad, you burned all your schoolbooks in a bonfire at the back of the school. In our year, Fionn was the only one who kept his books – and he actually read them, the snake.

I consider texting Sorcha and telling her. Then I think, no, I'll find out what he's up to first.

So it's, like, standing room only in the main assembly hall in Mount Anville. The room is full of children and their parents and it's a massive, massive day in the history of the school. As Mister Wade points out at the stort of his speech, they've become the first primary school in Ireland to have bathroom facilities for non-binary genders.

'Agender,' he goes, listing them off, 'Bigender, Gender Fluid, Gender Questioning, Transgender Male to Female and Transgender Female to Male. These are not just labels. Each represents someone's gender identity as it differs from the gender identity they were assigned at birth. We here at Mount Anville are happy to provide an environment that wraps itself around the student and makes *her*, or *him*, or indeed *they*, feel safe, respected and valued.'

God, it's taken its toll on the man, though. He looks like he's aged about twenty years since Christmas.

'We are very proud,' he goes, 'that the name of Mount Anville has become synonymous with advocacy on behalf of those whose voices might otherwise not be heard. Past pupils of the school include former President, Mary Robinson and former US Ambassador to the United Nations, Samantha Power – in addition to stars of stage and screen, such as Alison Doody.'

Sorcha, beside me, just shakes her head – I want to say – *witheringly?*

'To that proud list of high-achieving alumnae,' Mister Wade goes, 'I am confident that we will one day be adding a new name, that of the young student who very bravely brought to the school's attention a way in which we could make our genderqueer pupils –'

There's all of a sudden muttering in the room. It's the first time I notice that the atmos is less than happy-clappy. To create space for the new bathrooms, they had to get rid of the music room, and I'm slowly realizing that most of these parents aren't here to celebrate. They're here to complain.

'It's absolutely ridiculous,' I hear one mother go – she's very attractive as well. 'My daughter was learning the clarinet. Now there's nowhere for her to play.'

Mister Wade tries to rise above it – or at least his voice does, '– in which we could make our genderqueer pupils – *and* staff – feel secure and cherished within the school environment. Before he goes out into the corridor to cut the ribbon to officially open the new non-binary gender bathrooms, I want to invite Eddie Lalor up here to the stage to say a few words.'

Eddie stands up and walks to the stage. There's only, like, a tiny smattering of applause – most of it coming from Sorcha, who's also shouting, 'You're an advocate for justice, Eddie! And an advocate for change!'

A woman sitting behind us, out of the corner of her mouth, goes, 'Do you hear *her*? Twenty-seven votes she got!'

As Eddie steps up onto the stage, there's a sort of low hum – it's the sound of South Dublin disapproving of something. Eddie reaches the lectern and just smiles. It's funny because there's actually a port of him that seems to *enjoy* the notoriety – another way in which he's like me. If that was me up there, I'd probably be pulling up my shirt right now and giving them an eyeful of The Six.

Eddie goes, 'I just wanted to say a huge thank you to Mister Wade, the other members of the teaching staff and the Board of Management of the school for agreeing to provide bathroom facilities for a whole group of people who have been hitherto marginalized.'

'Hitherto marginalized?' a man two rows ahead of me shouts. 'I've never heard of anything so ridiculous in my life. What's it going to cost to clean all these extra bathrooms?'

That gets everyone's courage up.

'Absolutely nothing,' a woman at the back goes, 'because they'll never be used.'

The dude goes, 'They'll still have to be cleaned. You watch the fees go up next year. That's where this is heading.'

Sorcha storts shouting at people, going, 'Hear him out!' meaning Eddie. 'Let him speak!'

'What I wanted to say,' Eddie goes, 'is that these bathrooms should represent only the base camp of our ambitions . . .'

Sorcha definitely helped him with the speech. I've heard her use that phrase before – when she was talking about separating our domestic rubbish and I innocently asked whether four wheelie bins was possibly overkill?

Eddie's there, 'I hope, in the coming weeks, that the school will see its way to providing bathroom facilities for other sexual and gender identities that remain lavatorially unrecognized.'

I notice Mister Wade turn to another teacher on the stage and go, 'Other?'

Then some dude shouts out the question that seems to be on *everyone's* lips? He's like, 'How many of these things are there?'

And that's when Eddie launches into his list.

'There's Gransgender,' he goes, 'who are people who identify as the mother of one or either of their parents. There's Francegender – people who identify as French even if they have not necessarily ever visited that country. And Hansgender is the German equivalent. There's Standsgender – people who are asexual but choose to stand up when they go to the toilet. They just need a urinal, although we probably should put an actual bowl in there as well, as they can be fluid.'

'She's making these up!' the clarinet woman shouts – the big ride.

Half the people in the room already have their phones out and they're Googling like billyo.

'She's not making them up,' one of the other mothers goes. 'They all exist. Mostly in California – but they do exist.'

'There's Dodosexuals,' Eddie goes, 'whose sexuality has been extinct for generations. There's Bohosexuals, who are only attracted to scruffy people who live for the orts, and Hobosexuals, who are only attracted to scruffy people who live on the streets. There's Go-go-sexuals, who are only attracted to people who are assertive and dynamic, and Lolosexuals, who find the whole question of gender and sexuality to be laugh out loud funny.'

'There's quite a few of those in the room,' the dude who pulled her up on the phrase 'hitherto marginalized' goes.

Eddie just fixes the man with a look and goes, 'I have neither the time nor the crayons to explain the subject of gender identity to someone as ignorant as you.'

The entire room gasps as one. I'm always telling Sorcha that we should be keeping a book with all of Honor slash Eddie's funniest quotes. He could bring a whole room to silence – which is actually what he's just done, by the way.

Eddie continues. He's there, 'There's Androgynes, who are of indeterminate gender. There's Tannedrogynes, who are also of indeterminate gender but have a fantastic all-year-round colour. There's Blandrogynes, who are of indeterminate gender but who like to dress down and wear a lot of pastels.'

'But do they all need toilets?' the clarinet woman goes. I actually think she looks like Romee Strijd.

Sorcha is straight on her feet. 'Of course they need toilets! That's the most offensive question I've ever heard!'

'I mean do they all need individual toilets? Could some of them not, you know, double up?'

'Double up? Oh my God, you are *such* a Fascist!'

'Why am I a Fascist? Because I don't believe the same things as you?'

'You're a Fascist because you support the oppression of minorities.'

'And you're a Fascist because you don't believe in free speech.'

'What you said wasn't free speech. It was hate speech. Free speech comes with responsibilities.'

'What, the responsibility to believe all the same things as you believe?'

Jesus, so much for loving each other horder.

Eddie, by the way, is still on the stage, listing off genders who need toilets.

'There's Hermaphrodites,' Eddie goes, 'who have male and female sexual organs; Germaphrodites, who have male and female sexual organs and an obsession with bodily cleanliness; and Permaphrodites, who have male and female sexual organs and big hair. There's Drag Queens, Slag Queens, Skag Queens and Nag Queens.'

Some dude – again, another parent – stands up and goes, 'This is classic attention-seeking behaviour. I'm Googling some of them on my phone. She's not naming legitimate genders – she's just naming roles that people choose to play.'

'*She* happens to be a *he*,' I suddenly go. *I'm* on my feet now? 'My daughter is a boy and I would ask you to show him some respect.'

Eventually, Mister Wade steps over to the lectern and goes, 'Eddie, look, as you know, we have shown ourselves to be more than willing to accommodate people of alternative genders. Can you just put a final number on this for us, please? How many toilets do you want?'

'Sixty-four,' Eddie goes. 'And if you don't provide them, then you're a bigot.'

'But we'll have nowhere left to teach the children.'

Sorcha shouts, 'It's not *where* you teach children that matters. It's *what* you teach them.'

There's all of a sudden boos coming from the other parents and even the other kids. Someone shouts, 'This is the kind of wishy-washy rubbish you were talking before the election. You saw where it got you.'

But Sorcha stands her ground. 'You will provide these toilets – Eddie, give Mister Wade your list – or we will make a complaint to the Irish Human Rights and Equality Commission. And you can all account for your hate crimes in front of them.'

Eddie Hobbs says my old man is a dangerous lunatic. This is on the news while I'm driving out to Killiney to spend my weekly hour with the kids. He is urging Fianna Fáil and Fine Gael to come to a coalition arrangement, the dude on the radio says, to rescue Ireland from a dangerous Fascist who preaches intolerance and hatred and who threatens to lead Ireland into a century of isolationism and possibly even war. However, sources for both Fianna Fáil and Fine Gael said they considered their differences too great to ever contemplate a power-sharing arrangement.

I drive through the gates of Honalee and I pork next to Sorcha's old man's focking Flintstone cor. I kill the engine and I check myself out in the visor mirror. I look great, and I'm only stating that as a fact. I *feel* great as well? Things are definitely looking up for the Rossmeister. The issue of bathrooms for something-binary-whatever-the-phrase-is people has definitely brought me and Sorcha even closer together and it won't be long until I've got my famous size tens back under the table where they belong.

Sorcha's old man opens the door. He doesn't make a big show of checking his watch like he *usually* does? That should be my first warning that today is going to be different. I step into the house, giving him a bit of a shoulder nudge, but only because he's slow about moving out of my way. 'Are the kids upstairs?' I go.

He's like, 'No, they're not. Sorcha's mother has taken them to the library.'

I'm there, 'The library? What the fock are you talking about? Saturday is my day of having access.'

'We're in my study,' he goes – and he doesn't say who *we* are? He just storts walking and expects me to follow him.

I do follow him. Into the study we go. Sorcha is sitting in an orm-chair in the corner with a look of, like, confusion on her face. She goes, 'Ross, my dad said he has proof – that you did send those texts. Is it true?'

I think the bigger question is what the fock are my children doing in a library? But I let it go. I'm there, 'I already told you it wasn't true.'

He walks around his desk and sits down behind it, leaving me standing.

In a calm voice, he goes, 'Sorcha, how could your grandmother have sent those text messages at lunchtime if she died – according to the coroner – at eleven o'clock in the morning?'

'Sometimes that happens with my phone,' Sorcha goes, still wanting to give me the benefit of the doubt. 'I sometimes text Erika and my phone says it's sent but then it doesn't *actually* send? Then later on, she'll get, like, five messages from me all together.'

He opens his desk drawer. 'I asked an old friend of mine to look at those messages,' he goes. 'He's an expert in linguistics. I've used

303

him over the years in court. I printed them out and asked him to compare them with the language used in this.'

He pulls out my Rugby Tactics Book and puts it down on the desk. I notice there's, like, thirty or forty yellow Post-it notes sticking out of it.

I'm there, 'I've had enough of this. Which library did she take them to? I want to rescue them from whatever damage is being done to their minds.'

He goes, 'He read this from cover to cover, cross-referencing it with those text messages, looking for commonality between the two – recurring words and phrases, similarities in sentence construction, etcetera.'

'You shouldn't even have that book – never mind be passing it around to strangers.'

'And he found a great many matches. On the subject of the marriage equality referendum, your grandmother is supposed to have said in her text: "There's something that's been bugging me and I need to get it off my chest." And *he* writes, in relation to Declan Kidney –'

'Declan Kidney is a dick.'

'He writes, "There's something that's been bugging me. I need to get this off my chest."'

'Yeah, those two things are hordly identical.'

'Your grandmother supposedly wrote, "I'm a major, major fan of his and I think he definitely loves you. You won't do any better." And *he* writes, in respect of Ron Kearney –'

'*Rob* Kearney. Get his focking name right – after everything he's done for this country.'

'He writes, "I'm a major, major fan of his. We won't do any better." And there are many, many more. His use of words and phrases like "hey", "in terms of" and "basically". He's drawn up a report for me, in which he says he is one hundred percent certain that those text messages and this book of whatever-it's-supposed-to-be were written by the same hand.'

He produces the report from the same drawer. It's only about thirty pages long, but Sorcha's old man has gone to the trouble of having it bound between leather covers. I pick it up and I flick through it. I pick out phrases like 'same bad syntax' and 'identical grammatical errors'.

I can feel the weight of Sorcha staring at me, waiting for an explanation.

I'm realizing for the first time that I'm in genuine trouble here. But I also can't help but be impressed by someone who can tell so much from so little. I remember once, Sean O'Brien showed me how he could tell the time by just staring at a field of cows – he was accurate to within five minutes. It's why he's never owned a watch. That was one of the most impressive feats I'd ever seen. This thing is definitely in the same league.

Sorcha's there, 'Ross, is it true what he's saying?' and I can hear that she's on the verge of tears.

I go, 'All this report proves is the square root of fock-all,' and I throw it down on the desk. 'Sorcha, how did I get into the house to send those text messages, if – as your old man seems to be implying – the old lady was dead?'

He's there, 'She kept a key in the flowerpot shaped like a boot. I expect you knew that.'

'Such bullshit.'

'One of her neighbours saw a car very similar to yours parked outside that lunchtime.'

'Such, such bullshit.'

Sorcha goes, 'Did she take the reg?'

The really sad thing is that she's still hoping, against all the evidence, that I'm telling the truth. That's how much she deep down loves me.

'No,' her old man goes, 'she didn't take the reg. But she recognized the model because her son has the same one.'

I look at Sorcha. There are tears rolling down both her cheeks. She's there, 'Ross, did you text me, pretending to be my grandmother?'

I'm like, 'Sorcha, hand on hort, I never touched your grandmother's phone. I wouldn't even know what it looked like.'

Sorcha's old man reaches into his drawer and pulls out another file, which he also drops onto the desk. He goes, 'I asked an old friend – he has a private security firm – to check the phone for fingerprints. He found eight of your prints on the phone.'

I'm like, 'What are you talking about, my prints? You don't have my prints.'

'Yes, I do. Do you remember I showed you the framed photograph of Sorcha and her grandmother?'

'You sly focker.'

'I told you – this is what I do. And I'm very good at it.'

I decide to change tack, thinking, yeah, no, I can still talk my way out of this.

'What,' I go, 'you're trying to tell me that no two people have the exact same fingerprints? Come on!'

Sorcha just, like, properly bursts into tears. Her old man walks around the desk, leans down and tries to comfort her.

'Look,' I go, deciding to finally come clean, 'she rang me the day she died and she said she was going to tell you the truth – about what happened on the day of the marriage referendum. And she was going to tell you the truth about the scorf as well. So I called around to her and I found her – as you know – dead in the bed. And I thought, shit, she never got her final wish, which was to make a clean breast of things. That's why I did it – I was honouring her final wish.'

Sorcha goes, 'I wish I'd never heard the name O'Carroll-Kelly. Get out of this house, Ross. And get out of my life – and I mean, forever.'

Her old man is leaning over Sorcha, hugging her, while she cries uncontrollably. *He* looks over his shoulder at me. He goes, 'I'm going to make you a promise. You will never see Sorcha, or your children, or the inside of this house, ever again.'

'You did *what*?' she goes.

Erika is just in, like, shock.

I'm there, 'Hey, you're no angel yourself, can I just remind you?'

She goes, 'I've done some pretty shitty things in my life, Ross, but nothing like that.'

'Her old man says I'm never going to see my kids again.'

'He can't stop you seeing your kids. Why don't you talk to Hennessy?'

'Yeah, no, I may have burned my bridges there.'

We're on Baggot Street – in one of those burger joints that *pretends* to be Eddie Rocket's but actually *isn't*?

I'm there, 'In my defence, I didn't write anything that the woman wasn't going to say to Sorcha herself.'

'Ross,' she goes, 'you went into the woman's home, you found her dead in the bed, then you sent a bunch of text messages from her phone, pretending to be her.'

'I was honouring her final wishes.'

'You didn't even bother phoning an ambulance.'

'What focking use was an ambulance to her? She was dead. Anyway, Sorcha's old dear used to call in to see her everyday. I knew she'd find her.'

'It's seriously focked-up behaviour, Ross. And there's no mystery where you get it from.'

'Hey, he's your father as well.'

'I wasn't talking about Chorles. I was actually talking about Fionnuala.'

I think about that while I remove the gherkin that I didn't ask for from my hamburger and fock it over my shoulder onto the floor. Maybe I *am* like her.

I change the subject. 'How's Helen?' I go.

Erika's there, 'She's coping. She's going away for a little while.'

'What? I love Helen.'

'She's going to Adelaide to see her sister, Susan. She doesn't know when she's coming home.'

'Because of him.'

'She said she can't watch it. The TV soap that he's become.'

'Some of us still have to live with him.'

'Did you see what he tweeted this morning?'

'I've given up reading them.'

'He said his enemies would soon feel his wrath.'

'Someone like him shouldn't be on social media.'

'He's also threatening to build a wall around Eddie Hobbs.'

I laugh. 'Now something like that,' I go, 'I would definitely vote for!'

She laughs as well, in fairness to her.

I find another piece of gherkin – this time in my mouth. I expressly said no focking gherkin. I fish it out from between my teeth. *It* goes on the floor as well.

Even though she's breaking my balls, it's still great catching up with her. She looks incredible and I'm mentioning it not to be a pervert but just to add a bit of background colour to the story. She's wearing a tight black shirt that really shows off her hefties, especially when she leans forward to grab the salt, which I keep accidentally on purpose moving just out of her reach.

She goes, 'Oisinn and Magnus are having their stag this weekend.'

She says it out of the blue.

I'm there, 'A joint one.'

'Yes, a joint one. Why do you keep moving things so I have to stretch for them? Do you want to just take a photograph of my chest, Ross?'

'Not really.'

'Are you sure?'

'Yes, I'm sure. Continue what you were saying. The stag.'

She can be hord work, but we get on a lot better than we used to.

'They're doing the first ever naked sky-dive over Roscommon and South Leitrim,' she goes.

I laugh, then I just nod – sadly. I'm there, 'I really wish I hadn't opened my stupid mouth that day.'

She goes, 'You really are a focking idiot, aren't you, Ross?'

'Thick. Absolutely thick. But I swear to you, Erika – even though I lie about pretty much everything – I was talking about soccer.'

'So you keep saying.'

'Erika, I feel shit about it. I genuinely do. You know how close me and Oisinn used to be. I miss him. I miss having him as my friend.'

She looks at me like she might possibly even believe me. Then behind us, a waitress slips on one of the pieces of gherkin I focked over my shoulder, and she hits the deck – her tray of food going everywhere.

I look down at her and ask her if we can have our bill.

Twenty minutes later, we're walking up Waterloo Road. It's a nice night, so I decide to just walk her home. Erika tells me about how well the gallery is going and I do the whole nodding along and pretending to be genuinely interested thing. I tell her about Ronan riding the bormaid at his engagement porty and how I've figured out that the urge to do the dirt is something that neither me, nor Ronan, nor my old man can do anything about, no more than we can change the colour of our eyes.

There's a gang of six or seven dudes walking just ahead of us – same direction we're going – and there's, like, two dudes walking towards them. And that's when it happens. Two goys from the gang give the two dudes who are passing them a serious shoulder nudge each.

I can tell straightaway that's it not a rugby-related shoulder nudge. It's not the kind that, say, Alan Quinlan would have given me back in the day if he saw me in Renords – one that says, 'That's what you get for constantly talking shit about Munster – but at the same time I've got massive, massive respect for you and everything you achieved in the game, albeit at just schools level.'

No, this is a different *kind* of shoulder nudge? There's a real nastiness to it. They send these two poor dudes flying. Then one of them also gets a kick in the orse – for nothing, as far as I can see. And that's when the dude who deals out the kick goes, 'Faggots!'

Erika just freezes. She goes, 'Let's just cross over the road.'

But I'm like, 'No, let's not.'

'Ross, don't get involved.'

But I just totally ignore her. Maybe I'm remembering our conversation about Oisinn. Or maybe I'm thinking about my transgender son who's going to grow up without a father all because Sorcha's grandmother was – even though I hate to speak ill of the dead – a homophobic bitch.

Cross over the road? When has the Rossmeister ever crossed over the road?

'Why don't you leave them the fock alone?' I hear myself suddenly go.

They all turn around at the exact same time and they look at me. They're a lot younger than I thought they were – all about seventeen, maybe eighteen?

The dude who kicked the other dude up the orse and used the faggot word looks me up and down. He's a big dude – obviously fancies himself as a bit of a weights freak. He goes, 'What are you going to do about it?'

I'm there, 'What I'm going to do about it is ask you to apologize to these two gay goys –'

'Yeah,' one of the two goys goes, 'we're not actually gay.'

I'm there, 'And if you don't apologize, I'm afraid I'm going to have to deck you.'

This dude laughs in my actual face. He goes, 'Are you serious, old man?'

I'm like, 'Yeah, I'm serious. I'm deadly serious,' and that's when it all ends up coming out. 'There's too much hatred going on at the moment. Hatred of gay people. Hatred of Cork people. Hatred of GAA players. Hatred of women drivers, even though they *can* be annoying. Hatred of women who just want to be properly represented in our theatres and produce work that's challenging and – Jesus Christ – we can't even let them do that. I'm listening to hatred for the last I-don't-know-how-long. I was raised by it. And I'm sick of it. So I'm making a stand. Here on Waterloo Road. I'm saying you either apologize to these two gay dudes –'

'I actually have a girlfriend,' one of them goes.

'– or you will be the subject of a decking.'

The big dude goes, 'It looks like it's going to have to be a decking then,' and he beckons me with his two hands, the universal sign for okay, it's on – it's on like Lil Wayne's bong.

I feel like I used to feel when I was about to throw myself into a ruck. There's, like, a split-second of hesitation because you know there's a chance you're going to get seriously hurt here. But then you do it anyway because – utter fock-up though you are in almost every other respect – you've been brave all your life. I've never crossed over the road. It's not in my nature to cross over the road.

I throw a punch. It's a big punch as well. And that's the last thing I remember.

Christ, my head. It actually feels like my brain is about to explode. And my eyelids are too heavy to even open. Then I get this familiar smell, which I recognize straightaway as *Tom Ford Portofino*.

'Your perfume,' I mumble. 'Oh my God, it's turning me on in a big-time way.'

I hear a man – I'm guessing a doctor – go, 'Your brother is suffering from concussion.'

Then I hear Erika go, 'Unfortunately, he's not. He talks like that all the time. I've got his clothes here. We'll go as soon as he opens his eyes.'

I open my eyes. I'm like, 'Where am I? As in, what hospital?'

Erika is standing at the foot of my bed. She goes, 'St Vincent's.'

I'm there, 'Public or private?'

I really am my mother's son.

'Neither,' she goes. 'You're on a trolley in A&E.'

I'm there, 'How long was I in a coma for?'

'You weren't in a coma, you idiot. You threw a punch and missed. You fell face-forward onto the kerb and you knocked yourself unconscious.'

'Just tell me, did I stop those two dudes being gay-bashed?'

'They weren't gay, Ross.'

'I just think it's terrible that we live in a country where two men can't be open about their feelings for each other.'

'They were brothers. It was a rugby-related thing.'

'Let's just agree to differ.'

I close my eyes again.

Erika goes, 'Don't go to sleep. There's someone here to see you.'

I open my eyes and for about thirty seconds I'm wondering am I *actually* in a coma and dreaming this?

'Hey,' he goes.

It's Oisinn. And it's also Magnus.

I'm like, 'Hey yourself. What are you doing here?'

'Erika rang me,' Oisinn goes. 'Told me what happened.'

'I stopped a gay-bashing.'

'She said it was just a bashing, Ross.'

'I'm sticking by my assessment. One of them definitely looked gay. It was actually the one who said he had a girlfriend.'

'Erika told us about your little speech.'

'Don't worry about that. It was just top-of-the-head stuff.'

There's, like, silence for a good ten seconds. Then Magnus goes, 'Erika shays she thinksh you are telling the truth when you shay you were talking about shoccer that night.'

I'm there, 'Dude, I *was* talking about soccer. Oisinn, you know how much I despise that sport and the people who play it. I'd ban it in the morning.'

Oisinn just nods. He goes, 'You have been consistent on that point.'

I'm like, 'Dude, when have you ever heard me say anything bad about gay people in all the years we've known each other?' and – oh, shit – that's when the tears stort to come. 'I love gay people. It's just it's so easy to cause offence these days without meaning to. There's all these words and phrases that are, I don't know, scattered around like focking landmines, waiting for you to stagger clue-lessly up to them to blow you up. I'm not homophobic, Oisinn. I'm just a fockwit. I don't give a shit if you like men, women or fock-ing teapots, you're my friend and I'd focking die for you . . . rugby, Oisinn . . . focking rugby.'

I'm crying. He's crying. Magnus is crying. Even Erika is dabbing at her eyes. It's a real captain's speech. Oisinn hugs me. I hug Mag-nus. Everyone gets a hug. There ends up being a lot of healing in that Accident and Emergency room.

'Sho,' Magnus goes, 'if you are sho open-minded as you shay, perhapsh shome time you would like to watch a shoccer match with me.'

And I'm like, 'Don't focking push it, Magnus! Seriously, don't push it!'

We all have a good laugh at that as I throw on my clothes.

Oisinn goes, 'So what are you doing this weekend?'

And I'm like, 'Sorcha's old man is going to the High Court to seek an order preventing me from ever having contact with my children again and my solicitor has washed his hands of the case. So it looks like not a lot.'

'Fantastic,' he goes, clapping his two hands together. 'So you can come on the stag?'

And I'm like, 'Dude, I wouldn't miss it for the world.'

'Why did they vote No?' I go.

This is while I'm taking off my trousers and looking down on the countryside of Roscommon and South Leitrim.

'I actually don't think it's bigotry,' Oisinn goes, having to shout out over the noise of the airplane. 'It's just something that's outside their realm of experience, that's all. They've never been exposed to it before.'

'Well,' I go, 'they're going to get exposure today – indecent exposure!'

Everyone on board laughs.

I'd hesitate to use the phrase Gay Icon – that's for others to say – but there's no question that gay people have always liked me. And I'm totally *cool* with that, by the way?

'They're going to think God has sent them some kind of plague,' one of Magnus's friends shouts. 'Except it's not raining frogs or locusts – it's raining men!'

Again, everyone laughs. I actually clap – that's how funny *I* think it is? 'Brilliant!' I go. 'Absolutely brilliant!'

It's shaping up to be one memorable stag. We're circling over Ballinamore – that's according to the pilot.

'Okay, lishen up,' Magnus shouts, 'in jusht a moment, I am going to hend out the parachutesh. If anyone ish having shecond thoughts, thish ish okay, you can shtay onboard and we will all meet up in Galway ash planned.'

No one is staying on the plane. Everyone is up for it. Gay, straight and whatever you're having yourself. I take off my shirt, then suddenly – like the other forty-seven men on board – I'm standing there in just my jockeys, shivering with the cold. I'm checking out

JP and noticing that he has a serious Ned Kelly on him. Fionn has the beginnings of one as well.

When did we all get old?

'That's yet another great thing about rugby,' I go, handing Christian one last beer from the cooler. 'You can stand around naked talking to other naked men and it's not one bit weird. Not one bit weird at all.'

He laughs – he definitely seems to be over Muirgheal. 'Ross,' he goes, 'you don't have to keep mentioning how cool you are with "the gay thing" as you call it.'

I'm there, 'Have I been doing that?'

'Only about every thirty seconds since we took off. The best way to show you're cool with it is to maybe stop making an issue of it all the time.'

'Yeah, no, I'll try and do that. It's possibly just nerves. With the sky-diving thing, rather than the gay thing. Which I'm totally cool with. Fock, I'm doing it again.'

He changes the subject then. Totally out of the blue, he goes, 'Me and Lauren are going to give it another go.'

I'm like, 'What? I thought she was seeing some cinematographer called Loic who didn't give a shit about rugby?'

'It's over. It's been over for a long time.'

'What, so she comes crawling back to you? What kind of a name is Loic anyway? Dude, you should definitely tell her to fock off.'

'She's moving home next weekend.'

'Dude, you're seriously taking her back?'

'I miss her, Ross. I miss my kids.'

And that makes me feel suddenly worse about my own situation.

Then it turns out that JP is in the same boat as me. Or a similar boat. 'Yeah, no,' he goes, 'on the subject of relationships, just to let you know that me and Chloe broke up.'

We're all there, 'No! That's shit for you! Dude, I'm sorry!'

But he goes, 'It's fine. It was actually mutual. We just weren't getting on. But we still want to be the best parents we can be for Isa.'

Him and Chloe had this pact for years that if they were both still single at thirty-whatever, they'd have a baby together. I was always a bit – as Frank Sinatra might say – shooby-dooby-dubious about it.

'Living with someone is hord,' he goes. 'But it's ten times horder if there's no actual love.'

It's still shit, though. It's still shit.

I notice that Fionn is literally green in the face. I'd totally forgotten that he's scared of heights. Or more specifically, he's scared of falling from heights, which is what he's about to voluntarily do – fair focks to him.

I'm like, 'Are you going to be sick again?'

He just shakes his head.

I'm there, 'Do you want a Jack Daniel's or something – settle your stomach?'

He goes, 'No, I'll be okay . . . once I'm back . . . on the ground.'

He's talking like that because he keeps getting the heaves.

I'm there, 'So why were you playing golf with my old man last week? And Hennessy?'

He goes, 'He offered me a job . . . as a special advisor . . .'

I'm there, 'I thought you said he was a racist and a misogynist and loads of other different things?'

'I didn't say . . . yes . . . I'm thinking about it . . . I think I could maybe . . . do a good job, though . . . working from the inside . . . I could maybe temper . . . some of your old man's . . . more extreme policies . . . he wants me . . . to conduct the pre-talks . . . with the other party leaders . . . the talks about talks . . . while he's busy . . . attending your mother's trial . . .'

'Sorcha will have a focking conniption when she finds out.'

'Like I said . . . I'm only . . . thinking about it . . .'

Magnus storts handing out the parachutes – basically backpacks with the Gaycation Ireland logo on them. I throw mine on. I'm there, 'Can I just check again, Magnus, we pull this cord here and the chute should open, yeah?'

'For everybody elsh,' he goes, 'yesh. But yoursh, Rosh, ish jusht a ruckshack wish rocksh in it!'

Everyone laughs. He's joking. I'm pretty sure he's joking.

'Okay,' he then shouts, 'anybody shtill wearing any peesh of clothing, you musht loosh it now!'

So I whip off my boxers.

'Not an issue,' I go. 'Not an issue at all.'

Someone opens the door of the plane and suddenly it's nearly impossible to hear anything. It's all hand gestures now. Magnus beckons us all forward, then one by one, we all stort jumping out of the plane.

When I reach the door, I actually hesitate, because I realize I'm suddenly shitting it. I don't know how many feet up we are, but it looks like a lot. Then someone grabs my hand. It's Oisinn.

'Do you want to jump together?' he goes – he has to really roar to be heard and even then I'm kind of only lip-reading him.

I just nod.

He says something else then and I'm pretty sure it's, 'Will you be my best man?'

Then someone gives us each a shove in the back and we fall out of the plane. Our grip on each other is broken and we're spinning – bollock-naked, bear in mind – through the air. And after a few seconds, I manage to correct my position and I spot Oisinn maybe forty or fifty feet away and I give him the two thumbs-up as if to say, yeah, no, you better believe I'll be your best man.

It's amazing because I totally chillax then and just enjoy the view. It's just, like, fields and woods and obviously the bare orses of the men who jumped before me and are now hurtling towards the ground. The world looks so beautiful from up here. There's time to actually think. And I end up becoming a bit, I don't know, *philosophical*? Maybe this court order preventing me from ever having contact with Sorcha and my children ever again could turn out to be a good thing. The girl might just need time and space to come to the realization that what I did wasn't actually that bad.

I watch the parachutes open below me, one by one, like flowers, I don't know, blooming. They're all the colours of the rainbow. I pull my cord and I'm relieved to discover that Magnus *was* actually joking. A parachute thankfully comes out.

As we get closer to the ground, we can suddenly make out the people, squinting up at us – forty-eight naked men dropping out of the sky on top of them. Some of the people are laughing and waving at us. Some are shouting threats. Some are making the sign of the cross. One man in a balaclava tries to shoot us but his gun fails to go off and he runs off into some nearby woods.

Then we spot the Gorda cors. Eight of them. And at least twenty Gords. We all land safely in a field. One or two twisted ankles – nothing more serious than that. We all, like, roar and cheer as we hit the ground and no one seems to care that we're about to be arrested.

The Gords stort walking across the field towards us. We're all just, like, high-fiving and hugging each other and it doesn't feel weird at all. As the Gords get closer, we notice that they're laughing and they're carrying blankets. They throw them at us and tell us to make ourselves daycent, for fuck's sake outta that.

'Pack of eejits,' one of them goes. 'Where are ye headed?'

Oisinn's like, 'There's a bus waiting for us in Ballinamore. Our clothes are on that.'

We can't stop laughing. They can't stop laughing either.

'Well,' the dude goes, 'you're not walking into town like that. Yee'll be fooken kilt. Get in the cars.'

Eddie is at the door.

I'm like, 'Okay, what are you doing here?' but he just brushes past me into the gaff.

He goes, 'You look like shit.'

I'm there, 'Yeah, no, it was Oisinn's stag at the weekend. Eddie, you're not supposed to be here.'

'Er, I'm allowed to see my dad?'

'Yeah, you're kind of *not*, Eddie? I mean, that's the entire point of a court order.'

'What are they going to do – send me to jail?'

'I think I'm the one who could end up going to jail – although I'm not sure of the ins and outs of it. I don't have a solicitor anymore. Why aren't you in school, by the way?'

'They sent us home because they had to turn the water off. They've got, like, an ormy of plumbers in to fit the new toilets.'

'What number are we up to now?'

'Fifty-two.'

'Fifty-two? I'm so proud of you, Eddie.'

'They've had to get rid of the library, the gym and the cafeteria.'

'Well, people of different genders have to have somewhere to piss and shit. That just a fact, no matter how inconvenient it might be for some people.'

'We all just eat our lunch at our desks now and we do PE outside – even when it's raining.'

'That's hilarious. It's all about equality, though. That's the most important thing.'

'Also, First and Second Class are going to have to merge. And Third and Fourth. And maybe Fifth and Sixth.'

'They're going to be big, big classes.'

'Not really. Loads of parents have taken their children out of the school.'

'Bigots. That's all they are. How did you get here, by the way?'

'I called a Hailo using your credit cord. I was thinking we could watch my DVD of Leinster versus Northampton.'

Shit. She's making it very hord for me to say no – even with the threat of imprisonment.

'Eddie,' I go, 'you genuinely shouldn't be here. If *he* finds out, he *will* call the Feds.'

He's like, 'It's all his *focking* fault!' and I can see that he's on the point of tears.

I'm there, 'He definitely has questions to answer, Eddie. He definitely has questions to answer.'

He goes, 'You didn't do anything wrong.'

'That's not a hundred percent true.'

'All you did was text *her* pretending to be her dead granny.'

'Exactly.'

'So focking what? That was only because her granny was a homophobic bitch and she couldn't accept that fact. I thought it was – oh my God – *such* a clever thing to do.'

'Thanks, Eddie. That's a nice thing to hear.'

'It's actually like something *I* would have done?'

'That's because you and me are so alike. Unfortunately, not everyone sees the world like we do. Sorcha's old man being an example.'

I hear the letterbox suddenly snap behind me. I go and pick the post up off the floor and at the same time I'm like, 'You're going to have to go home, Eddie – tempting as watching that match sounds. You certainly know what buttons to press with me.'

Eddie goes, 'I'm not going home. I'm staying here with you.'

But I'm not really listening to him. Because I'm suddenly staring at this, like, letter? It's got an English stamp on it and it's addressed to Fionnuala and Ari Samuels. I'm curious. That's the reason I end up opening it and giving it the old left to right. It's from some couple they obviously met on honeymoon. He's called Bob and she's called Esther – which doesn't matter either way. They're just randomers. And they obviously have no idea what's been happening because they're asking how Ari's health is, and they wouldn't be doing that if they knew he was dead.

The letter is actually pretty boring – it's all news about their grandkids, which is of fock-all interest to me – but what does grab my attention are the photographs they've stuck in with the letter. There's, like, ten of them, all from their last night in Sordinia. The old dear, Ari and a bunch of other old folk. I'm flicking through them and I'm suddenly thinking, 'Oh . . . Holy . . . Shit.'

Eddie's like, 'What's wrong?'

And I'm there, 'She didn't do it, Eddie.'

He sounds actually disappointed. He's like, 'What? Why?'

I hand him one of the photographs. I'm there, 'What's that on Ari's shin?'

Eddie goes, 'Oh! My God!'

Because there's a bandage on his shin – covering, presumably, a burn mork.

And I go, 'There's the actual proof. She was telling the truth. She didn't kill him after all.'

And Eddie goes, 'I was kind of hoping she *did* do it?'

10. It'll Be Alt-right on the Night

It's her *leg* that I see first? Long and shapely, with a black Manolo on the end of it, sticking out of the back of a silver taxi. I tip over – ever the gent! – and I hold the door open while the woman bum-walks her way along the back seat and steps out onto the pavement in front of the Four Courts.

'Can you help me with this?' she goes, trying to hand me her briefcase like she thinks I'm the help.

And that's when I suddenly recognize her and – after a delay of a few seconds, followed by a sneer – she suddenly recognizes me. It's Tiffany-Blue – as in, Ari's granddaughter.

'Well, look who it is,' she goes to no one in particular. 'The murderer's son with the Twinkie for a penis.'

A Twinkie is an American thing. I had one when I was on my Jı. It wouldn't fill you.

I'm like, 'Hey, Tiffany-Blue. You're very welcome,' sounding weirdly like a *porty* greeter? 'The thing is, Tiffany-Blue, I actually don't think she *did* kill him?'

She's like, 'Oh, please! You have to say that because she's your mother.'

She slams the taxi door, then storts walking up the steps of the court. I let her go first – again, being a gentleman, but also – if I'm being honest – trying to see through her white trousers to find out if she's wearing regular knickers or a thong.

'That burn mork on your grandfather's shin,' I go. 'It didn't come from a two-bor electric heater. It did come from a piece of borbecue coal. He had it in Sordinia. I got my hands on a photograph. His leg is bandaged.'

She stops and goes, 'You are being manipulated. Like she manipulates everyone. She's going to spend the rest of her pitiful life rotting away in a prison cell.'

Some dude arrives over to us then. 'Hello, Tiffany-Blue,' he goes. It's O'Maonaigh. 'Is this man bothering you?'

She laughs. 'This little pussy,' she goes, 'with a dick like a packet of Life Savers?'

They're also American. They're *their* equivalent of Polos? It probably should be clear at this stage that me and Tiffany-Blue have been on intimate terms.

O'Maonaigh fixes me with a look and goes, 'You attempt to speak to her again and I'll arrest you for interfering with a witness.'

I'm there, 'I was trying to be a gentleman,' but off they walk, in through the doors of the court.

I follow a short distance behind them.

I find the old man and Hennessy in a little private office. The old man is on the phone. He's going, 'You can tell Enda Kenny that an Army presence at all GAA matches was what I promised the electorate and I am not prepared to accept some private security firm compromise. Referees are being murdered. Seven in Galway last month! Four in Wicklow last Saturday alone, Fionn!'

I don't believe it. Fionn must have said yes to him. What an actual Judas.

'And while you're at it,' he goes, 'you can also tell Michael Martin that I've decided to make it a precondition of talks that he accepts the wall! You can tell them from me that it's not going to be a chain-link fence! It's going to be made of solid bloody well brick!'

It's the second week in April, by the way, and still no Government. Not that it seems to matter. The sun hasn't stopped moving around the Earth.

Hennessy is talking to some dude who I'm guessing is the old dear's barrister. He looks at me and goes, 'And you are?'

'Ross,' I go. 'I'm Fionnuala's, I suppose, son.'

He's there, 'Fionnuala's I suppose son. It's nice to meet you, Fionnuala's I suppose son.'

They always think they're hilarious.

'Dermot Earley,' he goes, without bothering to offer me his hand. 'I'm going to be conducting your mother's defence. You found the evidence, I believe, that the burn on the deceased's leg was sustained a week earlier?'

I'm there, 'Will it be enough?'

'I'm more optimistic than I was when I took on the case. You did well, Fionnuala's I suppose son.'

He wanders over to my old man, who's finished chatting to Fionn. Hennessy doesn't say anything to me for about thirty seconds, then he goes, 'He's right. You did good.'

I'm there, 'I just hope it's enough to prove her innocence. I feel like a total tit, by the way.'

He has me dressed up like a dork – suit and tie, actual shoes instead of my famous Dubes, then my hair is combed to the side with no even *product* in it?

He goes, 'The State is calling you as a witness. We want the jury to like you.'

'Why wouldn't they like my usual shoes?'

He doesn't answer me. Instead, after a few seconds, he goes, 'Sorcha still sweet on you?'

I'm like, 'Er, no. It's a long story, but I basically texted her from her dead granny's phone.'

Hennessy's jaw just drops. Which is saying something – he's done some seriously iffy shit in his time.

'So, yeah, no,' I go, 'before you ask, she's cut off my access altogether.'

He's like, 'You miss them, right?'

I do – even though Eddie still calls to the gaff occasionally. I haven't seen the boys for literally a month and it's killing me. I don't even give a shit that they're into soccer. I want to be with them no matter what.

I'm like, 'Of course I miss them.'

'You put on the performance of a lifetime in that court,' he goes, 'and I'll forget about you stealing the plans for Aquatraz.'

'You'll help me get joint custody?'

'I'll help you get joint custody.'

Outside in the corridor, there's a definite air of something. I hear the shuffle of activity and the voices of boggers going, 'This way . . . That's it . . . Keep walking . . . In here . . .'

Then the door suddenly opens and in she walks. My old dear.

The old man makes a beeline for her and throws his orms around her. He's like, 'Fionnuala! How wonderful to see you! It's been a long road, but justice is within sight at last!'

A knob.

She spots me then. She's like, 'Ross?'

I'm there, 'Yeah, no, hi.'

'Have you a hug for your mother?'

I hug her. She ends up shaming me *into* it? 'Thank you,' she goes, 'for finding that photograph.'

I'm like, 'I didn't find it as such. I just happened to be noseying through your post.'

'And just to think, I was mad at Ari when he asked those people to join us that night. I thought they were common.'

'He must have exchanged addresses with them.'

'It certainly wasn't me. I had no interest in them. But how wonderful that they got in touch.'

She gives me another hug. I've had more affection out of her today than I had in my entire childhood.

'By the way,' I go, 'you'll never guess who I saw outside.'

She's like, 'Who?'

'What are your two least favourite words in the world?'

'Affordable housing?'

'I'm not talking about affordable housing. I'm talking about Tiffany-Blue. She's here.'

'Well, of course she's here. I presume she's going to give evidence.'

'Well, she's already said a few non-too-complimentary things about me.'

Someone steps into the room then – I'm presuming some kind of usher – and goes, 'Everyone ready?'

We all just look at each other – me, the old dear and the old man especially – and we all just nod.

She ends up being led out through one door and we end up being led out through another, into the public gallery, where her friend Delma is sitting along with some of her mates from The Gables, the golf club and her various campaigns against things that might destroy the unique character of Foxrock. Delma hugs me and the old man, and we take our seats at the front.

We're only, like, ten feet away from Tiffany-Blue, who's sitting next to O'Maonaigh.

About sixty seconds later, the old dear is led in by two prison officers. She spots Delma and mouths the words, 'I love your coat!'

And Tiffany-Blue suddenly can't contain herself. 'You fucking murderer!' she shouts. 'You murdered my grandfather, you fucking murdering bitch!'

The dude who performed the post-mortem on Ari is being given a serious grilling by the old dear's barrister – this Dermot Earley dude.

'Let's talks about the scar on Ari's right shin,' he goes, 'which played such a crucial role in persuading the prosecution that Ari was murdered. How long have you been performing autopsies?'

The dude's like, 'Twenty-two years.'

'Twenty-two years. So in that time, you've seen a lot of stiffs, have you not?'

'As a pathologist, yes, I see bodies on a daily basis.'

'So when you examined this one, when you observed the scar on the right shin and concluded – to quote from your report – that it was "a superficial burn that had no relevance in respect of death", this was the considered view of a pathologist with more than two decades of experience in the area of post-mortem examination?'

'Yes.'

'What else did your examination reveal? And may I draw your attention to page fifteen of your report?'

The dude flicks through it. 'Yes,' he goes, when he finds the right page, 'the deceased had a history of cardiac problems.'

'A history of cardiac problems!' the barrister goes. 'Could you offer the jury a potted version of that history, please?'

Barristers are a bit like teachers. They always seem cleverer than they actually are because they can talk shit to you and you're not allowed to talk shit back. I'd love to see how the average senior counsel would cope if the dude in the box was allowed to go, 'Shut the fock up, you dick with ears.'

The pathologist can't do that, though. He has to play the game. Which is good news for the old dear. 'The deceased had suffered six heart attacks,' he goes, 'and had quite a number of surgeries, including three bypass operations.'

'Six heart attacks! The one that killed him being the seventh?'

'The seventh, yes.'

'So it wasn't difficult to conclude – as you did – that this man expired due to natural causes. In other words, he died a non-violent death.'

'That was my conclusion.'

'Which is why you took the decision to immediately release the body to his next-of-kin.'

'That's right.'

'Then, a short time later, the Gardaí came to you and they said what?'

'They asked me about the burn mark on his right shin. They asked if, in my view, it might have been the result of an electrical appliance – specifically a two- or three-bar electric heater – being dropped into the bath for the purposes of inducing a heart attack.'

'And what did you tell them when they came to you with this fanciful story?'

'I told them that, in my view, Ari had died of natural causes. But that if his death was now the subject of a criminal investigation, I would be prepared to examine the body again.'

'And did you?'

'Yes.'

'And what did you discover?'

'With the natural decomposition that takes place, I was unable to make an accurate assessment of when the burn was sustained.'

'So you, who performed the job of examining his body, of dissecting his organs, determined that he died a natural death?'

'Yes.'

'With no violence?'

'With no evidence of violence.'

'The jury is being asked to consider evidence – not the absence of it.'

'Yes.'

'No further questions.'

I look at the old dear. She sort of, like, smiles, but in such a way that it's impossible to tell whether she's happy or not.

'This is such bullshit!' Tiffany-Blue shouts. 'Look at her sitting there playing the grieving fucking widow.'

The judge goes, 'Any further outbursts in this court will result in my jailing someone for contempt,' and he wallops his hammer slash whatever-the-actual-word-is off the desk.

Other witnesses come and go. It's mostly pretty boring. Lots of technical shit that goes way, way over my head. I actually spend most of the afternoon just spacing. Then, just after four o'clock, the final witness of the day is called. It's Bob, the English dude who sent the old dear the photograph of Ari with the bandage on his shin. The old dear's barrister throws him a nice easy one to stort off. He asks him if he remembers first meeting Ari and Fionnuala Samuels.

'Yes,' he goes, 'we were on us 'olidays and we were 'avin' us breakfast one morning when we got talking to this nice old duffer – American – who were sitting at next table int restaurant. And that were Ari. Like I said, he were a lovely fella. Said he were ont 'oneymoon, even though he were sitting ont his own at time. I think *she* were int toilet.

'Any road, like I said to you, I liked him and so did Esther – and we both call as we see. He ast us if we'd like to come up to his villa that night and I said, "Appen we will."

'So then *she* came back – Fionnuala – fromt toilet. And I didn't much like 'er, being honest. She were a bit stuck-up. She said to 'im, in front of us, "Why are you talking to them? They're not People Like Us!"'

The barrister decides he's probably losing the sympathy of the jury so he interrupts him. He goes, 'Could you tell us what happened that night?'

'Right you are! Well, it turned out we weren't t'only ones Ari'd invited. There were loadut other couples there. It were a good night, although I wanted to go 'ome at one point because I thought I 'eard 'er – Fionnuala – describe me and Esther as either scum or scum ut t'Earth. She were pretty plastered. Esther persuaded me that I'd mebbe mis-'eard it.'

He didn't mishear it. Take it from me.

The dude goes, 'It were during this conversation that Ari decided he were going to give barbercue a bit of a poke. He were a bit doddery, like. Wasn't fully with it, I thought. But that were when a load of coals fell out – he must have really gone at it – and one them burned 'im pretty badly ont shin.'

'You saw this yourself?' the barrister goes.

'I not only saw it. I were't one who dressed it.'

'You dressed it?'

'I were't one who't put bandage on it. I 'ave First Aid training, see. I were int t'Army.'

'On which shin did Ari sustain this burn injury?'

'Same one int photo.'

'Can you *tell* the jury which shin?'

'It were't right.'

'No further questions.'

The judge says that's it for the day. He'll see us back here on Tuesday morning. We all stand up. It seems to have been a good day for the old dear. She can't keep the smile from her face as she's led from the court by the same two prison officers who escorted her in.

Delma shouts, 'Don't worry, Fionnuala! We'll be eating carrot cake in Mount Usher before the end of next week!' and that seems to be pretty much the general vibe.

Tiffany-Blue shouts, 'This is some bullshit!'

On the way out of the court, the old man turns around to Hennessy and goes, 'This is some bullshit is right! This is distracting me from the important business of trying to form a Government! How the hell did the State even agree to take this case?'

And Hennessy goes, 'Don't go counting your chickens, Charlie. The DPP's got some big shit to throw at her next week.'

So it's, like, Friday night and the old crew is back together in Kielys of Donnybrook Town. We're talking me, Christian, Oisinn, JP and Fionn – and the famous Magnus, who is fast becoming one of the goys.

'Look,' I go, 'I know the wedding is still, whatever, a month away, but my gift to you, Magnus, is going to be a Leinster season

329

ticket. Even though rugby isn't your thing – you've obviously chosen the other bus – but it's the best way I know to express how I feel,
which is that I'm delighted you're in Oisinn's life and I'm delighted
you're in our lives as well. End of story.'

He goes, 'That'sh very shweet of you, Rosh,' and he puts his orm
around me and kisses me on the cheek.

And it's fine. It's fine. It's fine. It's fine.

Christian is telling Oisinn his news. Lauren is coming home
tomorrow. Her and the kids. For good. Christian has decided to
forgive her. He's a bigger man than me. I mention that as well. I'm
there, 'I'd have said to her, "You made your focking bed . . .", but
not this mug. Too nice for his own good.'

Oisinn goes, 'I'm delighted for you, Christian. Hey, it'll be great
having her and the kids at the wedding.'

JP has barely said a word all night. He's on Tinder. I've been there.
It's pretty addictive alright. At one point, he holds up his phone and
goes, 'What do you think?' and Oisinn takes it from him and nods – I
think it's a word – *approvally*? Christian, Fionn and Magnus all do the
same. Then it gets handed to me. And I have to stop myself from
actually laughing. Because it's Tilly. I think about telling him that
she's a focking bore. But then I think, no, let him find out for himself.

'She's nice,' I go. 'And birds called Tilly are usually pretty
open-minded, aren't they?'

He's there, 'I'm swiping right, so!'

It's nice to see him happy again, too.

Magnus gets the round in – like I said, he's fitting right in – and I turn
around to Fionn and tell him I can't believe he's now working for my
old man, after all the things he said about him, including that whole
blind leading the blonde thing. I'm there, 'Have you told Sorcha yet?'
because I'm guessing she's going to have a shit-fit when she finds out.

He goes, 'I haven't had an opportunity yet, but she'll understand
when she –'

He doesn't get the chance to finish his sentence. Because Sorcha
suddenly walks through the doors. She looks pretty pissed about
something.

I'm there, 'Now's your chance to break the news, Fionn.'

But it turns out she already knows. She makes a sudden beeline towards him. She covers the ground between them like Bryan Habana. From six feet away, she already has her hand cocked. Then she slaps him across the face.

'You bastard!' she goes.

It's an absolute peach as well. His glasses go flying off him.

He's like, 'Sorcha, if you'd just let me explain –'

She's there, 'How *could* you? He's a racist, Fionn! And a misogynist and a liar and . . . all the other things we said!'

Everyone in Kielys is suddenly looking over. It's great not being the centre of attention for once.

He tries to go, 'Sorcha, can we talk somewhere in private?'

And she's like, 'No, we can't! I trusted you! We said we were going to work together to try to make the world a more loving and environmentally aware place!'

I look down and I see Fionn's glasses on the ground. I accidentally on purpose stand on them, crushing them into the ground.

She goes, 'I can't believe you're actually working for him!'

He ends up suddenly losing it with her. He's there, 'Jesus Christ, I'm playing him, Sorcha!' and then he looks at me, like he suddenly regrets opening his mouth in front of me.

'Playing him?' Sorcha goes.

I'm there, 'Don't worry, I'm not going to say shit to him.'

He lowers his voice and everyone goes back to their drinks. 'Yes,' he goes, 'I'm playing him. I'm talking to Enda Kenny and I'm talking to Micheál Martin and I'm being deliberately difficult. I'm hoping that Fianna Fáil and Fine Gael will realize that maybe they should start talking to each other.'

'Fianna Fáil and Fine Gael?' Sorcha goes. 'But they've got – oh my God – *nothing* in common?'

'I know.'

'They, like, hate each other.'

'I know that, too. But I'm hoping, the longer we talk, the more they'll realize that they hate the alternative even more. Soldiers at GAA matches. A wall around Cork. Women drivers treated like second-class citizens.'

'Fionn, they'd sooner see all of those things than work together in Government.'

'It's still worth trying, Sorcha. Look, I haven't given up on that better world we talked about – a world without casual cruelty and meanness just for the sake of it.'

And I go, 'I, er, accidentally stood on your glasses, Fionn. And yeah, no, they're focked.'

It's O'Maonaigh's turn in the spotlight. The dude who pushed the case from day one. The dude who said he looked into my old dear's eyes and saw genuine evil where the rest of us just see dilated pupils, evidence of liver deterioration and greed.

There's a definite change in the atmos when he steps into the witness box.

'There he is!' the old man mutters under his breath. 'The man who cooked up this entire conspiracy to smear the name of a good woman and destroy the political fortunes of New Republic on behalf of the Establishment!'

Ronan is sitting beside me. He's come to offer his grandmother some moral support – although, from the time he arrived, he's seemed more interested in ogling some junior solicitor on the State's side, who I happen to think is a ringer for Iggy Azalea.

I give him a nudge and I whisper to him. I'm there, 'Are you following this?'

He goes, 'Course Ine foddying it.'

'It's just you haven't shouted a single threat at this cop. Or the judge. It's very unlike you.'

'I've me foorst yee-or exaddems cubbing up. I doatunt wanth to miss them for conthempth of cowurt.'

'It's not because you were scoping Iggy Azalea over there, no?'

'Just cos you've altreddy eaten, Rosser, dudn't mee-un you caddent look at the medu.'

I just, like, smile at him.

O'Maonaigh, by the way, is enjoying exactly what Ronan would like right now – a nice easy ride. But then he would be. The barrister asking the questions is Willie Murphy SC, who's on *his* actual side. He asks him about the history of the investigation from the moment that Tiffany-Blue first alleged that her grandfather had been offed by my old dear.

'Tell the jury,' the dude goes, 'when you first suspected that there may have been merit in these claims by the granddaughter of Ari Samuels?'

O'Maonaigh's there, 'It was when I examined Fionnuala O'Carroll-Kelly's laptop.'

I watch Hennessy turn to the old man and nod, as if to say, here it is – we knew this was coming.

'You examined her laptop,' this Willie Murphy dude goes, 'which you took away in the course of routine evidence collection.'

He's like, 'That's correct.'

'And on that laptop, you found a document file – did you not? – entitled How To Get Away With Murder.'

'That's correct.'

The old dear ends up totally losing her shit. 'I told you when I was arrested,' she roars, 'that was a sample chapter from a psychological thriller I was planning to pitch to my publisher.'

'Silence!' the judge shouts. 'I will not tolerate these interruptions!'

The barrister dude continues. 'Would you mind reading from that document for the jury, please? Page seventeen – the fifth paragraph onwards.'

'The *fifth*?' O'Maonaigh goes.

'If you would?'

So the dude storts reading from the document in front of him. He's there, '*She felt him inside her. All of him. It was as if a tree had been planted between her legs, its thick trunk reaching up through her cervix, its strong branches creeping into her uterus, its twigs tickling her ovaries. Then, all at once, the tree was withdrawn and he blew his sap all over her sweat-moistened belly.*'

'Jesus focking Christ!' I shout.

'I apologize,' this Willie Murphy goes. 'I meant the *sixth* paragraph onwards.'

I look at the jury. They all look like they want to vom.

O'Maonaigh returns to the story. He goes, '*It was when he left the room to run a bath that she decided to put her plan into action. She took the two-bar electric heater from underneath the bed where she'd hidden it.'*

I'm thinking, holy fock. And I doubt if I'm the only one.

He goes, *'Slowly, deliberately, she plugged the twenty-metre extension cord into the wall on the landing, then returned to the bedroom, unspooling the cord as she walked. She plugged the two-bar electric heater into the extension, then waited for the sound of the taps being switched off.*

'Moments later, she heard the flow of water stop, then his pleasured exhalation as he allowed his body to disappear under the surface of the hot and load-bearing bathwater. She stepped into the bathroom, holding the two-bar electric heater in front of her. He looked at her and raised a questioning eyebrow. "What's that, Darling?" he said. He was a very wealthy man. He had never seen a two-bar electric heater before.

'She smiled at him evenly and said, "It's your unlucky day." Then, without pausing to consider the enormity of what she was about to do, she dropped the two-bar electric heater into the water. There was a flash. The house was suddenly cast into darkness as the fuse blew. In the blackness of the bathroom, she heard him thrash around in the water until he was suddenly still – and suddenly dead.'

The old man lets a roar out of him – he can't *help* himself? 'It's only a bloody well story!' he goes. 'Nothing more!'

The judge is like, 'Please continue.'

O'Maonaigh goes, *'She pulled the extension cord out of the wall, then she went downstairs and replaced the fuse. Light returned to the house. She went back to the bathroom, emptied the bath, then dried his body as it lay there, limp and still. With great difficulty, she managed to pull the body out of the bath and lay it down on the tiled floor. She dressed it in the tracksuit that she had laid out earlier.'*

There's, like, genuine gasps from the jury.

'You murdering bitch!' Tiffany-Blue roars. 'You fucking murdering fucking bitch!'

'Please – keep reading,' the judge goes.

O'Maonaigh's there, *'She dragged the body downstairs, feet first, slowly, so as not to cause any giveaway contusions to his head. Then she dragged it down a second flight of stairs to the basement, where she laid it down beside the treadmill. She switched the machine on and pushed the speed up to high.'*

Willie Murphy just smiles and goes, 'No further questions.'

I'm looking at the jury and they're all in just, like, *shock*? They're looking at each other with their mouths wide open, like they've just listened to my old dear confess – which, I suppose, in some of their minds, they actually *have*?

The old man goes, 'It's bloody well fiction, Hennessy! Like something Jeffrey Archer would write!'

But Hennessy's there, 'Jeffrey Archer's wife never turned up dead.'

The judge says the case will resume tomorrow morning at eleven o'clock.

Ronan turns around to me and goes, 'It's a dudden deal, Rosser. Your ma's toast. Untless when you're in that box, you can say sometin to chayunge that jewer doddy's moyunt.'

I don't need this. I *literally* don't need it? I'm supposed to be in court today, giving evidence that will hopefully stop my old dear from being sent down for a murder she possibly didn't – but maybe actually did – commit. And now I've got Mister focking Wade on the phone, in tears, asking me to come to the school. He's going, 'I need you to come to the school. You seem to be the reasonable one.'

I'm there, 'That's a nice thing for me to hear. But the courts have said I'm not allowed to go within one hundred yords of my children and I'm supposed to be giving evidence in my old dear's murder trial this afternoon.'

But he goes, 'Your wife has gone mad, Ross! She's gone absolutely mad! Please come to the school – I want to show you something.'

So I end up having no choice in the matter. I check Sorcha's Twitter feed while I'm on the Stillorgan dualler and I'm straightaway worried about the girl. She was awake until – it looks like – four o'clock this morning, arguing with total randomers, who don't even have names. They're called Avenger27 and YesImTHATGuy and they have eggs instead of profile pictures. And Sorcha has been arguing with twelve, thirteen, fourteen of these randomers at exactly the same time.

One of them will make some reasonable-sounding point about

Cork people, or women drivers, or how climate change is the will of the Baby Jesus, and Sorcha will fire straightaway back with some snorky comment about their grammar or their spelling and she'll tell them to go and educate themselves and then she'll include the hashtags #LoveMore and #LoveHorder. But then *they'll* say something back to her and, within two or three exchanges, she's going, 'You are focking vile Nazi scum.'

It's not the Sorcha I know and still love.

I reach the school and I find Mister Wade in his office. He looks wrecked. He doesn't say anything to me, except, 'I want to show you something,' and I follow him up the stairs.

We're suddenly walking along this long, winding corridor and I'm looking at all these doors – we're talking thirty or forty, maybe even more – with just, like, *symbols* on them? One is, like, a circle with four arrows sticking out of it. Then there's one with, like, two arrows sticking out of it and two squiggly lines underneath it. They're like cave drawings, or traffic signs – what they mean is anyone's guess.

I'm like, 'Are these all –?'

And he goes, 'These are toilets, Ross.'

'All of them?'

'Yes.'

'There's a lot of them, isn't there?'

'Sixty-four in total.'

'Sixty-four? Fock.'

He storts giving me a guided tour of them and at the same time he's talking about the school as he once *remembered* it? 'This used to be the computer room,' he goes. 'We were very proud of our computer room . . . And that was the music room in there. The girls were hoping to stage *The Pajama Game* at the end of the school year. That's all gone now . . . This was the science laboratory. We were the first primary school in Ireland to have a working science lab . . . Now it's a toilet for the – I don't know what that symbol means – I think it's lolosexual.'

'Which ones are they again?'

'They're the ones who find the whole notion of sexuality laugh out loud funny.'

'It's hord to keep track, isn't it?'

'You're probably wondering where all the children are?'

'Yeah, no, it did cross my mind that there doesn't seem to be anyone around to basically use these toilets.'

'They're all squeezed into what used to be the maintenance block. We've had to merge First Class with Second Class, Third Class with Fourth Class and Fifth Class with Sixth Class. Which in normal circumstances would lead to overcrowding. But parents are removing their children from the school and sending them elsewhere.'

'In which case, that's probably enough toilets. It's time for you to possibly draw a line. It looks to me like you've got everyone covered at this stage.'

'Not according to your wife and daughter.'

'Well, she's actually my son.'

'They want more.'

'More?'

'Apparently, we have nowhere for the hohosexuals to go.'

'Hohosexuals? Are they not the same as the lolosexuals? Because they do *sound* the same?'

'Lolosexuals find the notion of sexuality laugh out loud funny. Hohosexuals find the notion of sexuality side-splittingly hilarious.'

'See, they do definitely sound similar. I'm probably not being very politically correct here, but could they not piss and shit in the same place?'

'Your wife doesn't think so. That's why she screamed at me on the phone. That's why she's on her way here now.'

'She's coming here?'

'Please stay, Ross. I need an ally. I'm not strong enough to fight them on my own.'

He suddenly bursts into tears and – I swear to fock – storts literally sobbing on my shoulder. I'm sort of, like, hugging him, going, 'Dude, I know it's easy for me to say, but you have to stand up to them.'

Eventually he pulls away from me, wipes his cheeks with his palm and goes, 'They want the staff canteen. And, understandably, the teachers are in revolt because I told them that they may have to eat their lunch sitting in their cars. They said, "No way – you've got to stop appeasing this one student." It seems the computer room was the Sudetenland – but the canteen is Poland.'

'I've no idea what that even means.'

A voice from the other end of the corridor goes, 'He's comparing me to Hitler.'

We both turn around at the exact same time. It's Sorcha. She's wearing her black Alexander Wang blazer – which she always throws on her when she means business – and black, four-inch Loubs, which click off the tiles as she walks down the corridor towards us. It's pretty intimidating, it has to be said.

Mister Wade suddenly gets his courage up. Yes, I'm *that* good at hugs. 'You *are* like Hitler,' he goes, 'with your regular lists of demands that must be met without question.'

Sorcha goes, 'You're the one who oppresses minorities. I think it's pretty obvious who Hitler is in this scenario.'

'You're the one who's Hitler.'

'I think you'll find you're the one who's Hitler.'

'Hill! Air!'

It's another voice from the opposite end of the corridor slash toilet block. It's Eddie.

Sorcha goes, 'Hi, Darling – I was just telling Mister Wade that we are not going to give in to his Gestapo tactics. *First they came for the hohosexuals and I did not speak out . . .'*

And that's when Eddie says *the* most unbelievable thing. 'There's no such thing as hohosexuals,' he goes. 'It's totally made-up.'

Sorcha's there, 'What do you mean it's made-up? Hohosexuals *are* a thing – we read their amazing, amazing stories on the Internet.'

'Yeah, they're only a thing in America. They're the children of divorced parents who are looking for attention.'

It's a moment. There's no doubt about that. No one says anything for a good, like, sixty seconds. Sorcha is just, like, staring at Eddie with a look of horror spreading across her face. She goes, 'Eddie, are you saying *you* did this for attention too?'

'*And* for a laugh,' Eddie goes. 'Er, so-so-sexuals? People who think that the issue of sexuality is neither a very good thing nor a very bad thing? *Hello?'*

Sorcha just looks instantly hortbroken.

Mister Wade goes, 'Are you saying this was all just a joke to you?'

It is *kind* of funny? But I've decided to definitely hold the laughter in.

Sorcha's there, 'I don't know what kind of a boy we raised –'

'I'm not a focking boy!' Eddie goes. 'I'm a focking girl!'

We're all like, 'What?'

'Yeah, mic drop!' he goes – or *she* goes, it seems to be again. 'I was just taking the piss out of the whole transgender thing. I wanted to see how far I could push you.'

Sorcha can't accept it, though. I watch her eyes fill up with tears and she's like, 'Eddie, you couldn't have been just taking the piss! You were saving up your pocket money for gender reassignment surgery, remember?'

But Honor – I'm calling her that again because she seems to be serious – just laughs in her face and goes, 'I totally had you. Hobo-sexuals? I thought I'd gone too far with that one, but you actually believed me!'

I'm like, 'What about being interested in rugby, Honor? Was that an act?'

Sorcha goes, 'Stay out of this, Ross!' and she actually roars it at me. 'Honor, I can't believe you would do something like this. Having a genderqueer son was a huge port of my election platform.'

'Yeah,' Honor goes, 'every second sentence out of your mouth was, "Speaking as the mother of a transgender child . . ."'

'That's because I was brought up to embrace diversity, not to make a joke out of it.'

'No wonder no one voted for you – you bogus bitch.'

I decide the moment calls for a firm word from me. I'm there, 'Honor, maybe don't speak to your mother like that.'

Her and Sorcha are just, like, eyeballing each other. I can immediately tell that, as far as Sorcha is concerned, this is definitely the worst thing she's ever done – even worse than the time she infested her previous school with rats.

Mister Wade goes, 'I'll leave you to your conversation. I'm

going to go and ring the plumber. Get rid of all these ridiculous lavatories.'

Off he heads – the poor focker.

Honor's there, 'I don't want to live with you anymore – you, your focking knob of a mother and your focking dickhead of a father.'

I snort. Can't be helped.

She goes, 'I want to live with him,' and – pretty flattering, it has to be said – she means me.

'You can't live with him,' Sorcha goes. 'He's the reason you've turned out to be the horrible little girl you are.'

'No, he isn't,' Honor goes, in fairness to her. 'I'd be a bitch anyway. But he's my dad. And he doesn't give a shit what I am. He just loves me for me.'

That's actually true. I wouldn't mind a straight answer to that rugby question, though.

I'm there, 'Honor, you can't live with me. Like your mother said, I encouraged you to break that other kid's collarbone – even though I still maintain it was a technically legal tackle.'

'I want to live with you,' she goes – there's, like, pleading in her voice. And her eyes. 'We could find another club for me. Maybe Bective. Or even Seapoint – you're a hero out there. Oh my God, I'd love to follow in the great Ross O'Carroll-Kelly's footsteps.'

And a terrible thing happens then. I look into her eyes, and I realize that I can't one hundred percent believe that she means it. I'm thinking, this might be as much of an act as the whole Eddie Lalor thing.

I'm there, 'I'm sorry, Honor. Look, I have to go. I'm in the witness box this afternoon.'

Sorcha goes, 'I hope your mum gets off,' which is the nicest thing she's said to me in a long time.

I'm just like, 'Thanks.'

As I walk away, I hear Honor go, 'You can't stop me from seeing my dad. If you don't let me see him, I'm going to make your life – oh my God – *so* focking unbearable.'

And Sorcha's there, 'You already have, Honor. You already have.'

*

'Can I remind you,' the barrister cross-examining me goes, 'that you are under oath?'

I'm there, 'Yeah, no, I know what swearing on the *Bible* means?'

'Then I'm going to ask you the question again. Did you or did you not tell Tiffany-Blue Samuels that you considered your mother capable of anything – including murdering her grandfather?'

The old dear is looking at me with just, like, pleading eyes. Hennessy is mouthing the word 'No!' at me, over and over again. Tiffany-Blue shouts, 'Tell the fucking truth!'

'Yeah, no,' I go. 'I did say that.'

There's, like, gasps in the courtroom.

I'm there, 'But I said it in the course of trying to get the girl into the sack.'

Willie Murphy SC is, like, genuinely shocked, and I'd say he's heard a few things in his time. 'In the course of trying to get her into *the sack*,' he goes, 'you told her that you thought your mother might kill her grandfather?'

'I told her I thought she was capable of it. I was trying to let her think I was on her side. She was convinced that my old dear only married him because he was worth, I don't know, two billion snots. She met my old dear in rehab and my old dear apparently told her that the next time she got married, it would be to a rich man who was about to fall off the perch.'

'And you suggested she was the kind of woman who might perhaps . . . push him off the perch?'

'I can't remember my exact words but I said, yeah, no, don't be surprised if he's found dead in suspicious circumstances.'

'Ross,' the old dear shouts, 'how *could* you?'

The old man goes, 'You're putting words in the boy's mouth! I'm calling for a mistrial!'

'In my defence,' I go, 'this was to make her think – like I said – that I was on *her* side? It was a tactic. And one that worked because we did end up . . .'

I look at Tiffany-Blue.

She goes, 'You and your little Tootsie Roll dick – you were in and out in thirty seconds.'

Everyone in the court laughs. Tootsie Roll. The girl is snack-food obsessed.

The judge goes, 'Can we have order in the court, please?'

The barrister goes, 'You said something else to Tiffany-Blue as well, didn't you? Another piece of pillow talk that might also interest the jury.'

I'm there, 'Is this something to do with me naming Leinster XVs to try to, er, hold back the tide?'

Again, there's laughter in the court. They're getting their money's worth, in fairness to them.

The dude goes, 'Perhaps we might like to hear that another time. I'm interested in what you told her about Alma Goad – another elderly person you said your mother killed for money.'

The old man jumps to his feet and roars across the courtroom at our barrister, who he's paying good money to supposedly defend the old dear. He's like, 'Are you going to object to this line of questioning or am I going to have to go down there and do it myself?'

It's only then that Dermot Earley SC stands up and goes, 'Yes, objection. This is hearsay. *Dúirt bean liom go ndúirt bean léi.* Fionnuala O'Carroll-Kelly is not on trial for murdering Alma Goad. She's on trial for murdering Ari Samuels.'

The judge goes, 'I'm going to allow the question – if there *is* a question?'

The barrister is like, 'My question is this: was your certainty that your mother was capable of killing Ari Samuels based on your knowledge that she had already performed a similar act – albeit for considerably lesser stakes – when she killed Alma Goad?'

I'm there, 'I didn't say she killed Alma Goad!' and I pretty much roar it at him. 'I said she conned her out of her floristry business and Alma died a broken woman! Big difference!'

'You told Tiffany-Blue that your mother "literally" killed her.'

'Yeah, by literally, I meant basically. I would have thought that was obvious.'

'In your mind, you held your mother responsible for the death of this woman, who – as you said – owned a florist shop where your mother worked and which she eventually came to own herself?'

I look at the old dear. She's got, like, tears streaming down – I'm guessing – the small of her back. I'm focking this up in a big-time way. I *know* I am? But I can't lie. And it has nothing to do with being under oath.

'Yeah, no,' I go, 'I did hold her responsible. Alma was a nice old lady who didn't deserve what my old dear did to her. And she definitely went downhill afterwards.'

The old man shouts, 'They're putting words in your mouth, Kicker!'

I'm there, 'Me and my old dear have a very complicated relationship.'

The barrister's like, 'It would certainly seem so.'

'A lot of it goes back to her not wanting me when I was a baby. We've never really got on. I'm her horshest critic. She'll tell you that herself. I always, *always* think the worst of the woman and – to be honest – she very rarely disappoints me. She's greedy. She's stuck-up. She's insincere. She's self-serving. She's – what was the phrase? – incapable of human feeling? She's a drunk and she's got a head like a stuffed pocket. But there's no way she would be capable of killing someone.'

'I expect you'd be telling me a different story,' he goes, 'if you were trying to get *me* into the sack.'

And I go, 'That's actually a bit homophobist.'

The entire jury laughs. And I realize something in that moment. They like me. I don't know what way they feel about the old dear, but they definitely like me.

I'm there, 'The woman is a wagon. She's a weapon of mass destruction. If she'd thrown me to wolves on the day I was born, they would have made a better fist of raising me than her. But she's not a killer.'

'No further questions,' the dude goes.

As I step out of the box, I look at the old dear. She's dabbing at her eyes with a handkerchief, even though they're basically bone-dry. And she mouths the words 'Thank you, Ross. Thank you.'

We're sitting in The Chancery Inn – we're talking me, the old man and Hennessy – having just listened to the two sides summing up.

'An inspired idea of yours!' the old man goes.

I'm there, 'I don't know about inspired. It was the nearest pub to the court.'

'I'm referring to your moment on the stand! All those names you called your mother! A drunk! A weapon of mass what's-it! I said to your godfather there, "You can see what he's doing, can't you? He's leading the jury to believe that he hates Fionnuala so that any testimony he offers in her favour will carry additional weight!"'

'Yeah, no, I actually *meant* those things I said?'

'In-spired! I only hope it'll be enough!'

Hennessy knocks back his brandy in one. 'They've no forensics,' he goes. 'No murder weapon. The evidence that she was out of the house that lunchtime narrows the window of opportunity for the murder. We knocked out the evidence of Ari's burn injury. Her computer could be a problem. That story was very visual and identical in almost every detail to the way the prosecution say it happened. We can only hope that something *you* said in that box struck a chord with the jury.'

And hopefully not the bit about her being greedy and incapable of human feeling.

The old man's phone rings on the table in front of us. He looks at it. 'It's young Fionn!' he goes, looking at Hennessy. Then he answers it. 'What have you got for me?' After listening for ten seconds, he's like, 'I can't believe we're still talking about the wall! No, I will not accept a four-foot-high wall! What bloody use is a wall they can see over? You tell Michael Martin that it's going to be four metres high – and I'm going to get Israel to build the blasted thing!'

He hangs up, then I get this suddenly attack of – I don't know – something that *feels* like guilt? It's possibly loyalty, its first cousin.

'Fionn is playing games,' I automatically go. 'He's deliberately focking up the talks to try to push Fianna Fáil and, er, the other one that *sounds* like Fianna Fáil –?'

'Fine Gael,' Hennessy goes.

'That's them. He's trying to push the two of them together. Get them to see that they're not so different.'

I don't get the reaction I *think* I'm going to get? I'm expecting the old man to flip. Or at least say thank you. Except he doesn't. He just smiles at Hennessy and Hennessy smiles back at him. 'We know what Fionn is doing!' the old man eventually goes. 'Why do you think I asked *him* to conduct the negotiations and not young Muirgheal?'

I'm like, 'What, so you don't *want* to be the actual Taoiseach?'

He's there, 'We don't want to be part of some coalition arrangement that forces us into all sorts of compromises! No, we figured if we pushed Fianna Fáil and Fine Gael together, it'll make New Republic stronger in the long term!'

'So *you're* using *Fionn* rather than the other way around?'

Hennessy goes, 'We knew he wouldn't be an honest broker. He has too many principles. And he's too in love with your wife.'

I focking knew it.

The old man goes, 'Fianna Fáil and Fine Gael have already agreed to work together! As a matter of fact, they're going to announce it this afternoon! A minority Fine Gael Government supported by Fianna Fáil! It won't last two years! Which gives us time to build up even more support! And when the Government collapses – as it inevitably will – we will be in a position to deliver what we really want.'

I'm like, 'And what's that?'

'An overall majority, of course.'

Kennet suddenly comes running into the pub. He's like, 'The j . . . j . . . j . . . j . . .'

'What's he trying to say?' the old man goes.

It's like an episode of *Skippy*.

'The j . . . j . . . j . . . j . . . j . . . jewer doddy is arthur arriving at a v . . . v . . . v . . . v . . . verdict,' he goes.

We're up off our stools, across the road and back in the court before he even finishes the last word. It takes about three minutes, in other words.

There's a definite buzz in the room. Someone in the press gallery, who obviously expects the news to be bad for the old dear, leans forwards and asks the old man, 'Will there be an appeal?'

The old man goes, 'Good Lord! Let's have the verdict first, shall we?'

The old dear is escorted in by the same two screws who've brought her in every day of the trial. She blows a kiss at the old man and then one at me.

I pretend not to notice.

The judge walks in and we all stand up. Then about two minutes later, the jury arrive in. None of them looks at the old dear and none of them looks in our direction either. I can't tell if that's a good or bad thing. It's just something I happen to *notice?*

The judge bangs his little hammer. He loves that focking thing. Delma puts her hand on my shoulder and goes, 'This is it, Ross! Let's hope our prayers are answered!'

Ronan arrives just in time and I make space for him between me and the old man. I notice he's got a massive Denis Hickie on his neck. I'm wondering did Shadden give it to him. And if not, how did he explain it to her?

'Soddy Ine late,' he goes.

I'm there, 'You haven't missed anything.'

I grab his hand. He grabs my old man's hand. My old man grabs Hennessy's hand.

The foreman of the jury is told to stand up. It's a woman.

'In the case of the State versus Fionnuala O'Carroll-Kelly,' the judge goes, 'do you find the defendant, Fionnuala O'Carroll-Kelly, guilty or not guilty?'

The woman doesn't hesitate.

She goes, 'Not guilty.'

The old dear screams. Tiffany-Blue screams. You wouldn't blame her either. Not only has the old dear got off, she's going to walk away with the two billion snots that *she* would have otherwise *inherited?* The old man shouts, *'Fiat justitia et pereat mundus!'* before hugging me, then Ronan, then Hennessy.

'Thank you!' the old dear is saying to the jury. 'Thank you! Thank you! Thank you!'

Tiffany-Blue screams, 'I'm going to fucking kill you! You fucking murdering bitch!' and she jumps the rail at the front of the public gallery and it takes five Gords and one Lady Gorda to hold her back.

I notice O'Maonaigh just staring at me with a look of, like, disappointment on his face. And that's when I know that it was my doing. It was my testimony that basically swung it for her.

Outside the court, everyone is saying pretty much the same *thing*? The old dear goes, 'She looked at you, Ross! The foreman of the jury, when she said, "Not guilty!" she looked at you!' and she hugs me for, like, the five hundredth time.

Then we're all herded in front of the TV cameras. The old man, the old dear, Ronan, who's trying to hide the hickie from the camera, then me in my dorky clothes – Luke Fitzgerald is going to destroy me if he happens to see the news tonight – with all of the old dear's friends and the old man's supporters standing behind us. Vivienne Traynor is doing the interview. She asks the old dear how she feels.

'Happy,' the old dear goes. 'Relieved. Vindicated. All of those things. And grateful – to the jury, to my wonderful family and friends. My beautiful, beautiful son, Ross, who's been my rock. My ex-husband, Charles, a dear, dear friend who never for one moment believed I was capable of doing what I was accused of doing. Now, I just want to go home and pour myself a nice, long gin –'

It always comes back to gin.

'– and tonic.'

She won't go near the tonic.

Vivienne turns to the old man then. 'Charles O'Carroll-Kelly,' she goes, 'there are reports this afternoon that Fine Gael and Fianna Fáil may be on the verge of an historic deal, with Micheál Martin agreeing to support a minority Government led by Enda Kenny. How much did the trial distract you from the job of trying to form a Government?'

The old man goes, 'I said it from day one that Fionnuala's trial was an attempt by the Establishment to destroy our movement! And I made it clear, too, that winning her freedom was my number one priority! From what you're saying, it sounds like the Establishment has achieved its goal of preventing New Republic from leading the next Government! But this I will also add – people have long memories! But I don't wish to dwell on any of that now. I want to go home with my dear, dear friend Fionnuala and celebrate this wonderful verdict!'

★

Enda Kenny is set to be elected as Taoiseach when the Dáil meets next week. That's according to the news. He's done a deal with Fianna Fáil and a handful of independent TDs, thwarting the ambitions of Charles O'Carroll-Kelly and his New Republic porty, who had promised, amongst other things, to take Ireland out of the European Union and to build a wall around Cork.

I switch off the radio and I drive the last fifteen minutes home in silence. I'm thinking about the kids. About Brian, Johnny and Leo, but – can I be honest? – I'm mostly thinking about Honor. And that's me being biased. People who tell you that they love all their children exactly the same are lying. I miss them all, but I miss Honor most of all.

And maybe that's a rugby thing.

She phoned me an hour ago and she went, 'I'm going to focking kill him!'

Of course, I had to laugh. I was like, 'Are you talking about Sorcha's old man?'

She went, 'I'm going to drop something in his bath – like Fionnuala did to that old man.'

It's kind of funny – the old dear turning out to be a role model for her.

'Honor,' I went, 'you heard the verdict. Your grandmother didn't actually *do* it?'

And she was like, 'I still think she did.'

'Look, maybe hold off on murdering him for a little while longer. I'm pretty confident of getting a result in court as well.'

Hennessy couriered a letter to Sorcha this morning, telling her that I intended to challenge the existing court order and seek joint custody in front of a judge with known sympathies towards rugby. Honor promised not to kill Sorcha's old man until all legal avenues have been exhausted.

I'm just pulling into the driveway when my *phone* all of a sudden rings? At first I think it might be Honor again. Except it's not. It ends up being Shadden. She's like, 'Howiya?'

I'm there, 'Hey, Shadden, how are the wedding plans coming along?'

There's, like, two or three seconds of silence on the other end. Then she goes, 'Is Ronan dare wit you?'

I'm there, 'Ronan? Er, yeah, no, he is actually.'

He's obviously up to his tricks again.

She goes, 'He ditn't come home last neet – arthur coddidge.'

I'm there, 'Yeah, no, I met him for a few pints out this direction. He, er, crashed here – on account of him being gee-eyed.'

'Is he besoyut you? Put me onto um.'

'Bear in mind, you're breaking up, Shadden.'

'Gib the phowun to um, Rosser.'

'I'm in a bad area.'

I'm not. I'm on Torquay Road.

'Rosser, put me onto um reet –'

And that's when I hang up on her and switch my phone off. That's my next job, after I get access to my children again – to persuade Ronan not to get married.

One miracle at a time, as Father Fehily used to say.

I put my key in the front door and open it. It's, like, weird being back here living with the old pair again. But then I see something that suddenly makes it – this is *my* word – *doubly* weird? And what I see is the old dear's shoes discorded on the hallway floor and her tights in a ball on the stairs. And I'm thinking, oh no – not again.

You've got to be focking kidding me!

I tiptoe up the stairs and I find more items of her clothing – then one or two items of his. Including his focking Y-fronts! Then I hear it, through the door of what used to be their bedroom. My old pair going at it like dinosaurs fighting.

She's going, 'Slow down, Charles! I think I bruised my tailbone doing that last thing you asked me to do!' and I actually think I'm going to get sick.

And then I hear *him* go, 'Let me take another one of these little blue pills that Hennessy gave me!'

In the name of all that is *focking* decent!

I tip downstairs, my plan being to fill a bucket with water and literally fock it over the two of them. But then their noises grow louder and louder and I think, no, I can't actually stay in the gaff and listen to my old pair humping themselves hoarse. Which is why I decide to step outside. I head for the air-raid shelter at the bottom of the gorden, which seems somehow, I don't know, appropriate in the circumstances.

I haven't been in there for years. I got it done up for me and Ronan to use as a sort of, like, man cave, but then Ronan met Shadden and he stopped coming to Foxrock as much. I can see him spending many nights in here when Shadden finds out what he's really like.

The front of the shelter is all, like, covered over with bushes and I end up having to pull them back to find the actual door. I still have the key on my key ring. I put it in the keyhole and I turn it but the door won't budge, and I end up having to put my shoulder against it to get it open.

It gives way and in I go. There's, like, a seriously musty smell in the place. It's also, like, pitch dork. I feel around for the light switch. Then I find it and flick it and the room is suddenly bright. I'm looking around. It's just as me and Ronan left it.

And that's when I spot it. I end up getting such a fright that – I'm going to admit something here – I end up literally pissing my chinos. Because there, on top of the pool table, all dirty and blackened, is the weapon my old dear used to murder Ari Samuels.

It's a two-bor electric heater.

Epilogue

So what do I end up doing? The answer is I end up deciding to hide the thing. Until I know what I'm going to actually do with it. So I go back into the gaff and I look under the stairs for something – I don't even know *what* yet? My hands are literally shaking. And then I find a trowel. I have no idea why we own such a thing. I can only presume the old dear uses it to put on her foundation.

I pick it up and I take it down to the air-raid shelter, then I use it to scrape away the cement holding an entire section of bricks together – again, my hands trembling the entire time. I'm thinking, how the fock did the Feds not think to search this place? Maybe they didn't know it was even here. Like I said, it was covered with bushes and the mad focker who built it in – I don't know – the 1950s or something did it without actual planning permission.

It takes a good hour before I manage to pull about eight bricks out of the wall at sort of, like, chest height. I pick up the heater and I shove it through the hole. It drops on the other side, in the space between the inner and outer walls. I think it's called a cavity.

I just put the bricks back roughly, obviously without using actual cement. Then I go back into the house, thinking, what do I do? How can I ever look her in the eye again? What if she finds out that I know? Would she kill me next? How can I ever look at her in the same way again?

I'm standing in the hallway, thinking, well, at least they've stopped riding upstairs. Then there's suddenly a ring on the door and I end up nearly soiling myself again with the fright. For some reason, I stort to think it's the Feds. But then I'm thinking, can she even be chorged with the same crime once she's already been found not guilty? There's a second ring and I think, fock it, I'm going to have to answer it. So I do.

It ends up being Sorcha.

The first line out of her mouth is, 'Oh my God, Ross, are you okay? You look like you've just seen a ghost!'

I'm like, 'What?'

Then I watch her little nose doing its thing. She's there, 'Ross, did you . . . have you . . . wet yourself?'

And I go, 'Er, no, I think it's, er, damp here in the hallway . . . yeah, no, the gaff *was* empty for a long time . . . while my old dear was, you know . . .'

She smiles. She goes, 'Oh my God, I was *so* pleased for her.'

I'm there, 'Yeah, no, she got your flowers.'

'I said it from day one that Fionnuala wasn't capable of killing someone.'

'Hmmm.'

'Ross, are you sure you're okay? You're *actually* white.'

'Yeah, no, I'm just having a weird day . . . how are you?'

'I'm much better now. Did you hear, Enda Kenny offered me a seat in the Seanad?'

'The Seanad? He obviously thinks the world of you.'

I have no idea what the Seanad even does, but she seems to be definitely pleased.

She goes, 'He wants to make me one of his nominees. He said he was impressed by the way I conducted myself during the election campaign.'

'That's, em, great.'

There's, like, an awkward *silence* between us then?

'Anyway,' she goes, 'there *was* a reason I wanted to talk to you.'

I'm there, 'Okay?'

'My dad had a letter from Hennessy this morning –'

'Right.'

'– saying you were going to be seeking joint custody.'

'I miss the kids, Sorcha. Look, I know I acted like a dick, but not seeing my children is too big a price to pay. It's too big a price.'

'What if I told you there was no need to go to court? What if I told you I was happy to let you see the kids whenever you want?'

'What? What would your old man say?'

'This has nothing to do with him. This is my decision.'

'What changed your mind?'

She sighs. I like that top on her – it really shows off her dugs.

'Honor needs you,' she goes. 'And even though it pains me to say it, she doesn't need me.'

I'm there, 'There's a definite bond between us.'

'I thought my dad might serve that role. I hoped she'd develop the same relationship with him that I had as a little girl.'

'She's not a fan.'

'I know. I genuinely think she could hurt him. I was looking at the search history on her laptop last night and . . .'

She doesn't finish her sentence. I'm thinking, she possibly should warn him not to go taking any baths, but then I think, fock him.

I'm there, 'I don't think Honor is capable of actually hurting someone – other than, you know, *mentally*?'

'I came to a terrible realization that day at the school,' she goes. 'My daughter doesn't love me.'

'I'm sure she does, Sorcha – deep, deep, deep, deep down.'

'She doesn't. You're the one she loves. You're the only one who can talk to her. And denying you access to her is only going to make things worse. So, as far as I can see, we have two options.'

'What are they?'

'Honor can either come and live with you here –'

'I, er, don't think that would be a good idea, Sorcha. I would have serious concerns about my old dear becoming a role model for her.'

'– or you can move back to Honalee.'

She says it so casually, so matter-of-factly, that for a good ten seconds I'm actually *stunned*? What a focking day this is turning out to be. Of course, I don't even know the half of it yet.

I'm like, 'Move back? Back in with you?'

She goes, 'Back home, Ross.'

'Jesus Christ, am I dreaming this? What about your old pair?'

'The antagonism between Honor and my dad isn't good for her, Ross. I've spoken to him and he's agreed that it would be best all round if they found somewhere else to live.'

'I can't wait to see him again. Rub his focking nose in it.'

There's another long silence before I eventually go, 'So what about us?'

She's like, 'Ross, I don't think I'll ever be able to forgive you for sending those texts from my grandmother's phone.'

'I was just trying to get you to see that she was a homophobist bigot who believed all gay people go to Hell.'

'I'm not offering you anything, Ross, other than the opportunity to be a father to your children . . .'

'Right.'

'. . . while I pursue my political career.'

'Kind of like Bill and Hillary Clinton – a sort of, like, marriage of convenience?'

'For you, Ross, it always has been a marriage of convenience.'

'Okay, then – I'll take it.'

I'm moving back home. I'm going to get to see my daughter all the time. I'm going to spend every minute of every day with my boys, slowly chipping away at their love of soccer and reintroducing them subtly to the game of rugby.

'There's one other thing you should know,' she goes.

I'm like, 'Yeah, no, shoot!' thinking she's going to tell me that she's changed the alorm code, or she's switched Internet providers.

'I'm pregnant,' she goes.

She says it as coolly as that. I just laugh. But then I realize, from her expression, that she's actually serious.

I'm there, 'That's, er, random. And I'm saying random in a good way.'

She goes, 'I thought you'd be angry.'

'Why would I be angry? I mean, I'm presuming it's mine.'

She looks at me like she's just found a severed finger in her arugula salad. 'How *could* it be yours?' she goes. 'You had a vasectomy.'

I'm like, 'Okay, full disclosure. I didn't.'

'Excuse me?'

She's pretty shocked, it has to be said.

I'm there, 'Look, when it came to it, I couldn't go through with it.'

She goes, 'So you're saying it *could* be yours?'

'I'm saying I'm still firing live rounds, yeah.'

And that's when it suddenly hits me – what she's actually *saying* here?

I'm there, 'Whoa, hang on a second – if it wasn't mine, whose baby did you think it might be?'

She goes, 'I only slept with him once, Ross. And we both realized it was a mistake. It was the night that Gran died.'

I'm like, 'No, Sorcha. Please don't say it. Don't say *his* name.'

But she does. She says it anyway.

She goes, 'Ross, I slept with Fionn.'

Acknowledgements

Heartfelt thanks to the team of very talented people who, every year for almost twenty years now, have helped turn the misadventures of a South Dublin rugby jock into books of which I am enormously proud. Special thanks to my editor Rachel Pierce, my agent Faith O'Grady, the artist Alan Clarke, as well as Michael McLoughlin, Patricia Deevy, Cliona Lewis, Patricia McVeigh, Brian Walker, Aimée Johnston and all the staff at Penguin Ireland. Thanks to my father, David, and my brothers, Mark, Vincent and Richard. And thanks most of all to my very wonderful wife, Mary.